Homegoing

Homegoing

Yaa Gyasi

BOND
STREET
BOOKS
DOUBLEDAY
CANADA

Library and Archives Canada Cataloguing in Publication

Gyasi, Yaa, author
Homegoing / Yaa Gyasi.

Issued in print and electronic formats.
ISBN 978-0-385-68613-6 (bound).--ISBN 978-0-385-68614-3 (epub)

I. Title.

PS3607.Y37H65 2016   813'.6   C2015-906282-9
                                            C2015-906283-7

Grateful acknowledgment is made to Alfred Music and Hal Leonard Corporation for permission to reprint lyric excerpts of "I Loves You, Porgy" (from "Porgy and Bess"). Words and music by George Gershwin, DuBose and Dorothy Heyward, and Ira Gershwin. Copyright © 1935, renewed by Ira Gershwin Music, DuBose and Dorothy Heyward Memorial Fund Publishing, George Gershwin Music, Nokawi Music, and Frankie G. Songs. All rights on behalf of Ira Gershwin Music administered by WB Music Corp. All rights for Nokawi Music administered by Imagem Sounds. All rights for Frankie G. Songs and DuBose and Dorothy Heyward Memorial Fund Publishing administered by Songs Music Publishing. All rights reserved. Reprinted by permission of Alfred Music and Hal Leonard Corporation.

Jacket design by Peter Mendelsund
Printed and bound in the USA

Bond Street Books and colophon are registered trademarks of Penguin Random House Canada Limited

Published in Canada by Bond Street Books,
a division of Penguin Random House Canada Limited

www.penguinrandomhouse.ca

10 9 8 7 6 5 4 3 2 1

BOND
STREET   Penguin
BOOKS   Random
           House

For my parents and for my brothers

Abusua te sɛ kwaɛ: sɛ wo wɔ akyire a wo hunu sɛ ɛbom; sɛ wo bɛn ho a na wo hunu sɛ nnua no bia sisi ne baabi nko.

The family is like the forest: if you are outside it is dense; if you are inside you see that each tree has its own position.

—AKAN PROVERB

Maame

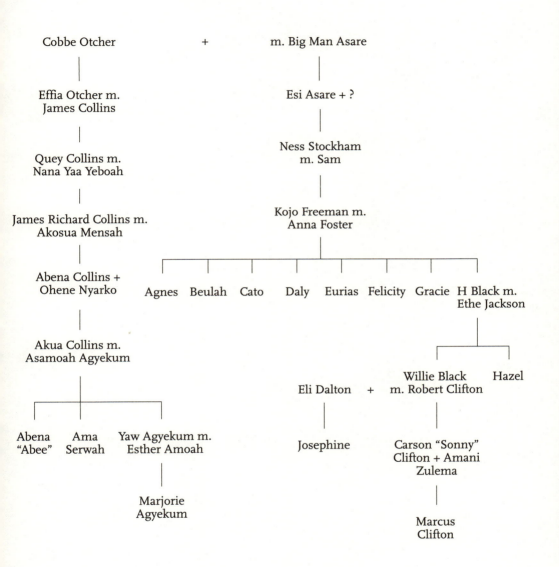

Cobbe Otcher + m. Big Man Asare

Effia Otcher m.
James Collins

Esi Asare + ?

Quey Collins m.
Nana Yaa Yeboah

Ness Stockham
m. Sam

James Richard Collins m.
Akosua Mensah

Kojo Freeman m.
Anna Foster

Abena Collins +
Ohene Nyarko

Agnes   Beulah   Cato   Daly   Eurias   Felicity   Gracie   H Black m.
Ethe Jackson

Akua Collins m.
Asamoah Agyekum

Willie Black   Hazel
Eli Dalton   +   m. Robert Clifton

Abena
"Abee"   Ama
Serwah   Yaw Agyekum m.
Esther Amoah

Josephine

Carson "Sonny"
Clifton + Amani
Zulema

Marjorie
Agyekum

Marcus
Clifton

Part One

Effia

THE NIGHT EFFIA OTCHER was born into the musky heat of Fanteland, a fire raged through the woods just outside her father's compound. It moved quickly, tearing a path for days. It lived off the air; it slept in caves and hid in trees; it burned, up and through, unconcerned with what wreckage it left behind, until it reached an Asante village. There, it disappeared, becoming one with the night.

Effia's father, Cobbe Otcher, left his first wife, Baaba, with the new baby so that he might survey the damage to his yams, that most precious crop known far and wide to sustain families. Cobbe had lost seven yams, and he felt each loss as a blow to his own family. He knew then that the memory of the fire that burned, then fled, would haunt him, his children, and his children's children for as long as the line continued. When he came back into Baaba's hut to find Effia, the child of the night's fire, shrieking into the air, he looked at his wife and said, "We will never again speak of what happened today."

The villagers began to say that the baby was born of the fire, that this was the reason Baaba had no milk. Effia was nursed by Cobbe's second wife, who had just given birth to a son three months before. Effia would not latch on, and when she did, her sharp gums would tear at the flesh around the woman's nipples until she became afraid to feed the baby. Because of this, Effia grew thinner, skin on small bird-like bones, with a large black hole of a mouth that expelled a hungry cry which could be heard throughout the village, even on the days Baaba did her best to smother it, covering the baby's lips with the rough palm of her left hand.

"Love her," Cobbe commanded, as though love were as simple an act as lifting food up from an iron plate and past one's lips. At night, Baaba dreamed of leaving the baby in the dark forest so that the god Nyame could do with her as he pleased.

Effia grew older. The summer after her third birthday, Baaba had her first son. The boy's name was Fiifi, and he was so fat that sometimes, when Baaba wasn't looking, Effia would roll him along the ground like a ball. The first day that Baaba let Effia hold him, she accidentally dropped him. The baby bounced on his buttocks, landed on his stomach, and looked up at everyone in the room, confused as to whether or not he should cry. He decided against it, but Baaba, who had been stirring *banku*, lifted her stirring stick and beat Effia across her bare back. Each time the stick lifted off the girl's body, it would leave behind hot, sticky pieces of *banku* that burned into her flesh. By the time Baaba had finished, Effia was covered with sores, screaming and crying. From the floor, rolling this way and that on his belly, Fiifi looked at Effia with his saucer eyes but made no noise.

Cobbe came home to find his other wives attending to Effia's wounds and understood immediately what had happened. He and Baaba fought well into the night. Effia could hear them through the thin walls of the hut where she lay on the floor, drifting in and out of a feverish sleep. In her dream, Cobbe was a lion and Baaba was a tree. The lion plucked the tree from the ground where it stood and slammed it back down. The tree stretched its branches in protest, and the lion ripped them off, one by one. The tree, horizontal, began to cry red ants that traveled down the thin cracks between its bark. The ants pooled on the soft earth around the top of the tree trunk.

And so the cycle began. Baaba beat Effia. Cobbe beat Baaba. By the time Effia had reached age ten, she could recite a history of the scars on her body. The summer of 1764, when Baaba broke yams across her back. The spring of 1767, when Baaba bashed her left foot with a rock, breaking her big toe so that it now always pointed away from the other toes. For each scar on Effia's body, there was a companion scar on Baaba's, but that didn't stop mother from beating daughter, father from beating mother.

Matters were only made worse by Effia's blossoming beauty. When she was twelve, her breasts arrived, two lumps that sprung from her chest, as soft as mango flesh. The men of the village knew that first blood would soon follow, and they waited for the chance to ask Baaba and Cobbe for her hand. The gifts started. One man tapped palm wine better than anyone else in the village, but another's fishing nets were never empty. Cobbe's family feasted off Effia's burgeoning woman-hood. Their bellies, their hands, were never empty.

In 1775, Adwoa Aidoo became the first girl of the village to be proposed to by one of the British soldiers. She was light-skinned and sharp-tongued. In the mornings, after she had bathed, she rubbed shea butter all over her body, underneath her breasts and between her legs. Effia didn't know her well, but she had seen her naked one day when Baaba sent her to carry palm oil to the girl's hut. Her skin was slick and shiny, her hair regal.

The first time the white man came, Adwoa's mother asked Effia's parents to show him around the village while Adwoa prepared herself for him.

"Can I come?" Effia asked, running after her parents as they walked. She heard Baaba's "no" in one ear and Cobbe's "yes" in the other. Her father's ear won, and soon Effia was standing before the first white man she had ever seen.

"He is happy to meet you," the translator said as the white man held his hand out to Effia. She didn't accept it. Instead, she hid behind her father's leg and watched him.

He wore a coat that had shiny gold buttons down the middle; it strained against his paunch. His face was red, as though his neck were a stump on fire. He was fat all over and sweating huge droplets from his forehead and above his upper lip. Effia started to think of him as a rain cloud: sallow and wet and shapeless.

"Please, he would like to see the village," the translator said, and they all began to walk.

They stopped first by Effia's own compound. "This is where we live," Effia told the white man, and he smiled at her dumbly, his green eyes hidden in fog.

He didn't understand. Even after his translator spoke to him, he didn't understand.

Cobbe held Effia's hand as he and Baaba led the white man through the compound. "Here, in this village," Cobbe said, "each wife has her own hut. This is the hut she shares with her children. When it is her husband's night to be with her, he goes to her in her hut."

The white man's eyes grew clearer as the translation was given, and suddenly Effia realized that he was seeing through new eyes. The mud of her hut's walls, the straw of the roof, he could finally see them.

They continued on through the village, showing the white man the town square, the small fishing boats formed from hollowed-out tree trunks that the men carried with them when they walked the few miles down to the coast. Effia forced herself to see things through new eyes, too. She smelled the sea-salt wind as it touched the hairs in her nose, felt the bark of a palm tree as sharp as a scratch, saw the deep, deep red of the clay that was all around them.

"Baaba," Effia asked once the men had walked farther ahead of them, "why will Adwoa marry this man?"

"Because her mother says so."

A few weeks later, the white man came back to pay respects to Adwoa's mother, and Effia and all of the other villagers gathered around to see what he would offer. There was the bride price of fifteen pounds. There were goods he'd brought with him from the Castle, carried on the backs of Asantes. Cobbe made Effia stand behind him as they watched the servants come in with fabric, millet, gold, and iron.

When they walked back to their compound, Cobbe pulled Effia aside, letting his wives and other children walk in front of them.

"Do you understand what just happened?" he asked her. In the distance, Baaba slipped her hand into Fiifi's. Effia's brother had just turned eleven, but he could already climb up the trunk of a palm tree using nothing but his bare hands and feet for support.

"The white man came to take Adwoa away," Effia said.

Her father nodded. "The white men live in the Cape Coast Castle. There, they trade goods with our people."

"Like iron and millet?"

Her father put his hand on her shoulder and kissed the top of her forehead, but when he pulled away the look in his eyes was troubled and distant. "Yes, we get iron and millet, but we must give them things in return. That man came from Cape Coast to marry Adwoa, and there will be more like him who will come and take our daughters away. But you, my own, I have bigger plans for you than to live as a white man's wife. You will marry a man of our village."

Baaba turned around just then, and Effia caught her eyes. Baaba scowled. Effia looked at her father to see if he had noticed, but Cobbe did not say a word.

Effia knew who her choice for husband would be, and she dearly hoped her parents would choose the same man. Abeeku Badu was next in line to be the village chief. He was tall, with skin like the pit of an avocado and large hands with long, slender fingers that he waved around like lightning bolts every time he spoke. He had visited their compound four times in the last month, and later that week, he and Effia were to share a meal together.

Abeeku brought a goat. His servants carried yams and fish and palm wine. Baaba and the other wives stoked their fires and heated the oil. The air smelled rich.

That morning, Baaba had plaited Effia's hair. Two long braids on either side of her center part. They made her look like a ram, strong, willful. Effia had oiled her naked body and put gold in her ears. She sat across from Abeeku as they ate, pleased as he stole appreciative glances.

"Were you at Adwoa's ceremony?" Baaba asked once all of the men had been served and the women finally began to eat.

"Yes, I was there, but only briefly. It is a shame Adwoa will be leaving the village. She would have made a good wife."

"Will you work for the British when you become chief?" Effia asked.

Cobbe and Baaba sent her sharp looks, and she lowered her head, but she lifted it to find Abeeku smiling.

"We work *with* the British, Effia, not for them. That is the meaning of trade. When I am chief, we will continue as we have, facilitating trade with the Asantes and the British."

Effia nodded. She wasn't exactly sure what this meant, but she could tell from her parents' looks that it was best to keep her mouth shut. Abeeku Badu was the first man they had brought to meet her. Effia wanted desperately for him to want her, but she did not yet know what kind of man he was, what kind of woman he required. In her hut, Effia could ask her father and Fiifi anything she wanted. It was Baaba who practiced silence and preferred the same from Effia, Baaba who had slapped her for asking why she did not take her to be blessed as all the other mothers did for their daughters. It was only when Effia didn't speak or question, when she made herself small, that she could feel Baaba's love, or something like it. Maybe this was what Abeeku wanted too.

Abeeku finished eating. He shook hands with everyone in the family, and stopped by Effia's mother. "You will let me know when she is ready," he said.

Baaba clutched a hand to her chest and nodded soberly. Cobbe and the other men saw Abeeku off as the rest of the family waved.

That night, Baaba woke Effia up while she was sleeping on the floor of their hut. Effia felt the warmth of her mother's breath against her ear as she spoke. "When your blood comes, Effia, you must hide it. You must tell me and no one else," she said. "Do you understand?" She handed Effia palm fronds that she had turned into soft, rolled sheets. "Place these inside of you, and check them every day. When they turn red, you must tell me."

Effia looked at the palm fronds, held in Baaba's outstretched hands. She didn't take them at first, but when she looked up again there was something like desperation in her mother's eyes. And because the look had softened Baaba's face somehow, and because Effia also knew desperation, that fruit of longing, she did as she was told. Every day, Effia checked for red, but the palm fronds came out greenish-white as always. In the spring, the chief of the village grew ill, and everyone watched Abeeku carefully to see if he was ready for the task. He married two women in those months, Arekua the Wise, and Millicent, the half-caste daughter of a Fante woman and a British soldier. The soldier had died from fever, leaving his wife and two children much wealth to do with as they pleased. Effia prayed for the day all of the villagers would call her Effia the Beauty, as Abeeku called her on the rare occasions when he was permitted to speak to her.

Millicent's mother had been given a new name by her white husband. She was a plump, fleshy woman with teeth that twinkled against the dark night of her skin. She had decided to move out of the Castle and into the village once her husband died. Because the white men could not leave money in their wills to their Fante wives and children, they left it to other soldiers and friends, and those friends paid the wives. Millicent's mother had been given enough money for a new start and a piece of land. She and Millicent would often come visit Effia and Baaba, for, as she said, they would soon be a part of the same family.

Millicent was the lightest-skinned woman Effia had ever seen. Her black hair reached down to the middle of her back and her eyes were tinged with green. She rarely smiled, and she spoke with a husky voice and a strange Fante accent.

"What was it like in the Castle?" Baaba asked Millicent's mother one day while the four women were sitting to a snack of groundnuts and bananas.

"It was fine, fine. They take care of you, oh, these men! It is like they have never been with a woman before. I don't know what their British wives were doing. I tell you, my husband looked at me like I was water and he was fire, and every night he had to be put out."

The women laughed. Millicent slipped Effia a smile, and Effia wanted to ask her what it was like with Abeeku, but she did not dare.

Baaba leaned in close to Millicent's mother, but still Effia could hear, "And they pay a good bride price, eh?"

"Enh, I tell you, my husband paid my mother ten pounds, and that was fifteen years ago! To be sure, my sister, the money is good, but I for one am glad my daughter has married a Fante. Even if a soldier offered to pay twenty pounds, she would not get to be the wife of a chief. And what's worse, she would have to live in the Castle, far from me. No, no, it is better to marry a man of the village so that your daughters can stay close to you."

Baaba nodded and turned toward Effia, who quickly looked away.

That night, just two days after her fifteenth birthday, the blood came. It was not the powerful rush of the ocean waves that Effia had expected it to be, but rather a simple trickle, rain dripping, drop by drop, from the same spot of a hut's roof. She cleaned herself off and waited for her father to leave Baaba so that she could tell her.

"Baaba," she said, showing her the palm fronds painted red. "I have gotten my blood."

Baaba placed a hand over her lips. "Who else knows?"

"No one," Effia said.

"You will keep it that way. Do you understand? When anyone asks you if you have become a woman yet, you will answer no."

Effia nodded. She turned to leave, but a question was burning hot coals in the pit of her stomach. "Why?" she finally asked.

Baaba reached into Effia's mouth and pulled out her tongue, pinching the tip with her sharp fingernails. "Who are you that you think you can question me, enh? If you do not do as I say, I will make sure you never speak again." She released Effia's tongue, and for the rest of the night, Effia tasted her own blood.

The next week, the old chief died. The funeral announcements went out to all of the surrounding villages. The proceedings would last a month and end with Abeeku's chief ceremony. The women of the village prepared food from sunrise to sunset; drums were made out of the finest wood, and the best singers were called upon to raise their voices. The funeral attendants began dancing on the fourth day of the rainy season, and they did not rest their feet until the ground had completely dried.

At the end of the first dry night Abeeku was crowned Omanhin, chief of the Fante village. He was dressed in rich fabrics, his two wives on either side of him. Effia and Baaba stood next to each other as they watched, and Cobbe paced the crowd. Every so often, Effia could hear him muttering that she, his daughter, the most beautiful woman in the village, should be up there too.

As the new chief, Abeeku wanted to do something big, something that would bring attention to their village and make them a force to be reckoned with. After only three days in office, he gathered all of the men of the village to his compound. He fed them for two days straight, got them drunk on palm wine until their boisterous laughing and impassioned shouting could be heard from every hut.

"What will they do?" Effia asked.

"That does not concern you," Baaba said.

In the two months since Effia had begun to bleed, Baaba had stopped beating her. Payment for her silence. Some days, when they were preparing meals for the men, or when Effia would bring back the water she had fetched and watch Baaba dip in with cupped hands, she would think they were finally behaving as mothers and daughters were supposed to behave. But then, other days, the long scowl would return to Baaba's face, and Effia would see that her mother's new quiet was only temporary, her rage a wild beast that had been tamed for the moment.

Cobbe came back from the meeting with a long machete. The handle was gold with carvings of letters that no one understood. He was so drunk that all of his wives and children stood around him in a circle, at a distance of two feet, while he shuffled about, jabbing the sharp instrument this way and that. "We will make the village rich with blood!" he screamed. He lunged at Fiifi, who had wandered into the circle, and the boy, leaner and quicker than he had been in his days as a fat baby, swiveled his hips, missing the tip of the machete by only a few inches.

Fiifi had been the youngest one at the meeting. Everyone knew he would make a fine warrior. They could see it in the way he climbed the palm trees. In the way he wore his silence like a golden crown.

After her father left and Effia was certain that their mother had gone to sleep, she crawled over to Fiifi.

"Wake up," she hissed, and he pushed her away. Even in half sleep he was stronger than she was. She fell backward but, with the grace of a cat, flipped back onto her feet. "Wake up," she said again.

Fiifi's eyes flashed open. "Don't worry me, big sister," he said.

"What will happen?" she asked.

"It's the business of men," Fiifi said.

"You are not yet a man," Effia said.

"And you are not yet a woman," Fiifi snapped back. "Otherwise you would have been there with Abeeku this very evening as his wife."

Effia's lips began to quiver. She turned to go back to her side of the hut, but Fiifi caught her arm. "We are helping the British and the Asantes with their trade."

"Oh," Effia said. It was the same story she had heard from her father and Abeeku just a few months before. "You mean we will give Asante gold and fabric to the white men?"

Fiifi clutched her tighter. "Don't be stupid," he said. "Abeeku has made an alliance with one of the most powerful Asante villages. We will help them sell their slaves to the British."

And so, the white man came to their village. Fat and skinny, red and tanned. They came in uniform, with swords at their sides, their eyes looking sideways, always and ever cautious. They came to approve of the goods Abeeku had promised them.

In the days following the chief ceremony, Cobbe had grown nervous about the broken promise of Effia's womanhood, nervous that Abeeku would forget her in favor of one of the other women in the village. He had always said that he wanted his daughter to be the first, most important wife, but now even third seemed like a distant hope.

Every day he would ask Baaba what was happening with Effia, and every day Baaba would reply that she was not yet ready. In desperation, he decided to allow his daughter to go over to Abeeku's compound with Baaba once a week, so that the man could see her and remember how much he had once loved her face and figure.

Arekua the Wise, the first of Abeeku's wives, greeted them as they came in one evening. "Please, Mama," she said to Baaba. "We weren't expecting you tonight. The white men are here."

"We can go," Effia said, but Baaba clutched her arm.

"If you don't mind, we would like to stay," Baaba said. Arekua gave her a strange look. "My husband will be angry if we come back too early," Baaba said, as if that were enough of an explanation. Effia knew that she was lying. Cobbe had not sent them there that night. It was Baaba who had heard that the white men would be there and insisted that they go pay respects. Arekua took pity and left to ask Abeeku if the two of them might stay.

"You will eat with the women, and if the men come in, you will not speak," she said once she had returned. She led them deeper into the compound. Effia watched hut after hut pass by until they entered the one where the wives had gathered to eat. She sat next to Millicent, whose pregnant belly had begun to show, no bigger than a coconut, slung low. Arekua had prepared fish in palm oil stew, and they dug in until their fingers were stained orange.

Soon, a maidservant Effia had not noticed before came into the room. She was a tiny girl, only a child, whose eyes never lifted from the ground.

"Please, Mama," she said to Arekua. "The white men would like to tour the compound. Chief Abeeku says you are to make sure you are presentable for them."

"Go and fetch us water, quick," Millicent said, and when the servant came back with a bucket full of water, they all washed their hands and lips. Effia tidied her hair, licking her palms and rubbing her fingers along the tight baby curls that lined her edges. When she finished, Baaba had her stand between Millicent and Arekua, in front of the other women, and Effia tried her best to seem smaller so as not to draw attention to herself.

Before long the men came in. Abeeku looked as a chief should look, Effia thought, strong and powerful, like he could lift ten women above his head and toward the sun. Two white men came in behind him. There was one who Effia thought must be the chief of the white men because of the way the other glanced at him before he moved or spoke. This white chief wore the same clothes as the rest of them wore, but there were more shiny golden buttons running along his coat and on the flaps above his shoulders. He seemed older than Abeeku, his dark brown hair flecked with gray, but he stood up straight, as a leader should stand.

"These are the women. My wives and children, the mothers and daughters," Abeeku said. The smaller, more timid white man watched him carefully as he said this and then turned to the white chief and spoke their strange tongue. The white chief nodded and smiled at all of them, looking carefully at each woman and saying hello in his poor Fante.

When his "hello" reached Effia, she couldn't help but giggle. The other women shushed her, and embarrassment like heat began to move into her cheeks.

"I'm still learning," the white chief said, resting his eyes on Effia, his Fante an ugly sound in her ears. He held her gaze for what seemed like minutes, and Effia felt her skin grow even hotter as the look in his eyes turned into something more wanton. The dark brown circles of his irises looked like large pots that toddlers could drown in, and he looked at Effia just like that, as though he wanted to keep her there, in his drowning eyes. Color quickly flooded into his cheeks. He turned to the other white man and spoke.

"No, she is not my wife," Abeeku said after the man had translated for him, his voice not bothering to hide his annoyance. Effia hung her head, embarrassed that she had done something to cause Abeeku shame, embarrassed he could not call her wife. Embarrassed, too, that he had not called her by name: Effia the Beauty. She wanted desperately then to break her promise to Baaba and announce herself as the woman she was, but before she could speak, the men walked away, and her nerve faded as the white chief looked over his shoulder at her and smiled.

His name was James Collins, and he was the newly appointed governor of the Cape Coast Castle. Within a week, he had come back to the village to ask Baaba for Effia's hand in marriage. Cobbe's rage at the proposal filled every room like hot steam.

"She is all but promised to Abeeku!" he yelled at Baaba when Baaba told him that she was considering the offer.

"Yes, but Abeeku cannot marry her until her blood comes, and we have been waiting years now. I tell you, husband, I think she was cursed in that fire, a demon who will never become a woman. Think about it. What creature is that beautiful but cannot be touched? All of the signs of womanhood are there, and yet, still, nothing. The white man will marry her regardless. He does not know what she is."

Effia had heard the white man talking to her mother earlier that day. He would pay thirty pounds up front and twenty-five shillings a month in tradable goods to Baaba as bride gift. More than even Abeeku could offer, more than had been offered for any other Fante woman in this village or the next.

Effia could hear her father pacing all throughout the evening. She even awoke the next morning to that same sound, the steady rhythm of his feet on the hard clay earth.

"We must make Abeeku think it was his idea," he finally said.

And so, the chief was called to their compound. He sat beside Cobbe as Baaba told him her theory, that the fire that had destroyed so much of their family's worth had also destroyed the child.

"She has the body of a woman, but something evil lurks in her spirit," Baaba said, spitting on the ground for emphasis. "If you marry her, she will never bear you children. If the white man marries her, he will think of this village fondly, and your trade will prosper from it."

Abeeku rubbed his beard carefully as he thought about it. "Bring the Beauty to me," he said finally. Cobbe's second wife brought Effia into the room. She was trembling and her stomach pained her so much that she thought she might empty her bowels right there in front of everyone.

Abeeku stood up so that he was facing her. He ran his fingers along the full landscape of her face, the hills of her cheeks, the caves of her nostrils. "A more beautiful woman has never been born," he said finally. He turned to Baaba. "But I see that you are right. If the white man wants her, he may have her. All the better for our business with them. All the better for the village."

Cobbe, big, strong man that he was, began to weep openly, but Baaba stood tall. She walked over to Effia after Abeeku had left and handed her a black stone pendant that shimmered as though it had been coated in gold dust.

She slipped it into Effia's hands and then leaned into her until her lips were touching Effia's ear. "Take this with you when you go," Baaba said. "A piece of your mother."

And when Baaba finally pulled away, Effia could see something like relief dancing behind her smile.

*

Effia had passed by the Cape Coast Castle only once, when she and Baaba ventured out of their village and into the city, but she had never been in it before the day of her wedding. There was a chapel on the ground level, and she and James Collins were married by a clergyman who had asked Effia to repeat words she didn't mean in a language she didn't understand. There was no dancing, no feasting, no bright colors, slicked hair, or old ladies with wrinkled and bare breasts throwing coins and waving handkerchiefs. Not even Effia's family had come, for after Baaba had convinced them all that the girl was a bad omen, no one wanted anything to do with her. The morning she left for the Castle, Cobbe had kissed the top of her head and waved her away, knowing that the premonition of the dissolution and destruction of the family lineage, the premonition that he had had the night of the fire, would begin here, with his daughter and the white man.

For his part, James had done all he could to make Effia comfortable. She could see how much he tried. He had gotten his interpreter to teach him even more words in Fante so that he could tell her how beautiful she was, how he would take care of her as best he could. He had called her what Abeeku called her, Effia the Beauty.

After they were married, James gave Effia a tour of the Castle. On the ground floor of the north wall there were apartments and warehouses. The center held the parade ground, soldiers' quarters, and guardroom. There was a stockyard, a pond, a hospital. A carpenter's shop, smithy, and kitchen. The Castle was itself a village. Effia walked around with James in complete awe, running her hands along the fine furniture made from wood the color of her father's skin, the silk hangings so smooth they felt like a kiss.

She breathed everything in, stopping at the gun platform that held huge black canons facing out toward the sea. She wanted to rest before James led her up his private stairwell, and so she laid her head down against one of those cannons for just a moment. Then she felt a breeze hit her feet from small holes in the ground.

"What's below?" she asked James, and the mangled Fante word that came back to her was "cargo."

Then, carried up with the breeze, came a faint crying sound. So faint, Effia thought she was imagining it until she lowered herself down, rested her ear against the grate. "James, are there people down there?" she asked.

Quickly, James came to her. He snatched her up from the ground and grabbed her shoulders, looking straight into her eyes. "Yes," he said evenly. It was one Fante word he had mastered.

Effia pulled away from him. She stared back into his piercing eyes. "But how can you keep them down there crying, enh?" she said. "You white people. My father warned me about your ways. Take me home. Take me home right now!"

She didn't realize she'd been screaming until she felt James's hand on her mouth, pushing her lips as though he could force the words back in. He held her like that for a long time, until she had calmed. She didn't know if he understood what she said, but she knew then, just by the faint push of his fingers on her lips, that he was a man capable of hurting, that she should be glad to be on one side of his meanness and not another.

"You want to go home?" James asked. His Fante firm, though unclear. "Your home is no better."

Effia pulled his hand from her mouth and stared at him for a while longer. She remembered her mother's joy at seeing her leave, and knew that James was right. She couldn't go home. She nodded, only barely.

He hurried her up the stairs. On the very top floor were James's quarters. From the window Effia could see straight out to the sea. Cargo ships like black specks of dust in the blue, wet eye of the Atlantic floated so far out that it was difficult to tell how far away from the Castle the ships actually were. Some were maybe three days away, others merely an hour.

Effia watched a ship just like this once she and James finally got to his room. A flickering of yellow light announced its presence on the water, and with that light, Effia could just barely make out the boat's silhouette, long and curved like the hollowed-out skin of a coconut. She wanted to ask James what the ship was carrying and whether it was coming or going, but she had grown tired of trying to decipher his Fante.

James said something to her. He smiled when he spoke, a peace offering. The corners of his lips twitched almost imperceptibly. She shook her head, tried to tell him that she didn't understand, and finally he gestured to the bed in the left-hand corner of the room. She sat. Baaba had explained what would be expected of her on her wedding night before she had left for the Castle that morning, but it seemed no one had explained it to James. When he approached her, his hands were trembling, and she could see the sweat building on his forehead. She was the one who laid her body down. She was the one who lifted her skirt.

They went on like this for weeks until, eventually, the comfort of routine began to dull the ache that missing her family had left her with. Effia didn't know what it was about James that soothed her. Perhaps it was the way he always answered her questions, or the affection he showed her. Perhaps it was the fact that James had no other wives there to attend to and so every one of his nights belonged to her. She had cried the first time he brought her a gift. He had taken the black stone pendant that Baaba had given her and put it on a string so that Effia could wear it around her neck. Touching the stone always gave her great comfort.

Effia knew she was not supposed to care for James, and she kept hearing her father's words echoing through her mind, how he had wanted more for her than to be the Fante wife of a white man. She remembered, too, how close she had come to really *being* someone. Her whole life Baaba had beat her and made her feel small, and she had fought back with her beauty, a silent weapon, but a powerful one, which had led her to the feet of a chief. But ultimately, her mother had won, cast her out, not only of the house but of the village entirely, so that now the only other Fantes she saw regularly were the spouses of the other soldiers.

She'd heard the Englishmen call them "wenches," not wives. "Wife" was a word reserved for the white women across the Atlantic. "Wench" was something else entirely, a word the soldiers used to keep their hands clean so that they would not get in trouble with their god, a being who himself was made up of three but who allowed men to marry only one.

"What is she like?" Effia asked James one day. They had been trading languages. In the early mornings, before he went off to oversee the work of the Castle, James would teach her English, and at night, when they lay in bed, she taught him Fante. This night, he was tracing his finger along the curve of her collarbone while she sang him a song that Baaba used to sing Fiifi at night as Effia lay in the corner, pretending to be asleep, pretending not to care that she was never included. Slowly, James had started to mean more to her than a husband was supposed to mean to a wife. The first word he had asked to learn was "love," and he said it every day.

"Her name is Anne," he said, moving his finger from Effia's collarbone to her lips. "I haven't seen her in so long. We were married ten years ago, but I've been away for so many of those years. I hardly know her at all."

Effia knew that James had two children in England as well. Emily and Jimmy. They were ages five and nine, conceived in the few days he was on leave and able to see his wife. Effia's father had twenty children. The old chief had had nearly a hundred. That a man could be happy with so few seemed unfathomable to her. She wondered what the children looked like. She wondered, too, what Anne wrote James in those letters of hers. They came at unpredictable intervals, four months here, one month there. James would read them at his desk at night while Effia pretended to be sleeping. She didn't know what the letters said, but every time James read one, he would come back to bed and lie as far away from her as possible.

Now, without the force of a letter to keep him away, James was resting his head on her left breast. When he spoke, his breath was hot, a wind that traveled the length of her stomach, down between her legs. "I want children with you," James said, and Effia cringed, worried that she would not be able to fulfill this want, worried too that because she had a bad mother, she herself would become one. She had already told James about Baaba's scheme, how she had forced Effia to keep her womanhood a secret so that she would seem unfit for the men of her village, but James had just laughed her sadness away. "All the better for me," he said.

And yet, Effia had started to believe that perhaps Baaba was right. She'd lost her virginity on the night of her wedding, but months had passed without a pregnancy. The curse may have been rooted in a lie, but perhaps it bore the fruit of truth. The old people of her village used to tell a story about a woman who was said to have been cursed. She lived under a palm tree on the northwest side, and no one had ever called her by her name. Her mother had died so that she might live, and on her tenth birthday, she had been carrying a pot of boiling hot oil from one hut to another. Her father was napping on the ground and she, thinking that she could step over him instead of going around, tripped, spilling the hot oil onto his face and disfiguring him for the rest of his life, which lasted only twenty-five more days. She was banished from the house, and she wandered the Gold Coast for years, until she returned at age seventeen, a strange, rare beauty. Thinking that perhaps she no longer courted death wherever she went, a boy who had known her when she was young offered to marry her as she was, destitute and without family. She conceived within a month, but when the baby came out it was half-caste. Blue-eyed and light-skinned, it died four days later. She left her husband's house the night of the child's death and went to live under the palm tree, punishing herself for the rest of her life.

Effia knew that the elderly of her village only told this story to warn the children to take care when around hot oil, but she wondered about the end of the story, the half-caste child. How this child, both white and black, was an evil powerful enough to force the woman out into the forest of palms.

When Adwoa had married the white soldier, and when Millicent and her mother had wandered into the village, Cobbe turned up his nose. He had always said that the joining of a man and a woman was also the joining of two families. Ancestors, whole histories, came with the act, but so did sins and curses. The children were the embodiment of that unity, and they bore the brunt of it all. What sins did the white man carry with him? Baaba had said that Effia's curse was one of a failed womanhood, but it was Cobbe who had prophesied about a sullied lineage. Effia couldn't help but think that she was fighting against her own womb, fighting against the fire children.

"If you don't give that man children soon, he will take you right back," Adwoa said. She and Effia had not been friends when they lived in the village, but here they saw each other as often as possible, each happy to be near someone who understood her, to hear the comforting sounds of her regional tongue. Adwoa had already had two children since leaving the village. Her husband, Todd Phillips, had only gotten fatter since Effia had last seen him, sweaty and red in Adwoa's old hut.

"I tell you, oh, Todd has kept me flat on my back since I arrived in this place. I am probably expecting right now as we speak."

Effia shuddered. "But his stomach is so big!" she said, and Adwoa laughed until she choked on the groundnuts she was eating.

"Eh, but the stomach is not the part you use to make the baby," she said. "I will give you some roots from the woods. You put them under the bed when you lie with him. Tonight, you must be like an animal when he comes into the room. A lioness. She mates with her lion and he thinks the moment is about him when it is really about her, *her* children, *her* posterity. Her trick is to make him think that he is king of the bush, but what does a king matter? Really, she is king and queen and everything in between. Tonight, we will make you live up to your title, Beauty."

And so Adwoa came back with roots. They were no ordinary roots. They were large and swirled, and when you pulled back one strand, another would appear to take its place. Effia put them under the bed and they only seemed to multiply, spilling leg after leg out until it seemed the root would pick the bed up on its back and walk away, a strange new spider.

"Your husband should not be able to see any of it," Adwoa said, and they worked to push back the strands of root that insisted on peeking out, pushing and pulling until finally it was contained.

Then Adwoa helped Effia prepare for James. She plaited and smoothed her hair and spread oil on her skin, and red clay on the apples of her cheeks and the curve of her lips. Effia made sure that when James came in that night the room smelled earthy and lush, like something there could bear fruit.

"What's all this?" James asked. He was still in his uniform, and Effia could tell that he'd had a long day by the way his lapel drooped. She helped him pull off his coat and shirt and she pressed her body against his, as Adwoa had taught her. Before he could register his surprise, she grabbed his arms and pushed him to the bed. Not since their first night together had he been this timid, afraid of her unfamiliar body, the full-figured flesh, so different from how he had described his wife. Excited now, he pushed into her, and she squeezed her eyes as tightly as she could, her tongue circling her lips. He pushed harder, his breathing heavy and labored. She scratched his back, and he cried out. She bit his ear and pulled his hair. He pushed against her as though he were trying to move through her. And when she opened her eyes to look at him, she saw something like pain written across his face and the ugliness of the act, the sweat and blood and wetness they produced, became illuminated, and she knew that if she was an animal tonight, then he was too.

Once they had finished, Effia lay with her head on James's shoulder.

"What is that?" James asked, turning his head. They had moved the bed so that now three strands of the root were exposed.

"Nothing," Effia said.

James jumped up and peered underneath the bed. "What is it,

Effia?" he asked again, his voice more forceful than she had ever heard it before.

"It's nothing. A root that Adwoa gave me. For fertility."

His lips formed a thin line. "Now, Effia, I don't want any voodoo or black magic in this place. My men can't hear that I let my wench place strange roots under the bed. It's not Christian."

Effia had heard him say this before. Christian. That was why they had been married in the chapel by the stern man in black who shook his head every time he looked at her. He'd spoken before, too, of the "voodoo" he thought all Africans participated in. She could not tell him the fables of Anansi the spider or stories that the old people from her village used to tell her without his growing wary. Since moving to the Castle, she'd discovered that only the white men talked of "black magic." As though magic had a color. Effia had seen a traveling witch who carried a snake around her neck and shoulders. This woman had had a son. She'd sung lullabies to him at night and held his hands and kept him fed, same as anyone else. There was nothing dark about her.

The need to call this thing "good" and this thing "bad," this thing "white" and this thing "black," was an impulse that Effia did not understand. In her village, everything was everything. Everything bore the weight of everything else.

The next day Effia told Adwoa that James had seen the root.

"That is not good," Adwoa said. "Did he call it evil?" Effia nodded, and Adwoa clicked her tongue three times. "Todd would have said the same thing. These men could not tell good from evil if they were Nyame himself. I don't think it will work now, Effia. I'm sorry." But Effia wasn't sorry. If she was barren, so be it.

Soon, even James was too busy to worry about children. The Castle was expecting a visit from Dutch officers, and everything needed to run as smoothly as possible. James would wake up well before Effia to help the men with the imported store items and to see to the ships. Effia spent more and more time wandering around the villages surrounding the Castle, roaming the forests, and chatting with Adwoa.

The afternoon of the Dutch arrival, Effia met with Adwoa and some of the other wenches just outside the Castle. They stopped beneath the shade of a patch of trees in order to eat yams with palm oil stew. There was Adwoa, then Sarah, the half-caste wench of Sam York. There was also the new wench, Eccoah. She was tall and slender, and she walked as though her limbs were made of thin twigs, as though wind could snap and collapse her.

This day, Eccoah was lying in the slim shade of a palm tree. Effia had helped her coil her hair the day before, and in the sun, it looked like a million tiny snakes rising from her head.

"My husband cannot pronounce my name well. He wants to call me Emily," Eccoah said.

"If he wants to call you Emily, let him call you Emily," Adwoa said. Out of the four of them, she had been a wench the longest, and she always spoke her opinions loudly and freely. Everyone knew that her husband practically worshipped at her feet. "Better that than to listen to him butcher your mother tongue over and over."

Sarah dug her elbows into the dust. "My father was a soldier too. When he died, Mama moved us back to our village. I came to marry Sam, but he did not have to worry about my name. Do you know he knew my father? They were soldiers together in the Castle when I was just a small girl."

Effia shook her head. She was lying on her belly. She loved days like this one, where she could speak Fante as fast as she wanted. No one asking her to slow down, no one telling her to speak English.

"My husband comes up from the dungeons stinking like a dying animal," Eccoah said softly.

They all looked away. No one ever mentioned the dungeons.

"He comes to me smelling like feces and rot and looking at me like he has seen a million ghosts, and he cannot tell if I am one of them or not. I tell him he must wash before he touches me and sometimes he does, but sometimes he pushes me to the floor and pushes into me like he has been possessed."

Effia sat up and rested a hand against her stomach. James had received another letter from his wife the day after he'd found the root underneath their bed. They had not slept together since.

The wind picked up. The snakes in Eccoah's hair snapped this way and that, her twig arms lifted. "There are people down there, you know," she said. "There are women down there who look like us, and our husbands must learn to tell the difference."

They all fell silent. Eccoah leaned back against the tree, and Effia watched as a line of ants passed over a strand of her hair, the shape of it seeming, to them, to be just another part of the natural world.

After that first day in the Castle, James never spoke to Effia about the slaves they kept in the dungeon, but he spoke to her often about beasts. That was what the Asantes trafficked most here. Beasts. Monkeys and chimpanzees, even a few leopards. Birds like the king crowns and parrots that she and Fiifi used to try to catch when they were children, roaming the forests in search of the one odd bird, the bird that had feathers so beautiful it seemed to be set apart from the rest. They would spend hours on end looking for just one such bird, and most days they would find none.

She wondered what such a bird would be worth, because in the Castle all beasts were ascribed worth. She had seen James look at a king crown brought in by one of their Asante traders and declare that it was worth four pounds. What about the human beast? How much was he worth? Effia had known, of course, that there were people in the dungeons. People who spoke a different dialect than her, people who had been captured in tribal wars, even people who had been stolen, but she had never thought of where they went from there. She had never thought of what James must think every time he saw them. If he went into the dungeons and saw women who reminded him of her, who looked like her and smelled like her. If he came back to her haunted by what he saw.

Effia soon realized that she was pregnant. It was spring, and the mango trees outside the Castle had started to drop down mangoes. Her stomach jutted out, soft and fleshy, its own kind of fruit. James was so happy when she told him that he picked her up and danced her around their quarters. She slapped his back and told him to set her down, lest they shake the baby to pieces, and he had complied before bending and planting a kiss on her barely bulged stomach.

But their joy was soon tempered by news from her village. Cobbe had fallen ill. So ill that it was unclear whether or not he would still be alive by the time Effia made the journey back to see him.

She was not sure who had sent the letter from her village, for it was addressed to her husband and written in broken English. She had been gone two years, and she had not heard from anyone in her family since then. She knew that this was Baaba's doing, and indeed she was surprised that anyone had even thought to notify her of her father's illness.

The journey back to the village took about three days. James did not want her to make the trip alone in her condition, but he could not accompany her, so he sent along a house girl. When they arrived, everything in the village looked different. The colors of the treetop canopies seemed to have dulled, their vibrant browns and greens now muted. The sounds seemed different too. Everything that once rustled now stood still. Abeeku had made the village into one so prosperous that they would forever be known as one of the leading slave markets in all of the Gold Coast. He had no time to see Effia, but he sent along gifts of sweet palm wine and gold to meet her once she arrived at her father's compound.

Baaba stood in the entranceway. She looked to have aged a hundred years in the two that Effia had been gone. Her scowl was held in place by the hundreds of tiny wrinkles that pulled at her skin, and her nails had grown so long that they curled like talons. She didn't speak a word, only led Effia to the room where her father lay dying.

No one knew what sickness had struck Cobbe. Apothecaries, witch doctors, even the Christian minister from the Castle, had been called upon to give their opinions and pray over the man, and yet no measure of healing thoughts or medicines could spit him out of the lips of death.

Fiifi stood beside him, wiping the sweat off his forehead carefully. Suddenly, Effia was crying and shaking. She reached out her hand to her father's and began to stroke the sallow skin there.

"He cannot speak," Fiifi whispered, glancing quickly at her bulging belly. "He is too weak."

She nodded and continued to cry.

Fiifi dropped the drenched cloth and took Effia's hand. "Big sister, I am the one who wrote you the letter. Mama did not want you to come, but I thought you should get to see our father before he enters Asamando."

Cobbe closed his eyes, and a low murmur escaped his lips so that Effia could see that the Land of the Spirits was indeed calling him.

"Thank you," she said to Fiifi, and he nodded.

He began walking out of the room, but before he reached the hut's door, he turned. "She is not your mother, you know. Baaba. Our father had you by a house girl who ran away into the fire the night you were born. She is the one who left you that stone you wear around your neck."

Fiifi stepped outside. And soon, Cobbe died, Effia still holding his hand. The villagers would say that Cobbe had been waiting for Effia to come home before he could die, but Effia knew that it was more complex than that. His unrest had kept him alive, and now that unrest belonged to Effia. It would feed her life and the life of her child.

After she had wiped her tears, Effia walked out of the compound and into the sun. Baaba sat on the stump of a felled tree, her shoulders squared as she held hands with Fiifi, who stood beside her, now as quiet as a field mouse. Effia wanted to say something to Baaba, to apologize perhaps for the burden her father had made Baaba carry all of those years, but before she could speak, Baaba hacked from her throat, spit on the ground before Effia's feet, and said, "You are nothing from nowhere. No mother and now no father." She looked at Effia's stomach and smiled. "What can grow from nothing?"

Esi

THE SMELL WAS UNBEARABLE. In the corner, a woman was crying so hard that it seemed her bones would break from her convulsions. This was what they wanted. The baby had messed itself, and Afua, its mother, had no milk. She was naked, save the small scrap of fabric the traders had given her to wipe her nipples when they leaked, but they had miscalculated. No food for mother meant no food for baby. The baby would cry soon, but the sound would be absorbed by the mud walls, subsumed into the cries of the hundreds of women who surrounded it.

Esi had been in the women's dungeon of the Cape Coast Castle for two weeks. She spent her fifteenth birthday there. On her fourteenth birthday, she was in the heart of Asanteland, in her father's, Big Man's, compound. He was the best warrior in the village, so everyone had come to pay their respects to the daughter who grew more beautiful with each passing day. Kwasi Nnuro brought sixty yams. More yams than any other suitor had ever brought before. Esi would have married him in the summer, when the sun stretched long and high, when the palm trees could be tapped for wine, climbed by the spriest children, their arms holding the trunk in a hug as they shinnied to the top to pluck the fruits that waited there.

When she wanted to forget the Castle, she thought of these things, but she did not expect joy. Hell was a place of remembering, each beautiful moment passed through the mind's eye until it fell to the ground like a rotten mango, perfectly useless, uselessly perfect.

A soldier came into the dungeon and began to speak. He had to hold his nose to keep from vomiting. The women did not understand him. His voice didn't seem angry, but they had learned to back away at the sight of that uniform, that skin the color of coconut meat.

The soldier repeated himself, louder this time, as though volume would coax understanding. Irritated, he ventured further into the room. He stepped in feces and cursed. He plucked the baby from Afua's cradled arms, and Afua began to cry. He slapped her, and she stopped, a learned reflex.

Tansi sat next to Esi. The two had made the journey to the Castle together. Now that they weren't walking constantly, or speaking in hushed tones, Esi had time to get to know her journey friend. Tansi was a hardy and ugly woman, barely turned sixteen. She was thick, her body built on a solid foundation. Esi hoped, and dared not hope, that they would be allowed to stay together even longer.

"Where are they taking the baby?" Esi asked.

Tansi spit onto the clay floor and swirled the spittle with her finger, creating a salve. "They will kill it, I'm sure," she said. The baby was conceived before Afua's marriage ceremony. As punishment, the village chief had sold her to the traders. Afua had told Esi this when she first came into the dungeon, when she was still certain that a mistake had been made, that her parents would return for her.

Now, hearing Tansi speak, Afua resumed her crying, but it was as though no one heard. These tears were a matter of routine. They came for all of the women. They dropped until the clay below them turned to mud. At night, Esi dreamed that if they all cried in unison, the mud would turn to river and they could be washed away into the Atlantic.

"Tansi, tell me a story, please," Esi begged. But then they were interrupted again. The soldiers came in with the same mushy porridge that had been fed to them in the Fante village where Esi was held. Esi had learned to swallow it down without gagging. It was the only food they ever received, and their stomachs were empty more days than full. The porridge passed right through her, it seemed. The ground was littered with their waste, the unbearable smell.

"Ah! You're too old for stories, my sister," Tansi said once the soldiers left, but Esi knew she would give in soon. Tansi enjoyed the sound of her own voice. She pulled Esi's head into her lap and began playing with her hair, pulling at the strands that had been caked with dust, so brittle that they could be broken, each one snapped like a twig.

"Do you know the story of the kente cloth?" Tansi asked. Esi had heard it numerous times before, twice from Tansi herself, but she shook her head. Asking if the story had been heard before was a part of the story itself.

Tansi began to tell her. "Two Asante men went out into the forest one day. They were weavers by trade, and they had gone out to hunt for meat. When they got to the forest to collect their traps, they were met by Anansi, the mischievous spider. He was spinning a magnificent web. They watched him, studied him, and soon realized that a spider's web is a unique and beautiful thing, and that a spider's technique is flawless. They went home and decided to weave cloth the way Anansi weaves his web. From that, kente was born."

"You are a fine storyteller," Esi said. Tansi laughed and smoothed the salve she had created onto her knees and elbows to soothe the cracked skin there. The last story she had told Esi was of how she had been captured by the northerners, plucked from her marriage bed while her husband was off fighting a war. She had been taken with a few other girls, but the rest had not survived.

By morning, Afua had died. Her skin was purple and blue, and Esi knew that she had held her breath until Nyame took her. They would all be punished for this. The soldiers came in, though Esi was no longer able to tell what time. The mud walls of the dungeon made all time equal. There was no sunlight. Darkness was day and night and everything in between. Sometimes there were so many bodies stacked into the women's dungeon that they all had to lie, stomach down, so that women could be stacked on top of them.

It was one of those days. Esi was kicked to the ground by one of the soldiers, his foot at the base of her neck so that she couldn't turn her head to breathe anything but the dust and detritus from the ground. The new women were brought in, and some were wailing so hard that the soldiers smacked them unconscious. They were piled on top of the other women, their bodies deadweight. When the smacked ones came to, there were no more tears. Esi could feel the woman on top of her peeing. Urine traveled between both of their legs.

Esi learned to split her life into Before the Castle and Now. Before the Castle, she was the daughter of Big Man and his third wife, Maame. Now she was dust. Before the Castle, she was the prettiest girl in the village. Now she was thin air.

Esi was born in a small village in the heart of the Asante nation. Big Man had thrown an outdooring feast that lasted four nights. Five goats were slaughtered and boiled until their tough skins turned tender. It was rumored that Maame did not stop crying or praising Nyame for the entire duration of the ceremony, nor would she set baby Esi down. "You never know what could happen," she kept repeating.

At that time, Big Man was known only as Kwame Asare. Esi's father was not a chief, but he commanded just as much respect, for he was the best warrior the Asante nation had ever seen, and at age twenty-five he already had five wives and ten children. Everyone in the village knew his seed was strong. His sons, still toddlers and young children, were already tough wrestlers and his daughters were beauties.

Esi grew up in bliss. The villagers called her ripe mango because she was just on the right side of spoiled, still sweet. There was nothing her parents would refuse her. Even her strong warrior of a father had been known to carry her through the village at night when she couldn't sleep. Esi would hold the tip of his finger, to her as thick as a branch, as she toddled past the huts that made up each compound. Her village was small but growing steadily. In the first year of their walks, it wouldn't take but twenty minutes to reach the forest edge that cut them off from the rest of Asanteland, but that forest had been pushed farther and farther back until by the fifth year the journey there took nearly an hour. Esi loved walking to the forest with her father. She would listen, enraptured, as he told her how the forest was so dense it was like a shield, impenetrable to their enemies. He would tell her how he and the other warriors knew the forest better than they knew the lines of their own palms. And this was good. Following the lines of a palm would lead nowhere, but the forest led the warriors to other villages that they could conquer to build up their strength.

"When you are old enough, Esi, you will learn how to climb these trees with nothing but your bare hands," he said to her as they walked back to the village one day.

Esi looked up. The tops of the trees looked as though they were brushing the sky, and Esi wondered why leaves were green instead of blue.

When Esi was seven years old, her father won the battle that would earn him the name Big Man. There had been rumors that in a village just north of theirs, warriors had come back with splendors of gold and women. They had even raided the British storehouse, earning gunpowder and muskets in the process. Chief Nnuro, the leader of Esi's village, called a meeting of all the able-bodied men.

"Have you heard the news?" he asked them, and they grunted, slammed their staffs against the hard earth, and cried out. "The swine of the northern village are walking about like kings. All around Asante people will say, it is the northerners who stole guns from the British. It is the northerners who are the most powerful warriors in all of the Gold Coast." The men stomped their feet and shook their heads. "Will we allow this?" the chief asked.

"No!" they cried.

Kwaku Agyei, the most sensible among them, hushed their cries and said, "Listen to us! We may go to fight the northerners, but what have we? No guns, no gunpowder. And what will we gain? So many people will praise our enemies in the north, but will they not still praise us as well? We have been the strongest village for decades. No one has been able to break through the forest and challenge us."

"So will you have us wait until the northern snake slithers its way into our fields and steals our women?" Esi's father asked. The two men stood on opposite sides of the room, and all the other men stood between them, turning their heads from one to the other in order to see which gift would win: wisdom or strength.

"I only say, let us not be too hasty. Lest we appear weak in the process."

"But who is weak?" Esi's father asked. He pointed to Nana Addae, then Kojo Nyarko, then Kwabena Gyimah. "Who among us is weak? You? Or maybe you?"

The men shook their heads one by one, and soon they were all shaking their entire bodies into a rallying cry that could be heard throughout the village. From the compound where Esi stood helping her mother fry plantains, she heard them, and dropped two slices of plantains so quickly that oil jumped up and splashed her mother's leg.

"Aiieee!" her mother cried out, wiping the oil away with her hands and blowing on the burn. "Stupid girl! When will you learn to be careful around fire?" Maame asked. Esi had heard her mother say this or something like it many times before. Maame was terrified of fire. "Be careful of fire. Know when to use it and when to stay cold," she would often say.

"It was an accident," Esi snapped. She wanted to be outside, catching more of the warriors' discussion. Her mother reached over and yanked her ear.

"Who are you talking to that way?" she hissed. "Think before you act. Think before you speak."

Esi apologized to her mother, and Maame, who had never been able to stay mad at Esi for longer than a few seconds, kissed the top of her head as the men's cries grew louder and louder.

Everyone in the village knew the story. Esi had her father tell it to her every night for a whole month. She would lie with her head in his lap, listening as he spoke of how the men stole out for the northern village on the evening of the rallying cry. Their plan was thin: overtake the town and steal whatever had been stolen. Esi's father told her of how he led the group through the forest until they came upon the circle of warriors protecting the newly acquired goods. Her father and his warriors hid in the trees. Their feet moved with the lightness of leaves on the forest ground. When they came upon the warriors of the northern village, they fought bravely, but it was of no use. Esi's father and many others were captured and packed into huts that had been converted into a prison camp.

It was Kwaku Agyei and his few followers who had had the foresight to wait in the forest until after the eager warriors had rushed in. They found the guns that the northerners were hiding and loaded them quickly and quietly before moving in to where their fellow men were being held captive. Though there were only a few of them, Kwaku Agyei and his men were able to hold off the warriors with the stories they told of the many men they had waiting behind them. Kwaku Agyei said that if this mission failed, there would be one raid every night until the end of time. "If it isn't the West, it will be the whites," he reasoned, darkness glinting from the gap between his front teeth.

The northerners felt they had no choice but to give in. They released Esi's father and the others, who parted with five of the stolen guns. The men returned to their village in silence, Esi's father consumed by his embarrassment. When they reached the edge of their village, he stopped Kwaku Agyei, got down on both of his knees, and bowed his head before him. "I am sorry, my brother. I will never again rush into a fight when it is possible to reason."

"It takes a big man to admit his folly," Kwaku Agyei said, and they all continued into the village, the contrite and newly christened Big Man leading the way.

This was the Big Man who returned to Esi, the one she knew as she grew older. Slow to anger, rational, and still the strongest and bravest warrior of them all. By the time Esi turned twelve their small village had won more than fifty-five wars under Big Man's leadership. The spoils of these wars could be seen as the warriors carried them back, shimmering gold and colorful textiles in large tan sacks, captives in iron cages.

It was the prisoners that fascinated Esi the most, for after each capture they would be put on display in the center of the village square. Anyone could walk by and stare at them, mostly young, virile warriors, though sometimes women and their children. Some of these prisoners would be taken by the villagers as slaves, house boys and house girls, cooks and cleaners, but soon there would be too many to keep and the overflow would have to be dealt with.

"Mama, what happens to all the prisoners after they leave here?" Esi asked Maame as they passed by the square one afternoon, a roped goat, their dinner, trailing behind them.

"That's boys' talk, Esi. You don't need to think about it," her mother replied, shifting her eyes.

For as long as Esi could remember, and perhaps even before, Maame had refused to choose her own house girl or house boy from among the prisoners who were paraded through the village each month, but because there were now so many prisoners, Big Man had started to insist.

"A house girl could help you with the cooking," he said.

"Esi helps me with my cooking."

"But Esi is my daughter, not some common girl to be ordered about."

Esi smiled. She loved her mother, but she knew how lucky Maame was to have gotten a husband like Big Man when she had no family, no background to speak of. Big Man had saved Maame somehow, from what wretchedness Esi did not know. She knew only that her mother would do almost anything for her father.

"All right," she said. "Esi and I will choose a girl tomorrow."

And so they chose a girl and decided to call her Abronoma, Little Dove. The girl had the darkest skin Esi had ever seen. She kept her eyes low, and though her Twi was passable, she rarely spoke it. She didn't know her age, but Esi guessed Abronoma was not much older than she was. At first, Abronoma was horrible at the chores. She spilled oil; she didn't sweep under things; she didn't have good stories for the children.

"She's useless," Maame said to Big Man. "We have to take her back."

They were all outside, basking under the warm midday sun. Big Man tilted his head back and let out a laugh that rumbled like thunder in the rainy season. "Take her back where? *Odo*, there's only one way to train a slave." He turned to Esi, who was trying to climb a palm tree the way she'd seen the other kids do it, but her arms were too small to reach around. "Esi, go and get me my switch."

The switch in question was made from two reeds tied together. It was older than Esi's paternal grandfather, having been passed down from generation to generation. Big Man had never beaten Esi with it, but she had seen him beat his sons. She'd heard the way it whistled when it snapped back off of flesh. Esi moved to enter the compound, but Maame stopped her.

"No!" she said.

Big Man raised his hand to his wife, anger flashing quickly through his eyes like steam from cold water hitting a hot pan. "No?"

Maame stammered, "I—I just think that I should be the one to do it."

Big Man lowered his hand. He stared at her carefully for a while longer, and Esi tried to read the look that passed between them. "So be it," Big Man said. "But tomorrow I will bring her out here. She will carry water from this yard to that tree there, and if even so much as a drop falls, then *I* will take care of it. Do you hear me?"

Maame nodded and Big Man shook his head. He had always told anyone who would listen that he had spoiled his third wife, seduced by her beautiful face and softened by her sad eyes.

Maame and Esi went into their hut and found Abronoma, curled up on a bamboo cot, living up to her name of a little bird. Maame woke her and had her stand before them. She pulled out a switch that Big Man had given her, a switch she had never used. She then looked at Esi with tears in her eyes. "Please, leave us."

Esi left the hut and for minutes after could hear the sound of the switch and the harmonizing pitch of two separate cries.

The next day Big Man called everyone in his compound out to see if Abronoma could carry a bucket of water on her head from the yard to the tree without spilling a drop. Esi and her whole family, her four stepmothers and nine half siblings, scattered around their large yard, waiting for the girl to first fetch water from the stream into a large black bucket. From there, Big Man had her stand before all of them and bow before starting the journey to the tree. He would walk beside her to be certain there was no error.

Esi could see Little Dove shaking as she lifted the bucket onto her head. Maame clutched Esi against her chest and smiled at the girl when she bowed at them, but the look Abronoma returned was fearful and then vacant. When the bucket touched her head, the family began to jeer.

"She'll never make it!" Amma, Big Man's first wife, said.

"Watch, she will spill it all and drown herself in the process," Kojo, the eldest son, said.

Little Dove took her first step and Esi let out the breath she had been holding. She herself had never been able to carry so much as a single plank of wood on her head, but she had watched her mother carry a perfectly round coconut without it ever rolling off, steady as a second head. "Where did you learn to do that?" Esi had asked Maame then, and the woman replied, "You can learn anything when you have to learn it. You could learn to fly if it meant you would live another day."

Abronoma steadied her legs and kept walking, her head facing forward. Big Man walked beside her, whispering insults in her ear. She reached the tree at the forest's edge and pivoted, making her way back to the audience that awaited her. By the time she got close enough that Esi could make out her features again, there was sweat dripping off the ledge of her nose and her eyes were brimming with tears. Even the bucket on her head seemed to be crying, condensation working its way down the outside of it. As she lifted the bucket off of her head, she started to smile triumphantly. Maybe it was a small gust of wind, maybe an insect looking for a bath, or maybe the Dove's hand slipped, but before the bucket reached the ground, two drops sloshed out.

Esi looked at Maame, who had turned her sad, pleading eyes to Big Man, but by that point, the rest of the family was already shouting for punishment.

Kojo began to lead them into a song:

The Dove has failed. Oh, what to do? Make her to suffer or you'll fail too!

Big Man reached for his switch, and soon the song gained its accompaniment: the percussion of reed to flesh, the woodwind of reed to air. This time, Abronoma did not cry.

"If he didn't beat her, everyone would think he was weak," Esi said. After the event, Maame had been inconsolable, crying to Esi that Big Man should not have beaten Little Dove for so small a mistake. Esi was licking soup off of her fingers, her lips stained orange. Her mother had taken Abronoma into their hut and made a salve for her wounds, and now the girl lay on a cot sleeping.

"Weak, eh?" Maame said. She glared at her daughter with malice that Esi had never before seen.

"Yes," Esi whispered.

"That I should live to hear my own daughter speak like this. You want to know what weakness is? Weakness is treating someone as though they belong to you. Strength is knowing that everyone belongs to themselves."

Esi was hurt. She had only said what anyone else in her village would have said, and for this Maame yelled at her. Esi wanted to cry, to hug her mother, something, but Maame left the room then to finish the chores that Abronoma could not perform that night.

Just as she left, Little Dove began to stir. Esi fetched her water, and helped tilt her head back so that she could drink it. The wounds on her back were still fresh, and the salve that Maame had made stank of the forest. Esi wiped the corners of Abronoma's lips with her fingers, but the girl pushed her away.

"Leave me," she said.

"I—I'm sorry for what happened. He is a good man."

Abronoma spit onto the clay in front of her. "Your father is Big Man, eh?" she asked, and Esi nodded, proud despite what she had just seen her father do. The Dove let out a mirthless laugh. "My father too is Big Man, and now look at what I am. Look at what your mother was."

"What my mother was?"

Little Dove's eyes shot toward Esi. "You don't know?"

Esi, who had not spent more than an hour away from her mother's sight in her life, couldn't imagine any secrets. She knew the feel of her and the smell of her. She knew how many colors were in her irises and she knew each crooked tooth. Esi looked at Abronoma, but Abronoma shook her head and continued her laugh.

"Your mother was once a slave for a Fante family. She was raped by her master because he too was a Big Man and big men can do what they please, lest they appear *weak*, eh?" Esi looked away, and Abronoma continued in a whisper. "You are not your mother's first daughter. There was one before you. And in my village we have a saying about separated sisters. They are like a woman and her reflection, doomed to stay on opposite sides of the pond."

Esi wanted to hear more, but there was no time to ask the Dove. Maame came back into the room, and saw the two girls sitting beside each other.

"Esi, come here and let Abronoma sleep. Tomorrow you will wake up early and help me clean."

Esi left Abronoma to her rest. She looked at her mother. The way her shoulders always seemed to droop, the way her eyes were always shifting. Suddenly, Esi was filled with a horrible shame. She remembered the first time she'd seen an elder spit on the captives in the town square. The man had said, "Northerners, they are not even people. They are the dirt that begs for spit." Esi was five years old then. His words had felt like a lesson, and the next time she passed, she timidly gathered her own spit and launched it at a little boy who stood huddled with his mother. The boy had cried out, speaking a language that Esi didn't understand, and Esi had felt bad, not for having spit, but for knowing how angry her mother would have been to see her do it.

Now all Esi could picture was her own mother behind the dull metal of the cages. Her own mother, huddled with a sister she would never know.

In the months that followed, Esi tried to befriend Abronoma. Her heart had started to ache for the little bird who had now perfected her role as house girl. Since the beating, no crumb was dropped, no water spilled. In the evenings, after Abronoma's work was done, Esi would try to coax more information from her about her mother's past.

"I don't know any more," Abronoma said, taking the bundle of palm branches to sweep the floor, or straining used oil through leaves. "Don't worry me!" she screamed once she'd reached the height of her annoyance.

Still, Esi tried to make amends. "What can I do?" she asked. "What can I do?"

After weeks of asking, Esi finally received an answer. "Send word to my father," Abronoma said. "Tell him where I am. Tell him where I am and there will be no bad blood between us."

That night, Esi couldn't sleep. She wanted to make peace with Abronoma, but if her father knew what she had been asked to do, surely there would be war in her hut. She could hear her father now, yelling at Maame, telling her that she was raising Esi to be a small woman, weak. On the floor of her hut, Esi turned and turned and turned, until finally her mother hushed her.

"Please," Maame said. "I'm tired."

And all Esi could see behind her closed eyelids was her mother as house girl.

Esi decided then that she would send the message. Early, early, early the next morning she went to the messenger man who lived on the edge of the village. He listened to her words and the words of others before setting out into the forest every week. Those words would be carried from village to village, messenger man to messenger man. Who knew if Esi's message would ever reach Abronoma's father? It could be dropped or forgotten, altered or lost, but at the very least, Esi could say that she had done it.

When she got back, Abronoma was the only person yet awake. Esi told her what she had done that morning, and the girl clapped her hands together and then gathered Esi into her small arms, squeezing until Esi's breath caught.

"All is forgotten?" Esi asked once the Dove had released her.

"Everything is equal," Abronoma said, and relief rushed through Esi's body like blood. It filled her to the brim and left her fingers shaking. She hugged Abronoma back, and as the girl's body relaxed in her arms, Esi let herself imagine that the body she was hugging was her sister's.

Months went by, and Little Dove grew excited. In the evenings she could be found pacing the grounds and muttering to herself before sleep. "My father. My father is coming."

Big Man heard her mutterings and told everyone to beware of her, for she might be a witch. Esi would watch her carefully for signs, but every day it was the same thing. "My father is coming. I know it. He is coming." Finally, Big Man promised to slap the words out of the Dove if she continued, and so she stopped, and the family soon forgot.

Everyone went along as usual. Esi's village had never been challenged in Esi's lifetime. All fighting was done away from home. Big Man and the other warriors would go into nearby villages, pillaging the land, sometimes setting the grass on fire so that people from three villages over could see the smoke and know the warriors had come. But this time things were different.

It began while the family was sleeping. It was Big Man's night in Maame's hut, so Esi had to sleep on the ground in the corner. When she heard the soft moaning, the quickened breath, she turned to face the wall of the hut. Once, just once, she had watched them where they lay, the darkness helping to cover her curiosity. Her father was hovering over her mother's body, moving softly at first, and then with more force. She couldn't see much, but it was the sounds that had interested her. The sounds her parents made together, sounds that walked a thin line between pleasure and pain. Esi both wanted and was afraid to want. So she never watched again.

That night, once everyone in the hut had fallen asleep, the call went out. Everyone in the village had grown up knowing what each sound signified: two long moans meant the enemy was miles off yet; three quick shouts meant they were upon them. Hearing the three, Big Man jumped from the bed and grabbed the machete he stored under each of his wives' cots.

"You take Esi and go into the woods!" he screamed at Maame before running from the hut with little time to cover his nakedness.

Esi did what her father had taught her, grabbing the small knife that her mother used to slice plantains and tucking it into the cloth of her skirt. Maame sat at the edge of her cot. "Come on!" Esi said, but her mother didn't move. Esi rushed to the bed and shook her, but she still didn't move.

"I can't do it again," she whispered.

"Do what again?" Esi asked, but she was hardly listening. Adrenaline was coursing through her so urgently that her hands trembled. Was this because of the message she had sent?

"I can't do it again," her mother whispered. "No more woods. No more fire." She was rocking back and forth and cradling the fat flap of her stomach in her arms as though it were a child.

Abronoma came in from the slave quarters, her laugh echoing through the hut. "My father is here!" she said, dancing this way and that. "I told you he would come to find me, and he has come!"

The girl scurried away, and Esi didn't know what would become of her. Outside, people were screaming and running. Children were crying.

Esi's mother grabbed Esi's hand and dropped something into it. It was a black stone, glimmering with gold. Smooth, as if it had been scrubbed carefully for years to preserve its perfect surface.

"I have been keeping this for you," Maame said. "I wanted to give it to you on your wedding day. I—I left one like this for your sister. I left it with Baaba after I set the fire."

"My sister?" Esi asked. So what Abronoma said was true.

Maame babbled nonsense words, words she had never spoken before. Sister, Baaba, fire. Sister, Baaba, fire. Esi wanted to ask more questions, but the noise outside was growing louder, and her mother's eyes were growing blank, emptying somehow of something.

Esi stared at her mother then, and it was as though she were seeing her for the first time. Maame was not a whole woman. There were large swaths of her spirit missing, and no matter how much she loved Esi, and no matter how much Esi loved her, they both knew in that moment that love could never return what Maame had lost. And Esi knew, too, that her mother would die rather than run into the woods ever again, die before capture, die even if it meant that in her dying, Esi would inherit that unspeakable sense of loss, learn what it meant to be un-whole.

"You go," Maame said as Esi tugged at her arms, tried to move her legs. "Go!" she repeated.

Esi stopped and tucked the black stone into her wrapper. She hugged her mother, took the knife from her skirt, put it in her mother's hand, and ran.

She reached the woods quickly and found a palm tree that her arms could manage. She had been practicing, not knowing that it was for this. She wrapped her arms around the trunk, hugging it while using her legs to push her up, up, as far as she could go. The moon was full, as large as the rock of terror that was sitting in Esi's gut. What had she ever known of terror?

Time passed and passed. Esi felt like her arms were encircling fire instead of the tree, so badly were they burning. The dark shadows of the leaves on the ground had started to look menacing. Soon, the sound of screaming people falling from the trees like plucked fruit could be heard all around her, and then a warrior was at the bottom of her tree. His language was unfamiliar, but she knew enough to know what came next. He threw a rock at her, then another, then another. The fourth rock slammed into her side, but still she held on. The fifth hit the lattice of her clasped fingers; her arms came undone, and she fell to the ground.

She was tied to others; how many, she didn't know. She didn't see anyone from her compound. Not her stepmothers or half siblings. Not her mother. The rope around her wrists held her palms out in supplication. Esi studied the lines on those palms. They led nowhere. She had never felt so hopeless in her life.

Everyone walked. Esi had walked for miles with her father before and so she thought that she could take it. And indeed the first few days were not so bad, but by the tenth the calluses on Esi's feet split open and blood seeped out, painting the leaves she left behind. Ahead of her, the bloody leaves of others. So many were crying that it was difficult to hear when the warriors spoke, but she wouldn't have understood them anyway. When she could, she checked to see if the stone her mother had given her was still safely tucked in her wrapper. She didn't know how long they would be allowed to keep their clothes. The leaves on the forest ground were so damp with blood and sweat and dew that a child in front of Esi slipped on them. One of the warriors caught him, helped him to stand up, and the little boy thanked him.

"Why should he thank him? They are going to eat us all," the woman behind Esi said. Esi had to strain to hear through the haze of tears and buzz of insects that surrounded them.

"Who will eat us?" Esi asked.

"The white men. That is what my sister says. She says the white men buy us from these soldiers and then they cook us up like goats in soup."

"No!" Esi cried, and one of the soldiers was quick to run up to her and poke her side with a stick. Once he left, her flank throbbing, Esi pictured the goats that walked freely around her village. Then she pictured herself capturing one—the way she roped its legs and laid its body down. The way she slit its neck. Was this how the white men would kill her? She shuddered.

"What's your name?" Esi asked.

"They call me Tansi."

"They call me Esi."

And like that, the two became friends. They walked all day. The sores on Esi's feet had no time to heal, so soon were they reopened. At times, the warriors would leave them tied to trees in the forest so that they could go ahead and survey the people of new villages. At times, more people from those villages would be taken and added to the rest of them. The rope around Esi's wrists had started to burn. A strange burn, like nothing she had ever felt before, like cool fire, the scratch of salty wind.

And soon, the smell of that wind greeted Esi's nose, and she knew from stories she had heard that they were nearing Fanteland.

The traders slapped their legs with sticks, making them move faster. For almost half of that week, they walked both day and night. The ones who couldn't keep up were beaten with the sticks until suddenly, like magic, they could.

Finally, once Esi's own legs had started to buckle, they reached the edge of some Fante village. They were all packed into a dark and damp cellar, and Esi had time to count the group. Thirty-five. Thirty-five people held together by rope.

They had time to sleep, and when they awoke they were given food. A strange porridge that Esi had never eaten before. She didn't like the taste of it, but she could sense that there would be nothing else for a long while.

Soon, men came into the room. Some were the warriors that Esi had seen before, but others were new.

"So these are the slaves you have brought us?" one of the men said in Fante. It had been a long while since Esi had heard anyone speak that dialect, but she could understand him clearly.

"Let us out!" the others tied to Esi began to shout, now that they had an ear that could listen. Fante and Asante, fellow Akans. Two peoples, two branches split from the same tree. "Let us out!" they shouted until their voices grew hoarse from the words. Nothing but silence greeted them.

"Chief Abeeku," another said. "We should not be doing this. Our Asante allies will be furious if they know we have worked with their enemies."

The one called Chief threw up his hands. "Today their enemies pay more, Fiifi," he said. "Tomorrow, if they pay more, we will work with them too. This is how you build a village. Do you understand?"

Esi watched the one called Fiifi. He was young for a warrior, but already she could tell that one day he would be a Big Man too. He shook his head, but didn't speak again. He went out of the cellar and brought back more men.

They were white men, the first Esi had ever seen. She could not match their skin to any tree or nut or mud or clay that she had ever encountered.

"These people do not come from nature," she said.

"I told you, they have come to eat us," Tansi replied.

The white men approached them.

"Stand up!" the chief shouted, and they all stood. The chief turned to one of the white men. "See, Governor James," he said in fast Fante, so fast Esi hardly understood him and wondered how this white man could. "The Asante are very strong. You may check them for yourselves."

The men started to undress the ones who still had clothes on, checking them. For what? Esi didn't know. She remembered the stone tucked in her cloth wrapper, and when the one called Fiifi reached her to undo the knot she had tied at the top of it, she launched a long, full stream of spit into his face.

He did not cry like the boy captive she had spit on in her own village square. He did not whimper or cower or seek comfort. He simply wiped his face, never taking his eyes off her.

The chief came to stand next to him. "What will you do about this, Fiifi? Will you let this go unpunished?" the chief asked. He spoke low, so that only Esi and Fiifi could hear.

Then, the sound of the smack. It was so loud, it took a moment for Esi to determine whether the pain she felt was on her ear or inside it. She cowered and sank to the ground, covering her face and crying. The smack had popped the stone from her wrapper, and she found it there, on the ground. She cried even harder, trying to distract them now. Then she laid her head against the smooth black stone. The coolness of it soothed her face. And when the men had finally turned their backs and left her there, forgetting for a moment to take off her wrapper, Esi took the stone from against her cheek and swallowed it.

*

Now the waste on the dungeon floor was up to Esi's ankles. There had never been so many women in the dungeon before. Esi could hardly breathe, but she moved her shoulders this way and that, until she had created some space. The woman beside her had not stopped leaking waste since the last time the soldiers fed them. Esi remembered her first day in the dungeon, when the same thing had been true of her. That day, she had found her mother's stone in the river of shit. She had buried it, marking the spot on the wall so that she would remember when the time came.

"Shh, shh, shh," Esi cooed to the woman. "Shh, shh, shh." She had learned to stop saying that everything would be all right.

Before long, the door of the dungeon opened and a sliver of light peeked through. A couple of soldiers walked in. Something was wrong with these soldiers. There was less order to their movements, less structure. She had seen men drunk from palm wine before, the way their faces flushed and their gestures grew wilder. The way their hands moved as though ready to collect even the very air around them.

The soldiers looked around and the women in the dungeon began to murmur. One of them grabbed a woman on the far end and pushed her against the wall. His hands found her breasts and then began to move down the length of her body, lower and lower still, until the sound that escaped her lips was a scream.

The women in the stack started to hiss then. The hiss said, "Quiet, stupid girl, or they will beat us all!" The hiss was high and sharp, the collective cry of a hundred and fifty women filled with anger and fear. The soldier who had his hands on the woman began to sweat. He shouted back at them all.

Their voices hushed to a hum, but did not stop. The murmur vibrated so low, Esi felt as though it were coming from her own stomach.

"What are they doing!" they hissed. "What are they doing!" The hissing grew louder, and soon the men were shouting something back at them.

The other soldier was still walking around, looking at each woman carefully. When he came upon Esi, he smiled, and for one quick second, she confused that act as one of kindness, for it had been so long since she'd seen someone smile.

He said something, and then his hands were on her arm.

She tried to fight him, but the lack of food and the wounds from the beatings had left her too weak to even collect her saliva and spit at him. He laughed at her attempt and dragged her by the elbow out of the room. As they walked into the light, Esi looked at the scene behind her. All those women hissing and crying.

He took her to his quarters above the place where she and the rest of the slaves had been kept. Esi was so unused to light that now it blinded her. She couldn't see where she was being taken. When they got to his quarters, he gestured toward a glass of water, but Esi stood still.

He gestured to the whip that sat on his desk. She nodded, took one sip of the water, and watched it slip out of her numb lips.

He put her on a folded tarp, spread her legs, and entered her. She screamed, but he placed his hand over her lips, then put his fingers in her mouth. Biting them only seemed to please him, and so she stopped. She closed her eyes, forcing herself to listen instead of see, pretending that she was still the little girl in her mother's hut on a night that her father had come in, that she was still looking at the mud walls, wanting to give them privacy, to separate herself. Wanting to understand what kept pleasure from turning into pain.

When he had finished, he looked horrified, disgusted with her. As though he were the one who had had something taken from him. As though he were the one who had been violated. Suddenly Esi knew that the soldier had done something that even the other soldiers would find fault with. He looked at her like her body was his shame.

Once night fell and the light receded, leaving only the darkness that Esi had come to know so well, the soldier snuck her out of his quarters. She had finished her crying, but still he shushed her. He wouldn't look at her, only forced her along, down, down, back to the dungeons.

When she got there, the murmur had subsided. The women were no longer crying or hissing. There was only silence as the soldier returned her to her spot.

Days went on. The cycle repeated. Food, then no food. Esi could do nothing but replay her time in the light. She had not stopped bleeding since that night. A thin trickle of red traveled down her leg, and Esi just watched it. She no longer wanted to talk to Tansi. She no longer wanted to listen to stories.

She had been wrong when she'd watched her parents that night as they worked together in her mother's hut. There was no pleasure.

The dungeon door opened. A couple of soldiers walked in, and Esi recognized one of them from the cellar in Fanteland. He was tall and his hair was the color of tree bark after rain, but the color was starting to turn gray. There were many golden buttons along his coat and on the flaps above the shoulders. She thought and thought, trying to push out the cobwebs that had formed in her brain and remember what the chief had called the man.

Governor James. He walked through the room, his boots pressing against hands, thighs, hair, his fingers pinching his nose. Following behind him was a younger soldier. The big white man pointed to twenty women, then to Esi.

The soldier shouted something, but they didn't understand. He grabbed them by their wrists, dragged them from atop or underneath the bodies of other women so that they were standing upright. He stood them next to each other in a row, and the governor checked them. He ran his hands over their breasts and between their thighs. The first girl he checked began to cry, and he slapped her swiftly, knocking her body back to the ground.

Finally, Governor James came to Esi. He looked at her carefully, then blinked his eyes and shook his head. He looked at her again, and then began checking her body as he had the others. When he ran his hands between her legs, his fingers came back red.

He gave her a pitying look, as though he understood, but Esi wondered if he could. He motioned, and before she could think, the other soldier was herding them out of the dungeon.

"No, my stone!" Esi shouted, remembering the golden-black stone her mother had given her. She flung herself to the ground and started to dig and dig and dig, but then the soldier was lifting her body, and soon all that she could feel instead of dirt in her steadily moving hands was air and more air.

They took them out into the light. The scent of ocean water hit her nose. The taste of salt clung to her throat. The soldiers marched them down to an open door that led to sand and water, and they all began to walk out onto it.

Before Esi left, the one called Governor looked at her and smiled. It was a kind smile, pitying, yet true. But for the rest of her life Esi would see a smile on a white face and remember the one the soldier gave her before taking her to his quarters, how white men smiling just meant more evil was coming with the next wave.

Quey

QUEY HAD RECEIVED A MESSAGE from his old friend Cudjo and didn't know how he would answer it. That night, he pretended the heat was keeping him awake, an easy lie for he was drenched in sweat, but then, when wasn't he sweating? It was so hot and humid in the bush that he felt like he was being slowly roasted for supper. He missed the Castle, the breeze from the beach. Here, in the village of his mother, Effia, sweat pooled in his ears, in his belly button. His skin itched, and he imagined mosquitoes crawling up his feet to his legs to his stomach, to rest at the watering hole of his navel. Did mosquitoes drink sweat, or was it only blood?

Blood. He pictured the prisoners being brought into the cellars by the tens and twenties, their hands and feet bound and bleeding. He wasn't made for this. He was supposed to have an easier life, away from the workings of slavery. He was raised among the whites in Cape Coast, educated in England. He should still be in his office in the Castle, working as a writer, the junior officer rank that his father, James Collins, had secured for him before his death, logging numbers that he could pretend didn't represent people bought and sold. Instead, the Castle's new governor had summoned him, sent him here, to the bush.

"As you know by now, Quey, we've had a long-standing working relationship with Abeeku Badu and the other Negroes of his village, but of late, we've heard that they have begun trading with a few private companies. We would like to set up an outpost in the village that would act as a residence for a few of our employees, as a way of, say, gently reminding our friends there that they have certain trade obligations to our company. You've been specially requested for the position, and given your parents' history with the village and given your comfort and familiarity with the language and local customs, we thought that you might be a particular asset to our company while there."

Quey had nodded and accepted the position, because what else could he do? But inside he resisted. His comfort and familiarity with the local customs? His parents' history with the village? Quey was still in Effia's womb the last time he or his mother had been there, so scared was she of Baaba. That was in 1779, nearly twenty years ago. Baaba had died in those years, and yet, still, they had stayed away. Quey felt his new job was a kind of punishment, and hadn't he been punished enough?

The sun finally came up, and Quey went to see his uncle Fiifi. When they'd met for the first time, only a month before, Quey could hardly believe that a man like Fiifi was related to him. It wasn't that he was handsome. Effia had been called the Beauty her whole life, and so Quey was accustomed to beauty. It was that Fiifi looked powerful, his body a graceful alliance of muscles. Quey had taken after his father, skinny and tall, but not particularly strong. James was powerful, but his power had come from his pedigree, the Collinses of Liverpool, who'd gained their wealth building slave ships. His mother's power came from her beauty, but Fiifi's power came from his body, from the fact that he looked like he could take anything he wanted. Quey had known only one other person like that.

"Ah, my son. You are welcome here," Fiifi said when he saw Quey approaching. "Sit. Eat!"

Summoned, the house girl came out with two bowls. She started to set one bowl in front of Fiifi, but he stopped her with only a glance. "You must serve my son first."

"Sorry," she mumbled, setting the bowl in front of Quey instead.

Quey thanked her and looked down at the porridge.

"Uncle, we've been here a month already and yet, still, you haven't discussed our trade agreements. The company has the money to buy more. Much more. But you have to let us. You have to stop trading with any other company."

Quey had given this very speech or one like it many times before, but his uncle Fiifi always ignored him. The first night they were there, Quey had wanted to talk to Badu about the trade agreements straight-away. He thought the sooner he could get the chief to agree, the sooner he could leave. That night, Badu had invited all the men to drink at his compound. He brought them enough wine and *akpeteshie* to drown in. Timothy Hightower, an officer eager to impress the chief, drank half a caskful of the home brew before he passed out underneath a palm tree, shaking and vomiting and claiming to see spirits. Soon, the rest of the men also littered the forest of Badu's front yard, vomiting or sleep-ing or searching for a local woman to sleep with. Quey waited for his chance to speak to Badu, sipping his drink all the while.

He had had only two cups of wine before Fiifi approached him. "Careful, Quey," Fiifi said, pointing at the scene of men before them. "Stronger men than these have been brought down by too much drink."

Quey looked at the cup in Fiifi's hand, his eyebrow raised.

"Water," Fiifi said. "One of us must be ready for anything." He motioned to Badu, who had fallen asleep in his gold throne, his chin nestled down into the round flesh of his belly.

Quey laughed, and Fiifi cracked a smile, the first that Quey had seen since meeting him.

Quey never talked to Badu that night, but as the weeks went on he learned that it was not Badu he needed to please. While Abeeku Badu was the figurehead, the Omanhin who received gifts from the political leaders of London and Holland alike for his role in their trade, Fiifi was the authority. When he shook his head, the whole village stopped.

Now Fiifi was as silent as he was every other time Quey had brought up trade with the British. He looked out into the forest in front of them, and Quey followed his gaze. In the trees, two vibrant birds sang loudly, a discordant song.

"Uncle, the agreement Badu made with my father—"

"Do you hear that?" Fiifi asked, pointing to the birds.

Frustrated, Quey nodded.

"When one bird stops, the other one starts. Each time their song gets louder, shriller. Why do you think that is?"

"Uncle, trade is the only reason we're here. If you want the British out of your village, you have to—"

"What you cannot hear, Quey, is the third bird. She is quiet, quiet, listening to the male birds get louder and louder and louder still. And when they have sung their voices out, then and only then will she speak up. Then and only then will she choose the man whose song she liked better. For now, she sits, and lets them argue: who will be the better partner, who will give her better seed, who will fight for her when times are difficult.

"Quey, this village must conduct its business like that female bird. You want to pay more for slaves, pay more, but know that the Dutch will also pay more, and the Portuguese and even the pirates will pay more too. And while you are all shouting about how much better you are than the others, I will be sitting quietly in my compound, eating my *fufu* and waiting for the price I think is right. Now, let us not speak of business anymore."

Quey sighed. So he would be here forever. The birds had stopped singing. Perhaps they sensed his exasperation. He looked at them, their blue, yellow, orange wings, their hooked beaks.

"There were no birds like this in London," Quey said softly. "There was no color. Everything was gray. The sky, the buildings, even the people looked gray."

Fiifi shook his head. "I don't know why Effia let James send you to that nonsense country."

Quey nodded absently and returned to the porridge in his bowl.

Quey had been a lonely child. When he was born, his father built a hut close to the Castle so that he, Effia, and Quey could live more comfortably. In those days trade had been prosperous. Quey never saw the dungeons, and he had only the faintest idea of what went on in the lower levels of the Castle, but he knew that business was good because he rarely saw his father.

Every day was for him and Effia. She was the most patient mother in all of Cape Coast, in all of the Gold Coast. She spoke softly yet assuredly. She never hit him, even when the other mothers taunted her, telling her that she would spoil him and that he would never learn.

"Learn what?" Effia would answer. "What did I ever learn from Baaba?"

And yet Quey did learn. He sat in Effia's lap as she taught him to speak, repeating a word in both Fante and English until Quey could hear in one language and answer in the other. She had only learned how to read and write herself in the first year of Quey's life and yet she taught him with vigor, holding his small, fat fist in hers as they traced lines and lines and lines together.

"How smart you are!" she exclaimed when Quey learned to spell his name without her help.

In 1784, on Quey's fifth birthday, Effia first told him about her own childhood in Badu's village. He learned all of the names—Cobbe, Baaba, Fiifi. He learned there was another mother whose name they would never know, that the shimmering black stone Effia always wore about her neck had belonged to this woman, his true grandmother. Telling this story, Effia's face darkened, but the storm passed when Quey reached up and touched her cheek.

"You are my own child," she said. "Mine."

And she was his. When he was young that had been enough, but as he grew older, he began to lament the fact that his family was so small, unlike all of the other families in the Gold Coast, where siblings piled on top of siblings in the steady stream of marriages each powerful man consummated. He wished that he could meet his father's other children, those white Collinses who lived across the Atlantic, but he knew that it would never be. Quey had only himself, his books, the beach, the Castle, his mother.

"I'm worried because he has no friends," Effia said to James one day. "He doesn't play with the other Castle children."

Quey had almost stepped in the door after a day of building sand castle replicas of the Cape Coast Castle when he heard Effia mention his name, and so he had remained outside to listen.

"What are we supposed to do about that? You've coddled him, Effia. He's got to learn to do some things on his own."

"He should be playing with other Fante children, village children, so that he can get away from here from time to time. Don't you know anyone?"

"I'm home!" Quey announced, perhaps a bit too noisily, not wanting to hear what his father would say next. By the end of the day, he'd forgotten all about it, but weeks later, when Cudjo Sackee came with his father to visit the Castle, Quey remembered his parents' conversation.

Cudjo's father was the chief of a prominent Fante village. He was Abeeku Badu's biggest competitor, and he had begun meeting with James Collins to discuss increasing trade when the governor asked him if he might bring his eldest son to one of their meetings.

"Quey, this is Cudjo," James said, giving Quey a small push toward the boy. "You two play while we talk."

Quey and Cudjo watched their fathers walk off to a different side of the Castle. Once they could hardly make them out anymore, Cudjo turned his attention to Quey.

"Are you white?" Cudjo had asked him, touching his hair.

Quey recoiled at Cudjo's touch, though many others had done the same thing, asked him the same question. "I'm not white," he said softly.

"What? Speak up!" Cudjo said, and so Quey had repeated himself, nearly shouting. From the distance, the boys' fathers turned to observe the commotion.

"Not so loud, Quey," James said.

Quey could feel color flood into his cheeks, but Cudjo had just looked on, clearly amused.

"So you're not white. What are you?"

"I'm like you," Quey said.

Cudjo held his hand out and demanded that Quey do the same, until they were standing arm to arm, skin touching skin. "Not like me," Cudjo said.

Quey had wanted to cry, but that desire embarrassed him. He knew that he was one of the half-caste children of the Castle, and, like the other half-caste children, he could not fully claim either half of himself, neither his father's whiteness nor his mother's blackness. Neither England nor the Gold Coast.

Cudjo must have seen the tears fighting to escape Quey's eyes.

"Come now," he said, grabbing Quey's hand. "My father says they keep big guns here. Show me where!"

Though he'd asked Quey to show him, Cudjo was the one who began to lead the way, running until the two boys had zipped past their fathers, toward the cannons.

It was in this way that Quey and Cudjo became friends. Two weeks after the day they first met, Quey had received a message from Cudjo asking if he would like to visit his village.

"Can I go?" Quey asked his mother, but Effia was already pushing him out the door, overjoyed at the prospect of a friend.

Cudjo's was the first village that Quey had ever spent a lot of time in, and he was amazed at how different it was from the Castle and from Cape Coast. There was not even one white person there, no soldiers to say what one could or could not do. Though the children were no strangers to beatings, they were still rowdy, loud and free. Cudjo, who was eleven like Quey, was already the oldest of ten children, and he ordered his siblings about as though they were his tiny army.

"Go and fetch my friend something to eat!" he shouted at his youngest sister when he saw Quey approaching. The girl was but a toddler, thumb still inseparable from mouth, but she always did as Cudjo said as soon as he said it.

"Hey, Quey, look what I've found," Cudjo said, hardly waiting for Quey to reach him before opening his palm.

Two small snails were in his hands, their tiny, slimy bodies wriggling between Cudjo's fingers.

"This one is yours, and this one is mine," Cudjo said, pointing them out. "Let's race them!"

Cudjo closed his palm again and started to run. He was faster, and Quey had a hard time keeping up. When they got to a clearing in the forest, Cudjo got down on his stomach and motioned for Quey to do the same.

He gave Quey his snail, then marked a line in the dirt as the starting point. The two boys put their snails behind the line, then released them.

At first, neither snail moved.

"Are they stupid?" Cudjo asked, prodding his snail with his index finger. "You're free, stupid snails. Go! Go!"

"Maybe they're just shocked," Quey said, and Cudjo looked at him like he was the one who was stupid.

But then Quey's snail started to move past the line, followed, seconds later, by Cudjo's snail. Quey's snail didn't move like a snail usually did, slowly and deliberately. It was as though he knew he was racing, as though he knew he was free. It didn't take long for the boys to lose sight of him, while Cudjo's snail ambled along, even turning in a circle several times.

Suddenly, Quey was nervous. Maybe Cudjo would be angry at his loss and tell him to leave the village and never come back. Quey had only just met Cudjo, but already he knew that he didn't want to lose him. He did the only thing he could think to do. He stuck out his hand as he'd often seen his father do after business deals, and, to his surprise, Cudjo took it. The boys shook.

"My snail was very stupid, but yours did well," Cudjo said.

"Yes, mine did very well," Quey agreed, relieved.

"We should name them. We'll call mine Richard because it's a British name and he was bad like the British are bad. Yours can be named Kwame."

Quey laughed. "Yes, Richard is bad like the British," he said. He forgot in that second that his own father was British, and when he remembered later, he realized that he didn't care. He felt only that he belonged, fully and completely.

. . .

The boys grew older. Quey grew four inches in one summer, while Cudjo grew muscle. His legs and arms rippled, so that sweat flowing down them looked like cresting waves. He became known far and wide for his wrestling prowess. Older boys from neighboring villages were brought to challenge him, and still he won every match.

"Eh, Quey, when will you wrestle me?" Cudjo asked.

Quey had never challenged him. He was nervous, not of losing, for he knew he would lose, but because he'd spent the last three years carefully watching, and knew better than anyone what Cudjo's body was capable of. The elegance of Cudjo's movements as he circled around his opponents, the mathematics of the violence, how an arm plus a neck could equal breathlessness, or an elbow plus a nose meant blood. Cudjo never missed a step in this dance, and his body, both forceful and controlled, awed Quey. Lately, Quey had been thinking about Cudjo's strong arms encircling him, dragging him down to the ground, Cudjo's body on top of his.

"Get Richard to wrestle you," Quey said, and Cudjo let out his exuberant laugh.

After the snail race, the boys had started to name everything, good or bad, Richard. When they got in trouble with their mothers for saying something crude, they blamed Richard. When they ran the fastest or won a wrestling match, it was thanks to Richard. Richard was there the day Cudjo had swum too far out and his strokes had started to fail him. It was Richard who had wanted him to drown and Richard who had saved him, helping him to regain his rhythm.

"Poor Richard! I would destroy him-oh," Cudjo said, flexing his muscles.

Quey reached over to squeeze Cudjo's arm. Though the muscle did not give way, he said, "Why? Because of this small thing?"

"Enh?" Cudjo said.

"I said this arm is small. It feels soft in my hand, brother."

Without warning, quick as a stroke of heat lightning, Cudjo locked Quey's neck into his arms. "Soft?" he asked. His voice was hardly more than a whisper, a wind in Quey's ear. "Careful, friend. There is nothing soft here."

Though Quey was losing his breath, he could feel his cheeks flushing. Cudjo's body was pressed so close to him that he felt, for a moment, that they were one body. Each hair on Quey's arms stood at attention, waiting for what would happen next. Finally, Cudjo let him go.

Quey took in deep gulps of air as Cudjo looked on, a smile playing on his lips.

"Were you scared, Quey?" Cudjo asked.

"No."

"No? Don't you know every man in Fanteland is scared of me now?"

"You wouldn't hurt me," Quey said. He looked straight into Cudjo's eyes and could feel something in them falter.

Quickly, Cudjo regained his composure. "Are you sure?"

"Yes," Quey said.

"Challenge me, then. Challenge me to wrestle."

"I won't."

Cudjo walked up to Quey until he was standing only inches from his face. "Challenge me," he said, and his breath danced on Quey's own lips.

The next week Cudjo had an important match. While drunk, a soldier in the Castle had boasted that Cudjo would never be able to beat him.

"Negroes fighting other Negroes is not a challenge. Put a savage against a white man, then you'll see."

One of the servants, a man from Cudjo's own village, had heard the white soldier's boast and reported it back to Cudjo's father. The next day, the chief arrived to deliver his message personally.

"Any white man who thinks he can beat my son, let him try. In three days' time we will see who is better."

Quey's father had tried to forbid the match, saying that it was uncivilized, but the soldiers were bored and restless. Uncivilized fun was exactly what they craved.

Cudjo came at the end of that week. He brought with him his father and his seven brothers, no one else. Quey had not spoken to him since the week before, and he found himself inexplicably nervous, the feeling of Cudjo's breath still present on his lips.

The soldier who had made the boast was also nervous. He paced, and his hand shook, as all the men of the Castle looked on.

Cudjo stood across from his challenger. He looked him up and down, assessing him. Then his eyes found Quey's in the audience. Quey nodded at him, and Cudjo smiled, a smile that Quey knew to mean "I will win this."

And he did. Only a minute after the match started, Cudjo had his arms wrapped around the soldier's fat belly, flipping him over and pinning him down.

The crowd roared with excitement. More challengers stepped in, soldiers whom Cudjo defeated with varying degrees of ease until, finally, all the men were drunk and spent, and Cudjo alone was unruffled.

The soldiers started to leave. After congratulating Cudjo loudly and raucously, his own brothers and father also left. Cudjo was to spend the night in Cape Coast with Quey.

"I'll wrestle you," Quey said when it looked like everyone had gone. The night air was starting to move into the Castle, cooling it, but only a bit.

"Now that I'm too tired to win?" Cudjo asked.

"You've never been too tired to win."

"Okay. You want to wrestle me? Come catch me first!" And with that Cudjo broke into a run. Quey was faster than he was in the early years of their friendship. He caught up to Cudjo at the cannons and dove toward him, locking his legs and pulling him down to the ground.

Within seconds, Cudjo was on top of him, panting heavily while Quey struggled to turn him over.

Quey knew he should tap the ground three times, the signal to end the match, but he didn't want to. He didn't want to. He didn't want Cudjo to get up. He didn't want to miss the weight of him.

Slowly, Quey relaxed his body, and he felt Cudjo do the same. The boys drank in each other's gazes; their breathing slowed; the feeling on Quey's lips grew stronger, a tingling that threatened to draw his face up toward Cudjo's.

"Get up right now," James said.

Quey didn't know how long his father had been standing there watching them, but he recognized a new tone in his father's voice. It was the same measured control he used when he spoke to servants and, Quey knew though he'd never seen, to slaves before he struck them, but now there was fear mixed in.

"Go home, Cudjo," James said.

Quey watched his friend leave. Cudjo didn't even look back.

The next month, just before Quey's fourteenth birthday, while Effia cried and fought and fought some more, going so far, once, as to strike James across the face, Quey boarded a ship bound for England.

*

"I heard you're back from London. Can I see you, old friend?"

Quey couldn't stop thinking about the message he'd received from Cudjo. He stared into his bowl and saw that he'd hardly eaten any of the porridge. Fiifi had already finished one bowl and asked for another.

"Maybe I should have stayed in London," Quey said.

His uncle looked up from his meal and gave him a funny look. "Stayed in London for what?"

"It was safer there," Quey said softly.

"Safer? Why? Because the British don't tramp through bushland finding slaves? Because they keep their hands clean while we work? Let me tell you, the work they do is the most dangerous of all."

Quey nodded, though it wasn't what he'd meant. In England he'd gotten to see the way black people lived in white countries, Indians and Africans who were packed twenty or more to a room, who ate the slop the pigs left behind, who coughed and coughed and coughed endlessly, all together, a symphony of sickness. He knew the dangers that waited across the Atlantic, but he knew too the danger in himself.

"Don't be weak, Quey," Fiifi said, staring at him intently, and for just a second Quey wondered if his uncle had understood him after all. But then Fiifi returned to his porridge and said. "Isn't there work for you to do?"

Quey shook his head, trying to collect himself. He smiled at his uncle and thanked him for the meal and then he set off.

The work wasn't difficult. Quey and his fellow company men's official duties included meeting Badu and his men weekly to go over the inventory, overseeing the bombboys who loaded the canoes with cargo, and updating the Castle's governor with news of Badu's other trade partners.

Today it was Quey's turn to oversee the bombboys. He walked the several miles to the edge of the village and greeted the young Fante boys who worked for the British, shuttling slaves from the coastal villages to the Castle. On this day there were only five slaves, bound and waiting. The youngest, a small girl, had messed herself, but everyone ignored it. Quey had grown accustomed to the smell of shit, but fear was one smell that would stand out forever. It curled his nose and brought tears to his eyes, but he had learned long ago how to keep himself from crying.

Every time he saw the bombboys set off with a canoe full of slaves, he thought of his father standing on the shores of the Cape Coast Castle, ready to receive them. On this shore, watching the canoe push off, Quey brimmed with the same shame that accompanied each slave departure. What had his father felt on his shore? James had died soon after Quey arrived in London. The ship ride there had been uncomfortable at best, harrowing at worst, with Quey alternating steadily between crying and vomiting. On the ship, all Quey could think about was how this was what his father did to the slaves. This was what his father did to his problems. Put them on a boat, shipped them away. How had James felt every time he watched a ship push off? Was it the same mix of fear and shame and loathing that Quey felt for his own flesh, his mutinous desire?

Back in the village, Badu was already drunk. Quey said hello, and then tried to move quickly past him.

He wasn't fast enough. Badu grabbed him by the shoulder and asked, "How's your mother? Tell her to come and see me, enh?"

Quey pursed his lips into what he hoped looked like a smile. He tried to swallow his disgust. When he'd accepted his assignment here,

Effia had cried out, begging him to refuse, begging him to run away, all the way into Asante as his never-known grandmother before him had done if that was what he needed to do in order to escape the obligation.

She'd fingered the stone pendant on her neck as she spoke to him. "There is evil in that village, Quey. Baaba—"

"Baaba is long dead," Quey said, "and you and I are both too old to still believe in ghosts."

His mother had spit on the ground at his feet, and shook her head so quickly he thought it might spin off. "You think you know, but you don't know," she said. "Evil is like a shadow. It follows you."

"Perhaps my mother will come visit soon," Quey said now, knowing that she would never want to see Badu. Though his parents had fought, mostly about him, it was obvious to all that they had cared for each other. And, though a part of Quey hated his father, another part still wanted ardently to please him.

Quey finally freed himself from Badu and kept on walking. Cudjo's message repeated in his head.

"I heard you're back from London. Can I see you, old friend?"

When Quey had returned from London, he'd been too nervous to ask after Cudjo, but he hadn't needed to. Cudjo had taken over as chief of his old village, and they still traded with the British. Quey had recorded Cudjo's name in the Castle ledgers nearly every day when he was still working as a writer. It would be easy enough now to go see Cudjo, to talk as they used to, to tell him that he had hated London as he had hated his father, that everything about the place—the cold, the damp, the dark—had felt like a personal slight against him, designed for the sole purpose of keeping him away from Cudjo.

But what good could come of seeing him? Would one look have him back where he'd been six years ago, back on that Castle floor? Maybe London had done what his father had hoped it would do, but then again, maybe it hadn't.

Weeks went steadily on, and still Quey sent no answer to Cudjo. Instead, he devoted himself to his work. Fiifi and Badu had numerous contacts in Asanteland and further north. Big Men, warriors, chiefs, and the like who would bring in slaves each day by the tens and twenties. Trade had increased so much, and the methods of gathering slaves had become so reckless, that many of the tribes had taken to marking their children's faces so that they would be distinguishable. Northerners, who were most frequently captured, could have upwards of twenty scars on their faces, making them too ugly to sell. Most of the slaves brought to Quey's village outpost were those people captured in tribal wars, a few were sold by their families, and the rarest kind of slave was the one that Fiifi captured himself in his dark night missions up north.

Fiifi was preparing himself for one such journey. He wouldn't tell Quey what the mission was, but Quey knew it had to be something particularly treacherous, for his uncle had sought help from another Fante village.

"You can keep all the captives but one," Fiifi was saying to someone. "Take them back with you when we split up in Dunkwa."

Quey had just been summoned to his compound. Before him, warriors were dressing for battle, muskets, machetes, and spears in hand.

Quey moved further in, trying to see the man his uncle spoke to.

"Ah, Quey, you've finally come to greet me, enh?"

The voice was deeper than Quey remembered and yet he knew it immediately. His hand trembled as he held it out to shake with his old friend. Cudjo's grip was firm, his hand soft. The handshake took Quey back to Cudjo's village, to the snail race, to Richard.

"What are you doing here?" Quey asked. He hoped his voice didn't betray him. He hoped he sounded calm and sure.

"Your uncle has promised us a good mission today. I was eager to accept."

Fiifi clapped Cudjo's shoulder and moved on to speak to the warriors.

"You never returned my message," Cudjo said softly.

"I didn't have time."

"I see," Cudjo said. He looked the same, taller, broader, but the same. "Your uncle tells me you haven't yet married."

"No."

"I married last spring. A chief must be married."

"Oh, right," Quey said in English, forgetting himself.

Cudjo laughed. He took up his machete and leaned in closer to Quey. "You speak English like a British man, just like Richard, enh? When I have finished up north with your uncle, I will return to my own village. You are always welcome there. Come and see me."

Fiifi gave one last cry to gather the men, and Cudjo went running. As he sped off, Cudjo glanced back and smiled at Quey. Quey didn't know how long they would be gone, but he knew he would not sleep until his uncle returned. No one had told him anything about the mission. Indeed, Quey had seen the warriors go out a handful of times and never questioned it, but now his heart thumped so hard it felt like a toad had replaced his throat. He could taste every beat. Why had Fiifi told Cudjo that Quey wasn't married? Had Cudjo asked? How could Quey be welcomed in Cudjo's village? Would he live in the chief's compound? In his own hut, like a third wife? Or would he be in a hut on the edge of the village, alone? The toad croaked. There was a way. There was no way. There was a way. Quey's mind raced back and forth with every thump.

One week passed. Then two. Then three. On the first day of the fourth week, Quey was finally summoned to the slave cellar. Fiifi was lying against the wall of the cellar, his hand covering his flank as it oozed blood from a large gash. Soon one of the company doctors arrived with a thick needle and thread and began sewing Fiifi up.

"What happened?" Quey asked. Fiifi's men were guarding the cellar door, clearly shaken. They held both machetes and muskets, and when so much as a leaf rustled in the woods, they would clutch each weapon tighter.

Fiifi began laughing, a sound like the last roar of a dying animal. The doctor finished closing up the wound and poured a brown liquid over it, causing Fiifi to stop laughing and cry out.

"Quiet!" one of Fiifi's soldiers said. "We don't know who may have followed us."

Quey knelt down to meet his uncle's eyes. "What happened?"

Fiifi was gnashing his teeth against the slow-moving wind. He lifted an arm and pointed to the cellar door. "Look what we have brought, my son," he said.

Quey stood up and went to the door. Fiifi's men handed him a lamp and then moved aside so that he could enter. When he did, the darkness echoed around him, reverberating against him as though he had stepped inside a hollowed drum. He lifted the lamp higher and saw the slaves.

He didn't expect to see many, for the next shipment was not set to arrive until early the following week. He knew immediately that these were not slaves the Asantes brought in. These were people Fiifi had stolen. There were two men tied together in the corner, big warriors, bleeding from minor flesh wounds. When they saw Quey, they began to jeer in Twi, thrashing against their chains so that they broke fresh flesh, bleeding anew.

On the opposite wall sat a young girl who made no noise. She looked up at Quey with large moon eyes, and he knelt down beside her to study her face. On her cheek was a large oval-shaped scar, a medical mark James had taught Quey years before, before he'd shipped him off to England, a mark of the Asantes.

Quey got up, looking at the girl still. Slowly, he backed away, realizing who the girl must be. Outside, his uncle had passed out from the pain, and the soldiers had loosened their grips on their weapons, content that no one had followed them.

Quey looked at the one closest to the door, grabbed his shoulder, shook him. "What in God's name are you doing with the Asante king's daughter?"

The soldier lowered his eyes, shook his head, and did not speak. Whatever Fiifi had planned, it could not fail, or the entire village would pay with their lives.

Every night after that night, Quey sat with Fiifi as he healed. He heard the story of the capture, how Fiifi and his men had stolen into Asante in the dead of night, informed by one of their contacts as to when the girl would have the fewest guards around her, how Fiifi had been slit around like a coconut by the tip of her guard's machete when he reached for her, how they had dragged their captives south, through the forest, until they reached the Coast.

Her name was Nana Yaa and she was the eldest daughter of Osei Bonsu, the highest power in the Asante Kingdom, a man who commanded respect from the queen of England herself for his sway over the Gold Coast's role in the slave trade. Nana Yaa was an important political bargaining tool, and people had been trying to capture her since her infancy. Wars had been started over her: to get her, to free her, to marry her.

Quey was so worried he didn't dare ask how Cudjo had fared. Soon, Quey knew, Fiifi's informant would be caught and tortured until he told who had taken her. It was only a matter of time until the consequences came to meet them.

"Uncle, the Asantes will not forgive this. They will—"

Fiifi cut him off. Since the night of the capture, every time Quey tried to broach the topic of the girl, to gauge Fiifi's intentions, the man clutched his side and grew quiet or told one of his long-winded fables.

"The Asantes have been angry with us for years," Fiifi said. "Ever since the time they found out we traded other Asantes brought to us by some northerners Badu found. Badu told me then that we trade with the ones who pay more. It is the same thing I told the Asantes when they found out, the same thing I told you. Asante anger is to be expected, Quey, and you are right that it is not to be underestimated. But trust me, they are wise where we are cunning. They will forgive."

Fiifi stopped talking and Quey watched as his uncle's youngest daughter, a girl of only two, played in the yard. After a while, a house girl came by with a snack of groundnuts and bananas. She approached Fiifi first, but he stopped her. With a level voice and leveled gaze, he said, "You must serve my son first."

The woman did as she was told, bowing before Quey, and reaching out with her right hand. After they had both received their fill, the girl left while Quey watched the measured sway of her ample hips.

"Why do you always say that?" Quey asked once he was sure she had gone.

"Why do I say what?"

"That I'm your son." Quey looked down, spoke so softly that he hoped the ground would swallow his sound. "You never claimed me before."

Fiifi split the shell of a groundnut with his teeth, separating it from the nut itself and spitting it onto the ground before them. He looked toward the thin dirt road that led away from his compound and toward the village square. He looked as though he were expecting someone.

"You were in England too long, Quey. Maybe you have forgotten that here, mothers, sisters, and their sons are most important. If you are chief, your sister's son is your successor because your sister was born of your mother but your wife was not. Your sister's son is more important to you than even your own son. But, Quey, your mother is not my sister. She is not the daughter of my mother, and when she married a white man from the Castle, I began to lose her, and because my mother had always hated her, I began to hate her too.

"And this hate was good, at first. It made me work harder. I would think about her and all of the white people in the Castle, and I would say, My people here in this village, we will be stronger than the white men. We will be richer too. And when Badu became too greedy and too fat to fight, I began to fight for him, and even then I hated your mother and your father. And I hated my own mother and I hated my own father too for the kind of people I knew that they were. I suppose I even began to hate myself.

"The last time your mother came to this village I was fifteen years old. It was for my father's funeral, and after Effia had gone, Baaba told me that because she was not truly my sister, I owed her nothing. And for many years I believed that, but I am an old man now, wiser, but weaker. In my youth, no man could have touched me with his machete, but now : . ." Fiifi's voice trailed off as he gestured to his wound. He cleared his throat and continued. "Soon, all that I have helped to build in this village will no longer belong to me. I have sons but I have no sisters, and so all that I have helped to build will blow away like dust in a breeze.

"I am the one who told your governor to give you this job, Quey, because you are the person I am supposed to leave all of this to. I loved Effia as a sister once, so even though you are not of my mother, you are the closest thing to a firstborn nephew that I have. I will give you all that I have. I will make up for my mother's wrongdoings. Tomorrow night, you will marry Nana Yaa, so that even if the Asante king and all of his men come knocking on my door, they cannot deny you. They cannot kill you or anyone in this village, because it is now your village as it was once your mother's. I will make sure you become a very powerful man, so that even after the white men have all gone from this Gold Coast—and believe me, they will go—you will still matter long after the Castle walls have crumbled."

Fiifi began to pack a pipe. He blew out of it until white smoke formed little roofs above the pipe's bowl. The rainy season was coming and soon the air would start to thicken, and the people of the Gold Coast would have to relearn how to move in a climate that was always hot and wet, as though it intended to cook its inhabitants for dinner.

This was how they lived there, in the bush: Eat or be eaten. Capture or be captured. Marry for protection. Quey would never go to Cudjo's village. He would not be weak. He was in the business of slavery, and sacrifices had to be made.

Ness

THERE WAS NO DRINKING GOURD, no spiritual soothing enough to mend a broken spirit. Even the Northern Star was a hoax.

Every day, Ness picked cotton under the punishing eye of the southern sun. She had been at Thomas Allan Stockham's Alabama plantation for three months. Two weeks before, she was in Mississippi. A year before that, she was in a place she would only ever describe as Hell.

Though she had tried, Ness couldn't remember how old she was. Her best guess was twenty-five, but each year since the one when she was plucked from her mother's arms had felt like ten years. Ness's mother, Esi, had been a solemn, solid woman who was never known to tell a happy story. Even Ness's bedtime stories had been ones about what Esi used to call "the Big Boat." Ness would fall asleep to the images of men being thrown into the Atlantic Ocean like anchors attached to nothing: no land, no people, no worth. In the Big Boat, Esi said, they were stacked ten high, and when a man died on top of you, his weight would press the pile down like cooks pressing garlic. Ness's mother, called Frownie by the other slaves because she never smiled, used to tell the story of how she'd been cursed by a Little Dove long, long ago, cursed and sisterless, she would mutter as she swept, left without her mother's stone. When they sold Ness in 1796, Esi's lips had stood in that same thin line. Ness could remember reaching out for her mother, flailing her arms and kicking her legs, fighting against the body of the man who'd come to take her away. And still Esi's lips had not moved, her hands had not reached out. She stood there, solid and strong, the same as Ness had always known her to be. And though Ness had met warm slaves on other plantations, black people who smiled and hugged and told nice stories, she would always miss the gray rock of her mother's heart. She would always associate real love with a hardness of spirit.

Thomas Allan Stockham was a good master, if such a thing existed. He gave them five-minute breaks every three hours, and the field slaves were allowed onto the porch to receive one mason jar full of water from the house slaves.

This day in late June, Ness waited in line for water beside TimTam. He was a gift to the Stockham family from their neighbors, the Whitmans, and Tom Allan often liked to say that TimTam was the best gift he'd ever received, better even than the gray-tailed cat his brother had given him for his fifth birthday or the red wagon he'd received for his second.

"How your day been?" TimTam asked.

Ness turned toward him just slightly. "Ain't all days the same?"

TimTam laughed, a sound that rumbled like thunder built from the cloud of his gut and expelled through the sky of his mouth. "I s'pose you right," he said.

Ness was not certain she would ever get used to hearing English spill out of the lips of black people. In Mississippi, Esi had spoken to her in Twi until their master caught her. He'd given Esi five lashes for every Twi word Ness spoke, and when Ness, seeing her battered mother, had become too scared to speak, he gave Esi five lashes for each minute of Ness's silence. Before the lashes, her mother had called her Maame, after her own mother, but the master had whipped Esi for that too, whipped her until she cried out "My goodness!"—the words escaping her without thought, no doubt picked up from the cook, who used to say it to punctuate every sentence. And because those had been the only English words to escape Esi's mouth without her struggling to find them, she believed that what she was saying must have been something divine, like the gift of her daughter, and so that goodness had turned into, simply, Ness.

"Where you comin' from?" TimTam asked. He chewed the chaffy end of a wheat stalk and spit.

"You ask too many questions," Ness said. She turned away. It was her turn to receive water from Margaret, the head house slave, but the woman poured only enough to fill a quarter of the glass.

"We ain't got enough today," she said, but Ness could see that the buckets of water on the porch behind her were enough to last a week.

Margaret looked at Ness, but Ness got the feeling that she was really looking through her, or rather, that she was looking five minutes into Ness's past, trying to discern whether or not the conversation Ness had just had with TimTam meant that the man was interested in her.

TimTam cleared his throat. "Now, Margaret," he said. "That ain't no kinda way to treat somebody."

Margaret glared at him and plunged her ladle into the bucket, but Ness didn't accept the offering. She walked away, leaving the two people to stew. While there may have been a piece of paper declaring that she belonged to Tom Allan Stockham, there was no such paper shackling her to the whims of her fellow slaves.

"You ain't gotta be so hard on him," a woman said once Ness resumed her position in the field. The woman seemed older, mid to late thirties, but her back hunched even when she stood up straight. "You new here, so you don't know. TimTam done lost his woman long while ago, and he been taking care of little Pinky by hisself ever since."

Ness looked at the woman. She tried to smile, but she had been born during the years of Esi's unsmiling, and she had never learned how to do it quite right. The corners of her lips always seemed to twitch upward, unwillingly, then fall within milliseconds, as though attached to that sadness that had once anchored her own mother's heart.

"Ain't we all done lost someone?" Ness asked.

Ness was too pretty to be a field nigger. That's what Tom Allan said to her the day he'd taken her back to his plantation. He'd bought her on good faith from a friend of his in Jackson, Mississippi, who said she was one of the best field hands he'd ever seen, but to make quite sure to only use her in the field. Seeing her, light-skinned with kinked hair that raced down her back in search of her round shelf of buttocks, Tom Allan thought his friend must have made some kind of mistake. He pulled out the little outfit he liked for his house niggers to wear, a white button-down with a boat neckline and capped sleeves, a long black skirt attached to a little black apron. He'd had Margaret take Ness into the back room so that she could change into it, and Ness had done what she was told. Margaret, seeing Ness all done up, clutched her hand to her heart and told Ness to wait there. Ness had to press her ear to the wall to hear what Margaret said.

"She ain't fit for da house," Margaret told Tom Allan.

"Well, let me see her, Margaret. I'm sure I can decide for myself whether or not somebody's fit to work in my own house, now can't I?"

"Yessuh," Margaret said. "I reckon you is, but it ain't something you gon' want to see, is what I'm sayin'."

Tom Allan laughed. His wife, Susan, came into the room and asked what all the fuss was about. "Why, Margaret's got our new nigger locked up in the back and won't let us see her. Stop this nonsense now and go fetch her here."

If Susan was like any of the other masters' wives, she must have known that her husband's bringing a new nigger into the house meant she had better pay attention. In this and every other southern county, men's eyes, and other body parts, had been known to wander. "Yes, Margaret, bring the girl so we can see. Don't be silly about it."

Margaret shrugged her shoulders and went back to the room, and Ness pulled her ear from the wall. "Well, you bess come out" was all Margaret said.

And so Ness did. She walked out to her audience of two, her shoulders bared, as well as the bottom halves of her calves, and when Susan Stockham saw her, she fainted outright. It was all Tom Allan could do to catch his wife while shouting at Margaret to go change Ness at once.

Margaret rushed her into the back room, and left in search of field clothes, and Ness stood in the center of that room, running her hands along her body, reveling in her ugly nakedness. She knew it was the intricate scars on her bare shoulders that had alarmed them all, but the scars weren't just there. No, her scarred skin was like another body in and of itself, shaped like a man hugging her from behind with his arms hanging around her neck. They went up from her breasts, rounded the hills of her shoulders, and traveled the full, proud length of her back. They licked the top of her buttocks before trailing away into nothing. Ness's skin was no longer skin really, more like the ghost of her past made seeable, physical. She didn't mind the reminder.

Margaret came back in the room with a head scarf, a brown top that covered the shoulders, a red skirt that went all the way to the floor. She watched Ness put them on. "It a shame, really. For a second, I's thought you mighta been prettier than me." She clucked her tongue twice and left the room.

And so Ness worked in the field. It was not new to her. In Hell, she'd worked the land too. In Hell, the sun scorched cotton so hot it almost burned the palms of your hands to touch it. Holding those small white puffs almost felt like holding fire, but God forbid you let one drop. The Devil was always watching. Hell was where she had learned to be a good field hand, and the skill had carried her all the way to Tuscumbia.

It was her second month at the Stockham plantation. She lived in one of the women's cabins, but she had made no friends. Everyone knew her as the woman who had snubbed TimTam, and the ladies, angry when they thought that she was the object of his desire and even angrier when they realized she didn't want to be that object, treated her as though she were little more than a strong wind, an annoyance that you could still push through.

In the mornings, Ness prepared her pail to take out to the field with her. Cornmeal cakes, a bit of salt pork, and, if she was lucky, some greens. In Hell, she had learned to eat standing up. Picking cotton with her right hand, shoveling food in with her left. It wasn't something she was required to do here at Tom Allan's, work while eating, but she didn't know any other way.

"Look like she think she better den us," one woman called, just loudly enough so Ness could hear.

"Tom Allan sho gon' think so," another said.

"Nuh-uh, Tom Allan ain't paid her no mind since she got kicked out da big house," the first one said.

Ness had learned how to tune the voices out. She tried to remember the Twi that Esi used to speak to her. Tried to still her mind until all that was left was the thin, stern line of her mother's lips, lips that used to usher out words of love in a tongue that Ness could no longer quite grasp. Phrases and words would come to her, mismatched or lopsided, wrong.

She worked all day like this, listening to the sounds of the South. The insistent buzz of mosquitoes, that screech of cicadas, the hum of slave gossip. At night, she would return to her quarters, beat out her pallet until dust billowed from it, wrapping around her like a hug. She would set it back down again and wait for a sleep that rarely came, trying her best to still the harrowing images that danced behind her closed eyelids.

It was on a night like this, just when she had snapped her pallet into the air, that the pounding started, fists beating against the door of the women's cabin in a steady, urgent rhythm. "Please!" a voice called. "Please, help us."

A woman named Mavis opened the door. TimTam stood there cradling his daughter, Pinky, in his arms. He pushed into the room, his voice choked though there were no tears in his eyes. "I think she got what her mama had," he said.

The women cleared a spot for the girl and TimTam set her down before he started to pace. "Oh Lord, oh Lord, oh Lord," he cried.

"You bess go fetch Tom Allan so's he can get the doctor," Ruthie said.

"Doctor ain't helped last time," TimTam said.

Ness stood behind a row of women, their shoulders squared as if headed into battle. She pushed her way through to the center to catch a glimpse of the child. Pinky was small and sharp-edged, as though her body were built from sticks with no bend to them. Her hair was tied up in two big puffs. The whole time the women were watching her, she made no noise save for a quick intake of breath.

"Ain't nothing wrong wid her," Ness said.

Suddenly, TimTam stopped his pacing as everyone turned to stare at Ness. "You ain't been round here long," TimTam said. "Pinky ain't spoke a word since her mama died and now she can't stop with these hiccups."

"Ain't nothing but hiccups," Ness said. "Those ain't killed anyone yet, far's I know." She looked around at all the women shaking their heads at her disapprovingly, but she couldn't tell what she had done wrong.

TimTam pulled her aside. "These women ain't told you?" he whispered, and Ness shook her head. The women so rarely spoke to her, and she had finally gotten good at tuning out their gossip. TimTam cleared his throat and hung his head a little lower. "See, we know ain't nothing wrong wid her but the hiccups, but we been tryin' to get her to speak, so . . ."

His voice trailed off as Ness began to understand that the whole thing had been nothing more than a plot to trick little Pinky into utterance. Ness pulled away from TimTam and looked at the small congregation of women carefully, from one to the next and then the next. She made her way to the center of the room, where Pinky lay on the pallet, her eyes staring up at the ceiling. The girl turned her eyes toward Ness and hiccuped once more.

Ness addressed the room. "Lord, I don't know what kinda foolishness I done walked into at this here plantation, but y'all need to leave this girl alone. Maybe she don't want to speak cuz she know just how crazy it make you or maybe she ain't got nothin' to say yet, but I reckon she ain't gon' start tonight just because y'all makin' like you actors in a travelin' show."

The women wrung their hands and shifted their feet, and Tim-Tam's head sunk a little lower.

Ness walked back to her pallet, finished beating the dust out, and lay down.

TimTam walked over to Pinky. "Well, les go," he said, reaching for the girl, but she pulled away. "I said, les go," he repeated, shame coloring his voice gray, but the girl snatched herself away again. She went over to where Ness lay, her eyes shut tightly as she begged sleep to come quick. Pinky's hand brushed Ness's shoulder, and she opened her eyes to see the girl staring at her, round moon eyes imploring. And because Ness understood loss, and because she understood mother-lessness and wanting and even silence, she reached for the girl's hand and pulled her down onto the bed.

"You go on 'head," she said to TimTam, Pinky's head already nes-tled between the soft cushions of her breasts. "I got her tonight."

From that day forward, Pinky could not be separated from Ness. She had even moved from the other women's cabin into Ness's. She slept with Ness, ate with Ness, took walks with Ness, and cooked with Ness. Still, she didn't speak, and Ness never asked her to, knowing full well that Pinky would speak when she had something to say, laugh when something was truly funny. For her part, Ness, who had not known how much she missed company, took comfort in the girl's quiet presence.

Pinky was the water girl. On any given day she would make as many as forty trips to the small creek on the edge of the Stockhams' planta-tion. She carried a plank of wood across her back, arms folded over it from behind so that she looked like a man holding a cross, and on each end of the plank hung two silver pails. Once she had reached the creek, Pinky would fill those pails, bring them back to the main house, and then empty them into the large water buckets that lived on the Stock-ham porch. She would fill the basins in the house so that the Stockham children would have fresh water for their afternoon baths. She would water the flowers that sat on Susan Stockham's dressing table. From there, she went to the kitchen to give two pailfuls to Margaret for the day's cooking. She walked the same worn path every day, down to the creek, back up to the house. By the end of the day, her arms would throb so hard Ness could feel her heart beat in them when the girl crawled into bed with Ness at night and the woman hugged her close.

The hiccups had not stopped, continuing since the day TimTam had brought her into Ness's cabin hoping to scare the child into speak-ing. Everyone pitched in with a remedy.

"Stand da girl upside down!"

"Tell her hold her breath and swall-ah!"

"Cross two straws on top her head!"

The last remedy, put forth by a woman named Harriet, was the one that seemed to work. Pinky made thirty-four trips to the creek without a single hiccup. Ness was on the porch getting her fill of water on Pinky's thirty-fifth trip back. The two redheaded Stockham children were out and about that day. The boy, named Tom Jr., and the girl, Mary. They were running up the stairs just as Pinky rounded the corner, and Tom Jr. knocked the plank so that one of the pails went flying into the air, water raining down on everyone on the porch. Mary started to cry.

"My dress is all wet!" she said.

Margaret, who had just finished ladling out water for one of the other slaves, set the ladle down. "Hush now, Miss Mary."

Tom Jr., who had never been much for gallantry, decided to try it just then for his sister's sake. "Well, apologize to Mary!" he said to Pinky. The two were the same age, though Pinky was about a foot taller.

Pinky opened her mouth, but no words came out.

"She sorry," Ness said quickly.

"I wasn't talking to you," Tom Jr. said.

Mary had stopped crying and was staring at Pinky intently. "Tom, you know she don't talk," Mary said. "It's all right, Pinky."

"She'll talk if I tell her to talk," Tom Jr. said, shoving his sister. "Apologize to Mary," he repeated. The sun was high and hot that day. Indeed, Ness could see that the two wet drops on Mary's dress had already dried.

Pinky, eyes welling with tears, opened her mouth again and a wave of hiccups came out, frantic and loud.

Tom Jr. shook his head. He went into the house while everyone watched and returned with the Stockham cane. It was twice his length, made of a dull birchwood. It wasn't thick, but it was so heavy that Tom Jr. could hardly hold it with both of his hands, let alone the one it would take to snap it back.

"Speak, nigger," Tom Jr. said, and Margaret, who had long since stopped her ladling, ran into the house crying, "Ooh, Tom Junior, I'm gon' find yo daddy!"

Pinky was sobbing and hiccuping all at once, the hiccups blocking whatever speech she might have given. Tom Jr. lifted the cane in his right hand with great effort and tried to snap it over his shoulder, but Ness, who was standing behind him, caught the tip of it in her hand. It tore through her palms as she tugged so hard that Tom Jr. fell to the ground. She dragged him half an inch.

Tom Allan appeared on the porch with Margaret, who was breathless and clutching her chest. "What's this?" he asked.

Tom Jr. started crying. "She was gonna hit me, Daddy!" he said.

Margaret tried to speak up, "Massa Tom, you lie! You was—"

Tom Allan raised his hand to stop Margaret's speech and looked at Ness. Maybe he remembered the scars on her shoulders, remembered how they had kept his wife laid up in bed for the rest of that day and put him off his dinner for a week. Maybe he wondered what a nigger had to do to earn stripes like that, what trouble a nigger like that must be capable of. And there his son was on the ground with dirt on his shorts and the mute child Pinky crying. Ness was sure that he could see clear as day what had happened, but it was the memory of her scars that made him doubt. A nigger with scars like that, and his son on the ground. There wasn't anything else he could do.

"I'll deal with you soon enough," he said to Ness, and everyone wondered what would happen.

That evening, Ness returned to the women's quarters. She crawled into her bed and closed her eyes, waiting for the images that played every night behind her lids to still to darkness. Beside her, Pinky began to hiccup.

"Oh Lord, here she go! Ain't we had enough trouble fo one day?" one of the women said. "Can't get no kinda rest when dis girl start to hiccup."

Ashamed, Pinky slapped a hand to her mouth as though, with it, she could erect a wall to block the sound's escape.

"Don't pay dem no mind," Ness whispered. "Thinking 'bout it only make it worse." She didn't know if she was speaking to Pinky or to herself.

Pinky squeezed her eyes tight as a series of hiccups exploded from her lips.

"Leave her be," Ness said to the chorus of groans, and they listened. The events of the day had planted a little dual seed of respect and pity for Ness that they watered with deference of their own. They didn't know what Tom Allan would do.

In the night, once they had all finally reached sleep, Pinky rolled over and snuggled into the soft skin of Ness's gut. Ness allowed herself to hold the girl, and she allowed herself to drift off into memory.

She is back in Hell. She is married to a man they call Sam, but who comes straight from the Continent and speaks no English. The master of Hell, the Devil himself, with red-leather skin and a shock of gray hair, prefers his slaves married "for reasons of insurance," and because Ness is new to Hell and because no one has claimed her, she is given to calm the new slave Sam.

At first they do not speak to each other. Ness doesn't understand his strange tongue, and she is in awe of him, for he is the most beautiful man that she has ever seen, with skin so dark and creamy that looking at it could very well be the same thing as tasting it. His is the large, muscular body of the African beast, and he refuses to be caged, even with Ness as his welcoming gift. Ness knows that the Devil must have paid a great deal of money for him, and therefore expects hard work, but nothing anyone does seems to tame him. On his first day he fights with another slave, spits on the overseer, and is stood on a platform and whipped in front of everyone until the blood on the ground is high enough to bathe a baby.

Sam refuses to learn English. Each night, in retribution for his still-black tongue, the Devil sends him back to their marriage bed with lashes that are reopened as soon as they heal. One night, enraged, Sam destroys the slave quarters. Their room is savaged from wall to wall, and when the Devil hears of the destruction he comes to serve punishment.

"I did it," Ness says. She has spent the night hidden in the left corner of the room, watching this man she's been told is her husband become the animal he's been told that he is.

The Devil shows no mercy, even though he knows she is lying. Even though Sam tries time and again to accept the blame. She is beaten until the whip snaps off her back like pulled taffy, and then she is kicked to the ground.

When he leaves, Sam is crying and Ness is barely conscious. Sam's words come out in a thick and feverish prayer, and Ness can't understand what he's saying. He picks her up gingerly and places her on their pallet. He leaves the house in search of the herbal doctor, five miles away, who comes back with the roots and leaves and salves that are smeared into Ness's back as she slips in and out of consciousness. It is the first night that Sam sleeps in the cot with her, and in the morning, when she wakes to fresh pain and festered sores, she finds him sitting at her feet, peering at her face with his big, tired eyes.

"I'm sorry," he says. They are the first English words he ever speaks to her, to anyone.

That week, they work side by side in the fields, and the Devil, though watchful, does not act against them. In the evenings, they return to their bed, but they sleep on opposite sides of it, never touching. Some nights, they fear that the Devil is watching them as they lie, and those are the nights Sam hugs her body to his, waiting for the metronome of fear that keeps her heart's drumbeat moving quickly to slow. His vocabulary has grown to include her name and his, "don't worry" and "quiet." In a month, he will learn "love."

In a month, once the wounds on both of their backs have hardened to scars, they finally consummate their marriage. He picks her up so easily, she thinks she must have turned into one of the rag dolls she makes for the children to play with. She has never been with a man before, but she imagines that Sam is not a man. For her, he has become something much larger than a man, the Tower of Babel itself, so close to God that it must be toppled. He runs his hands along her scabby back, and she does the same along his, and as they work together, clutching each other, some scars reopen. They are both bleeding now, both bride and bridegroom, in this unholy holy union. Breath leaves his mouth and enters hers, and they lie together until the roosters crow, until it's time to return to the fields.

Ness awoke to Pinky's finger poking her shoulder. "Ness, Ness!" she spoke. Ness turned to face the girl, trying to hide her surprise. "Was you having a bad dream?" she asked.

"No," Ness said.

"It looked like you was having a bad dream," the girl said, disappointed because when she was lucky Ness told her stories.

"It was bad," Ness replied. "But it wasn't no dream."

*

Morning announced its presence through the roosters' cries, and the women in the slave quarters readied themselves for the day, all the while whispering about Ness's fate.

No one had ever seen Tom Allan do a public whipping before, not like the ones they saw, or experienced, at other plantations. Their master had a river for a stomach, and he hated the sight of blood. No, when Tom Allan wished to punish one of his slaves, he did it in private, somewhere he could close his eyes during, lie down after. But this seemed different. Ness was one of the few slaves that he had ever publicly berated, and she knew that she had embarrassed him, what with his own child lying in the dirt while Pinky stood silent and unscathed.

Ness returned to the same row of field that she was in the day before as everyone stared. It was rumored that Tom Allan's plantation stretched longer than any of the other small plantations in the county, and to finish picking one row of cotton took two good days. Without warning, TimTam was back behind Ness. He touched her shoulder and she turned.

"They tol' me Pinky spoke yesterday. I s'pose I should say thank you for that. And for the other thing."

Ness looked at him and realized that every time she'd ever seen the man, he was chewing on something, his mouth always working its way around in a circle. "You ain't got to do nothing," Ness said, bending again. TimTam looked up to check if Tom Allan had arrived on the front porch yet.

"Well, I'm grateful anyway," he said, and he sounded it. When Ness turned her face up, she saw that he was grinning again, his wide lips pulling back to make way for teeth. "I can talk to Massa Tom for you. He ain't gon' do nothin'."

"I reckon I ain't needed anyone to fight my battles for me before. Don't see why I should start now," Ness said. "Now, you go bother somebody else with your gratefulness. Margaret sure seemed like she'd be happy to take it."

TimTam's face fell. He nodded at Ness and then returned to his own row. After a few minutes, Tom Allan arrived on the porch and peered out. Everyone looked at Ness from the corners of their eyes. She felt like she sometimes felt at night, in the dark in high mosquito season, when she could feel the presence of something ominous but could not see the danger itself.

She looked at Tom Allan, not more than a speck on the porch from where she stood in the field, and wondered how long it would take for him to act, if he would call her up this very morning or spend days letting it pass, making her wait. It was waiting that bothered her, that had always bothered her. She and Sam had spent so much time waiting, waiting, waiting.

Ness had made Sam wait outside when she was in labor. She gave birth to Kojo during a strange southern winter. An unheard-of snow had blanketed the plantations for a full week, threatening the crops, angering the landowners, making the slaves' hands idle.

Ness was holed up in the birthing room the night of the heaviest snowfall, and when the midwife finally arrived and opened the door, a cold wind moved through the room, bringing with it a flurry of snowflakes that melted on the tables and chairs and on Ness's stomach.

Throughout the pregnancy, Kojo was the kind of baby who fought the walls of his mother's womb, and the journey out had been no different. Ness had screamed her throat raw, remembering with each push the stories the other slaves told about her own birth. They said Esi hadn't told anyone that Ness was coming; she'd just gone out behind a tree and squatted. They said a strange sound had preceded Ness's newborn wail, and for years after, Ness had listened to them argue about what that sound was. One slave thought it was the flutter of birds' wings. Another that it was a spirit, come to help Ness out and then gone with a rumble. Yet another said that the sound had come from Esi herself. That she had gone out to be alone, to have her own private moment of joy with her baby before anyone came to snatch both joy and baby away. The sound, that slave had said, was of Esi laughing, which was why they hadn't recognized it.

Ness couldn't imagine anyone laughing through a birth until the midwife finally pulled Kojo out into the world and her baby boy had wailed, louder than little lungs should have allowed him to wail, and Sam, who had been pacing outside in the snow, thanked his ancestors in Yoruba and waited for the chance to hold him. Then Ness understood.

Following the birth of their son, Sam had come to be all that the Devil had wanted him to be. Tame, a good, hard worker who rarely fought or caused trouble. He would remember the way the Devil had beaten Ness for his folly, and when he held Kojo, called Jo, for the first time, he'd promised himself that no harm would come to the boy on his account.

Then Ness found Aku and told Sam that he would be able to keep that promise. Ness had been sitting in the back of the church on Easter Sunday, the only Sunday the Devil allowed his slaves to walk the fifteen miles to the black Baptist church on the edge of town, waiting for the sermon to start. Without thinking, she began singing a little Twi tune her mother used to sing sorrowfully on nights when the work of slavery was particularly grueling, when she had been beaten for supposed insolence or laziness or failure.

The Dove has failed. Oh, what to do? Make her to suffer, or you'll fail too.

Ness didn't know what she was singing, for Esi had never taught her what the words of the song meant, but in the pew in front of her, a woman turned and whispered something.

"I'm sorry. I don't understand," Ness said. The words the woman spoke had been in her mother's tongue.

"So you are an Asante, and you don't even know," the woman said. Her accent was still thick, like Esi's had been, gleaming with the lightness of the Gold Coast.

She introduced herself as Aku, and she explained that she was from Asanteland and had been kept in the Castle just like Ness's mother had, before being shipped to the Caribbean and then to America.

"I know the way back out," Aku said. The sermon was about to begin and Ness knew she wouldn't have much time. Easter Sunday would not come again for another year, and by that time she or Aku or both could be sold; dead, even. Theirs was the kind of life that did not guarantee living. They had to act fast.

Aku talked softly, told Ness about how she had taken Akan people north to freedom many times, so many times that she had earned the Twi nickname *Nyame nsa*, hand of God, of help. Ness knew that no one had ever escaped the Devil's plantation, but listening to this woman, who sounded like her mother had, who praised the god her mother had praised, Ness knew that she wanted her family to be the first.

Jo was one year old when Ness began planning her family's freedom. The woman had assured her that she had taken children north before, babies who were still screaming and whining for their mothers' tits. Jo would be no problem.

Ness and Sam talked about it every night they were together. "You can't raise a baby in Hell," Ness repeated over and over again, thinking about the way she'd been stolen from her own mother. Who knew how long she'd have with her perfect child before he forgot the sound of her voice, the details of her face, the way she had forgotten Esi's. And when Sam finally agreed, they sent word to Aku, telling her that they were ready, that they would wait for her signal, an old Twi song, sung softly in the woods as though carried by windswept leaves.

And so they waited. Ness and Sam and Kojo, working longer and harder in the fields than any of the other slaves so that even the Devil began to smile at the mention of their names. They waited out fall and then winter, listening for the sound that would tell them it was time, praying that they wouldn't be sold and separated before their chance came.

They weren't, but Ness often wondered if it wouldn't have been better if they had been. The song came in the spring, so light Ness thought that perhaps she had imagined it, but soon Sam was grabbing Jo in one arm and Ness in the other, and the three of them were out beyond the Devil's land for the first time that they could remember.

That first night, they walked so long, so far, that the cracked soles of Ness's feet opened up. She bled on the leaves, and hoped for rain so that the dogs that were surely coming wouldn't be able to catch her scent. When the sun came up, they climbed the trees. Ness hadn't done it since childhood, but the skill came back to her quickly. She wrapped Jo around her back with cloth and reached for the highest branch. When he cried, she smothered him against her chest. Sometimes, after she had done this, he would get so still, she would worry, long for his cries. But they were all practicing stillness there, stillness like the kind Esi used to talk about in her stories about the Big Boat. Stillness like death.

Days passed this way, the four of them playing trees in the woods or grass in the fields, but soon Ness could feel a heat rising from the earth, and she knew, the way a person knew air or love just by feeling, that the Devil was after them.

"Would you take Kojo tonight?" Ness asked Aku while Sam and the boy had wandered off in search of water to drink. "Just fo' tonight. My back can't take much more of him."

Aku nodded, giving her a strange look, but Ness knew what she wanted and she wouldn't change her mind.

That morning the dogs came, their panting heavy and labored as their paws slapped against the tree where Ness hid.

From afar there was a whistle, an old Dixie tune that lifted from the ground before the sound could be attached to a body. "I know you're here somewhere," the Devil said. "And I'm glad to wait you out."

In broken Twi, Ness called to Aku, who was further up in the distance, holding baby Jo. "Don't come down, whatever you do," Ness said.

The Devil continued approaching, his hum low and patient. Ness knew he would wait there forever and soon the baby would cry, need food. She looked over at the tree Sam was in and hoped he would forgive her for all that she was about to bring upon them, and then she climbed down the tree. She was on the ground before she realized that Sam had done the same.

"Where's the boy?" the Devil asked while his men tied the two of them up.

"Dead," Ness said, and she hoped her eyes had that look in them, that look that mothers got sometimes when they came back from running, having killed their children to set them free.

The Devil raised one eyebrow and laughed a slow laugh. "It's a shame, really. I thought I mighta had me some trustworthy niggers. Just goes to show."

He marched Ness and Sam back to Hell.

Once they got there, all of the slaves were called out to the whipping post. He stripped them both bare, tied Sam so tight he couldn't even wiggle his fingers, and made him watch as Ness earned the stripes that would make her too ugly to work in a house ever again. By the end of it, Ness was on the ground, dust covering her sores. She could not lift her head, so the Devil lifted it for her. He made her watch. He made them all watch: the rope come out, the tree branch bend, the head snap free from body.

And so this day, while Ness waited to see what punishment Tom Allen had in store for her, she couldn't help but remember that day. Sam's head. Sam's head tilted to the left and swinging.

Pinky carried water up to the porch where Tom Allen sat, waiting. When the little girl turned back around, her eyes caught Ness's, but Ness didn't hold her gaze for long. She just continued to pick cotton. She thought of the act of cotton picking as she had since the day she saw Sam's head, like a prayer. With the bend, she said, "Lord forgive me my sins." With the pluck, she said, "Deliver us from evil." And with the lift, she said, "And protect my son, wherever he may be."

James

OUTSIDE, THE SMALL CHILDREN were singing *"Eh-say, shame-ma-mu"*
and dancing around the fire, their smooth, naked bellies glistening
like little balls catching light. They were singing because word had
arrived—the Asantes had Governor Charles MacCarthy's head. They
were keeping it on a stick outside the Asante king's palace as a warning
to the British: this is what happens to those who defy us.

"Eh, small children, do you not know that if the Asantes defeat the
British they will come for us Fantes next?" James asked. He lunged
at one of the little girls and tickled her until all of the children were
giggling and begging for mercy. He released the girl and then put on
a somber face, continuing his lecture. "You will be safe here in this village because my family is royal. Do not forget that."

"Yes, James," they said.

Down the road, James's father was approaching with one of the
white men from the Castle. He motioned to James to follow them into
the compound.

"Should the boy hear this, Quey?" the white man asked, glancing
quickly at James.

"He is a man, not a boy. He will take over my responsibilities here
when I've finished. Whatever you say to me, you may also say to him."

The white man nodded, and looked at James carefully as he spoke.
"Your mother's father, Osei Bonsu, has died. The Asantes are saying
we killed their king to avenge Governor MacCarthy's death."

"And did you?" James asked, returning the man's stare with force, anger beginning to boil up in his veins. The white man looked away. James knew the British had been inciting tribal wars for years, knowing that whatever captives were taken from these wars would be sold to them for trade. His mother always said that the Gold Coast was like a pot of groundnut soup. Her people, the Asantes, were the broth, and his father's people, the Fantes, were the groundnuts, and the many other nations that began at the edge of the Atlantic and moved up through the bushland into the North made up the meat and pepper and vegetables. This pot was already full to the brim before the white men came and added fire. Now it was all the Gold Coast people could do to keep from boiling over again and again and again. James wouldn't be surprised if the British had killed his grandfather as a way to raise the heat. Ever since his mother had been stolen and married to his father, his village had been swelteringly hot.

"Your mother wants to go to the funeral," Quey said. James unclenched the fist he hadn't realized he'd made.

"It's too dangerous, Quey," the white man said. "Even Nana Yaa's royal status might not protect you. They know your village has been allied to us for years. It's just too dangerous."

James's father looked down, and suddenly James could hear his mother's voice in his ear again, telling him that his father was a weak man with no respect for the land he walked on.

"We will go," James said, and Quey looked up. "Not attending the Asante king's funeral is a sin the ancestors would never forgive."

Slowly, Quey nodded. He turned to the white man. "It is the least we can do," he said.

The white man shook hands with the two of them, and the next day, James, his mother, and his father headed north for Kumasi. His grandmother Effia would stay home with the younger children.

James held the gun in his lap as they rode through the forest. The last time he'd held one was five years before, in 1819, for his twelfth birthday. His father had taken him out into the woods to shoot at swaths of fabric he had tied to various trees in the distance. He told James that a man should learn to hold a gun the same way he held a woman, carefully, tenderly.

Now, looking at his parents as they rode through the bush, James wondered if his father had ever held his mother that way, carefully or tenderly. If war had been the way of the world of the Gold Coast, it had also defined the world inside his compound.

Nana Yaa wept as they rode inside the carriage. "If it weren't for my son, would we even be going?" she asked.

James had made the mistake of telling her what his father and the white man had talked about the day before.

"If it weren't for me, would you even have this son?" his father muttered.

"What?" his mother said. "I could not understand that ugly Fante you speak."

James rolled his eyes. They would go on like this for the rest of the trip. He could still remember the fights they had when he was a small boy. His mother screaming loudly about his name.

"James Richard Collins?" his mother would shout. "James Richard Collins! What kind of Akan are you that you give your son three white names?"

"And so what?" his father would reply. "Will he not still be a prince to our people and to the whites too? I have given him a powerful name."

James knew now, as he knew then, that his parents had never loved each other. It was a political marriage; duty held them together, though even that seemed to be barely enough. By the time they passed the town of Edumfa, his mother was going on about how Quey wouldn't even be a man were it not for James's late great-uncle Fiifi. So many of their arguments led to Fiifi and the decisions he had made for Quey and their family.

After days of travel, they stopped to spend the night in Dunkwa with David, a friend from Quey's time in England who had moved back to the Gold Coast years before with his British wife. Days, even weeks, would pass before they reached the interior where James's grandfather's body was being held so that all could celebrate his life.

"Quey, old friend," David said as James's family approached. He had a round belly like an oversized coconut. For a second, remembering the way he had grown up slicing the fruit and drinking what awaited inside, James wondered what a man like David would spill if punctured.

His father and David shook hands and began talking. James always noticed that the longer it had been since the two men saw each other, the louder and more impassioned their voices got, as though the volume was trying to make up for distance, or reach back in time.

Nana Yaa nodded at David's wife, Katherine, and then loudly cleared her throat.

"My wife is very tired," Quey said, and the servants came to show her to her room. James began to walk with them, hoping that he too could get some rest, but David stopped him.

"Eh, James, you are a big man now. Sit. Talk."

The handful of times James had seen David, David had called him a big man. He could remember back to when he was just four years old and had tripped on something invisible, an ant maybe, and had fallen to the ground, tearing the flesh of his upper lip. He had immediately begun crying, a violent cry that began somewhere inside his chest. David picked him up with one hand, dusted off his butt with the other, and stood him on a table in front of him so that the two were staring eye to eye. "You are a big man now, James. You can't cry at every little thing that comes your way."

The three men sat around a fire the servants had built, sipping palm wine. James's father looked older to him, but only slightly, as though the three-day journey had added three years. If the trip took thirty days, Quey would look almost as old as James's grandfather had before he died.

"So she is still giving you trouble, eh? Even though you are taking her to Osei Bonsu's funeral?" David asked.

"Nothing is ever enough for this wife of mine," Quey said.

"That is what happens when you marry for power instead of marrying for love. The Bible says—"

"I don't need to know what the Bible says. I studied the Bible too, remember? In fact, I recall going to religion class more often than you did," Quey said with a short laugh. "I have no use for that religion. I chose this land, these people, these customs over those of the British."

"You chose it, or it was chosen for you?" David said quietly. Quey stole a glance at James, and then looked away. It was as his mother always yelled at Quey when she was truly angry: "You are so soft, you break apart. Weak man."

"And you, James? You are almost old enough for the marriage festivities to start. Should we begin looking for a bride for you, or have you got a woman in mind?" David winked at him and then, as though the wink were the pulling of a switch that led to his throat, began to laugh so hard he choked on his own spittle.

"Nana Yaa and I have chosen a nice wife for him to marry when the time comes," Quey said,.

David nodded carefully and tipped the calabash of wine back, his Adam's apple bobbing against the stream of liquid that ran down it. Watching him, James cringed. Before his great-uncle Fiifi had died, when James was still just a small boy, Fiifi had conspired with Quey to choose the woman whom James would marry. She was called Amma Atta, the daughter of Chief Abeeku Badu's successor to the stool. Their joining would be the last thing on the list of rectifications that Fiifi had promised himself he would fulfill for Quey. It would be the realization of a promise that Cobbe Otcher had made to Effia Otcher Collins years ago: that her blood would be joined with the blood of Fante royals. James would marry her on the eve of his eighteenth birthday. She would be his first, his most important, wife.

Because Amma had also grown up in the village, James had known her all his life, and when they were young, he used to play with her outside Chief Abeeku's compound. But the older they got, the more Amma started to annoy him. Little things, like the way she always laughed just a second too long after he told a joke, just long enough for him to know she didn't find him funny at all, or the way she put so much coconut oil in her hair that if the strands brushed against his shoulder while they were together, his shoulder would continue to smell of oil when they were apart. He was only fifteen when he knew that he could never truly love a woman like that, but it didn't matter what he thought.

The men continued sipping the wine in silence for a while. In the trees, the birds were calling each other to sleep. A spider crawled over James's bare foot, and he thought of the Anansi stories his mother used to tell him, and still told his younger brothers and sisters. "Have you heard the story of Anansi and the sleeping bird?" she would ask them, mischief dancing behind her eyes, and they would all shout "No!" and giggle into their hands, thrilled by the lie they were telling, for they had all heard it many times before, learning then that a story was nothing more than a lie you got away with.

David tipped the calabash back again, his head tipping back with it so that he could completely empty the contents. He belched, then wiped his mouth with the back of his hand. "Is it true?" he asked. "The rumors about the British abolishing slavery soon?"

Quey shrugged his shoulders. "The year James was born, they told everyone in the Castle that the slave trade was abolished and that we could not sell our slaves to America anymore, but did that stop the tribes from selling? Did that make the British leave? Don't you see this war the Asantes and the British are fighting now and will continue to fight for far longer than you or I or even James can live to see? There's more at stake here than just slavery, my brother. It's a question of who will own the land, the people, the power. You cannot stick a knife in a goat and then say, Now I will remove my knife slowly, so let things be easy and clean, let there be no mess. There will always be blood."

James had heard this speech or something like it many times before. The British were no longer selling slaves to America, but slavery had not ended, and his father did not seem to think that it would end. They would just trade one type of shackles for another, trade physical ones that wrapped around wrists and ankles for the invisible ones that wrapped around the mind. James hadn't understood this when he was younger, when the legal slave exportation had ended and the illegal one had begun, but he understood now. The British had no intention of leaving Africa, even once the slave trade ended. They owned the Castle, and, though they had yet to speak it aloud, they intended to own the land as well.

.   .   .

They set out again the next morning. James thought his mother looked as though the night's rest had lifted her spirits. She even hummed while they traveled. They passed small towns and villages that were built of little more than mud and sticks. They relied upon the kindness of people whom Quey had once worked with, or cousins of cousins whom Nana Yaa had never met, people who offered their floors and a bit of palm wine. The further into the country they moved, the more James noticed how his father's skin attracted attention among the bush people. "Are you a white man?" one little girl had asked, reaching out with her index finger and swiping Quey's light brown skin as though she could capture a little bit of the color on it.

"What do you think?" Quey had asked, his Twi rusty but passable.

The little girl giggled, then shook her head slowly before running away to report back to the other children who were gathered around the fire staring, too intimidated to ask him themselves.

They reached Kumasi at dusk and were greeted by Nana Yaa's eldest brother, Kofi, and his guards.

"Akwaaba," he said. "You are welcome here."

They were taken to the new king's large palace, where the servants had prepared a room at the corner of the structure. Kofi sat with them while they ate the welcome food and updated them on what had passed in the town since they had left their own village.

"I'm sorry, sister, but we could not wait so long to bury him," Kofi said, and Nana Yaa nodded. She had known that the body would be buried before they got there so that the new king could take office. She had only wanted to make it to the funeral.

"And Osei Yaw?" she asked. Everyone was worried about the new king. Because they were at war, they had had to choose him quickly, just after the burial of James's grandfather, and no one knew whether or not this would be bad luck for the people and the war that they were fighting.

"He is doing a fine job as Asantehene," Kofi said. "Don't worry, little sister. He will make sure our father is honored as he should be honored."

As his uncle spoke, James noticed that Kofi paid no attention to his father. His eyes never once reached Quey's eyes, not even when wandering. He was like the blind cat that moved through the dark forest solely on instinct, avoiding the logs and rocks that threatened it or had hurt it once before.

The funeral proceedings began the next day. Nana Yaa left the palace long before James and the other men were awake so that she could join with the women of the family in mournful wailing, wailing that announced to everyone in the town that the celebration day had indeed arrived. By noon, these women were dressed in their red cloths, nyanya leaves and raffia braided about their clay-stained foreheads as they walked up and down the streets, wailing for all the townspeople to hear.

In the meantime, James, his father, and all of the other men put on their black and red mourning cloths. There was a line of drummers that began at one corner of the Royal Palace and ended at the other. They would drum until dawn. The men began chanting, then dancing the Kete, the Adowa, the Dansuomu. They would dance until dawn.

The dead king's family sat in a row so that they could be greeted by all the mourners as they came in. A single-file line of people began at James's grandfather's first wife and went all the way into the middle of the town square. Everyone in line shook the hand of each family member, and offered their condolences. James stood next to his father. He tried to remember to keep his shoulders squared and to look each mourner directly in the eyes so that they knew he was a man whose blood was as important as they expected it to be. They shook his hand and murmured their sorries, and James accepted, even though he had never lived in Asanteland and had known his grandfather only as a person knows his shadow, as a figure that is there, visible but untouchable, unknowable.

By the time the last of the mourners were coming through, the sun was at its highest point in the sky. James reached up briefly to wipe sweat out of his eyes, and once he had, he opened them to the loveliest girl he had ever seen.

"May the old king find peace in the land of the spirits," the girl said, but she did not reach for his hand.

"What's this?" James asked. "You do not shake?"

"Respectfully, I will not shake the hand of a slaver," she said. She looked him in the eye as she spoke, and James studied her face. Her hair was worn in a puff at the top of her head and her words had whistled through a gap between her front teeth. Though her mourning cloth was wrapped tightly, it had slid a little low so that James could just make out the tops of her breasts. He should have slapped her for her insolence, reported her, but the line continued on behind her and the funeral had to continue too. James let her move on, tried to watch her as she continued down the line, but before long he lost her in the crowd.

He lost her, but he could not forget her, even as the line moved on and the rest of the people came by to shake his hand. James was by turns annoyed and ashamed by what she had said. Did she shake his father's hand? His uncle's? Who was she to decide what a slaver was? James had spent his whole life listening to his parents argue about who was better, Asante or Fante, but the matter could never come down to slaves. The Asante had power from capturing slaves. The Fante had protection from trading them. If the girl could not shake his hand, then surely she could never touch her own.

They finally laid Osei Bonsu, the old king, to rest. The gong was rung to let the townspeople know that it was done, that they could all return to their normal lives. It would not be over for the family members for another forty days. For another forty days, they would wear the mourning clothes, sort through and divide the gifts, and worry over the king's successor.

James's parents would be leaving within the next couple of days, and James knew that he didn't have much time to find the girl who had refused to shake his hand.

He went to his cousin Kwame. Kwame was approaching twenty years old and had already married twice. He was a fat, dark man who spoke loudly and drank often, but he was kind and loyal. James and his family had visited once when James was only seven. He and Kwame had been playing in their grandfather's Golden Stool room, a room men had been killed for entering uninvited, a room that had been expressly forbidden to them. While playing, James had knocked over one of their grandfather's canes. In one of those coincidences that could only be attributed to evil spirits, the cane had landed in the palm oil lamp, catching fire, and the two boys had worked quickly to put it out. Smelling the fire, the whole family had come to see what was going on.

"Who is responsible for this?" their grandfather shouted. He had been the Asante king so long that his voice seemed no longer human, more like the roar of a lion.

James had looked down immediately, expecting Kwame to tell on him. He was the outsider, only in town once every few years. Kwame was the one who had to live there, with their lion of a grandfather and his quick, powerful rage. But Kwame had said nothing. Even as their mothers laid them across their laps and beat them in unison, Kwame still had said nothing.

"Kwame, I need to find a girl," James said.

"Eh, cousin, you have come to the right place," Kwame said, laughing loudly. "I know every girl who walks this town. Describe her to me."

So James did, and when he finished, his cousin told him who she was and where he could find her. James went out into the town he barely knew, looking for the girl he'd met but once. He knew his cousin would keep his secret for him.

When James found her, she was carrying water in a bucket on the top of her head, heading back toward her family's hut.

She did not seem surprised to see him, and he was confident that whatever he'd felt during their brief time together, she had felt too.

"Can I help you with that?" James asked, pointing to the bucket.

She shook her head, horrified. "No, please. You shouldn't be doing this kind of work."

"Call me James."

"James," she repeated, rolling the strange name around in her mouth, tasting it as though it were bitter melon hitting the back of her tongue. "James."

"And you are?"

"Akosua Mensah," she said. The two kept walking. The few towns-people who recognized James stopped to bow or stare, but mostly peo-ple went about their daily lives, fetching water and carrying wood back for their fires.

It was a ten-mile walk from the stream to Akosua's hut in the bush on the outskirts of town, and James was determined to learn everything there was to know about her.

"Why would you not shake my hand at the king's funeral?" James asked.

"I told you. I will not shake the hand of a Fante slaver."

"And am I a slaver?" James asked, trying to keep his anger from entering his voice. "If I am Fante, am I not also Asante? Was my grand-father not your king?"

She smiled at him. "I am one of thirteen children. Now there are only ten of us who remain. When I was a small girl, there was war between my village and another. They took three of my brothers."

They walked in silence for a few minutes longer. James was sorry for her loss, but he knew too that all loss was just a part of life. Even his mother, important as she was, had once been captured, stolen from her family and planted in another's. "If your village had won that war, would you not have taken three of someone else's brothers?" James asked, unable to resist the question.

Akosua looked away. The bucket on her head was so steady, James wondered what it would take to knock it down. Maybe wind? Maybe an insect? "I know what you are thinking," she finally said. "Everyone is a part of this. Asante, Fante, Ga. British, Dutch, and American. And you are not wrong to think like this. It is how we are all taught to think. But I do not want to think this way. When my brothers and the other people were taken, my village mourned them as we redoubled our military efforts. And what does that say? We avenge lost lives by taking more? It doesn't make sense to me."

They stopped walking so that she could adjust her wrapper. For the second time that day, James tried as hard as he could not to look at her breasts. She continued. "I love my people, James," she said, and his name on her tongue was indescribably sweet. "I am proud to be

Asante, as I am sure you are proud to be Fante, but after I lost my brothers, I decided that as for me, Akosua, I will be my own nation."

As James listened to her speak, he felt something well up inside him as it had never done before. If he could, he would listen to her speak forever. If he could, he would join that nation she spoke of.

They walked farther. The sun was getting even lower in the sky, and James knew it would be impossible for him to make it home before nightfall. Still, they slowed down so that it seemed their feet were not even moving at all really, just coasting slowly, as though their bodies were being lifted and flown awkwardly by the mosquitoes they could feel buzzing around them.

"Are you promised to anyone?" James asked.

Akosua glanced shyly at him. "My father does not believe in promising a girl before her body has shown that she is ready, and I have not yet received my blood."

James thought about his own wife-to-be back home in his village, selected for him because of her status. He would never be happy with her, and his marriage would be as loveless and biting as that of his parents. But he knew his parents would never approve of Akosua, not even as a third or fourth wife. She had nothing, and she came from nowhere.

Nothing from nowhere. It was something his grandmother Effia used to say on nights when she seemed most sad. James couldn't remember a day when he hadn't seen Effia in all black, nor a night when he hadn't heard her faint crying.

When he was still just a small boy, he'd spent a weekend with her at her house near the Castle. In the middle of the night, he had woken up and heard her crying in her room. He'd gone to her, and wrapped her into a hug as tight as his little arms could muster.

"Why are you crying, Mama?" he'd asked, touching his fingers to her face, trying to catch some of the tears to blow and make a wish on as his mother sometimes did when he cried.

"Have you heard the story of Baaba, my own?" she asked, pulling him up onto her lap and rocking him back and forth.

That was the first night James heard it, but it wasn't the last.

Now James grabbed Akosua's hand, stopped her from moving. The bucket on her head began to sway, and she lifted her hands to steady it. "I want to marry you," James said.

They were only steps away from the girl's hut. He could see it through the bushes. Young children were wrestling with each other in the mud, coming up with their faces caked in brown. A man stood chopping the tall grass with his machete. Each time the blade hit the ground it shook the earth. James thought he could feel it move under his feet.

"How can you marry me, James?" the girl said. She looked worried now, her eyes stealing over to where her family waited. If she was too late with the water, her mother would beat her, then yell at her until dawn. No one would believe that she had been with the Asante king's grandson, and if they did believe it, they would only smell trouble.

"When your blood comes, you must tell no one. You must hide it. I am leaving tomorrow, but I will come back for you, and we will leave this town together. Start a new life in a small village where no one knows us."

Akosua was still looking at her family, and he knew how crazy he sounded, and he knew how much he was asking her to give up. The Asante puberty rites were a serious matter. There was a weeklong ceremony to bless the girls' fresh womanhood. The rules thereafter were strict. Women in menses could not visit the stool houses, could not cross certain rivers. They lived in separate houses and painted their wrists with white clay on the days they bled. If anyone found out a woman had bled but not told, the punishment would be great.

"Do you trust me?" James asked, knowing it was a question he had no right to ask.

"No," Akosua answered finally. "Trust is a thing to be earned. I don't trust you. I have seen what power can do to men, and you are from one of the most powerful families."

James's head grew light. He felt faint, like he would soon fall.

"But," Akosua continued, "if you come back for me, then you will earn my trust."

James nodded slowly, understanding. He would be back in his village by the end of the month, at his own wedding by the end of the year. The war would continue, and nothing, not his life nor his heart, was guaranteed. But listening to Akosua speak, he knew he would make a way.

*

James could not explain to Amma why he did not want to sleep in her hut. They had been married for three months and his excuses were wearing thin. On their wedding night, he had told her he was ill. For the entire week after, his body had taken over the excuse-making for him, his penis lying limp between his legs each time he went to her, even on the nights she braided her hair the way he liked it and rubbed coconut oil on her breasts and between her thighs. After that week, he had spent another two pretending to be too embarrassed to go to her, but soon, that too had failed him.

"You must go to see the apothecary. There are herbs you can take to help with this. If I do not get pregnant soon, people will start to believe there is something wrong with me," Amma said.

He felt bad for her. It was true. Failure to conceive was always believed to be the woman's fault, a punishment for infidelity or loose morals. But, in these few short months, James had gotten to know his wife well. She would soon tell everyone in the village that there was something wrong with *him,* and word would get back to his father and mother that he had not fulfilled his husbandly duties. He could hear his mother now. "Oh, Nyame, what have I done to deserve this? First a weak husband and now a weak son!" James knew he would have to fig-ure something out soon if he wanted to remain faithful to the memory of Akosua.

It was a memory he gripped tightly. It had been nearly a year since James had promised Akosua that he would come back for her, and he had come no closer to creating a plan to fulfill that promise. The Asantes were winning battle after battle against the British and the peo-ple of his village had begun to murmur that maybe the Asantes would win against the white men. And then what? Would more white men come to replace the ones who had died? Who would protect them if the Asantes came to meet them, to finally exact revenge for Abeeku Badu and Fiifi's grievances toward them? They had made an alliance with the British so long ago, maybe the white men had already forgotten.

James had not forgotten Akosua. He could see her every night when he slept, her lips and eyes and legs and buttocks moving across the field of his closed eyes. In his own hut on the outer edge of the compound, which he had built for himself and Amma and the other wives who were supposed to follow. He had not forgotten how much he had loved being in his grandfather's town, among the Asantes, the warmth he'd felt from his mother's people. The longer he stayed in Fanteland, the sooner he wished to get away. To lead a simpler life, as a farmer like Akosua's father, not as a politician like his own father, whose work for the British and the Fantes so many years before had left him with money and power, but little else.

"James, are you listening to me?" Amma said. She was stirring a pot of pepper soup, a wrapper slung across her waist, her back leaning forward so that it seemed her bare breasts would dip into the broth.

"Yes, darling, you are right," James said. "Tomorrow, I will go to see Mampanyin."

Amma nodded her head, satisfied. Mampanyin was the premier apothecary for hundreds of miles around. Junior wives went to her when they wished to quietly kill the senior wives. Younger brothers went when they wanted to be chosen as successor over their elder brothers. From the ocean's edge to the inland forests, people went to her when they had a problem that prayers alone could not fix.

James saw her on a Thursday. His father and many others had always called the woman a witch doctor, and she seemed to physically embody that role. She was missing all but her four front teeth, evenly spaced, as though they had chased all of the other teeth out of her mouth and then joined together in the middle, triumphant. Her back was perpetually hunched forward, and she walked with a cane made out of a rich black wood, carved to look like a snake was coiled around it. One of her eyes always looked away, and try as hard as he might, moving his head this way and that, James could not convince that eye to greet him.

"What is this man doing here?" Mampanyin asked the air.

James cleared his throat, unsure if he should speak.

Mampanyin spit on the ground, more phlegm than saliva. "What does this man want with Mampanyin? Can he not leave her in peace? He who does not even believe in her powers."

"Aunty Mampanyin, I have come from my village at my wife's request. She would like me to take some herbs so that we can make a baby." He had rehearsed a speech on the journey there—about how he wanted to make his wife happy while also making himself happy—but the words eluded him. He could hear the uncertainty, the fear, in his voice, and he cursed himself for it.

"Eh, he calls me aunty? He whose family sells our people to the whites abroad. He dares to call me aunty."

"That was my father and grandfather's work. It is not mine." He didn't add that because of their work, he didn't have to work, but instead could live off the family name and power.

She watched him with her good eye. "In your mind, you call me witch, eh?"

"Everyone calls you witch."

"Tell me, is Mampanyin the one who lay down for a white man to open her legs? The white men might have left had they not tasted our women."

"The white man will stay until there is no more money to be made."

"Eh, now you speak of money? Mampanyin has already said she knows how your family makes money. By sending your brothers and sisters over to Aburokyire to be treated like animals."

"America is not the only place with slaves," James said quietly. He'd heard his father say it to David before, when they talked about the atrocities of the American South that he'd read about in the abolitionist British papers. "The way they treat the slaves in America, my brother," David had said. "It is unfathomable. Unfathomable. We do not have slavery like that here. Not like that."

James's skin was starting to feel warm, but the sun had already dipped underneath the Earth. He wished he could turn and leave. Mampanyin's wandering eye had landed on a tree in the distance, then moved up to the sky, then just past James's left ear.

"I don't want to do the work of my family. I don't want to be one with the British."

She spit again, and then focused her roving eye directly onto him, and he began to sweat. Once she had finished, her eye returned to its ambling, finally satisfied with what it had seen in him. "Your penis does not work because you don't want it to work. My medicine is only for those who want. You speak of what you don't want, but there is something you want."

It was not a question. James didn't think he could trust her, and yet he knew that with her bad eye, she had seen him. Really seen him. And since he had not been able to make the Earth move on his own, he decided to trust the witch doctor to help him move it.

"I want to leave my family and move to Asanteland. I want to marry Akosua Mensah and work as a farmer or something small-small."

Mampanyin laughed. "The son of Big Man wants to live small-small, eh?"

She left him standing outside and went into her hut. When she came back she was carrying two small clay pots that had flies buzzing around the tops of them. James could smell them from where he stood. She sat on a chair and began swirling her index finger inside one of the pots. She pulled her finger back out and licked what was on it. James gagged.

"If you do not want your wife, why did you marry her?" Mampanyin asked.

"I was required to marry her so that our families could finally join," James said. Wasn't it obvious? She herself had said it. He was the son of a Big Man. There were things he had to do. Things he had to be seen doing so that everyone would know that his family was still important. What he wanted, what he most wanted, was to disappear. His father had seven other sons who could carry on the Otcher-Collins legacy. He wanted to be a man without a name. "I want to leave my family without them knowing I have left them," he said.

Mampanyin spit into the pot and then mixed it again. Her good eye looked up at James. "Is this possible?"

"Aunty, they say that you make impossible things possible."

She laughed again. "Eh, but they say that about Anansi, about Nyame, about the white man. I can only make the possible attainable. Do you see the difference?"

He nodded, and she smiled—the first smile she'd given him since his arrival. She beckoned him toward her, and he went, hoping that she would not ask him to eat whatever it was that was stinking in the pot. She motioned for him to sit before her, and he did so wordlessly. His parents would not like how he was stooped below her in her seat so that it seemed that she was a higher-born one than him. He could hear his mother's voice saying, "Stand." But he kept kneeling. Perhaps Mampanyin could make it so that neither his mother's voice nor his father's would ever be in his head again.

"You have come here asking me what to do, but you already know how to leave without anyone knowing you've left," Mampanyin said.

James was quiet. It was true he had thought of ways to make his family think he'd gone to Asamando when really he had journeyed elsewhere. The best idea, the most dangerous, was to join the never-ending Asante-British War. Everyone knew about the war, how it seemed it would never end, how the white men were weaker than everyone had once thought, even with their large Castle made of stone.

"People think they are coming to me for advice," Mampanyin said, "but really, they come to me for permission. If you want to do something, do it. The Asantes will be in Efutu soon, this I know."

She was no longer looking at him. Instead, she focused on the contents of the pot. There was no way this woman could know what the plans of the Asantes were. Theirs was the most powerful army in all of Africa. It was said that when the white men first came upon the Asante warriors with their bare chests and their loose cloth wraps, they had laughed, saying, "Are these not the cloths our women would wear?" They had prided themselves on their guns and their uniforms: the button-down jackets and trousers. Then the Asantes had slaughtered them by the hundreds, cut out the hearts of their military leaders and eaten them for strength. After that, at least one British soldier could be seen wetting those trousers they once praised as he retreated from the men they once underestimated.

If all that they said about the Asante army was true, it was impossible that they would be poorly organized enough to let a Fante fetish woman know of their plans. James knew that her roving eye had found itself in Efutu, in the future, and had seen him there, just as it had seen his heart's desire just then.

But still James did not go to Efutu. Amma was waiting for him when he went back home.

"What did Mampanyin say?" his wife asked.

"She said you must be patient with me," he said, and his wife huffed, dissatisfied. James knew she would spend the rest of the day gossiping with her girlfriends about him.

For a week James was miserable. He started to have doubts about Akosua, about his wish to live a small life. Was his life now so bad? He could stay in the village. He could continue the work of his father.

James had all but decided to do this when his grandmother came over to eat one night.

Effia was an old lady, and yet it was still possible to see the youth that once was somewhere beneath the many lines of her face. She had insisted on living in Cape Coast, in the house her husband had built, even after Quey had grown prominent in her village. She said she would never again live in the village that evil had built.

As they all ate outside in Quey's compound, James could feel his grandmother watching him, and after the house girls and boys had all come to collect their dishes, and James's father and mother had retired for the evening, he could feel his grandmother watching him still.

"What's wrong, my own child?" she asked when the two of them were finally alone.

James didn't speak. The *fufu* they had eaten sat like a rock at the bottom of his belly, and he thought it would make him sick. He looked at his grandmother. They said she was once so beautiful that the Castle governor would have burned their whole village down just to get to her.

She touched the black stone necklace she wore at her neck and then reached for James's hand. "You are not content?" she asked.

And James could feel the pressure build behind his eyes as tears threatened to break through. He squeezed his grandmother's hand. "I've heard my mother call my father weak my whole life, but what if I'm just like him?" James said. He expected his grandmother to react, but she remained silent. "I want to be my own nation." He knew she wouldn't be able to understand what he said, and yet it seemed that she had heard him. Even though he spoke in a whisper, she heard him.

His grandmother didn't speak at first, just watched him. "We are all weak most of the time," she said finally. "Look at the baby. Born to his mother, he learns how to eat from her, how to walk, talk, hunt, run. He does not invent new ways. He just continues with the old. This is how we all come to the world, James. Weak and needy, desperate to learn how to be a person." She smiled at him. "But if we do not like the person we have learned to be, should we just sit in front of our *fufu*, doing nothing? I think, James, that maybe it is possible to make a new way."

She kept smiling. The sun was setting behind them, and James finally let himself cry in front of his grandmother.

And so, the next day, James told his family that he was going back to Cape Coast with Effia, but instead he went to Efutu. He found work with a doctor whom his grandmother knew, who had worked for the British when she lived in the Castle. All James had to do was tell him that he was James Collins's grandson, and he immediately received work and a place to stay.

The doctor was Scottish and so old he could hardly walk upright, let alone heal illnesses without catching them. He had moved to Efutu after working for the company for only one year. He spoke fluent Fante, had built his compound himself from the ground up, and had remained unmarried, even though many of the local women had brought their young daughters to him as offerings. To the townspeople he was a mystery, but they had grown fond of him, affectionately calling him the White Doctor.

It was James's job to help keep the medicine room clean. The White Doctor's medical hut was next door to his living quarters, and it was small enough so that he didn't really need James's help at all. James swept, organized the medicines, washed the rags. Sometimes, in the evenings, he would cook a simple meal for the two of them, and they would sit in the yard, facing the dirt stretch of road, while the White Doctor told stories about his time in the Castle.

"You look just like your grandmother. What was that the locals used to call her?" He scratched his fine white hair. "The Beauty. Effia the Beauty, right?"

James nodded, trying to see her through the doctor's eyes.

"Your grandfather was so excited to marry her. I remember the night before she was to come to the Castle, we took James over to the company store just as the sun was going down and drank up almost all of the new liquor shipment. James had to tell the bosses back in England that the ship that had transported the liquor had sunk or been taken over by pirates. Something like that. It was a great night for all of us. A little rabble-rousing in Africa." A dreamy look came over his face, and James wondered if the old man had gotten the adventure he seemed to have been chasing here in the Gold Coast.

In a month, James would get what he had been chasing. The call came in the middle of the night. Fast-paced, high-pitched panting and shrieking as the watchmen of Efutu went from hut to hut, shouting that the Asantes were coming. The British and Fante armies stationed there sent out word for backup to join them, but the panic in the watchmen's eyes told James that the Asantes were closer than any help could be. Already by that point, villages throughout Fanteland, Ga-land, and Denkyira had been living in fear of Asante raids. British soldiers had been stationed intermittently in the towns and villages surrounding Cape Coast. Their goal was to keep the Asantes from storming the Castle, lest they do it successfully, but Efutu, only a week's journey from the Coast, was far too close for comfort.

"You must run!" James shouted at the White Doctor. The old man had lit a palm oil lamp next to his cot and pulled out a leather-bound book, reading with his spectacles perched at the tip of his nose. "They will kill you when they see you. They will not care that you are old."

The White Doctor turned the page. He didn't look up at James as he waved goodbye.

James shook his head and left the hut. Mampanyin had told him that he would know what to do when the time came, and yet here he was, so panicked that he could hardly breathe. He could feel the warm liquid traveling down his legs as he ran. He could not think. He could not think quickly enough to devise a plan, and before he knew it, shots were being fired all around him. The birds took flight, a black and red and blue and green cloud of wings, ascending. James wanted to hide. He couldn't remember what had been so bad about his old life. He could learn to love Amma. He'd spent so much time seeing the bad in his parents' marriage that he'd assumed there had to be something better. What if there wasn't? He had trusted a witch with his happiness. With his life. Now he would surely die.

James woke up in the bush of some unknown forest. His arms and legs ached, and his head felt as though it had been beaten by a rock. He sat there, disoriented, for countless minutes. Then an Asante warrior was beside him, so quiet in his approach that James did not notice him until he was standing over him.

"You are not dead?" the warrior asked. "Are you hurt?"

How could James tell a warrior like this that he had a headache? He said no.

"You are Osei Bonsu's grandson, are you not? I remember you from his funeral. I have never forgotten a face."

James wished he would lower his voice, but he didn't say anything.

"What were you doing in Efutu?" the warrior asked.

"Does anyone know I'm alive?" James asked, ignoring the man's question.

"No, a warrior hit your head with a rock. You didn't move, so they threw you in the dead pile. We aren't supposed to touch the pile, but I recognized your face and took you out so that I could send your body back to your people. I hid you here so no one would know I touched the dead. I didn't know you were still alive."

"Listen to me. I died in this war," James said.

The man's eyes grew so wide they looked like echoes of the moon. "What?"

"You must tell everyone that I died in this war. Will you do that?"

The warrior shook his head. He said no over and over and over again, but ultimately he would do it. James knew he would do it. And when he did, it would be the last time James would ever use his power to make another do his bidding.

For the rest of the month, James traveled to Asanteland. He slept in caves and hid in trees. He asked for help when he saw people in the bushland, telling them he was a lowly farmer who had gotten lost. And when he finally got to Akosua, on the fortieth day of his travels, he found her waiting for him.

Kojo

SOMEBODY HAD ROBBED old *Alice,* which meant the police would come sniffing around the boat, asking all the ship workers if they knew anything about it. Jo's reputation was spotless. He'd been working on the ships in Fell's Point for nearly two years and had never given anybody any trouble. But still, whenever a boat was robbed, all the black dockworkers were rounded up and questioned. Jo was tired of it. He was always jumpy around police, or anyone in uniform. Even the appearance of the postman had once sent him running behind a lace curtain. Ma Aku said he'd been like this since their days in the woods, running from catchers, from town to town, until they'd hit the safe house in Maryland.

"Cover for me, would ya, Poot?" Jo asked his friend, but he knew the police wouldn't miss him. They couldn't tell one black face from another. Poot would answer when they called his own name and then answer when they called Jo's too, and they wouldn't know the difference.

Jo jumped off the boat and looked behind him at the beautiful Chesapeake Bay, at the large, imposing ships that lined the Fell's Point shipyards. He loved the look of those boats, loved that his hands helped build and maintain them, but Ma Aku always said it was bad juju, him and all the other freed Negroes working on ships. She said there was something evil about them building up the things that had brought them to America in the first place, the very things that had tried to drag them under.

Jo walked down Market Street and bought some pigs' feet from Jim at the corner store near the museum. As he was leaving, a horse broke free from its buggy and ran wild, nearly trampling an old white woman who had been lifting her skirt, just about to step into the street.

"You all right, ma'am?" Jo asked, running over to her and offering his arm.

She looked dazed for a second, but then she smiled at Jo. "Fine, thank you," she said.

He continued on. Anna would still be cleaning house with Ma Aku. He knew he should go over there and help the two women, what with Anna being pregnant again and Ma Aku being so old the never-ending coughs and aches had set in, but it had been too long since he'd let himself enjoy Baltimore, the cool sea breeze, the Negroes, some slave but some free as can be, who worked and lived and played around him. Jo had been a slave once. He was only a baby then, and yet every time he saw a slave in Baltimore, he felt like he remembered. Every time Jo saw a slave in Baltimore, he saw himself, saw what his life would have been like had Ma Aku not taken him to freedom. His free papers named him Kojo Freeman. Free man. Half the ex-slaves in Baltimore had the name. Tell a lie long enough and it will turn to truth.

Jo only knew the South from the stories Ma Aku told him, same way he knew his mother and father, Ness and Sam. As stories and nothing more. He didn't miss what he didn't know, what he couldn't feel in his hands or his heart. Baltimore was tangible. It wasn't endless crops and whippings. It was the port, the ironworks, the railroads. It was the pigs' feet Kojo was eating, the smiles of his seven children with number eight on the way. It was Anna, who'd married him when she was just sixteen and he nineteen, and had worked every day of the nineteen years since.

Thinking of Anna again, Jo decided to swing by the Mathison house, where she and Ma were cleaning that day. He bought a flower from Ol' Bess on the corner of North and Sixteenth and, holding it, he felt like he could finally forget the thought of the police on his ship.

"Why, if it ain't my husband, Jo, comin' up the walk," Anna said when she saw him. She was sweeping the porch with what looked like a new broom. The handle was a handsome brown, only a few shades darker than her own skin, and the bristles all stood at attention. Ma Aku always liked to tell them that in the Gold Coast brooms had no handles. The body was the handle, and it moved and bent much easier than a stick ever could.

"Brought you somethin'," Jo said, handing her the flower. She took it and breathed it in and smiled. The stalk hit her stomach just where her belly started to strain against her dress. Jo put his hand there and rubbed.

"Where's Ma?" he asked.

"Inside doin' the kitchen."

Jo kissed his wife and took the broom from her hands. "You go on and help her now," he said, giving her butt a squeeze and a push as he sent her inside. It was the butt that had done it nineteen years ago, was still doing it now. He'd seen it coming around Strawberry Alley and had followed it four whole blocks. It was mesmerizing, the way it moved, independent of the rest of her body, as though operating under the influence of another brain entirely, one cheek knocking into the other cheek so that that cheek had to swing out before knocking back.

When he was seven years old, Jo had asked Ma Aku what a man was supposed to do when he liked a woman, and she had laughed. His ma had never been like the other mothers. She was a little strange, a little off, still dreaming of the country she'd been ripped from years and years before. She could often be found looking out at the water, looking as if she would jump in, try to find her way home.

"Why, Kojo, in the Gold Coast, they say if you like a woman you have to go to her father with an offering." Back then, Jo had been in love with a girl named Mirabel, and in church the next Sunday, he'd brought her father a frog that he'd caught by the water the night before, and Ma Aku had laughed and laughed and laughed, until the pastor and the father said she was teaching Jo the ways of old African witchcraft and kicked them out of the congregation.

With Anna, Jo simply followed the sway of her butt, until it stopped still. He'd gone up to her and seen her face. Her sweet caramel skin and black, black hair, as dark and long as a horse tail, always worn in a single braid. He'd told her his name was Jo, and asked if he could walk with her a ways. She'd said yes, and they walked the whole length of Baltimore. It wasn't until months later that Jo learned Anna had gotten in trouble with her mother that night, having skipped out on all the chores she had promised to do.

The Mathisons were an old white family. Mr. Mathison's father's house had once been a stop on the Underground Railroad, and he'd taught his son to always lend a helpful hand. Mrs. Mathison was the one with the family money, and when the two had gotten together they'd bought a large house and employed Anna, Ma Aku, and a host of other black folk from in and around Baltimore.

The house was two stories and ten rooms. It took hours to clean, and the Mathisons liked it spotless. Kojo took up some of the work that day, and while washing the windows in the drawing room he could hear Mathison and the other abolitionists talking.

"If California joins the Union as a free state, President Taylor will have his hands full with Southern secessionists," Mathison said.

"And Maryland will be caught in the middle," another voice said.

"That's why we've got to do all we can to make sure more slaves are emancipated right here in Baltimore."

They could go on for hours talking this way. In the beginning, Jo had liked to listen to them. It had given him hope, seeing all those powerful white people take up for him and his, but the more years went on, the more he knew that even kindhearted people like the ones in the Mathison house could only do so much.

When they finished cleaning the house, Jo, Anna, and Ma Aku headed back toward their little apartment on Twenty-Fourth Street.

"My back—oh, my back," Ma said, clutching at the body part that had been paining her for years now. She turned to Jo and in Twi said, "Haven't we grown tired?" It was an old, worn expression for an old and worn feeling. Jo nodded and gave the woman his hand to help her up the stairs.

Inside, the kids were playing. Agnes, Beulah, Cato, Daly, Eurias, Felicity, and Gracie. It seemed like he and Anna were going to have one child for every letter of the alphabet. They would teach their children to read those letters, grow them up to be the kind of people who could teach those letters to other people. Now everyone in the house called the new baby "H," as a placeholder until it came out and brought its name along with it.

Being a good father felt like a debt Jo owed to his parents, who couldn't get free. He used to spend many nights trying to conjure up an image of his own father. Was he brave? Tall? Kind? Smart? Was he a good and fair man? What kind of father would he have been if he'd ever gotten the chance to be a father, free?

Now Jo spent most nights with his ear against his wife's barely there stomach, trying to get to know Baby H a little before it arrived. He had made a promise to Anna that he would be there for them, the way his own father had not been able to be there for him. And Anna, who had never wanted her own father to be there for her, knowing the kind of man he was and the kind of trouble his presence would have brought, had just smiled and patted his back.

But Jo meant what he had said. He studied his children, the few hours of every night that he got to see them before they went to bed or every morning before he went off to the docks. Agnes was the helper. He'd never known a kinder, gentler spirit. Not Anna and certainly not his world-weary mother. Beulah was a beauty, but she didn't know it yet. Cato was soft for a boy, and Jo tried every day to put a little grit into him. Daly was a fighter and Eurias was too often his target. Felicity was so shy she wouldn't tell you her own name if you asked her, and Gracie was a round ball of love. His life with them, with Anna and Ma and the kids, was all that he had ever wanted on those days he'd spent as a lonely child, going from safe house to safe house, job to job, trying to help the woman he called mother do the mothering work she hadn't asked for but never complained about.

Ma Aku started coughing, and Agnes came over right away to help her into the bed. The apartment had two rooms: one for Jo and Anna, separated by a curtain, and one for everyone and everything else. Ma Aku went down onto the mattress with a heavy sigh, and within minutes she was coughing and snoring in equal measure.

Gracie, the baby, was pawing at the leg of Jo's trousers. "Daddy, Daddy!"

Jo swooped down and picked her up in one arm as easily as if she were the toolbox he'd left on the boat. Pretty soon, she'd be too big for babying. Probably just in time for the new baby to come.

Soon, Agnes and Anna had gotten all the little kids to sleep, and Agnes was finally sleeping herself. Jo was sitting in the bedroom with the curtain drawn when Anna came in, rubbing the belly that was so small it was little more than a feeling.

"Police came by the boat today. Said somebody had robbed her," Jo said. Anna was taking off her clothes and folding them, then placing them on the chair that sat beside their mattress. She would wear the same ones tomorrow. She hadn't had time to do the wash that week, and she hadn't had the money to do it the week before. All she could do was hope that the children didn't smell when they went off to the Christian school.

"Did it scare you?" she asked, and Jo stood, quick as a flash, and grabbed her into his arms, pulling her down onto the mattress with him.

"Ain't nothing scare me, woman," he said while she laughed and thrashed, pretending to fight him off.

They kissed, and whatever clothes Anna hadn't gotten to, Jo made quick work of removing. He tasted her and could feel more than hear the pleasure it sent through her body like a current, the way she stifled her moans so the kids wouldn't wake up, an expert at this after many nights and seven children. They worked quickly and quietly together, hoping the dark would mask their motions if one of the children happened to be peering through the curtain, unable to sleep. Jo grabbed onto Anna's butt with both of his hungry hands. As long as he lived, it would always be a pleasure and a gift to fill his hands with the weight of her flesh.

The next morning, Jo went back to work on *Alice*. Poot came by to split his breakfast with Jo: a little cornbread and some fish.

"Did they come around?" Jo asked. Earlier that morning he had gotten the oakum ready for the deck, soaking the hemp in pine tar. He'd twisted it like rope, laying it down in the seams between the planks. Jo had been working with the same tools since he first started caulking. His very own iron and mallet. He loved the sound those two tools made together when he laid the oakum into the seams, tapping the iron gently to coerce the oakum to stay, the seam to fill, the boat to keep from leaking.

"Yeah, they came. Just asked the usual questions, though. Wasn't bad. I hear they found the man that done it." Poot was born free, lived in Baltimore his whole life. He'd worked on *Alice* for about a year, and before that he'd worked on just about every other ship in the port. He was one of the best caulkers around. People said he could just put his ear to a ship and it would tell him where it needed work. Jo had come up under him, and because of that he knew just about everything there was to know about ships.

He payed the hull, spreading hot pitch over the whole thing and then covering it with copper plates. When he was first starting out, Jo had almost died heating the pitch. The fire had been magnificent, and so hot it was like the Devil's breath, and before Jo knew it, it had started to chase the wood of the deck. He'd looked down at all that water floating in the bay, and then back up at the fire that was threatening to take the whole boat down with it, and he'd asked for a miracle. That miracle was Poot. Quick as can be, Poot had put out the fire and calmed the boss down by telling him that if Jo couldn't stay, he wouldn't either. Now whenever Jo lit a fire on the boat, he knew how to tend it.

Jo had just finished the hull and was wiping the sweat out of his eyes when he saw Anna standing and waving from the dock. It was rare for her to meet him after a workday because he usually finished before she did, but he was pleased to see her.

As he grabbed his tools and started walking toward her, he realized something was wrong.

"Mr. Mathison says for you to come to the house quick as you can," she said. She was wringing her handkerchief in her hands, a nervous habit he detested, for seeing it always had the effect of making him nervous too.

"Is Ma all right?" he asked, grabbing her hands in his and shaking them until they finally stilled.

"Yes."

"Then what is it?"

"I don't know," she said.

He looked at her hard but could see that she was telling the truth. She was nervous because Mathison had never asked to see Jo before, not in the seven years that she and Ma had been cleaning house for him, and she didn't know what it could mean that he was asking her now.

They walked the few miles to the Mathison house so quickly that the contents of Jo's toolbox rattled uncomfortably against the box walls. Jo was walking a little ahead of Anna, and he could hear the patter of her small feet struggling to stay in step with his long legs.

When they reached the house, Ma Aku was waiting on the porch, her cough their only welcome from her. She and Anna led Jo into the parlor, where Mathison and a handful of other white men were sitting on the plush white couches, the cushions so full they looked like small hills, or the backs of elephants.

"Kojo!" Mathison said, standing to shake his hand. He'd heard Ma Aku call Jo that once, and had asked them what it meant. When Ma had explained it was the Asante name for a boy born on Monday, he'd clapped his hands together as though hearing a good song, and insisted on calling Jo by his full name every time he saw him. "Taking away your name is the first step," he'd said somberly. So somberly that Jo hadn't felt it wise to ask what he was thinking—the first step to what?

"Mr. Mathison."

"Please, have a seat," Mr. Mathison said, pointing to an empty white chair. Jo suddenly felt nervous. His trousers were covered in dry pitch, so black it looked like hundreds of holes lined them. Jo worried the pitch would stain the chair, making it so that Anna and Ma Aku would have more work to do the next day when they came in. If they came in at all.

"I'm so sorry to bring you all the way over here, but my colleagues have informed me of some very troubling news."

A fatter white man cleared his throat, and Jo watched the jiggle of his neck as he spoke. "We've been hearing about a new law being drafted by the South and the Free-Soilers, and if it was to pass, law enforcement would be required to arrest any alleged runaway slave in the North and send them back south, no matter how long ago they escaped."

The men were all watching him, waiting for him to react, and so he nodded.

"My concern is for you and your mother," Mr. Mathison said, and Jo looked over to the door where Anna had been standing just moments ago. She was probably back to the cleaning by now, worried about whatever it was Mathison had to say to Jo. "As runaways, you might have more trouble than Anna and the children, who are free in their own right."

Jo nodded. He couldn't imagine who would be looking for him or Ma Aku after all of these years. Jo didn't even know the name or the face of his own old master. All Ma could remember was that Ness had called him the Devil.

"You should get your family further north," Mr. Mathison said. "New York, Canada, even. If this thing passes, there's no telling what kind of chaos it'll cause."

"Are they gon' fire me?" Anna asked. They were sitting on their mattress later that night, after the children had all gone to sleep, and Jo was finally able to explain to her what Mathison had called him over for.

"No, they just want to warn us, is all."

"But your ma's old master died. Ruthie tol' us, remember?"

Jo remembered. Anna's cousin Ruthie had sent word from one plantation to another to a safe house and finally to Ma Aku that the man who had owned her had died. And they had all breathed easier that night.

"Mr. Mathison say that don't matter. His people can still get her if they want to."

"What about me and the kids?"

Jo shrugged. Anna's master had fathered her, then set her and her mother free. She had real free papers, not forged ones like Jo and Ma

Aku. The kids had all been born right there in Baltimore, free. No one would be looking for them. "Just me and Ma that gotta worry. Don't you think about this none."

As for Ma Aku, Jo knew she would never leave Baltimore. Unless she could go back to the Gold Coast, there would be no new countries for her—not Canada, not even Paradise if it existed on Earth. Once the woman had decided to get free, she had also decided to stay free. When he was a child, Jo would often marvel at the knife Ma Aku always kept tucked inside her wrapper, which she'd been keeping inside her wrapper since her days as an Asante slave, then an American slave, then, finally, free. The older Jo got, the more he understood about the woman he called Ma. The more he understood that sometimes staying free required unimaginable sacrifice.

In the other room, Beulah started whimpering in her sleep. The child had night terrors. They came at unpredictable intervals: one month here, two days there. Some days they were so bad she would wake herself up to the sound of her own screams or she'd have scratches along her arms from where she'd fought invisible battles. Other days she slept still as death, tears streaming down her face, and the next day, when asked what she'd dreamed about, she always shrugged and said, "Nothing."

This day, Jo looked out and saw the girl's little legs start to move: a bend at the knee, an outward kick, repeat. Beulah was running. Maybe this was where it started, Jo thought. Maybe Beulah was seeing something more clearly on the nights she had these dreams, a little black child fighting in her sleep against an opponent she couldn't name come morning because in the light that opponent just looked like the world around her. Intangible evil. Unspeakable unfairness. Beulah ran in her sleep, ran like she'd stolen something, when really she had done nothing other than expect the peace, the clarity, that came with dreaming. Yes, Jo thought, this was where it started, but when, where, did it end?

*

Jo decided to keep his family in Baltimore. Anna was too pregnant to haul up from the city to which they were all rooted, and Baltimore still felt safe. People kept whispering about the law. A few families even made moves, packing up and heading north for fear that the law would pass. Ol' Bess who sold the flowers on North Street went. So did Everett, John, and Dothan, who worked on *Alice*.

"Damn shame," Poot said the day three Irishmen walked onto the boat to replace them.

"You ever think 'bout leavin', Poot?" Jo asked.

Poot snorted. "They gon' bury me in Baltimore, Jo. One way or another. They gon' throw my body down into the Chesapeake Bay."

Jo knew he meant it. Poot always said that Baltimore was a great city to be a black man in. There were black porters and teachers, preachers and hucksters. A free man didn't have to be a servant or a coach driver. He could make something with his own hands. He could fix something, sell something. He could build something up from the ground, then send it out to sea. Poot had taken up caulking when he was only a teenager, and he often joked that the only thing he liked better than holding a mallet was holding a woman. He was married but he had no children, no son to teach his trade to. The ships were his pride. He would never leave Baltimore.

And for the most part, everyone else in Baltimore stayed put too. They were tired of running and used to waiting. And so they waited to see what would come.

Anna's belly continued to swell. Baby H was making itself known every day with ferocious kicks and punches to the inside of Anna's gut. "H is gon' be a boxer," ten-year-old Cato said, resting his ear against his mother's stomach.

"Nuh-uh," Anna said. "There won't be no violence in *this* house." Five minutes later, Daly kicked Eurias in the shins, and Anna spanked him so hard he winced every time he sat down that day.

Agnes turned sixteen and took a job cleaning the Methodist church on Caroline Street, and Beulah relished her new role as oldest child in the house for the one hour of every evening before Agnes returned home from work.

"Timmy say he and Pastor John ain't going nowhere," Agnes reported one night. It was August 1850 and Baltimore had taken on a sticky heat. Agnes would come home every night with sweat licking at her upper lip, her neck, her forehead. Timmy was the pastor's son, and every day Jo and the rest of the family were subjected to Agnes's reports on what Timmy had thought, done, or said that day.

"So I guess that means you ain't going nowhere neither?" Anna said with a smirk, and Agnes huffed out of the house. She said it was in search of some chocolate for the kids, but they all knew that Anna had struck a nerve.

Ma Aku laughed as the door slammed. "That child don't know nothin' 'bout love," she said. Her laugh turned into a cough, and she had to bend forward to let the cough fall out.

Jo kissed Anna's forehead and looked at Ma. "What d'you know 'bout love, Ma?" he asked, taking over the laugh where she left it.

Ma wagged her finger at him. "Don't go askin' me what I know an' don't know," she said. "You ain't the only one who ever touched or been touched by somebody."

It was Anna's turn to laugh, and Jo dropped the hand that he had been squeezing, feeling a bit betrayed. "Who, Ma?"

Ma shook her head, slowly. "Don't matter."

Two weeks later, Timmy came by the docks to ask Jo for Agnes's hand in marriage.

"You know a trade, boy?" Jo asked.

"I'm gonna be a preacher like my daddy," Timmy said.

Jo grunted. He'd been to a church only once since the day he and Ma Aku were kicked out for witchcraft, and that was the day of his own wedding. If Agnes married this preacher's son, he'd have to go again for her wedding and then who knew how many more times.

The day they'd walked the five miles home from the Baptist church, after Jo had given Mirabel's father the frog, Jo had cried and cried. Ma Aku had let him carry on for a few minutes, and then she snatched his ear up with her hand, dragged him into an alley, looked at him hard, and said, "Whatchu cryin' fo', boy?"

"Pastor say we was doin' African witchcraft." He wasn't old enough to know what that meant, but he was old enough to know shame, and that day, he was full up to his ears with it.

Ma Aku spit behind her left shoulder, something she only did when truly disgusted. "Who tol' you to cry fo' that?" she asked, and he shrugged his shoulders, tried to keep his nose from running, for it seemed to make her more angry. "I tell you, if they had not chosen the white man's god instead of the gods of the Asante, they could not say these things to me."

Jo knew he was supposed to nod, and so he did. She continued. "The white man's god is just like the white man. He thinks he is the only god, just like the white man thinks he is the only man. But the only reason he is god instead of Nyame or Chukwu or whoever is because we *let* him be. We do not fight him. We do not even question him. The white man told us he was the way, and we said yes, but when has the white man ever told us something was good for us and that thing was really good? They say you are an African witch, and so what? So what? Who told them what a witch was?"

Jo had finished crying, and Ma Aku scrubbed at the white salt stains along his cheek with the hem of her dress. She pulled him back into the street, dragging him along by the arm and muttering the whole time.

Timmy's hands were trembling, and Jo watched them shake. He was a lanky, skinny boy with soft hands that had never been burned by hot pitch or callused by a caulking iron. Timmy came from a line of free folk: born and raised in Baltimore to parents who were also born and raised in Baltimore. "If that's what Aggie wants," Jo finally said.

The couple married the next month, on the morning the Fugitive Slave Act passed. Anna sewed Agnes's dress in the night by candlelight. In the mornings, Jo would find her, bleary-eyed, blinking herself awake as she got ready to go to the Mathison house. Baby H was so big in her belly that she could no longer walk without waddling, her feet so swollen that when she shoved them into her work slippers they folded back out and over, like bread that had too much yeast and could not be contained by its pan.

The wedding was at Timmy's father's church, and all the female congregants had cooked a meal fit to feed a king, even though there were whispers about Timmy marrying a girl whose folks didn't attend a church, not even the rival Methodist one across the street.

Beulah stood next to Agnes in a purple dress, and Timmy's brother, John Jr., stood next to him. Timmy's father, Pastor John, married them. He didn't close the usual way, announcing the new Mr. and Mrs. and telling them to kiss, but instead had the congregation reach their hands out toward Timmy and Agnes while he said a blessing. And just as he spoke the words "And all God's people said," a little boy ran by the door of the church shouting, "The law passed! The law passed!"

And the answer, "Amen," came muffled and insincere from some. From others, it didn't come at all. A few began to squirm in their seats and one even left, getting up so quickly that the whole pew rocked, thrown, as it was, off-balance.

Agnes looked at Jo with a shadow of nervousness hanging behind her eyes, and he looked at her as steadily as he knew how. Then her fear melted away as the collective fear grew. Pastor John finished marrying the couple, and everyone ate the feast that Anna, Ma, and the rest of the women had prepared.

Within a couple of weeks, word came in that James Hamlet, a Baltimore runaway, had been kidnapped and convicted in New York City. The white folks wrote about it in the *New York Herald* and in the Baltimore *Sun*. He was the first, but everyone knew there would be more. People began moving up to Canada by the hundreds. Jo went to Fell's Point one week, and what used to be a sea of black faces against the backdrop of the blue-green bay had turned into nothing. Mathison had made sure Jo's whole family had their free papers together, but he knew others with papers too, and even they had fled.

Mathison spoke to Jo again. "I want to make certain you know what's at stake here, Jo. If they catch you, they'll take you to trial, but you won't get any kind of say at all. It'll be the white man's word against no word at all. You all make sure you carry your papers at all times, understand?" Jo nodded.

There were rallies and protests throughout the North, and not just among the Negroes. White people were joining in like Jo had never seen them join in about anything before. The South had brought this fight to the Northern welcome mat, when many of them had wanted nothing to do with it. Now white people could be fined for giving a Negro a meal, or a job, or a place to stay, if the law said that Negro was a runaway. And how were they to know who was a runaway and who was not? It had created an impossible situation, and those who had been determined to stay on the fence found themselves without a fence at all.

In the mornings, before Jo and Anna went off to work, Jo made the children practice showing their papers. He would play the federal marshall, hands on his hips, walking up to each of them, even little Gracie, and saying, in a voice as stern as he could muster, "Where you goin'?" And they would reach into the pockets Anna had sewn onto their dresses and pants, and without any backtalk, always silently, thrust those papers into Jo's hands.

When he'd first started doing this, the children would burst into laughter, thinking it was a game. They didn't know about Jo's fear of people in uniform, didn't know what it was like to lie silent and barely breathing under the floorboards of a Quaker house, listening to the sound of a catcher's bootheel stomp above you. Jo had worked hard so that his children wouldn't have to inherit his fear, but now he wished they had just the tiniest morsel of it.

"You worry too much," Anna said. "Ain't nobody lookin' for them kids. Ain't nobody lookin' for us neither." The baby was due any day now, and Jo had noticed that his wife had become crankier than ever, snapping at him for the tiniest of things. She craved fish and lemons. She walked with her hands on her lower back, and she forgot things. The keys one day, the broom the next. Jo worried she would forget her papers next. He'd seen her leave them, rumpled and worn, on her side of the mattress one day when she went to the market, and he'd yelled at her for it. He'd yelled at her until she cried. Bad as he felt that day, he knew she would never forget again.

Then one day Anna didn't come home. Jo ran to the room to see if she'd left her papers again, but he couldn't find them anywhere, and he heard Anna's sweet voice saying, "You worry too much. You worry too much," in his ear. Beulah came home with the rest of the kids in tow, and Jo asked if they had seen their mother.

"Is Baby H comin', Daddy?" Eurias asked.

"Maybe," Jo said absently.

Then Ma Aku came home, her hands massaging the nape of her neck. It didn't take long for her to survey the room.

"Where Anna? She said she was gonna get some sardines before comin' home," Ma said, but Jo was already halfway out the door.

He went to the grocer, the corner store, the fabric shop. He went to the fish market, the cobbler, the hospital. The shipyards, the museum, the bank.

"Anna? She ain't been by today," said one after the other.

Then, for the first time in his life, Jo knocked on a white man's door at night. Mathison himself opened the door.

"She ain't been home since mornin'," Jo said, his throat catching on the words. It had been a long time since he'd cried, and he didn't want to do it in front of a white man, no matter how the man had helped him.

"Go home to your kids, Kojo. I'll start looking for her right now. You go home."

Jo nodded, and in his dazed walk home, he began to think about what life would be like without his wife, the woman he had loved hard and long. Everyone had been keeping up with what was becoming known as the "Bloodhound Law." They'd heard about the dogs, the kidnappings, the trials. They'd heard it all, but hadn't they earned their freedom? The days of running through forests and living under floorboards. Wasn't that the price they had paid? Jo didn't want to accept what he was already starting to know in his heart. Anna and Baby H were gone.

Jo couldn't stand by and wait for Mathison to look for Anna. Mathison may have had all the wealthy white connections a person could want, but Jo knew the black and the poor immigrant white people of Baltimore, and at night, after he had finished working on the ships, he went out to talk to them, trying to gather information.

But everywhere he went, the answer was the same. They had seen Anna that morning, the day before, three nights ago. The day she went missing, she'd been at Mathison's until six o'clock. After that, nothing. No one had seen her.

Agnes's new husband, Timmy, was a good artist. He drew up a picture of Anna from memory that looked as close to her as any Jo had ever seen. In the morning, Jo took the picture to Fell's Point with him. He got on every last boat in the shipyard, showing people Anna's face drawn in heavy charcoal.

"Sorry, Jo," they all said.

He took the picture onto *Alice* with him, and even though all the other men already knew what she looked like, they humored him, studying the picture carefully before telling Jo what he already knew. They hadn't seen her either.

Jo took to carrying the picture in his pocket while he worked. He lost himself in the sound of mallet hitting iron, that steady rhythm he knew so well. It soothed him. Then, one day, when he was getting the oakum ready, the picture slipped out of his pocket, and by the time Jo caught it, the bottom edges were soaked in pine tar. As he worked to get it off, the tar stuck to his fingers, and when he reached up to wipe sweat from his eye, his face shimmered with it.

"I gotta go," Jo said to Poot, waving the picture frantically, hoping the wind would dry it.

"You can't miss no more days, Jo," Poot said. "They gon' give yo job to one of them Irishmen and then what, huh? Who gon' feed them kids, Jo?"

Jo was already running toward dry land.

By the time Jo got to the furniture store on Aliceanna Street, he was showing the picture to every person he passed. He didn't know what he was thinking when he shoved it in the face of the white woman coming out of the store.

"Please, ma'am," he said. "Have you seen my wife? I'm looking for my wife."

The woman backed away from him slowly, her eyes widening with fear but never leaving his own, as though if she was to turn from him he would be free to attack her.

"You stay away from me," the woman said, holding her hand out in front of her.

"I'm looking for my wife. Please, ma'am, just look at the picture. Have you seen my wife?"

She shook her head and the held-out hand too. She didn't even glance at the picture once. "I've got children," she said. "Please don't hurt me."

Was she even listening to a word he said? Suddenly, Jo felt two strong arms grab him from behind. "This nigger bothering you?" a voice asked.

"No, officer. Thank you, officer," the woman said, breathing easier and then taking her leave.

The policeman swung Jo around to face him. Jo was so scared he couldn't lift his eyes, so instead he lifted the picture. "Please, my wife, sir. She's eight months pregnant and I ain't seen her in days."

"Your wife, huh?" the policeman said, snatching the picture from Jo's hands. "Pretty nigger, ain't she?"

Still Jo couldn't look at him.

"Why don't you let me take this picture with me?"

Jo shook his head. He'd almost lost the picture once that day and didn't know what he would do if he lost it again. "Please, sir. It's the only one I got."

Then Jo heard the sound of paper tearing. He looked up to see Anna's nose and ears and strands of hair, the shredded bits of paper flying off in the wind.

"I'm tired of all these runaway niggers thinking they're above the law. If your wife was a runaway nigger, then she got what she deserved. What about you? You a runaway nigger? I can send you on to see your wife."

Jo held the policeman's gaze. His whole body felt like it was shaking. He couldn't see it, but he could feel it inside him, an unstoppable quaking. "No, sir," he said.

"Speak up," the policeman said.

"No, sir. I was born free, right here in Baltimore."

The policeman smirked. "Go home," he said. The policeman turned and walked away, and the quaking that had been held somewhere inside Jo's bones started to escape until he was sitting on the hard ground, trying to hold himself together.

"Tell him what you told me," Mathison said. Jo was standing in Mathison's parlor three weeks later. Ma Aku had fallen ill and could no longer go to work, but Jo still stopped by the Mathison house on his way home to see if the man had any news about Anna.

This day, Mathison was holding a scared Negro child by his shoulders. The boy could not have been much older than Daly, and if he was any more scared of being called in by a white man, his skin would have been gray instead of its cool tar black.

He stood, hands trembling, and looked up at Jo. "I saws a white man takes a pregnant woman into his carriage. Says she too pregnant to walk home, so he takes her."

Jo bent down until his eyes were level with the shaking child's. He grabbed the boy's chin in his hand and made him look at him, and he searched the boy's eyes for what seemed like days, three whole weeks to be exact, searching for Anna.

"They sold her," Jo said to Mathison, standing back up.

"Now, we don't know that, Jo. Could be that they had to rush medical care. Anna was rightfully free, and she was pregnant," Mathison answered, but his voice was uncertain. They had checked every hospital, every midwife, even the witch doctors. No one had seen Anna or Baby H.

"They sold her and the baby too," Jo said, and before he or Mathison could stop or thank him, the child pulled away and ran out of the Mathison house quicker than a flash. He would likely tell his friends all about it, being in the grand home of a white man who had been asking questions about a Negro woman. He would make himself sound better in them. He would say he stood tall and spoke firmly, that the man shook his hand after and offered him a quarter.

"We'll keep looking, Jo," Mathison said, observing the empty space the boy had left behind. "This isn't over. We'll find her. I'll go to court if I have to, Jo. I promise you that."

Jo couldn't hear him anymore. The wind was coming in through the door the child had left ajar. It was moving around the big white pillars that held up the house, curving around them, bending until it fit into the thin space of Jo's ear canal. It was there to tell him that fall had come to Baltimore and that he would have to spend it alone, taking care of his ailing Ma and his seven children without his Anna.

When he went home, the kids were all waiting. Agnes had come over with Timmy. The girl was pregnant, Jo could just tell, but he knew that she was scared to tell him, to hurt him or the three-week-old memory of her mother, scared her small piece of joy was almost shameful.

"Jo?" Ma Aku called. Jo had given her the bedroom once her pain had started worsening.

He went to her. She was lying on her back, staring up at the ceiling, her hands folded over her chest. She turned her head toward him and spoke in Twi, something she used to do often when he was a child but had stopped almost completely since he married Anna.

"She's gone?" Ma asked, and Jo nodded. She sighed. "You will make it through this, Jo. Nyame did not make weak Asantes, and that is what you are, no matter what man here, white or black, wishes to erase that part of you. Your mother came from strong, powerful people. People who do not break."

"You're my mother," Jo said, and Ma Aku, with great effort, turned her whole body toward him and opened her arms. Jo crawled into bed with her and cried as he rested his head on her bosom, as he had not done since he was a young child. Back then, he used to cry for Sam and Ness. The only thing that would pacify him was stories about them, even if the stories were unpleasant. So Ma Aku would tell him that Sam hardly spoke, but when he did it was loving and wise, and that Ness had some of the most gruesome whip scars she had ever seen. Jo used to worry that his family line had been cut off, lost forever. He would never truly know who his people were, and who their people were before them, and if there were stories to be heard about where he had come from, he would never hear them. When he felt this way, Ma Aku would hold him against her, and instead of stories about family she would tell him stories about nations. The Fantes of the Coast, the Asantes of the Inland, the Akans.

When he lay against this woman now, he knew that he belonged to someone, and that had once been enough for him.

. . .

Ten years passed. Ma Aku passed with them. Agnes had three children, Beulah was pregnant, and Cato and Felicity were married. Eurias and Gracie, the youngest of the bunch, both found live-in work as soon as they could. They said it was to help take off some of the burden, but Jo knew the truth. His children could not stand to be around him anymore, and, though he hated to admit it, he could not stand to be around them.

The problem was Anna. The fact that he saw her everywhere in Baltimore, at every shop, on every road. He would sometimes see ample buttocks coming around a corner and follow them for blocks on end. He'd gotten slapped once doing this. It was winter, and the woman, so light her skin looked like cream with just a drop of coffee, had turned a corner and waited for him there. Slapped him so quick, he didn't even notice who had done it until she turned back around and he'd seen that generous swish of her hips.

He went to New York. It didn't matter that he had become one of the best ship caulkers the Chesapeake Bay area had ever seen; he couldn't look at a boat again. He couldn't pick up a chisel or smell oakum or hemp or tar without thinking about the life he had once had, the woman and the children he had once had, and the thought was too much.

In New York he did whatever work he could do. Mostly carpentry, plumbing when he could get it, though he was often underpaid. He rented a bedroom from an elderly Negro woman who cooked his meals and did his laundry, unbidden. Most nights he spent at the all-black bar.

He came in one blustery December day and sat down in his usual spot, running his hand over the smooth wood of the bar. The workmanship was impeccable, and he'd always suspected that some Negro had done it, perhaps during his first days of freedom in New York, so happy that he was able to do something for himself rather than for someone else that he put his whole heart into it.

The bartender, a man with an almost imperceptible limp, poured Jo his drink before Jo could even ask for it, and set it down. The man sitting next to him was whipping out that morning's paper, now crumpled, wet from the damp of the bar or the few slung drops of the man's drink.

"South Carolina seceded today," the man said, to no one in particular. And, getting no particular response, he looked up from the paper and glanced around at the few people who were there. "War's coming."

The bartender started wiping down the bar with a rag that looked to Jo to be dirtier than the bar itself. "There won't be a war," he said calmly.

Jo had been hearing talk of war for years. It didn't mean much to him, and he tried to veer away from the conversation whenever he could, leery of Southern sympathizers in the North or, worse, overly enthusiastic white Northerners who wanted him to be angrier and louder, to defend himself and his right to freedom.

But Jo wasn't angry. Not anymore. He couldn't really tell if what he had been before was angry. It was an emotion he had no use for, that accomplished nothing and meant even less than that. If anything, what Jo really felt was tired.

"I'm telling you, this is a bad sign. One Southern state secedes and the rest of them are gonna follow. Can't call us the United States of America if half the states are gone. You mark my words, war's coming."

The bartender rolled his eyes. "I'm not marking a thing. And unless you got money for another drink, I think it's time for you to stop marking and get going."

The man huffed loudly as he rolled his paper in his hand. As he walked by, he tapped Jo on the shoulder with it, and when Jo turned to look at him, he winked as if he and Jo were in on some scheme together, as though they knew something the rest of the world didn't, but Jo couldn't figure out what that could possibly be.

Abena

AS ABENA MADE THE JOURNEY back to her village, new seeds in hand, she thought, yet again, about how old she was. An unmarried twenty-five-year-old woman was unheard of, in her village or any other on this continent or the next. But there were only a few men in her village, and none of them wanted to take a chance with Unlucky's daughter. Abena's father's crops had never grown. Year after year, season after season, the earth spit up rotted plants or sometimes nothing at all. Who knew where this bad luck came from?

Abena felt the seeds in her hand—small, round, and hard. Who would suspect that they could turn into a whole field? She wondered if, this year, they would do so for her father. Abena was certain that she must have inherited the thing that had earned her father his nickname. They called him the man without a name. They called him Unlucky. And now his troubles had followed her. Even her childhood best friend, Ohene Nyarko, would not take her as his second wife. Though he would never say it, she knew what he was thinking: that she was not worth the loss of yams and wine a bride price would cost him. Sometimes, while sleeping in the private hut her father had built for her, she would wonder if she herself was a curse, not the untilled land that lay around them, but her own self.

"Old Man, I have brought you the seeds you were asking for," Abena announced as she entered her parents' hut. She had gone to the next village over because her father thought, yet again, that a change in seeds might bring about a change in luck.

"Thank you," he said. Inside the hut, Abena's mother was sweeping the floor, bent forward, one hand on the small of her back, the other gripped tightly around the palm bristles as she swayed to music that only she could hear.

Abena cleared her throat. "I would like to visit Kumasi," she said. "I would like to see it just once before I die."

Her father looked up sharply. He had been examining the seeds in his hands, turning them over, putting them to his ear as though he could hear them, putting them to his lips as though he could taste them. "No," he said firmly.

Her mother didn't stand up, but she stopped sweeping. Abena could no longer hear the bristles brushing the hard clay.

"It is time I make the journey," Abena said, eyes level. "It is time I meet people from other villages. I will soon be an old lady with no children, and I will know nothing but this village and the next. I want to visit Kumasi. See what a large city is like, walk by the Asante king's palace."

Hearing the words "Asante king," her father clenched his fists, crushing the seeds in his hands to a fine powder that slipped through the small spaces between his fingers. "See the Asante king's palace for what?" he yelled.

"Am I not an Asante?" she asked, daring him to tell her the truth, to explain the Fante in his accent, the white in his skin. "Do my people not come from Kumasi? You have kept me here like a prisoner with your bad luck. Unlucky, they call you, but your name should be Shame, or Fearful, or Liar. Which is it, Old Man?"

With that, her father slapped her firmly across her left cheek, and the seeds in his hand powdered her face. She reached up to where the pain was. He had never hit her before. Every other child in their village had been beaten for something as small as dropping water from a bucket or as large as sleeping with someone before marriage. But her parents never hit her. Instead, they treated her as an equal, asking her opinion and discussing their plans with her. The only thing they had ever forbidden her from doing was going to Kumasi, land of the Asante king, or down into Fanteland. And while she had no use for the Coast, no respect for Fante people, her pride in the Asante was great. It was growing every day as word came of the Asante soldiers' valiant battles against the British, their strength, their hope for a free kingdom.

For as long as she could remember her parents had made up one excuse after the other. She was too young. Her blood had not come. She was not married. She was never getting married. Abena had begun to believe that her parents had killed someone in Kumasi or were wanted by the king's guards, maybe even by the king himself. She no longer cared.

Abena wiped the seed powder from her face and made her hand into a fist, but before she could use it, her mother came up behind her and snatched her arm.

"Enough," she said.

Old Man had his head down as he walked out of their hut, and when the cool air from outside hit the exposed nape of her neck, Abena started to cry.

"Sit down," her mother said, gesturing to the stool her father had just left. Abena did as she was told, and watched her mother, a woman of sixty-five, who looked no older than she herself did, still so beautiful that the village boys whispered and whistled when she bent down to lift water. "Your father and I are not welcome in Kumasi," she said. She was speaking as one speaks to an old woman whose memories, those things that used to be hard-formed chrysalises, had turned into butter-flies and flown away, never to return. "I am from Kumasi, and when I was young, I defied my parents to marry your father. He came to get me. He came all the way from Fanteland."

Abena shook her head. "Why didn't your parents want you to marry him?"

Akosua put one hand on top of hers and began stroking it. "Your father was a . . ." She stopped, searching for the right words. Abena knew her mother didn't want to tell a secret that was not hers to tell. "He was the son of a Big Man, the grandson of two very Big Men, and he wanted to live a life for himself instead of a life that was chosen for him. He wanted his children to be able to do the same. That is all I can say. Go and visit Kumasi. Your father will not stop you."

Her mother left the hut in search of her father, and Abena stared at the red clay walls around her. Her father should have been a Big Man, but he had chosen this: red clay formed in the shape of a circle, a packed straw roof, a hut so small it fit nothing more than a few tree stump stools. Outside, the ruined earth of a farm that had never earned its title as a farm. His decision had meant her shame, her unmarried, childless shame. She would go to Kumasi.

In the evening, once she was certain her parents had gone to sleep, Abena slipped away to Ohene Nyarko's compound. His first wife, Mefia, was boiling water outside her hut, the steam from the air and the pot making her sweat.

"Sister Mefia, is your husband in?" Abena asked, and Mefia rolled her eyes and pointed toward the door.

Ohene Nyarko's farms were fruitful every year. Though their village was no more than two miles by two miles, though there was no one to even call Chief or Big Man, so small were their land and their status, Ohene was well respected. A man who could have done well elsewhere, had he not been born here.

"Your wife hates me," Abena said.

"She thinks I am still sleeping with you," Ohene Nyarko said, his eyes twinkling with mischief. It made Abena want to hit him.

She cringed when she thought of what had happened between them. They were only children then. Inseparable and mischievous. Ohene had discovered that the stick between his legs could perform tricks, and while Abena's father and mother were out begging for a share of the elders' food, as they did every week, Ohene had showed Abena those tricks.

"See?" he said as they watched it lift when she touched it. They had both seen their fathers' this way, Ohene on those days his father went from one wife's hut to the next, and Abena in the days before she got her own hut. But they had never known Ohene's to do the same.

"What does it feel like?" she had asked.

He shrugged, smiled, and she knew what he felt was a good thing. She was born to parents who let her speak her mind, go after what she wanted, even if that thing was limited to boys. Now she wanted this.

"Lie on top of me!" she demanded, remembering what she'd seen her parents do so many times. Everyone in the village had always laughed at her parents, saying that Unlucky was too poor to get a second wife, but Abena knew the truth. That on those nights when she had slept on the far side of their small hut, pretending not to listen, she could hear her father whisper, "Akosua, you are my one and only."

"We cannot do that until we have had our marriage ceremony!" Ohene said, mortified. All children had heard the fables about people who lay together before they had their marriage ceremonies: the far-fetched one about the men whose penises turned into trees while still inside the woman, growing branches into her stomach so that he could not exit her body; the simpler, truer ones about banishment, fines, and shame.

Finally that night, Abena had been able to convince Ohene, and he had fumbled around, thrusting at the entrance until he broke through and she hurt, thrusting inside: once, twice, then nothing. There was no loud moan or whimper as they had heard escape their fathers' mouths. He simply left the same way he had arrived.

Back then, she had been the strong, unshakable one, the one who could talk him into anything. Now Abena stared at Ohene Nyarko as he stood broad-shouldered and smirking, waiting for the favor he knew was tugging at her lips.

"I need you to take me to Kumasi," she said. It wasn't wise for her to travel alone and unmarried, and she knew her father would not take her.

Ohene Nyarko laughed, a large and boisterous sound. "My darling, I cannot take you to Kumasi now. It is more than two weeks' journey and the rains will soon be coming. I must tend to my farm."

"Your sons do most of the work anyway," she said. She hated when he called her his "darling," always spoken in English, as she had taught him when they were children after she'd heard her father say it once and asked him what it meant. She hated that Ohene Nyarko should call her his beloved while his wife was outside cooking his evening meal and his sons were outside tending to his farm. It didn't seem right that he should let her walk in shame as he had done all those years, not when she knew by looking at his fields that he would soon have enough wealth for a second wife.

"Eh, but who supervises my sons? A ghost? I cannot marry you if the yams don't grow."

"If you have not married me by now, you will never marry me," Abena whispered, surprised at the hard lump that had so quickly formed in her throat. She hated when he joked about marrying her.

Ohene Nyarko clicked his tongue and pulled her to his chest. "Don't cry now," he said. "I will take you to see the Asante capital, all right? Don't cry, my darling."

Ohene Nyarko was a man of his word, and at the end of that week, the two set out for Kumasi, the home of the Asantehene.

Everything felt new to Abena. Compounds were actually compounds, built from stone with five or six huts apiece, not one or two at most. These huts were so tall they resurrected the image of ten-foot-tall giants from the stories her mother used to tell. Giants who swooped down to pluck tiny children up from the clay earth when they were misbehaving. Abena imagined the families of giants who lived in the town, fetching water, building fires to boil the bad children in their soups.

Kumasi sprawled before them endlessly. Abena had never been to a place where she did not know everyone's name. She had never been to a farm that she could not measure with her own eye, so small was each family's plot. Here, the farmlands were large and luscious and filled with men to work them. People sold their wares in the middle of the town, things she had never seen before, relics from the old days of steady trade with the British and the Dutch.

In the afternoon they walked by the Asantehene's palace. It stretched so long and wide she knew it could fit over a hundred people: wives, children, slaves, and more.

"Can we see the Golden Stool?" Abena asked, and Ohene Nyarko took her to the room where it was kept, locked away behind a glass wall so that no one could touch it.

It was the stool that contained the *sunsum,* the soul, of the entire Asante nation. Covered in pure gold, it had descended from the sky and landed in the lap of the first Asantehene, Osei Tutu. No one was allowed to sit on it, not even the king himself. Despite herself, Abena felt tears sting her eyes. She had heard about this stool her entire life from the elders of her village, but she had never seen it with her own eyes.

After she and Ohene Nyarko had finished touring the palace, they exited through the golden gates. Entering at the same time was a man not much older than Abena's father, wrapped in kente and walking with a cane. He stopped, staring at Abena's face intently.

"Are you a ghost?" he asked, almost shouting. "Is that you, James? They said you had died in the war, but I knew that could not be!" He reached out with his right hand and grazed Abena's cheek, touching her so long and so familiarly that Ohene Nyarko finally had to remove his hand.

"Old Man, can you not see this is a woman? There is no James here."

The man shook his head as if to clear his eyes, but when he looked at Abena again there was only confusion. "I'm sorry," he said before hobbling away.

Once he had gone, Ohene Nyarko pushed Abena along, out of the gates, until they were firmly back in the bustle of the city. "That old man was probably half-blind," he muttered, steering Abena by the elbow.

"Shhh," Abena said, though there was no way the man could still hear them. "That man is probably a royal."

And Ohene Nyarko snorted. "If he is a royal, then you are a royal too," he said, laughing boisterously.

They kept walking. Ohene Nyarko wanted to buy new farming tools from some people in Kumasi before they headed back, but Abena couldn't bear the thought of wasting time with people she didn't know when she could be enjoying Kumasi, and so she and Ohene Nyarko parted ways, promising to meet again before nightfall.

She walked until the tough skin of her soles started to burn, and then she stopped for a moment, taking solace under the shade of a palm tree.

"Excuse me, Ma. I would like to talk to you about Christianity."

Abena looked up. The man was dark and sinewy, his Twi broken or rusty, she couldn't tell which. She took him in but could not place his face among any of the tribes she knew. "What is your name?" she asked. "Who are your people?"

The man smiled and shook his head. "It does not matter what my name is or who my people are. Come, let me show you the work we are doing here." And because she was curious, Abena followed him.

He took her to a patch of dirt, a clearing that was waiting, begging, for something to be built there so that the city sprawl around it wouldn't seem like a broken circle. At first Abena could not see much, but then more dark men with unplaceable faces walked over to the clearing carrying tree stumps for stools. Then a white man appeared. He was the first white man Abena had ever seen. Even though everyone whispered that there was white in her father, to her, he had always just looked like a lighter version of herself.

Here was the man the villagers really spoke of, the man who had come to the Gold Coast seeking slaves and gold however he could get them. Whether he stole, whether he lied, whether he promised alliance to the Fantes and power to the Asantes, the white man always found a way to get what he wanted. But the slave trade had finally ended, and two Anglo-Asante wars had passed. The white man, whom they called Abro Ni, wicked one, for all the trouble he had caused, was no longer welcome there.

And yet Abena saw him, sitting on the stump of a felled tree, talking to the tribeless dark men.

"Who is that?" she asked the man next to her.

"The white man?" he said. "He is the Missionary."

The Missionary was looking at her now, smiling and motioning for them to approach, but the sun was beginning to set, ducking under the palm tree canopies that marked the west side of the city, and Ohene Nyarko would be waiting for her.

"I have to go," she said, already pulling away.

Abena

"Please!" the dark man said. Behind him, the Missionary stood up, ready to come after her. "We are trying to build churches throughout the Asante region. Please, come find us if you ever need us."

Abena nodded, though she was already running. When she got to the meeting spot, Ohene Nyarko was buying roasted yams from a bush girl. A girl who, like Abena, had come from some small Asante village, hoping to see something new, to change her circumstances.

"Eh, Kumasi woman," Ohene Nyarko said. The girl had hoisted her big clay pot of yams back onto her head and was walking away, her hips keeping a steady, swaying pace. "You're late."

"I saw a white man," she said, pressing her palm against the wall of someone's compound as she tried to steady her breath. "A church man."

Ohene Nyarko spit on the ground, sucked his teeth. "Those Europeans! Don't they know to stay out of Asante? Did we not just beat them in this last war? We don't want whatever it is they are trying to bring us! They can take their religion to the Fantes before we finish them all."

Abena nodded absently. The men of her village often spoke of the ongoing conflict between the Asantes and the British, saying that the Fantes were sympathizers, and that no white man could come into their country and tell them that they no longer owned it. These were village people, farmers who had never seen war, most of whom had never seen the coast of the Gold Coast they so wanted to protect.

It was on a night like this that Papa Kwabena, one of the oldest men in their village, had started speaking about the slave trade. "You know, I had a cousin in the North who was stolen from his hut in the middle of the night. Swoosh! Just taken, and we don't know by whom. Was it an Asante warrior? Was it a Fante? We don't know. We don't know where they took him!"

"To the Castle," Abena's father said, and everyone had turned to look at him. Unlucky. Who always sat in the back of the village meetings, holding his daughter in his lap as though she were a son. They allowed this because they pitied him.

"What castle?" Papa Kwabena asked.

"There's a castle on the coast in Fanteland called the Cape Coast Castle. That is where they used to keep the slaves before they sent them away, to Aburokyire: America, Jamaica. Asante traders would bring in their captives. Fante, Ewe, or Ga middlemen would hold them, then sell them to the British or the Dutch or whoever was paying the most at the time. Everyone was responsible. We all were . . . we all are."

The men all nodded, though they did not know what a castle was, what America was, but they did not want to look foolish in front of Unlucky.

Ohene Nyarko spit out a burned portion of the yam and put his hand on Abena's shoulder. "Are you well?" he asked.

"I was thinking about my father," she said.

A smile broke across Ohene Nyarko's face. "Oh, Unlucky. What would he say if he saw you here with me now, eh? His precious 'son,' Abena, doing something he has long forbidden her to do." He laughed. "Well, let me get you home to him now."

They traveled quickly and quietly, Ohene Nyarko and his large, full frame making a way, tearing a path through terrain that had dangers Abena dared not think of. By the end of the second week, they could just make out the skyline of their own village, small though it was.

"Why don't we rest here?" Ohene Nyarko asked, pointing to a spot just in front of them. Abena could tell that others had rested there before. There was a small cave that had formed from the ruin of fallen trees, and the space on the ground had been cleared to make room for it.

"Can't we keep going?" Abena asked. She had begun to feel home-sick for her mother and father. She had told them everything from the day she spoke her first word, and she could not wait to tell them about this, even though she knew her father would still be angry. He would want to hear it. Her parents were getting older, and she knew they had no time to harbor bad feelings.

Ohene Nyarko was already setting his things down. "It's another day's journey," he said, "and I'm too tired, my darling."

"Don't call me that," Abena said, dropping her own things to the ground as she sat down in the small tree cave.

"But you are."

She didn't want to say it. Instead, she wanted to force the words to stay inside her mouth but could feel them coming up her throat, pressing against her lips. "Then why won't you marry me?"

Ohene Nyarko sat down next to her. "We've talked about that. I will marry you when I have my next big harvest. My parents always used to say that I shouldn't marry a woman whose clan I didn't know. They said you would bring nothing but dishonor to my children, if we had children at all, but they don't speak for me anymore. I don't care what the villagers say. I don't care if your mother was thought barren until she had you. I don't care that you are the daughter of a nameless man. I will marry you as soon as my land tells me that I am ready to marry you."

Abena couldn't look at him. She was staring at the bark on the palm trees, the rounded diamonds crisscrossing against each other. Each one different; each one the same.

Ohene Nyarko turned her chin toward him. "You must be patient," he said.

"I have been patient while you married your first wife. My parents are so old that their backs have begun to curve. Soon they will fall like these trees, and then what?" She didn't know if it was the thought of being alone without her parents or the fact of her present loneliness, but before she could fight them, tears were rolling down her face.

Ohene Nyarko placed his hands on both of her cheeks and wiped her tears with his thumbs, but they fell quicker than he could sweep them away, and so he used his lips, kissing the salty trail that had begun to form.

Soon her lips were meeting his. They were not the lips she remembered from their childhood, the ones that were thin and always dry because he refused to oil them. They were thicker, a trap for her own lips, her own tongue.

Soon they were lying down in the shadow of the cave. Abena took off her wrapper and heard Ohene Nyarko suck in his breath, removing his own. At first they just stared at each other, taking their bodies in, comparing them with what they'd known before.

He reached for her, and she flinched, remembering the last time he had touched her. How she had lain on the floor of her parents' hut, staring up at the straw roof and wondering if there was more to it than that, the pain of it so outweighing the pleasure that she could not understand why it happened in huts across her village, the Asante, the world.

Now Ohene Nyarko pinned her arms down to the hard red clay. She bit his arm and he growled, letting go, until she hugged him back toward her. He moved like he knew the scenes that were playing inside her head. And she let him inside her. And she let herself forget everything but him.

When they had finished, when they were sweaty and spent and catching their breath, Abena laid her head against his chest, that panting pillow, his heart drumming into her ear.

Abena once spent an entire day fetching water for her father's farm: going to the stream, dipping her bucket in, coming back and filling their basin. It was nearing nightfall, and no matter how much water she got, it never seemed to be enough. The next morning, the plants had all died, withered to brown leaves littering the land in front of their hut.

She was only five then. She did not understand that things could die, despite one's best efforts to keep them alive. All she knew was that every morning her father watched over the plants, prayed over them, and that each season when the inevitable happened, her father, a man whom she had never seen cry, who greeted each turn of bad luck as though it were a new opportunity, would lift his head high and begin again. And so, that time, she cried for him.

He found her in the hut and sat down beside her. "Why are you crying?" he asked.

"The plants have all died, and I could have helped them!" she said between sobs.

"Abena," he asked, "what would you have done differently if you knew the plants would die?"

She thought about this for a moment, wiped her nose with the back of her hand, and answered, "I would have brought more water."

Her father nodded. "Then next time bring more water, but don't cry for this time. There should be no room in your life for regret. If in the moment of doing you felt clarity, you felt certainty, then why feel regret later?"

She nodded as he spoke to her even though she didn't understand his words, because she knew, even then, that he was speaking more for himself.

But now, letting her head move in rhythm with Ohene Nyarko's breath and heart, the slow trickle of combined sweat that slid between them, she remembered those words, and she regretted nothing.

*

The year Abena visited Kumasi, everyone in her village had a bad harvest. Then the year after. And for four more years on top of those. Villagers began to move away. Some were so desperate they even went to the dreaded North, crossing the Volta in search of unclaimed land, land that hadn't forsaken them.

Abena's father was so old he could no longer straighten his back or hands. He could no longer farm. So Abena did it for him, watching as the ruined land spit up death year after year. The villagers were not eating. They said it was an act of penance but knew it was their only choice.

Even Ohene Nyarko's once lush lands had turned barren, and so his promise to marry Abena after the next good harvest had been set aside.

They continued to see each other. In the first year, before they knew what the harvest would bring, they had done so brazenly. "Abena, be careful," her mother would say in the mornings after Ohene Nyarko snuck out of Abena's hut. "This is bad juju." But Abena didn't care. So what if people knew? So what if she got pregnant? Soon enough she would be Ohene Nyarko's wife, not just his oldest friend turned mistress.

But that year, Ohene Nyarko's plants were the first to spoil, and people scratched their heads, wondering why. Until their own plants died, and they said there must be a witch among them. Had the trouble they thought Unlucky would bring them been so long delayed? It was a woman named Aba who first saw Ohene Nyarko walking the path back from Abena's hut at the end of the second bad year.

"It's Abena!" Aba cried at the next village meeting, bursting into the room full of old men, her hand clutching her heaving bosom. "She brought evil to Ohene Nyarko, and that evil is spreading to us all!"

The elders gathered accounts from Ohene Nyarko and Abena themselves, and then, for the next eight hours, they debated what to do. It was reasonable that Ohene Nyarko had promised to marry her after the next good harvest. They saw no harm in that, but they could not let the fornication go unpunished lest the children grow up to think such things were acceptable, lest the more superstitious among them continue to blame Abena for the faults of the land. All they knew was, the woman had to be as barren as the land itself for her to not have conceived, and they knew too that if they banished her from the village now, Ohene Nyarko would be too angry to help them get the earth to recover once she had left. Finally, they reached their decision and announced it to all. Abena would be removed from the village when she conceived a child or after seven bad years. If a good harvest came before either outcome, they would let her stay.

"Is your husband home?" Abena asked Ohene Nyarko's wife on the third day of the sixth bad year. She had walked the short distance as the sky dropped around her, but by the time she got there, it had stopped.

Mefia didn't look at her, nor did she speak. In fact, Ohene Nyarko's first wife had not spoken to Abena since the night she fought with her husband, begging him to end his affair, to end their family's shame, and he replied that he wouldn't go back on his word. Still, Abena tried being nice to the woman any chance she could.

Finally, after the moment of silence grew too awkward for Abena to bear, she went into Ohene Nyarko's hut. When she saw him, he was packing some things into a small kente cloth sack.

"Where are you going?" she asked, standing in the doorway.

"I'm going to Osu. They say someone there has brought over a new plant. They say it will grow well here."

"And what will I do while you are in Osu? They'll probably kick me out the second you're gone," Abena said.

Ohene Nyarko set down his things and lifted Abena into his arms so that their faces were level. "Then they will have to deal with me when I get back."

He put her down again. Outside, his children were picking bark from the Tweapia trees so that they could make chewing sticks to take to Kumasi and sell for food. Abena knew this shamed Ohene Nyarko— not that his children had found something useful to do, but that they had done so because of his inability to feed them.

They made love quickly that day, and Ohene Nyarko set out shortly after. Abena went home to find her parents sitting in front of a fire, roasting groundnuts.

"Ohene Nyarko says there is a new plant in Osu that is growing very well. He has gone to get it and bring it back to us."

Her mother nodded. Her father shrugged. Abena knew she had shamed them. When the pronouncement of her future exile was made, her parents had gone to the elders to try to reason with them, to make them reconsider. At that time, and still, Unlucky was the oldest man in the village. Deference was still owed, even if he wasn't allowed to be an elder because he wasn't originally from the village.

"We have only one child," Old Man had said, but the elders just turned their heads.

"What have you done?" Abena's mother asked her at dinner that night, crying into her hands before lifting them up to the heavens. "What have I done to deserve this child?"

But at that point, only two bad years had gone by, and Abena assured them that the plants would grow, and Ohene Nyarko would marry her. Now their only solace was the fact that it seemed Abena had inherited her mother's supposed barrenness, or Old Man's family's curse, or whatever it was that kept her from conceiving a child.

"Nothing will grow here," Old Man said. "This village is finished. No one can keep living like this. No one can take one more year eating nothing but nuts and tree bark. They think they are exiling just you, but really this land has condemned us all to exile. You watch. It's only a matter of time."

Ohene Nyarko came back a week later with the new seeds. The plant was called cocoa, and he said it would change everything. He said the Akuapem people in the Eastern Region were already reaping the benefits of the new plant, selling it to the white men overseas at a rate that was reminiscent of the old trade.

"You don't know how much these little seeds cost me!" Ohene Nyarko said, holding them in his palm so that everyone around him could see and feel and smell them. "But it will be worth it for the village. Trust me. They will have to stop calling us the Gold Coast and start calling us the Cocoa Coast!"

And he was right. Within months Ohene Nyarko's cocoa trees had sprouted, bearing their gold and green and orange fruit. The villagers had never seen anything like it, and they were so curious, so eager to touch and open the pods before they were ready, that Ohene Nyarko and his sons had taken to sleeping outside so that they could keep watch.

"But will this feed us?" the villagers wondered after they had been shooed away by the children or yelled at by Ohene Nyarko himself.

Abena saw less and less of Ohene Nyarko in those first few months of his cocoa farming, but the absence comforted her. The harder he worked on the farm, the sooner his harvest would be good; and the sooner the harvest was good, the sooner they could marry. On the days she did see him, he would speak of nothing other than the cocoa and what it had cost him. His hands smelled of that new smell, sweet and dark and earthy, and after she had left him, she would continue to smell it on the places he had touched, the full dark circles of her nipples or just behind her ears. The plant was affecting them all.

Finally, Ohene Nyarko said that it was time for the harvest, and all the men and women from the village came to do as he instructed, as he had been instructed by the farmers in the Eastern Region. They cracked open the cocoa fruit to find the sweet white pulp that surrounded the small purple beans, and placed the pulpy beans on a bed of banana leaves, then covered them with more leaves. After that, Ohene Nyarko sent them home.

"We can't live off of this," the villagers whispered as they walked back to their houses. Some of the families had already started packing up their huts, discouraged by what they had seen inside the cocoa pods. But the rest of them came back after five days to spread the fermented beans in the sun so that they would dry. The villagers had each donated their kente sacks, and once dry, the cocoa beans were packed into these sacks.

"Now what?" they asked each other, glancing around as Ohene Nyarko put the sacks into his hut.

"Now we rest," he announced to the group waiting outside. "Tomorrow I will go to the trading market and sell what I can."

He slept in Abena's hut that night, as brazenly and openly as if they had been married for forty years or more, and this gave Abena hope that soon they would be. But the man beside her on the floor was not the confident man who had promised an entire village redemption. In her arms, the man she had known since before they wore cloth to cover their loins trembled.

"What if this doesn't work? What if I can't sell them?" he asked, his head buried in her bosom.

"Shh! Stop that talk," she said. "They will sell. They have to sell."

But he kept crying and shaking so that she could not hear him when he said, "I'm afraid of that too," and she would not have understood even if she had.

He was gone by the time she woke up the next morning. The villagers had found and killed a scrawny young goat in preparation for his return, cooking the tough meat for days as best they could in the hope that it would turn tender. The younger children, thinking they were fast and clever, would try to snatch small pieces of partially cooked meat from the animal when their mothers weren't looking, but the women, born with a sixth sense for children's mischief, would swat their hands, then clutch them at the wrists, holding them over the fire until the children cried out and swore to behave.

Ohene Nyarko did not come back that night or the next. He came back in the afternoon of the third day. Behind him, being led by rope, were four fat and obstinate goats, bleating as though they could smell the iron of the slaughter knife. The sacks he had carried out, full of cocoa beans, had come back to them filled with yams and kola nuts, some fresh palm oil, and plenty of palm wine.

The villagers threw a celebration the likes of which they had not thrown in years, with dancing and shouting and bare, jiggling breasts. The old men and women danced the Adowa, lightly swaying their hips and bringing their hands up and over, as though ready to receive from the Earth and then give back to her.

Their stomachs had grown smaller, it seemed, and so the food they ate filled them quickly, and they filled the crevices that were left between the food with sweet palm wine.

Unlucky and Akosua were so happy the bad years had finally ended that they held each other close, watching the others dance, watching the children drum against their full bellies in time with the music.

In the middle of all the celebration, Abena looked over at Ohene Nyarko as he surveyed the people of the village they all loved so fiercely, his face full of pride and something she couldn't quite place.

"You've done well," she said, approaching him. He had kept his distance all night, and she thought it was because he didn't want to draw attention to the two of them in the middle of the celebration, didn't want the villagers to start wondering what this meant for Abena's exile. But the meaning was all Abena was able to think about. She had not told anyone yet, but she was four days late. And though she had been four days late before in her life, and imagined that she would be four days late again before she died, she wondered if this time was *the* time.

What she wanted was for Ohene Nyarko to shout his love for her from the rooftops. To say, now that the whole village has been fed and feted, I will marry you. And not tomorrow, but today. This very day. This celebration will be for us.

Instead, he said, "Hello, Abena. Did you get enough to eat?"

"Yes, thank you."

He nodded and drank from a calabash of palm wine.

"You have done well, Ohene Nyarko," Abena said, reaching out to touch his shoulder, but her hand grazed nothing but air. He wouldn't meet her eyes. "Why did you move?" she asked, stepping away from him.

"What?"

"Don't say 'what' like I am crazy. I tried to touch you and you moved."

"Quiet, Abena. Don't make a scene."

She didn't make a scene. Instead, she turned and began walking, walking past the people dancing, past her parents crying, walking until she found the floor of her hut and lay down upon it, one hand clutching her heart and the other clutching her stomach.

This was how the elders found her the next day when they came to announce that she could remain in the village. The bad years had ended before her seventh year of adultery and she had not yet conceived a child. And, they said, Ohene Nyarko's harvest had been so profitable that now he could finally fulfill his promise.

"He will not marry me," Abena said from her spot on the floor, rolling this way and that, one hand on her stomach, the other on her heart, holding the two places that hurt.

The elders scratched their heads and looked at each other. Had she finally gone mad from all the years of waiting?

"What is the meaning of this?" one of the elders asked.

"He will not marry me," she repeated, and then she rolled away, giving them nothing more than her back.

The elders rushed over to Ohene Nyarko's hut. He was already preparing for the next season, preparing and separating the seeds so that he could pass out a share to all of the other village farmers.

"So she has told you," he said. He didn't look up at the elders, just continued to work on the seeds. One pile for the Sarpongs, one for the Gyasis, one for the Asares, another for the Kankams.

"What is this about, Ohene Nyarko?"

He had made all of the piles, and in the afternoon, the head of each family would come to collect them, spread them onto their own small plots of land, and wait for the strange new trees to grow and flourish so that soon the village would be restored to what it once was, or surpass it.

"To get the cocoa plants, I had to promise a man in Osu that I would marry his daughter. I will have to use all of the leftover goods from my cocoa trade to pay her bride price. I cannot marry Abena this season. She will have to wait."

From her hut, where Abena had finally risen off of the hard ground and dusted off her knees and back, she knew she would not wait.

"I'm leaving, Old Man," Abena said. "I can't stay here and be made a fool of. I have suffered enough."

Her father blocked the exit of the hut with his body. He was so old, so frail, that Abena knew she had only to touch him and he would fall, the path would clear, and she could make her way on.

"You can't leave yet," he said. "Not yet."

He slowly backed out of the doorway, watching to see if she would stay. When she didn't move, he picked up his shovel, went out to a spot on the edge of their land, and started digging.

"What are you doing?" Abena asked. Unlucky was sweating. He moved so slowly, Abena took pity on him. She took the shovel and began to dig for him. "What are you looking for?" she asked.

Her father got down on his knees and started raking away the dirt with both of his hands, holding it awhile, then letting it sift through his fingers. When he stopped, all that was left in his palms was a black stone necklace.

Abena sank down beside him and looked at the necklace. It shimmered gold and was cool to the touch.

Her father huffed loudly, trying to catch his breath. "This belonged to my grandmother, your great-grandmother Effia. It was given to her by her own mother."

"Effia," Abena repeated. It was the first time she had heard the name of one of her ancestors, and she savored the taste of the name on her tongue. She wanted to say it again and again. Effia. Effia.

"My father was a slaver, a very wealthy man. When I decided to leave Fanteland, it was because I did not want to take part in the work my family had done. I wanted to work for myself. I see how these townspeople call me Unlucky, but every season I feel lucky to have this land, to do this honorable work, not the shameful work of my family. When the villagers here gave me this small bit of land, I was so happy that I buried this stone here to give thanks.

"I won't stop you if you want to go, but please take this with you. May it serve you as well as it has served me."

Abena put on the necklace and hugged her father. Her mother was in the doorframe, watching them out in the dirt. Abena got up and hugged her mother too.

The next morning Abena set out for Kumasi, and when she arrived at the missionary church there, she touched the stone at her neck and said thank you to her ancestors.

Part Two

H

IT TOOK THREE POLICEMEN to knock H down, four to put him in chains.

"I ain't done nothing!" he shouted once they got him to the jail cell, but he was speaking only to the air they had left behind. He'd never seen people walk away so quickly, and he knew he had scared them.

H rattled the bars, certain that he could bend or break them if only he tried.

"Stop that 'fore they kill you," his cellmate said.

H recognized the man from around town. Maybe he'd even share-cropped with him once on one of the county farms.

"Can't nobody kill me," H said. He was still pressing on the bars, and he could hear the metal start to give between his fingers. Then he could feel his cellmate's hands on his shoulder. H turned around so quick, the other man didn't have time to move or think before H had him lifted by the throat. H was over six feet tall, and he had the man so high up, his head brushed the top of the ceiling. If H lifted him any higher, he would have broken through. "Don't you touch me again," H said.

"You think dem white folks won't kill you?" the man said, his words coming out small and slow.

"What I done?" H said. He lowered the man to the ground, and he fell to his knees, gasping up long sips of breath.

"Say you was studyin' a white woman."

"Who say?"

"The police. Heard 'em talkin' 'bout what to say 'fore they went out to get you."

H sat down next to the man. "Who they say I was talkin' to?"

"Cora Hobbs."

"I wasn't studyin' no Hobbs girl," H said, his rage lit anew. If there were rumors about him and a white woman, he would have hoped it would be someone prettier than his old sharecropping boss's daughter.

"Boy, look atcha," his cellmate said, his gaze so spiteful now that H grew suddenly, inexplicably afraid of the smaller, older man. "Don't matter if you was or wasn't. All they gotta do is say you was. That's all they gotta do. You think cuz you all big and muscled up, you safe? Naw, dem white folks can't stand the sight of you. Walkin' round free as can be. Don't nobody want to see a black man look like you walkin' proud as a peacock. Like you ain't got a lick of fear in you." He rested his head against the cell wall and closed his eyes for a second. "How old you was when the war ended?"

H tried to count back, but he'd never been very good at numbers, and the Civil War was so long ago that the numbers climbed higher than H could reach. "Not sure. 'Bout thirteen, I reckon," he said.

"Mm-hmm. See, that's what I thought. You was young. Slavery ain't nothin' but a dot in your eye, huh? If nobody tell you, I'ma tell you. War may be over but it ain't ended."

The man closed his eyes again. He let his head roll against the wall, this way, then that. He looked tired, and H wondered how long he'd been sitting in that cell.

"My name's H," he finally said, a peace offering.

"H ain't no kind of name," his cellmate said, never opening his eyes.

"It's the only one I got," H said.

Soon the man fell asleep. H listened to him snore, watched the rise and fall of his chest. The day the war ended, H had left his old master's plantation and began to walk from Georgia to Alabama. He'd wanted new sights and sounds to go with his newfound freedom. He was so happy to be free. Everyone he knew was just happy to be free. But it didn't last long.

H spent the next four days in the county jail. On the second day, the guards took his cellmate away. He didn't know where. When they finally came for H, the guards wouldn't tell him what the charge was, only that he had to pay the ten-dollar fine by the end of the night.

"I only got five dollars saved," H said. It had taken him nearly ten years of sharecropping to put away that much.

"Maybe your family can help," the chief deputy said, but he was already walking away, on to the next person.

"Ain't got no family," H said to no one. He had made the walk from Georgia to Alabama by himself. He was used to being alone, but Alabama had turned H's loneliness into something like a physical presence. He could hold it when he went to bed at night. It was in the handle of his hoe, in the puffs of cotton that floated away.

He was eighteen when he met his woman, Ethe. By then he'd gotten so big that no one ever crossed him. He could walk into a room and watch it clear as men and women made way for him. But Ethe always stood her ground. She was the most solid woman he'd ever met, and his relationship with her was the longest he'd had a relationship with anyone at all. He would have asked her for her help now, but she hadn't talked to him since the day he called her by another woman's name. He had been wrong to cheat on her, wronger still to lie. He couldn't call Ethe now, not with this shame hanging over him. He'd heard of black women coming to the jailhouse to look for their sons or husbands and being taken into a back room by the policemen, told that there were other ways to pay a fine. No, H thought, Ethe would be better off without him.

By sunrise the next morning, on a sweltering July day in 1880, H was chained to ten other men and sold by the state of Alabama to work the coal mines just outside of Birmingham.

"Next," the pit boss shouted, and the chief deputy shoved H in front of him. H had been watching them check each of the ten men who'd been chained to him on the train ride there. H wasn't even sure he could call some of them men. He saw a boy no older than twelve, shivering in the corner of the train. When they'd pushed that boy in front of the pit boss, he'd peed himself, tears running down his face all the while, until he looked like he himself would melt down into the puddle of wet at his feet. The boy was so young, he'd probably never seen a whip like the one the pit boss had laid out on his desk, only heard about them in the nightmarish stories his parents told.

"He's a big one, ain't he?" the chief deputy said, squeezing H's shoulders so that the pit boss could see how firm they were. H was the tallest, strongest man in the room. He'd spent the whole train ride trying to figure out a way to break his chains.

The pit boss whistled. He got out of his chair and circled H. He grabbed H's arm, and H lunged at him before his shackles stopped him. He hadn't been able to break the chains, but he knew if his hands could only reach, it wouldn't take him but a second to snap the pit boss's neck.

"Hoo, hoo!" the pit boss said. "Looks like we'll have to teach this one some manners. How much you want for him?"

"Twenty dollars a month," the deputy said.

"Now, you know we don't pay more than eighteen, even for a first-class man."

"You said yourself he's a big one. This one will last you awhile, I bet. Won't die in the mines like the others."

"Y'all can't do this!" H shouted. "I'm free!" he said. "I'm a free man!"

"Naw," the pit boss said. He looked at H carefully and pulled out a knife from the inside of his coat. He began to sharpen the knife against an ironstone he kept on his desk. "No such thing as a free nigger." He walked slowly up to H, held the sharpened knife against his neck so that H could feel the cold, ridged edge of it, begging to break skin.

The pit boss turned to the chief deputy. "We'll give you nineteen for this one," he said. Then he ran the tip of the knife slowly across H's neck. A thin line of blood appeared, neat and straight, as if to underline the pit boss's words. "He may be big, but he'll bleed just like the rest of them."

H

. . .

It had never occurred to H, during those many years that he worked on plantations, that there was anything more than dirt and water, bugs and roots, under the earth. Now he saw that there was an entire city underground. Larger, more sprawling, than any county that H had ever lived or worked in, and this city was occupied almost entirely by black men and boys. This city had shafts for streets, and rooms for houses. And in every room, everywhere, there was coal.

The first thousand pounds of coal were the hardest to shovel. H spent hours, whole days, on his knees. By the end of the first month, the shovel felt like an extension of his arm, and indeed, his back had begun to ripple around the shoulder blades, growing, it seemed, to accommodate the new weight.

With his shovel arm, H and the other men were lowered some 650 feet down the shaft, into the mine. Once in the underground city, they traveled three, five, seven miles to the coal face where they were to work that day. H was large but nimble. He could lie on his flank and shinny himself into nooks and crannies. He could crawl on his hands and knees through tunnels of exploded rock until he got to the right room.

Once he reached the room, H shoveled some fourteen thousand pounds of coal, all while stooped down low, on his knees, stomach, sides. And when he and the other prisoners left the mines, they would always be coated in a layer of black dust, their arms burning, just burning. Sometimes H thought that burning pain would set the coal on fire, and they would all die there, from the pain of it. But, he knew, it wasn't just pain that could kill a man in the mine. More than once, a prison warden had whipped a miner for not reaching the ten-ton quota. H had seen a third-class man shovel 11,829 pounds of coal, weighed at the end of the workday by the pit boss. And when the pit boss had seen the missing 171 pounds, he'd made the man put his hands up against the cave wall, and then he'd whipped him until he died, and the white wardens did not move him that night or the rest of the next day, leaving the dust to blanket his body, a warning to the other convicts. Other times, mine stopes had collapsed, burying the prisoners alive.

Too many times, dust explosions would wipe out men and children by the hundreds. One day, H would be working beside a man he had been chained to the night before; the next day, that man would have died of God only knew what.

H used to fantasize about moving to Birmingham. He'd been a sharecropper since the war ended, and he'd heard that Birmingham was the place a black man could make a life for himself. He'd wanted to move there and finally start living. But what kind of life was this? At least when he was a slave, his master had needed to keep him alive if he wanted to get his money's worth. Now, if H died, they would just lease the next man. A mule was worth more than he was.

H could hardly remember being free, and he could not tell if what he missed was the freedom itself or the capacity for memory. Sometimes when he made it back to the bunk he shared with fifty-something men, all shackled together on long wooden beds so that they couldn't move while they slept unless they moved together, he would try to remember remembering. He would force himself to think of all the things his mind could still call up: Ethe mostly. Her thick body, the look in her eyes when he'd called her by another name, how scared he was to lose her, how sorry. Sometimes as he slept the chains would rub against his ankles in such a way that he would remember the feeling of Ethe's hands there, which always surprised him, since metal was nothing like skin.

The convicts working the mines were almost all like him. Black, once slave, once free, now slave again. Timothy, a man on H's chain link, had been arrested outside the house he had built after the war. A dog had been howling in a nearby field the whole night long, and Timothy had stepped out to tell the dog to hush up. The next morning the police had arrested him for causing a disturbance. There was also Solomon, a convict who had been arrested for stealing a nickel. His sentence was twenty years.

Occasionally one of the wardens would bring in a white third-class man. The new prisoner would be chained to a black man, and for the first few minutes all that white prisoner would do was complain. He'd say that he was better than the niggers. He'd beg his white brothers, the wardens, to have mercy on him, spare him from the shame of it all. He'd curse and cry and carry on. And then they would have to go down into the mine, and that white convict would soon learn that if he wanted to live, he would have to put his faith in a black man.

H had once been partnered with a white third-class man named Thomas whose arms had started shaking so badly, he couldn't lift the shovel. It was Thomas's first week, but he'd already heard that if you didn't make your quota, you and your buddy would be whipped, some-times to death. H had watched Thomas's trembling arms lift the few pounds of coal before giving way, and then Thomas had collapsed to the ground crying, stammering that he didn't want to die down there with nothing but niggers to bear witness.

Wordlessly, H had taken up Thomas's shovel. With his own shovel in one hand and Thomas's shovel in another, H had filled both men's quotas, the pit boss watching all the while.

"Ain't no man ever shoveled double-handed before," the boss had said after it was over, respect lacing his voice, and H had simply nod-ded. The pit boss had then kicked Thomas on the ground where he still sat, sniveling. "That nigger just saved your life," he said. Thomas looked up at H, but H said nothing.

That night, in a bunk with two men chained on either side of him, a bunk two feet above him, H realized that he couldn't move his arms.

"What's wrong?" Joecy asked, noticing H's awkward stillness.

"Can't feel my arms," H whispered, scared.

Joecy nodded.

"I don't want to die, Joecy. I don't want to die. I don't want to die. I don't want to die." H could not stop himself from repeating the words, and soon he realized that he was crying too, and he couldn't stop that either. The coal dust under his eyes started to run down his face, and silently H continued on. "I don't want to die. I don't want to die."

"Hush, now," Joecy said, hugging H to his body as best he could with the chains clanking and clacking as he moved. "Ain't nobody dying tonight. Not tonight." The two men looked around them to see if others had woken up from the noise. Everyone had heard about how H had saved the white third-class man, but they all knew, too, that this didn't mean the pit boss would show mercy. The next day, H would have to do his share all over again.

The next day H was assigned the morning shift, partnered again with Thomas. He and the other morning shift men woke up while the moon was still bright in the sky, sliced thin and arched upward as though it were the crooked, white-toothed smile of the dark-skinned night. They went over to the mess hall to get a cup of coffee and a slab of meat. They got a sack lunch to take with them, and then they were lowered some two hundred feet down below the Earth's surface until they hit the belly of the mine. From there, H and Thomas continued two miles in and further down, stopping finally in the room of the mine where they were to work that day. Usually, there were only two men to a room, but this one was particularly difficult, and the pit boss had paired H and Thomas with Joecy and his third-class man, a convict called Bull who had gotten his name not because of his frame, stocky and squat and commanding, but because Klansmen had burned his face one night—branded him, they said—so that everyone would know he was no good.

H had gone through all the motions of that morning, his arms achingly anchored to his sides as he refused the coffee and meat, couldn't pick up the lunch sack to hold it, shinnied onto the elevator shaft. He had made it through the morning without drawing attention, trying to save up his energy for when he would have to start working.

Joecy was the cutter that day. He was five feet four inches tall, a small man, but he understood the ways of the rock like no one H had ever worked with did. Joecy was a first-class man they all respected, working off year seven of his eight-year sentence as fervently as he had year one. He would often say how he was going to get free and start working in the mines for pay, as some of the other black men had done. They couldn't whip a free miner.

That day, the space between the rock was only about a foot high. H had seen men wiggle into spaces that small and shake and hyperventilate so badly they needed to leave. Once he'd seen a man get to the very middle and then stop, too scared to move forward or backward, too scared to breathe. They'd called Joecy over to try to fish him out, but by the time he got there the man had already died.

Joecy didn't even blink at the small space. He shinnied his small body under the rock and lay down on his back and started to undercut the bottom of the seam. Once he had finished that, he drove a hole into the rock, listening to it, he liked to say, so that he could find the spot that wouldn't crumble on top of him and kill him straightaway. Once the hole had been placed, Joecy put in the dynamite, lit it. The coal blew apart, and Thomas and Bull picked up their picks and started breaking the rock into manageable pieces so that they could all start to load the tramcar.

H tried to lift his shovel, but his arms would not budge. He tried again, focusing all his mind's power and energy on his shoulder, his forearm, his wrist, his fingers. Nothing happened.

At first, Bull and Thomas just stared at him, but before he knew it, Joecy was shoveling his pile for him, and then Bull. And then, finally, after what seemed like hours, Thomas too was pulling weight, until everybody in the room of that mine had shoveled his own pile and H's too.

"Thank you for your help the other day," Thomas said once they had finished.

H's arms were still aching at his sides. They felt like immovable stone, forced to his sides by some gravitational pull. H nodded at Thomas. He used to dream about killing white men the way they killed black men. He used to dream of ropes and whips, trees and mine shafts.

"Hey, how come they call you H?"

"Don't know," H said. He used to think of nothing else but escaping the mines. Sometimes he would study the underground city and wonder if there was somewhere, some way, he could break free, come out on another side.

"C'mon. Somebody must have named you."

"My old master say H is what my mama used to call me. They asked her to name me somethin' proper before she gave birth, but she refused. She killed herself. Master said they had to slice me out her belly 'fore she died."

Thomas didn't say anything then, just nodded his thank-you again. A month later, when Thomas died of tuberculosis, H couldn't remember his name, only the face he made when H had picked up his shovel for him.

This was how it went in the mines. H didn't know where Bull was now. So many were transferred at one point or another, contracted by one of the new companies or absorbed by another. It was easy to make friends but impossible to keep them. Last H had heard, Joecy had finished his sentence, and now all the convicts told stories about how their old friend had finally become one of those free miners they had all heard about but never dreamed of actually becoming.

*

H shoveled his last thousand pounds of coal as a convict in 1889. He had been working in Rock Slope for almost all of his incarceration, and his hard work and skill had shaved a year off his sentence. The day the elevator shaft took him up into the light and the prison warden unshackled his feet, H looked straight up at the sun, storing up the rays, just in case some cruel trick sent him back to the city underground. He didn't stop staring until the sun turned into a dozen yellow spots in his eyes.

He thought about going back home, but realized that he didn't know where home was. There was nothing left for him on the old plantations he'd worked, and he had no family to speak of. The first night of his second freedom, he walked as far as he could, walked until there was no mine in sight, no smell of coal clinging to his nostrils. He entered the first bar he saw that contained black people, and with the little money he had, he ordered a drink.

He had showered that morning, tried to rub the clench marks of the shackles from his ankles, the soot from underneath his nails. He had stared at himself in the mirror until he was confident that no one could tell he had ever been in a mine.

Sipping his drink, H noticed a woman. All he could think was that her skin was the color of cotton stems. And he missed that blackness, having only known the true blackness of coal for nearly ten years.

"Excuse me, miss. Could you tell me where I am?" he asked. He hadn't spoken to a woman since the day he called Ethe by another woman's name.

"You ain't looked at the sign 'fore you came in?" she asked, smiling.

"I reckon I ain't," he said.

"You in Pete's bar, Mr. . . ."

"H is my name."

"Mr. H is my name."

They talked for an hour. He found out her name was Dinah and she lived in Mobile but was visiting a cousin there in Birmingham, a very Christian woman who would not care to see her kin drinking. H had just about gotten it into his head to ask her to marry him when another man stepped in to join them.

"You look mighty strong," the man said.

H nodded. "I s'pose I am."

"How you got to be so strong?" the man asked, and H shrugged. "Go on," the man said. "Roll up yo sleeve. Show us some muscle."

H started laughing, but then he looked at Dinah, and her eyes were twinkling in that way that said maybe she wouldn't mind seeing. And so he rolled up his sleeve.

At first, both people were nodding appreciatively, but then the man came closer. "What's that?" he said, tugging where the sleeve met H's back until he'd made a rent in the fabric, and the whole cheap thing tore loose.

"Dear Lord!" Dinah said, covering her mouth.

H craned his neck trying to look at his own back, but then he remembered and knew he didn't need to. It had been nearly twenty-five years since the end of slavery, and free men were not supposed to have fresh scars on their backs, the evidence of a whip.

"I knew it!" the man said. "I knew he was one of them cons from over at the mines. Ain't nothin' else he could be! Dinah, don't you waste any more time talking to this nigger."

She didn't. She walked away with the man to stand on the other side of the bar. H rolled his sleeve back down and knew that he couldn't go back to the free world, marked as he was.

He moved to Pratt City, the town that was made up of ex-cons, white and black alike. Convict miners who were now free miners. His first night there, he asked around for a few minutes until he found Joecy, along with his wife and children, who had moved out to Pratt City to be with him.

"Ain't you got no one?" Joecy's wife said, frying up some salt pork for H, working hard to make up for the fact that he had not eaten a good meal for ten years, maybe more.

"Had a woman named Ethe, long time ago, but I reckon she ain't gon' wanna hear from me now."

The wife gave him a piteous look, and H figured she was thinking she knew the whole story of Ethe, having married a man herself before the white man came and labeled him con.

"Lil Joe!" the wife called, over and over, until a child appeared. "This our son, Lil Joe," she said. "He know how to write."

H looked him over. He couldn't have been more than eleven years old. He was knobby-kneed and clear-eyed. He looked just like his father, but he was different too. Maybe he wouldn't end up the kind of man who needed to use his body for work. Maybe he'd be a new kind of black man altogether, one who got to use his mind.

"He gon' write yo woman," the wife said.

"Naw," H said, thinking about how Ethe had fled the room the last time they were together, fled like a spirit was chasing her. "Ain't no need."

The wife clucked her tongue twice, three times. "I ain't gon' hear none of that," she said. "Somebody gotta know you free now. Somebody in this world need to know at least that."

"With all due respect, ma'am. I got myself, and that's all I ever needed."

Joecy's wife looked at him long and hard, and H could see all the pity and anger in that look, but he didn't care. He didn't back down, and so, finally, she had to.

The next morning, H walked with Joecy over to the mine to ask for work as a free laborer.

The boss man was called Mr. John. He asked H to take off his shirt. He inspected the muscles on his back and on his arms, and whistled.

"Any man what can spend ten years working at Rock Slope and live to tell about it's worth a-watching. Made some deal with the devil, have you?" Mr. John asked, looking at H with his piercing blue eyes.

"Just a hard worker, sir," Joecy said. "Hard and smart, too."

"You vouch for him, Joecy?" Mr. John asked.

"Ain't none better but me," Joecy said.

H left with a pick in his hands.

Pratt City life was not easy, but it was better than the living H had known anywhere else. He had never seen anything like it before. White men and their families next door to black men and theirs. Both colors joining the same unions, fighting for the same things. The mines had taught them that they had to rely on each other if they wanted to survive, and they had taken that mentality with them when they started the camp because they knew no one but a fellow miner, a fellow ex-con, knew what it was like to live in Birmingham and try to make something of a past that you would sooner forget.

The work H did was the same, only now he got paid for it. Proper wages, for he had once been a first-class man, contracted by coal companies from the state prison for nineteen dollars a month. Now that money went into his own pocket, sometimes as much as forty dollars in a single month. He remembered what little he had saved sharecropping for two years at the Hobbs plantation, and he knew that in some dark and twisted way the mine was one of the best things that had happened to him. It taught him a new skill, a worthy one, and his hands would never have to pick cotton or till land ever again.

Joecy and his wife, Jane, had been gracious enough to let H move in with them, but H had tired of living off of and around other people and their families. So he spent the better part of his first month in Pratt City coming back from the mine and then heading straight to the plot of land next to Joecy's place to start building his own house.

H was out there one night, hammering wood, when Joecy came to see him.

"Why ain't you joined the union yet?" Joecy asked. "We could use somebody with your temper."

He had gotten good lumber from another old friend from the mine and the only time he could work on building the house was between 8:00 p.m. and 3:00 a.m. At every other waking hour, he was down in the mines.

"I ain't like that no more," H said. Though he had no scar on his neck from that day the pit boss had sliced him, he still ran his hands there from time to time as a reminder that a white man could still kill him for nothing.

"Oh you ain't like that, huh? C'mon, H. We fightin' for things that you could use too. Ain't like you got anybody to keep you company in this here house you buildin'. Union might do you some good."

H sat in the very back of the first meeting he ever went to, his arms folded. At the front of the room a doctor spoke to them about black lung disease.

"The mineral dust that covers the outside of your bodies when you leave, well, that gets inside your body too. Makes you sick. Shorter hours, better ventilation, those are things that you should be fighting for."

It had taken about a month, but it wasn't just Joecy's talk that finally convinced H to join. The truth was, he was scared of dying in the mines and his freedom had not erased his fear. Every time H was lowered down into the mine, he would picture his own death. Men were getting diseases he had never before seen or heard of, but now that he was free he could make the danger worth something.

"More money's what we should be fighting for," H said.

A murmur started to pass through the room as people craned their necks to see who had spoken. "Two-Shovel H is here," "Is that Two-Shovel?" He'd gone so long without attending a meeting.

"Ain't no way to keep from breathing the dust, doc," H said. "Hell, most the men in this room are halfway to death as it is. Might as well get paid 'fore we go."

Behind H, the meeting door started to rustle and a child who'd had his leg blown off hobbled in. He couldn't have been more than fourteen years old, but already, H felt like he could picture the entire course of that boy's life. Maybe he'd started out as a breaker, sitting hunched over tons of coal, trying to separate it from slate and rock. Then maybe the bosses moved him up to spragger because they saw him running outside one day and knew that he was fast. The boy had to run along the cars, jamming sprags in the wheels to slow the cars down, but maybe one car didn't slow down. Maybe that one car jumped the track and took the boy's leg and his whole future with it. Maybe what saddened the boy most after the doctor sawed it off was the fact that he wouldn't ever get to be a first-class miner like his father.

The doctor looked from H to the crippled boy and back again. "Money's nice, don't get me wrong. But mining can be a whole lot safer than what it is. Lives are worth fighting for too." He cleared his throat, then continued to speak about the signs of black lung.

On his walk home that night, H started to think about the crippled boy, how easy it had been for H to make up his story. How easy it was for a life to go one way instead of another. He could still remember telling his cellmate that nothing could kill him, and now he saw his mortality all around him. What if H hadn't been so arrogant when he was a younger man? What if he hadn't been arrested? What if he'd treated his woman right? He should have had children of his own by now. He should have had a small farm and a full life.

Suddenly H felt like he couldn't breathe, like that decade's worth of dust was climbing up his lungs and into his throat and choking him. He hunched over and started to cough and cough and cough, and when he'd finished coughing, he stumbled his way to Joecy's house and knocked on the door.

Lil Joe answered with sleep in his eyes. "My daddy ain't back from the meeting yet, Uncle H," he said.

"I ain't here to see your daddy, son. I—I need you to write me a letter. Can you do that?"

Lil Joe nodded. He went into the house and came back out with the supplies he needed. He wrote as H dictated:

Deer Ethe. This is H. I am now free an livin in Prat City.

H mailed the letter the very next morning.

. . .

"What we need to do is call a strike," a white union member said.

H was sitting in the front row of the church house where the union meetings were held. There was an endless list of problems and the strike was the first solution. H listened carefully as a murmur of agreement began to rush through the room, as hushed as a hum.

"Who gon' pay attention to our strike?" H asked. He was becoming more vocal at the meetings.

"Well, we tell 'em we won't work until they raise our pay or make it safer. They gotta listen," the white man said.

H snorted. "When a white man ever listened to a black man?"

"I'm here now, ain't I? I'm listening," the white man said.

"You a con."

"You're a con, too."

H looked around the room. There were about fifty men there, over half of them black.

"Whatchu done wrong?" H asked, returning his gaze to the white man.

At first, the man wouldn't speak. He kept his head lowered, and cleared his throat so many times, H wondered if there was anything left in his mouth at all. Finally the words came out. "I killed a man."

"Killed a man, huh? You know what they got my friend Joecy over there for? He ain't cross the street when a white woman walk by. For that they gave him nine years. For killin' a man they give you the same. We ain't cons like you."

"We gotta work together now," the white man said. "Same as in the mine. We can't be one way down there and another way up here."

No one spoke. They all just turned to watch H, see what he would say or do. Everyone had heard the story of the time he'd picked up that second shovel.

Finally he nodded, and the next day the strike began.

Only fifty people showed up on that first day. They gave their bosses a list of their demands: better pay, better care for the sick, and fewer hours. The white union members had written up the list, and Joecy's boy, Lil Joe, had read it aloud to all the black members to make sure it said what they thought it said. The bosses had answered back that free miners could easily be replaced by convicts, and one week later a carriage full of black cons appeared, all under the age of sixteen, and looking so scared it made H want to quit the strike if only it meant more people wouldn't be arrested to fill in the gap. By the end of the week, the only thing both sides had agreed to was that there would be no killing.

And still, more convicts were rounded up and brought in. H wondered if there was a black man left in the South who hadn't been put in prison at one point or another, so many of them came to fill the mines. Even free laborers who weren't striking were being replaced, so soon more of them joined in the fight. H spent hours at Joecy and Jane's house, making signs with Lil Joe.

"What that say?" H asked, pointing to the tar-painted wood at Lil Joe's side.

"It say, more pay," the boy answered.

"And what that say?"

"It say, no more tuberculosis."

"Where you learn to read like that?" H asked. He had grown so fond of Lil Joe, but the sight of his friend's son only made him ache for a child of his own.

The smell of the tar Lil Joe was using to write clung to the hairs in H's nostrils. He coughed a little and a black string of mucus trailed from his mouth.

"I had a little school in Huntsville 'fore they took my daddy. When they arrested him, they said he and my whole family was gettin' too uppity. They said that was why Daddy didn't cross the street when the white woman passed by."

"And what you think?" H asked.

Lil Joe shrugged.

The next day, Joecy and H took the signs out with them to the strike. There were about 150 men standing out in the cold. They all watched while the new crop of cons walked by, waiting to be lowered down into the mines.

"Let them kids go!" H shouted loudly. A boy had peed himself waiting for the shaft, and H suddenly remembered the one who had been chained to him as they rode the train over, who had wet himself and cried endlessly when they stood before the pit boss. "They ain't but kids. Let 'em go!"

"Are you gonna stop this foolishness and get back to work?" came the reply.

Then, suddenly, the boy who had wet himself started to run. He was nothing but a blur in the corner of H's eye before the gunshot went off.

And the people on strike broke the line, swarming the few white bosses who were standing guard. They broke the shafts and dumped the coal from the tramcars before breaking those too. H grabbed a white man by the throat and held him over the vast pit.

"One day the world gon' know what you done here," he said to the man, whose fear was written plainly across his blue eyes, bulging now that H's grip had tightened.

H wanted to throw the man down, down to meet the city underneath the earth, but he stopped himself. He was not the con they had told him he was.

It took six more months of striking for the bosses to give in. They would all be paid fifty cents more. The running boy was the only one to die in the struggle. The pay increase was a small victory, but one that they would all take. After the day the running boy died, the strikers helped clean up the mess the fight had made. They picked up their shovels, found the boy who'd been gunned down, and buried him in the potter's field. H wasn't sure what the others were thinking when they finally laid the boy to rest among the hundreds of other cons who had died there, nameless, but he knew that he was thankful.

After the union meeting where the raise was announced, H walked home with Joecy. He saw his friend off to his house, and then he went next door to his own. When he got there, he saw that his front door was swinging open, and a strange smell was coming from inside. He still had his pick on him, caked with the dirt and coal from the mine. He lifted the pick over his head, certain that a pit boss had come to meet him. He crept in lightly, ready for whatever came next.

It was Ethe. Apron tied around her waist and handkerchief wrapped around her head. She turned from the stove, where she was cooking greens, and faced him.

"You might as well set that thing down," she said.

H looked at his hands. The pick was raised, just slightly, above his head, and he lowered it to his side and then to the floor.

"I got your letter," Ethe said, and H nodded and the two of them just stood there and stared at each other for a moment before Ethe found her voice again.

"Had to get Miz Benton from up the street to read it fo' me. First, I just let it sit there on my table. Every day, I would pass it, and I'd think 'bout what I was gon' do. I let two months go by that way."

The fatback at the bottom of the pot started to crackle. H didn't know if Ethe could hear it because she had not looked away from him, nor he from her.

"You have to understand, H. The day you called me that woman's name, I thought, *Ain't I been through enough?* Ain't just about everything I ever had been taken away from me? My freedom. My family. My body. And now I can't even own my name? Ain't I deserve to be Ethe, to you at least, if nobody else? My mama gave me that name herself. I spent six good years with her before they sold me out to Louisiana to work them sugarcanes. All I had of her then was my name. That was all I had of myself too. And you wouldn't even give me that."

Smoke began to form above the pot. It rose higher and higher, until a cloud of it was dancing around Ethe's head, kissing her lips.

"I wasn't ready to forgive you that for a long time, and by the time I was, the white folks was already payin' you back for somethin' I know you ain't done, but nobody would tell me how I could get you out. And what was I s'posed to do then, H? You tell me. What was I s'posed to do then?"

Ethe turned away from him and went to the pot. She began scraping the bottom of it, and the stuff she lifted up with the spoon was about as black as anything H had ever seen.

He went to her, took her body in his arms, let himself feel the full weight of her. It was not the same weight as coal, that mountain of black rock that he'd spent nearly a third of his life lifting. Ethe did not submit so easily. She did not lean back into him until the pot had been scraped clean.

Akua

EVERY TIME AKUA DROPPED a quartered yam into sizzling palm oil, the sound made her jump. It was a hungry sound, the sound of oil swallowing whatever it was given.

Akua's ear was growing. She had learned to distinguish sounds she had never before heard. She had grown up in the missionary school, where they were taught to go to God with all their worries and problems and fears, but when she came to Edweso and saw and heard a white man being swallowed alive by fire, she dusted off her knees, knelt down, and gave this image and sound to God, but God had refused to keep them. He returned her fear to her every night in horrible nightmares where fire consumed everything, where it ran from the coast of Fanteland all the way into Asante. In her dreams the fire was shaped like a woman holding two babies to her heart. The firewoman would carry these two little girls with her all the way to the woods of the Inland and then the babies would vanish, and the firewoman's sadness would send orange and red and hints of blue swarming every tree and every bush in sight.

Akua couldn't remember the first time she'd seen fire, but she could remember the first time she'd dreamed of it. It was in 1895, sixteen years after her mother, Abena, had carried her Akua-swollen belly to the missionaries in Kumasi, fifteen years after Abena had died. Then the fire in Akua's dream had been nothing more than a quick flash of ochre. Now the firewoman raged.

Akua's ear was growing, so at night she now slept flat on her back or stomach, never on her side, afraid of crushing the new weight. She was certain that the dreams entered through her growing ear, that they latched onto the sizzling sounds of fried things in the daytime and lodged themselves in her mind at night, and so she slept flat-backed to let them through. Because even though she feared the new sounds, she knew she needed to hear them too.

Akua knew she'd had the dream again that night when she woke up screaming. The sound escaped her mouth like breath, like pipe smoke. Her husband, Asamoah, woke up next to her and swiftly reached for the machete he kept beside him, looking at the ground to check for the children, then at the door to check for an intruder, and ending by look-ing at his wife.

"What is the meaning of this?" he asked.

Akua shivered, suddenly cold. "It was the dream," she said. She didn't realize she was crying until Asamoah pulled her into his arms. "You and the rest of the leaders should not have burned that white man," she said into her husband's chest, and he pushed her away.

"You speak for the white man?" he asked.

She shook her head quickly. She'd known since she picked him for marriage that her husband feared her time among the white mission-aries had made her weaker, less of an Asante somehow. "It's not that," she said. "It's the fire. I keep dreaming about fire."

Asamoah clicked his tongue. He had lived in Edweso his whole life. On his cheek he bore the mark of the Asante, and the nation was his pride. "What do I care of fire when they have exiled the Asantehene?"

Akua could not respond. For years, King Prempeh I had been refusing to allow the British to take over the Kingdom of Asante, insist-ing that the Asante people would remain sovereign. For this, he was arrested and exiled, and the anger that had been brewing all over the Asante nation grew sharper. Akua knew her dreams would not stop this anger from brewing in her husband's heart. And so she decided to keep them to herself, to sleep on her stomach or back, to never again let Asamoah hear her scream.

.   .   .

Akua spent her days in the compound with her mother-in-law, Nana Serwah, and her children, Abee and Ama Serwah. She started each morning by sweeping, a task she had always enjoyed for its repetitiveness, its calm. It had been her job in the missionary school too, but there, the Missionary used to laugh as he watched her, marveling at the fact that the school floor was made of clay. "Who ever heard of sweeping dust from dust?" he would say, and Akua would wonder what the floors looked like where he came from.

After she swept, Akua would help the other women cook. Abee was only four years old, but she liked to hold the giant pestle and pretend that she was helping. "Mama, look!" she would say, hugging the tall stick to her tiny body. It towered above her, and the weight of it threatened to throw her off-balance. Akua's toddler, Ama Serwah, had big, bright eyes that would glance from the top of the *fufu* stick to the trembling sister before sending her gaze to her mother.

"You are so strong!" Akua would say, and Nana Serwah would cluck her tongue.

"She'll fall and hurt herself," her mother-in-law would say, snatching the *fufu* stick from Abee's hands and shaking her head. Akua knew that Nana Serwah did not approve of her, often saying that a woman whose mother had left her to be taught by white men would never know how to raise children herself. It was usually around this time that Nana Serwah would send Akua out to the market to pick up more ingredients for the food they would make later for Asamoah and the other men who spent their days outside, meeting, planning.

Akua liked walking to the market. She could finally think, without the scrutinizing gaze of the women and elderly men, who stayed around the compound, making fun of her for all the time she spent staring at the same spot on a hut's wall. "She's not correct," they would say aloud, no doubt wondering why Asamoah would choose to marry her. But she wasn't just staring into space; she was listening to all the sounds the world had to offer, to all the people who inhabited those spaces the others could not see. She was wandering.

On her walk to the market, she would often stop at the spot where the townsmen had burned the white man. A nameless man, a wanderer himself, who had found himself in the wrong town at the wrong time.

At first he was safe, lying under a tree, shielding his face from the sun with a book, but then Kofi Poku, a child of only three, stumbled in front of Akua, who had been very close to asking the man if he was lost or needed help, pointed with his tiny index finger, and shouted, *"Obroni!"*

Akua's ears prickled at the word. She had been in Kumasi the first time she heard it. A child who didn't go to the missionary school had called the Missionary *"obroni,"* and the man turned as red as a burning sun and walked away. Akua was only six years old then. To her, the word had only ever meant "white man." She hadn't understood why the Missionary had gotten upset, and in times like those she wished she could remember her mother. Maybe she would have had the answers. Instead, Akua stole out that evening to the hut of a fetish priest on the edge of town who was said to have been around since the white man first came to the Gold Coast.

"Think about it," the man said, after she told him what happened. In the missionary school they called white people Teacher or Reverend or Miss. When Abena died, Akua had been left to be raised by the Missionary. He was the only one who would take her. "It did not begin as *obroni*. It began as two words. *Abro ni.*"

"Wicked man?" Akua said.

The fetish man nodded. "Among the Akan he is wicked man, the one who harms. Among the Ewe of the Southeast his name is Cunning Dog, the one who feigns niceness and then bites you."

"The Missionary is not wicked," Akua said.

The fetish man kept nuts in his pocket. This was how Akua had first met him. After her mother died, she had been wailing for her in the street. She hadn't yet understood loss. Crying was what she did every time her mother left her, to go to market, to go to sea. Wailing for the loss of her was commonplace, but this time it had lasted the entire morning, and her mother had not reappeared to shush her, hold her, kiss her face. The fetish man saw her crying that day and had given her a kola nut. Chewing it had pacified her, for a time.

Now he gave one to her again and said, "Why is the Missionary not wicked?"

"He is God's man."

"And God's men are not wicked?" he asked.

Akua nodded.

"Am I wicked?" the fetish man asked, and Akua didn't know how to answer. That first day she had met him, when he had given her the kola nut, the Missionary had come out and seen her with him. He had snatched her hand and pulled her away and told her not to talk to fetish men. They called him a fetish man because he was, because he had not given up praying to the ancestors or dancing or collecting plants and rocks and bones and blood with which to make his fetish offerings. He had not been baptized. She knew he was supposed to be wicked, that she would be in a sea of trouble if the missionaries knew that she still went to see him, and yet she recognized that his kindness, his love, was different from the people's at the school. Warmer and truer somehow.

"No, you're not wicked," she said.

"You can only decide a wicked man by what he does, Akua. The white man has earned his name here. Remember that."

She did remember. She remembered it even as Kofi Poku pointed at the white man sleeping under the tree and shouted *"Obroni!"* She remembered as the crowd formed and as the rage that had been building in the village for months came to a head. The men awoke the white man by tying him to the tree. They built a fire, and then they burned him. All the while he was screaming in English, "Please, if anyone here can understand me, let me go! I am only a traveler. I am not from the government! I am not from the government!"

Akua was not the only person in the crowd who understood English. She was not the only person in the crowd who did nothing to help.

When Akua returned to the compound, everyone was in an uproar. She could sense the chaos in the air that seemed to get thicker, heavier, with noise and fear, the smoke from sizzling food and the buzzing of flies. Nana Serwah was covered in a film of sweat, her wrinkled hands rolling *fufu* by the second to plate up for the large crowd of men who had come. The woman looked up and spotted Akua.

"Akua, what's wrong with you? Why are you just standing there? Come and help. These men need to be fed before the next meeting."

Akua shook herself out of the daze she had been in and sat beside her mother-in-law, rolling the mashed cassava into neat little circles and passing them along to the next woman, who filled the bowls with soup.

The men were shouting loudly, so loudly that it was nearly impossible to distinguish what one was saying from what the others were saying. The sound of it was all the same. Outrage. Rage. Akua could see her husband, but she did not dare look at him. She knew her place was with her mother-in-law, the other women, the old men, not begging questions of him with her eyes.

"What is going on?" Akua whispered to Nana Serwah. The woman was rinsing her hands in the calabash of water that sat beside her, then drying them on her wrapper.

She spoke in a hushed tone, her lips barely moving. "The British governor, Frederick Hodgson, was in Kumasi today. He says they will not return King Prempeh I from exile."

Akua sucked her teeth. This was what they had all been fearing.

"It's worse than that," her mother-in-law continued. "He said we must give him the Golden Stool so that he can sit on it or give it as a gift to his queen."

Akua's hands started to tremble in the pot, making a low rattling noise and marring the shape of the *fufu*. So it was worse than what they had all been fearing, worse than another war, worse than a few hundred more dead. They were a warrior people, and war was what they knew. But if a white man took the Golden Stool, the spirit of the Asante would surely die, and that they could not bear.

Nana Serwah reached out and touched her hand. It was one of the few gestures of kindness Asamoah's mother had shown her since the days of Asamoah and her courtship, then marriage. They both knew what was coming and what it meant.

By the next week there had already been a meeting among the Asante leaders in Kumasi. The stories that followed told of the men of the meeting being too timid, disagreeing about what to say to the British, what to do. It was Yaa Asantewaa, Edweso's own Queen Mother, who stood up and demanded that they fight, saying that if the men would not do it, the women would.

Most of the men were gone by morning. Asamoah kissed his daughters, and then he kissed her too, held her for just a moment. Akua watched him as he dressed. She watched as he left. Twenty other townsmen went with him. A few men stayed, sat in the compound waiting to be fed.

Nana Serwah's husband, Akua's father-in-law, had kept a machete with a golden handle beside him every night of his life, and after he died Nana Serwah had kept it in the place where he used to sleep. A machete in exchange for a body. After the Queen Mother's call to arms reached Edweso, she had pulled that machete out from the bed and taken it with her into the compound. And all the men who had not already gone to fight for the Asante took one look at the old woman holding the large weapon and left. And so began the war.

The Missionary kept a long, thin switch on his desk.

"You will no longer go to class with the other children," he told her. Only a few days had passed since a child had called the Missionary *obroni,* but Akua hardly remembered that. She had just learned to write her English name, Deborah, that very morning. It was the longest name of any of the children in the class, and Akua had worked very hard to write it. "From now on," the Missionary said, "you will take lessons from me. Do you understand?"

"Yes," she answered. Word must have gotten to him that she had mastered her name. She was getting special treatment.

"Sit down," the Missionary said.

She sat.

The Missionary took the switch from his desk and pointed it at her. The tip of it was just inches from her nose. When she crossed her eyes she could see it clearly, and it wasn't until then that the fear hit her.

"You are a sinner and a heathen," he said. Akua nodded. The teachers had told them this before. "Your mother had no husband when she came here to me, pregnant, begging for help. I helped her because that is what God would have wanted me to do. But she was a sinner and a heathen, like you."

Again Akua nodded. The fear was starting to settle somewhere in her stomach, making her feel nauseated.

"All people on the black continent must give up their heathenism and turn to God. Be thankful that the British are here to show you how to live a good and moral life."

This time, Akua did not nod. She looked at the Missionary, but she didn't know how to describe the look he returned to her. After he told her to stand up and bend over, after he lashed her five times and commanded her to repent her sins and repeat "God bless the queen," after she was permitted to leave, after she finally threw the fear up, the only word that popped into her head was "hungry." The Missionary looked hungry, like if he could, he would devour her.

Every day Akua woke her daughters up while the sun was still sleeping. She wrapped her wrapper, and then walked with her girls out into the dirt roads where Nana Serwah, Akos, Mambee, and all of the other women of Edweso had already begun to assemble. Akua's voice was the strongest, and so she led them in song:

> *Awurade Nyame kum dom*
> *Oboo adee Nyame kum dom*
> *Ennee yerekokum dom afa adee*
> *Oboo adee Nyame kum dom*
> *Soso be hunu, megyede be hunu.*

Up and down the streets they sang. Akua's toddler, Ama Serwah, sang the loudest and most off-key, her words a slew of gibberish until the song reached her favorite part, at which point she screamed more than sang, "CREATOR GOD, DEFEAT THE TROOPS!" Sometimes the women put her in the very front, and her little legs would stomp about valiantly until Akua picked her up to carry her the rest of the way.

After the singing, Akua went back to wash herself and the children, put white clay on her body as a symbol of her support for the war efforts, eat, then sing again. They cooked for the men in shifts so that there was always something to send away. At night, Akua would sleep alone, dreaming of the fire still. Screaming again, now that Asamoah was gone.

Akua and Asamoah had been married for five years. He was a tradesman, and he had business in Kumasi. He had seen her one day at the missionary school and had stopped to talk to her. And from then on he stopped to talk to her every single day. Two weeks later he was back to ask if she would marry him and come to live in Edweso, for he knew she was an orphan with no other place to live.

Akua found nothing particularly remarkable about Asamoah. He was not handsome like the man called Akwasi who came to church every Sunday, standing timidly in the back and pretending not to notice as the mothers threw their daughters at him. Asamoah also seemed to possess little mental intelligence, for his whole life had been about the intelligence of the body: what he could catch or build or lift to take with him to market. She had once seen him sell two kente for the price of one because he could not count the money correctly. Asamoah was not the best choice, but he was the sure one, and Akua was happy to accept his proposal. Up until then, she had thought she would have to stay with the Missionary forever, playing his strange game of student/ teacher, heathen/savior, but with Asamoah she saw that maybe her life could be something different from what she had always imagined it would be.

"I forbid it," the Missionary said when she told him.

"You can't forbid it," Akua said. Now that she had a plan, a hope for a way out, she felt emboldened.

"You . . . you are a sinner," the Missionary whispered, his head in his hands. "You are a heathen," he said, louder now. "You must ask God to forgive your sins."

Akua didn't respond. For nearly ten years, she had filled the Missionary's hunger. Now she wanted to attend to her own.

"Ask God to forgive your sins!" the Missionary yelled, throwing his switch at her.

The switch hit Akua on the left shoulder. She watched it drop to the floor, and then, calmly, she walked out. Behind her she could hear the Missionary saying, "He's not a man of God. He's not a man of God." But Akua cared nothing for God. She was sixteen, and the fetish priest had died only a year before. She used to go to him whenever she could get away from the Missionary. She used to tell him that the more she learned about God from the Missionary, the more questions she had. Big questions like, if God was so big, so powerful, why did he need the white man to bring him to them? Why could he not tell them himself, make his presence known as he had in the days written about in the Book, with bush fires and dead men walking? Why had her mother run to these missionaries, these white people, out of all people? Why did she have no family? No friends? Whenever she asked the Missionary these questions, he refused to answer her. The fetish man told her that maybe the Christian God *was* a question, a great and swirling circle of whys. This answer never satisfied Akua, and by the time the fetish man died, God no longer satisfied her either. Asamoah was real. Tangible. His arms were as thick as yams, and his skin as brown. If God was why, then Asamoah was yes and yes again.

Now that war had come for them, Akua noticed that Nana Serwah was nicer to her than she had ever before been. Word of this man and that man dying came in every day, and they were both holding their breath, certain that it was only a matter of time before the name out of the messenger's mouth was Asamoah.

Edweso was empty. The absence of the men felt like its own presence. Sometimes Akua would think that not much at all had changed, but then she would see the empty fields, the rotting yams, the wailing women. Akua's dreams were getting worse too. In them, the firewoman raged against the loss of her children. Sometimes she spoke to Akua, calling her, it seemed. She looked familiar, and Akua wanted to ask her questions. She wanted to know if the firewoman knew the white man who had been burned. If everyone touched by fire was a part of the same world. If she was being called. Instead, she didn't speak. She woke up screaming. In the midst of all this turmoil, Akua was pregnant. At least six months now, she figured by the shape and firm weight of her belly.

One day, more than halfway through the war, Akua was boiling yams to send to the soldiers, and she could not lift her eyes from the fire.

"This again?" Nana Serwah said. "I thought we had finished with your idleness. Are our people out fighting so that you can stare into the fire and scream at night for your children to hear?"

"No, Ma," Akua said, shaking herself out of her stupor. But the next day she did it again. And again her mother-in-law scolded her. The same thing happened the day after that, and then the one after that, until Nana Serwah decided that Akua was sick and that she must stay in her hut until the sickness had left her body. Her daughters would stay with Nana Serwah until Akua had fully healed.

The first day of her hut exile, Akua was thankful for the break. She had not had rest since the men left for war, always marching through town singing the war songs or standing on her feet sweating into a large pot. Her plan was to not sleep until night had fallen. To lie on the side of the hut where Asamoah usually lay, trying to conjure up the smell of him to keep her company until night fell over the hut, casting its awful darkness into the room. But within hours Akua was asleep, and the firewoman had reappeared.

She was growing, her hair a wild bush of ochre and blue. She was growing bolder. No longer simply burning the things that were around her, but now acknowledging Akua. Seeing her.

"Where are your children?" she asked. Akua was too afraid to answer her. She could feel that her body was in the cot. She could feel that she was dreaming, and yet she could not exert control over that feeling. She could not tell that feeling to grow hands, nudge her body into waking. She could not tell that feeling to throw water on the firewoman, put her out of her dreams.

"You must always know where your children are," the firewoman continued, and Akua shuddered.

The next day she tried to leave the hut, but Nana Serwah had the Fat Man sit at her door. His body, too fat to fight in the war that his peers were in, was just the right size for locking Akua in.

"Please!" Akua shouted. "Just let me see my children!"

But the Fat Man would not budge. Nana Serwah, standing next to him, shouted back, "You can see them once you are no longer sick!"

Akua fought for the rest of the day. She pushed but the Fat Man did not move. She screamed but he did not speak. She banged on the door but his ears would not hear.

Periodically, Akua could hear Nana Serwah coming to him, bringing him food to eat and water to drink. He said thank you, but nothing else. It was as though he felt like he had found his way to serve. The war had come to Akua's door.

By nightfall, Akua was afraid to speak. She crouched in the corner of the hut, praying to every god she had ever known. The Christian God whom the missionaries had always described in terms both angry and loving. Nyame, the Akan God, all-knowing and all-seeing. She prayed too to Asase Yaa and her children Bia and Tano. She even prayed to Anansi, though he was nothing more than the trickster people put in their stories to amuse themselves. She prayed aloud and feverishly so that she would not sleep, and by morning she was too weak to fight the Fat Man, too weak to know if he was even still there.

For a week she stayed like this. She had never understood the missionaries when they said they could sometimes spend a whole day in prayer, but now she did. Prayer was not a sacred or holy thing. It was not spoken plainly, in Twi or English. It need not be performed on the knees or with folded palms. For Akua, prayer was a frenzied chant, a language for those desires of the heart that even the mind did not recognize were there. It was the scraping up of the clay floor into her dark palms. It was the crouching in the shadow of the room. It was the one-syllable word that escaped her lips over and over and over again.

Fire. Fire. Fire.

The Missionary would not let Akua leave the orphanage to marry Asamoah. Since the day she told him of Asamoah's proposal, he had stopped his lessons, stopped telling her that she was a heathen or asking her to repent her sins, to repeat "God bless the queen." He only watched her.

"You can't keep me here," Akua said. She was gathering the last of her things out of her quarters. Asamoah would be back before nightfall to get her. Edweso was waiting.

The Missionary stood in the doorframe, his switch in his hand.

"What? Will you beat me until I stay?" she asked. "You'd have to kill me to keep me here."

"I'll tell you about your mother," the Missionary finally said. He dropped the switch to the floor and walked toward Akua until he was standing so close she could smell the faint stench of fish on his breath. For ten years, he had come no closer to her than the length of that switch. For ten years he had refused to answer her questions about her family. "I'll tell you about your mother. Anything you want to know."

Akua took a step back from him, and he did the same. He looked down.

"Your mother, Abena, she wouldn't repent," the Missionary said. "She came to us pregnant—you, her sin—but still she wouldn't repent. She spit at the British. She was argumentative and angry. I believe she was glad of her sins. I believe she did not regret you or your father, even though he did not care for her as a man should."

The Missionary was speaking softly, so softly that Akua couldn't be certain that she was hearing him at all.

"After you were born, I took her to the water to be baptized. She didn't want to go, but I—I forced her. She thrashed as I carried her through the forest, to the river. She thrashed as I lowered her down into the water. She thrashed and thrashed and thrashed, and then she was still." The Missionary lifted his head and looked at her finally. "I only wanted her to repent. I—I only wanted her to repent . . ."

The Missionary started crying. It was not the sight of tears that caught Akua's attention so much as the sound. The terrible sound, the heaving sound, like something wrenched from the throat.

"Where is her body?" Akua asked. "What did you do with her body?"

The sound stopped. The Missionary spoke. "I burned it in the forest. I burned it with all of her things. God forgive me! God forgive me!"

The sound returned. This time, shuddering came with it, a shaking so violent that soon the Missionary fell down to the ground.

Akua had to walk over his body to leave.

. . .

Asamoah returned at the end of the week. Akua could hear him with her growing ear, though she could not yet see him. She felt weighted to the ground, her limbs heavy logs on the floor of some dark forest.

At the door, Nana Serwah was sobbing and screaming. "My son-o! My son! My son-o! My son!" Then Akua's growing ear heard a new sound. Loud step. Space. Loud step. Space.

"What is the Fat Man doing here?" Asamoah asked. His voice was loud enough that Akua considered moving, but it was as though she were in the dream space again, unable to make her body do what her mind wanted it to.

Nana Serwah could not answer her son, so busy was she in her wailing. The Fat Man moved, his enormous girth a boulder rolling to reveal the door. Asamoah entered the room, but still Akua could not get up.

"What is the meaning of this?" Asamoah roared, and Nana Serwah was shaken from her wailing.

"She was sick. She was sick, so we . . ."

Her voice trailed. Akua could hear the sound again. Loud step. Space. Loud step. Space. Loud step. Space. Then Asamoah was standing in front of her, but instead of two legs, she only saw one.

He crouched down carefully so that their eyes could better meet, balancing so well that Akua wondered how long it had been since he'd last seen the missing leg. He seemed so well acquainted with the space.

He noticed her swollen belly and shuddered. He reached out his hand. Akua looked at it. She had not slept in a week. Ants had begun to pass over her fingers and she wanted to shake them off, or give them to Asamoah, lace her small fingers between his large ones.

Asamoah stood and turned to his mother. "Where are the girls?" he asked, and Nana Serwah, who had started crying anew, this time at the sight of Akua trapped on the ground, ran to fetch them.

Ama Serwah and Abee came in. To Akua they looked unchanged. Both girls still sucked their thumbs, despite the fact that Nana Serwah put hot pepper on the tips of them every morning, noon, and night to warn them away. The girls were developing a taste for heat. They looked from Asamoah to Akua, holding hands with their grandmother, thumbs in mouths. Then, wordlessly, Abee wrapped her entire little body around her father's leg as though it were a trunk, as though it were the *fufu* stick she was so fond of holding, stronger than she was, sturdier. The toddler, Ama Serwah, moved closer to Akua, and she could see that she had been crying; a thick line of snot trailed from her nose to lick her upper lip, her mouth gaping wide open. It looked like a slug exiting a cave in order to enter a cavern. She touched her father's knee, but kept moving to rest where Akua was. Then she lay down beside her. Akua could feel her little heart beating in time with her own broken one. She reached out to touch her daughter, to pull her into her arms, and then she stood and surveyed the room.

*

The war ended in September, and the earth around them began to register the Asante loss. Long fissures in the red clay formed about Akua's compound, so dry was the season. Crops died, and food was limited, for they had given all they had to the men who were fighting. They had given all they had, assured that it would come back to them in the abundance of freedom. Yaa Asantewaa, Edweso's warrior Queen Mother, was exiled to the Seychelles, never to be seen again by those who lived in the village. Sometimes Akua would walk by her palace in her wanderings and wonder: What if?

The day she had gotten up from the ground, she had not wanted to speak, nor would she let her children or Asamoah leave her sight. And so the broken family nestled into one another, each hoping the others' presences would fill the wound their personal war had left behind.

In the beginning, Asamoah did not want to touch her and she did not want to be touched. The space where his leg had been taunted her. She could not figure out how to situate her body next to his while they lay in bed at night. In the past, she would curl into him, one of her legs intertwined between his two, but now she could not get comfortable, and her restlessness fed his restlessness. Akua no longer slept through the night, but Asamoah hated to see her awake and tortured and so she pretended to sleep, allowing the waves of her breasts to rise and fall to the current of breaths. Sometimes Asamoah would turn and stare at her. She could feel him considering her while she pretended to sleep, and if she slipped, opened her eyes or lost her breathing rhythm, his big booming voice would command her to sleep. If she convinced him, she would wait for his real breathing to match her contrived one, and then she would lie there, wishing the firewoman away. If she slept, she would do so only lightly, dipping the ladle of sleep into the shallow pool of dreamland, hoping she would not see the firewoman there before she beckoned herself awake.

Then, one day, Asamoah no longer wanted to sleep. He nuzzled Akua's neck.

"I know you're awake," he said. "I know you do not sleep these days, Akua."

And still she tried to pretend, ignoring his hot breath against her skin, breathing still and the same.

"Akua," he said. He had turned his body so that his mouth now met her ear, and the sound of her name was a strong stick hitting a hollow drum.

She did not answer as he continued to speak her name. The first day she'd left the house after her week of exile, the townspeople had looked away as she passed, embarrassed and ashamed of how they had let Nana Serwah treat her. Her mother-in-law too could not see her without bursting into tears, her pleas for forgiveness muffled by the sound. It was only Kofi Poku, the child who had pointed out the white man, the evil one, and so consigned him to burn, who saw the silent Akua and whispered "Crazy Woman." Crazy Woman. Wife of Crippled Man.

That night, Crippled Man turned Crazy Woman onto her back and entered her, forcefully at first, and then more timidly. She opened her eyes to see him working more slowly than he used to, using his arms to push off, push in, his sweat dripping slowly off the bridge of his nose to land on her forehead and trickle down to meet the floor.

When he finished, Asamoah turned away from her and wept. Their daughters were asleep across from them, thumbs in mouths. Akua turned too. Exhausted, she slept. And in the morning, when she realized that she had not dreamed of fire, she felt that she would be all right. And weeks later, when Nana Serwah snatched baby Yaw from between Akua's legs with one hand and sliced the cord with the other, when Akua heard his loud and mewling cry, she knew that her son would be all right too.

Slowly Akua began to speak more. She slept rarely, but when she did, she would wander. Some days she woke up at the door, other days curled up between her daughters. The sleep time was short, quick, so that as soon as she had moved she was awake again. She would return to her place beside Asamoah, stare at the straw and mud of the roof above them until the sun began to peek through the cracks. Rarely, Asamoah would catch her in her night wanderings while he himself was in midsleep. He'd reach for his machete, then remember his missing leg and give up. Defeated, Akua thought, by his wife and his own misery.

Akua was wary of the villagers, and the only people who brought her any joy were her children. Ama Serwah was speaking real words now, leaving behind the fast and frantic nonsense speech of her early twos. Now no one questioned Akua when she wanted to take long walks with her children. They didn't question her when she thought a stick was a snake or when she left the food in the fire to burn. When they whispered "Crazy Woman," they had to do it behind Nana Serwah's back, because if the woman heard them, she would give them a tongue-lashing that would sting almost as much as the real thing.

Akua would start each walk by asking her daughters where they wanted to go. She would sling baby Yaw in a wrapper around her back and wait for the girls to direct her. Often, they would say the same things. They wanted to walk by Yaa Asantewaa's palace. The place had been preserved in her honor, and the girls liked to stand outside the gate, singing the postwar songs. Their favorite one was:

Koo koo hin koo
Yaa Asantewaa ee!
Obaa basia
Ogyina apremo ano ee!
Waye be egyae
Na Wabo Mmoden

Sometimes Akua would sing along softly, rocking Yaw back and forth in time with the music as she praised the woman who fought before cannons.

The girls would need to rest often, and their favorite spot to do it was underneath trees. Akua would spend long afternoons with them, napping in the small slices of shade provided by impossibly large trees.

"I want to be like Yaa Asantewaa when I am an Old Lady!" Ama Serwah declared on one such day. The girls had grown too tired to keep walking, and the only tree nearby was the one where the white man had burned. The blackness of the charred bark seemed to crawl up from the roots and toward the lowest branches. Akua resisted stopping there at first, but the baby's weight made her feel like she was carrying ten handfuls of yam. Finally she stopped, lying flat on her back, the small mountain of her not-yet-deflated belly hiding her girls from sight as they lay at her feet, Yaw at her side.

"Will they sing songs about you, my dear?" Akua asked, and Ama Serwah burst into giggles.

"Yes!" she said. "They'll say, Look at the Old Lady, Ama Serwah. Isn't she strong, and pretty too?"

"And what about you, Abee?" Akua asked, shielding her eyes from the mighty midday sun.

"Yaa Asantewaa was Queen Mother, daughter of a Big Man," Abee said. "That is why she gets a song. Ama Serwah and I are only the daughters of a Crazy Woman raised by white men."

Akua could not move as readily as she once used to. She didn't know if this was because of the baby that had grown in her stomach, demanding her food and energy, or if it was a result of her week spent in exile on the floor of her hut. She wanted to spring to her feet, to look her daughter in the eye, but all she could manage was a gentle torque of her lower back, first to the left and then to the right, until she had gathered enough force to sit up, and see Abee, who was playing with the peeling bark.

"Who told you I am crazy?" she asked, and the child, who could not yet tell if she was on the verge of getting in trouble, shrugged. Akua wanted to be angrier, but she couldn't find the energy anywhere in her body. She needed to sleep. Really sleep. Two days before, she had forgotten the yams she dropped into the oil, forgotten them as her eyes slept. By the time Nana Serwah shook her awake, the yams had burned to black. Her mother-in-law had said nothing.

"Everyone says you are crazy," she said. "Sometimes Nana yells at them when they say it, but they still do."

Akua rested her head against a rock, and did not speak until she heard the girls' soft and sleepy breaths floating about her like tiny butterflies.

That night Akua took the children home. Asamoah was eating in the middle of the compound when they walked in.

"How are my girls?" he asked as his daughters rushed toward him to receive their hugs. Akua hung back, her eyes following her daughters as they made their way into the hut. It had been a hot day, and Ama Serwah was already peeling off her wrapper as she ran inside. It waved behind her like a flag.

"And how is my son?" Asamoah asked Akua's back, where Yaw hung cradled in fabric. Akua walked toward her husband so that he could touch the baby.

"Nyame willing, he is good," she said, and Asamoah grunted his assent.

"Come get food to eat," he said. He called for his mother and she appeared within seconds. Her old age had not diminished her swiftness, nor had it diminished her ear's ability to distinguish the needy cry of her oldest son. She came out and nodded at Akua. She had stopped weeping at the sight of her only days before.

"You must eat so that your milk is rich," she said, dipping her hands into the washing bowl so that she could begin the *fufu*.

Akua ate until her stomach grew. It looked like it could be punctured, like sweet milk would flow from her belly button, and that was all that she could picture as she cleaned her hands. Milk flowing below her feet like a river. She thanked Nana Serwah, and twisted herself up off the stool that she had been sitting on. She reached out her hands to Asamoah so that he too could hop up, grabbed the baby, and then went into their hut.

The girls were already sleeping. Akua envied them. The ease with which they entered the dream world. They sucked their thumbs still, unfazed by the pepper their grandmother applied every morning.

Beside her, Asamoah rolled once, twice. He too had been sleeping better than he had in the early days of his return. Sometimes he would reach for the ghost of his leg in the middle of the night, and then, finding his hands empty, he would cry softly. Akua never mentioned this to him when he awoke.

Now, flat-backed in their hut, Akua allowed herself to close her eyes. She imagined that she was lying on the sand of the beaches of Cape Coast. Sleep came for her like waves. First licking her curling toes, her swollen feet, her aching ankles. By the time it hit her mouth, nose, eyes, she was no longer afraid of it.

When she entered the dreamland she was on the same beach. She had been there only once, with the missionaries from the school. They had wanted to start a new school in a nearby village but found the townspeople unwelcoming. Akua had been mesmerized by the color of the water. It was a color she had never had a word for because nothing like it appeared in her world. No tree green, no sky blue, no stone or yam or clay could capture it. In dreamland, Akua walked to the edge of the rolling ocean. She dipped her toe into water so cool she felt she could taste it, like a breeze hitting the back of the throat. Then the breeze turned hot as the ocean caught fire. The breeze from the back of Akua's throat began to swirl, round and round, gathering speed until it could no longer be contained within Akua's mouth, and so she shot it out. And the spit-out breeze began to move the fiery ocean, dipping down into the depths to collect itself until spiraling wind and fiery ocean became the woman that Akua now felt she knew so well.

This time, the firewoman was not angry. She beckoned Akua out onto the ocean, and, though afraid, Akua took her first step. Her feet burned. When she lifted one up she could smell her own flesh wafting from the bottom. Still, she moved, following the firewoman until she led her to a place that looked like Akua's own hut. Now in the firewoman's arms were the two fire children that she had held the first time Akua dreamed of her. They were locked into either arm, head resting on either breast. Their cries were soundless, but Akua could see the sound, floating out of their mouths like puffs of smoke from the fetish man's favored pipe. Akua had the urge to hold them, and she reached out her hands to them. Her hands caught fire, but she touched them still. Soon she cradled them with her own burning hands, playing with the braided ropes of fire that made up their hair, their coal-black lips. She felt calm, happy even, that the firewoman had found her children again at last. And as she held them, the firewoman did not protest. She did not try to snatch them away. Instead, she watched, crying from joy. And her tears were the color of the ocean water in Fanteland, that not-green, not-blue color that Akua remembered from her youth. The color began to gather. Blue and more blue. Green and more green. Until the torrent of tears began to put out the fire in Akua's hands. Until the children began to disappear.

"Akua, the Crazy Woman! Akua, the Crazy Woman!"

She felt the sound of her name in the growing pit of her stomach, the weight like worry. Her eyes began to open, and she saw Edweso around her. She was being carried. Ten men at least, lifting her above their heads. She registered all of this before she registered the pain she was in, looked down to see her burned hands and feet.

The wailing women were behind the men. "Evil woman!" some of them cried. "Wicked one," said others.

Asamoah was behind the wailing women, hopping with his stick, trying to keep up.

Then they were tying her to the burning tree. Akua found her voice.

"Please, brothers. Tell me what is going on!"

Antwi Agyei, an elder, began to bellow. "She wants to know what is going on?" he cried to the men who had gathered.

They wrapped the rope around Akua's wrists. Her burns screamed and then she.

Antwi Agyei continued. "What kind of evil does not know itself?" he asked, and the crowd stomped its many feet against the hard earth.

They slung the rope around Akua's waist.

"We have known her as the Crazy Woman, and now she has shown herself to us. Wicked woman. Evil woman. Raised by white men, she can die like one too."

Asamoah pushed his way to the front of the crowd. "Please," he said.

"You're on her side? The woman who killed your children?" Antwi Agyei screamed. His anger was echoed in the yells of the crowd, in the stomping feet and beating hands, the undulating tongues.

Akua could not think. The woman who killed her children? The woman who killed her children? She was asleep. She must still be asleep.

Asamoah began to weep. He looked Akua in the eyes, and with her own she begged him questions.

"Yaw is still alive. I grabbed him before he died, but I could only carry one," he said, looking at Akua still, but speaking to the crowd. "My son will need her. You cannot take her from me."

He looked at Antwi Agyei and then to the people of Edweso. The ones who had been sleeping were now awake, had filtered in to join the others waiting to see the evil woman burn.

"Have I not lost enough flesh?" Asamoah asked them.

Before long, they cut Akua down. They left her and Asamoah to get themselves back to the hut. Nana Serwah and the doctor were tending to Yaw's wounds. The baby was screaming, the sound seeming to come from somewhere outside of himself. They would not tell her where they had put Abee and Ama Serwah. They would not say anything at all.

Willie

IT WAS A SATURDAY, FALL. Willie stood in the back of the church, holding her songbook open with one hand so that she could clap the beat against her leg with the other. Sister Bertha and Sister Dora were the soprano and alto leads, generous, big-bosomed women who believed the Rapture was coming any day now.

"Willie, what you need to do is let yourself sing, girl," Sister Bertha said. Willie had come in straight from cleaning a house. She'd rushed to remove her apron as she walked in, but, though she didn't know it, a smear of chicken grease still lined her forehead.

Carson was sitting in the audience. Bored, Willie figured. He kept asking her about school, but she couldn't let him go until baby Josephine got old enough to go. He narrowed his eyes at her when she told him, and sometimes she dreamed about sending him down south to stay with her sister, Hazel. Maybe she wouldn't mind a child with that much hate floating around in his eyes. But Willie knew she could never actually do it. In her letters down home, she wrote about how things were going well, how Robert was getting on nicely. Hazel would write back that she would come visit soon, but Willie knew she never would. The South was hers. She wanted no part of the North.

"Yes, what you need to do is let the Lord take that cross you carryin'," Sister Dora said.

Willie smiled. She hummed the alto line.

"You ready to go?" she asked Carson when she got offstage.

"Been ready," he said.

She and Carson left the church. It was a cold fall day, a crisp wind coming toward them from the river. There were a few cars on the street, and Willie saw a rich, mahogany-colored woman walk by in a raccoon coat that looked as soft as a cloud. On Lenox, every other marquee said that Duke Ellington would be playing there: Thursday, Friday, Saturday.

"Let's walk a little longer," Willie said, and Carson shrugged, but he took his hands out of his pockets and his step picked up, so she could see that she had finally said the right thing.

They stopped to let some cars pass, and Willie looked up to see six little children looking down at her from an apartment building window. It was a pyramid of children, the oldest, tallest, lining the back row, the youngest in front. Willie reached her hand up and waved, but then a woman snatched them away and closed the curtains. She and Carson crossed the street. It seemed like there were hundreds of people out in Harlem that day. Thousands, even. The sidewalks were sinking with the weight, some literally cracking beneath them. Willie saw a man the color of milky tea singing on the street. Beside him a tree-bark woman clapped her hands and bounced her head. Harlem felt like a big black band with so many heavy instruments, the city stage was collapsing.

They turned south on Seventh, past the barbershop that Willie swept from time to time to earn a few cents, past several bars and one ice cream parlor. Wille reached into her purse and felt around until her hand hit metal. She tossed a nickel to Carson, and the boy smiled at her for what seemed like the first time in years. The sweetness of the smile was bitter too, for it reminded Willie of the days of his endless crying. The days when there was no one in the world except for the two of them, and she was not enough for him. She was barely enough for herself. He raced in to buy a cone, and when he came back out with it, the two of them kept walking.

If Willie could have taken Seventh Avenue south all the way back down to Pratt City, she probably would have. Carson licked his ice cream cone delicately, sculpting that round shape with his own tongue. He would lick all the way around, and then look at it carefully, lick again. She couldn't remember the last time she had seen him so happy, and how easy it was to make him that way. All it took was a nickel and a walk. If they walked forever, maybe she would start to get happy too. She might be able to forget how she'd wound up in Harlem, away from Pratt City, away from home.

Willie wasn't coal black. She'd seen enough coal in her lifetime to know that for sure. But the day Robert Clifton came with his father to the union meeting to hear Willie sing, all she could think was that he was the whitest black boy she had ever seen, and because she thought that, her own skin had started to look to her more and more like the thing her father brought home from the mines, under his fingernails and dusting his clothes, every single day.

Willie had been singing the national anthem at union meetings for the past year and a half. Her father, H, was the union leader, so it hadn't been very hard to convince him to let her sing.

The day Robert came in, Willie was in the back room of the church, practicing her scales.

"You ready?" her daddy asked. Before Willie had begged to sing, there was no anthem sung at union meetings.

Willie nodded and went out to the sanctuary, where all the union members were waiting. She was young, but she already knew that she was the best singer in Pratt City, maybe even in all of Birmingham. Everyone, women and children alike, came to the meetings just to hear that old world-weary voice come out of her ten-year-old body.

"Please stand for the anthem," H said to the crowd, and they did. Willie's father teared up the first time she'd sung it. Afterward, Willie could hear a man say, "Look at old Two-Shovel. Getting soft, ain't he?"

Now Willie sang the anthem, and the crowd watched, beaming. She imagined that the sound came from a cave at the very bottom of her gut, that like her father and all the men in front of her, she was a miner reaching deep down inside of her to pull something valuable out. When she finished, everyone in the room stood and clapped and whistled, and that was how she knew she had reached the rock at the bottom of the cave. Afterward, the miners went on with their meeting and Willie sat in her father's lap, bored, wishing she could sing again.

"Willie, you sang awfully pretty tonight," a man said after the meeting ended. Willie was standing with her little sister, Hazel, outside of the church, watching the people walk home while H closed up. Willie didn't recognize the man. He was new, an ex-con who'd worked the railroads before coming to work as a free man in the mines. "I'd like you to meet my son, Robert," the man said. "He's shy, but boy does he love to hear you sing."

Robert stepped out from behind his father.

"You go on and play for a bit," the man said, pushing Robert forward a little before walking on home.

His father was the color of coffee, but Robert was the color of cream. Willie was used to seeing white and black together in Pratt City, but she'd never seen both things in one family, both in one person.

"You got a nice voice," Robert said. He looked at the ground as he spoke, and kicked up a bit of dust. "I been coming to hear you sing."

"Thanks," Willie said. Finally, Robert looked at her and smiled, relieved, it seemed, to have spoken. Willie was startled by his eyes.

"Why your eyes look like that?" Willie asked while Hazel hid behind her leg, eyeing Robert from behind the bend of Willie's knee.

"Like what?" Robert asked.

Willie searched for the word, but realized there wasn't one word to describe it. His eyes looked like a lot of things. Like the clear puddles that stood over the mud that she and Hazel liked to jump in, or like the shimmering body of a golden ant she had once seen carrying a blade of grass across a hill. His eyes were changing before hers, and she didn't know how to tell him this, so instead she just shrugged.

"You a white man?" Hazel asked, and Willie pushed her.

"No. Mama say we got a lot of white in our blood, though. Sometimes it take a while to show up."

"That ain't right," Hazel said, shaking her head.

"Yo daddy's old as dirt. That ain't right neither," Robert said, and before Willie knew what she was doing, she pushed him. He stumbled, fell down onto his butt, and looked up at Willie with surprise in his brown, green, gold eyes, but she didn't care. Her daddy was one of the best miners Birmingham had ever seen. He was the light of Willie's life, and she was his. He told her all the time how he waited and waited and waited to have her, and when she'd come, he'd been so happy his big coal heart had melted.

Robert stood back up and dusted himself off.

"Ooh," Hazel said, turning toward Willie, never missing an opportunity to shame her. "I'm telling Mama on you!"

"No," Robert said. "That's all right." He looked at Willie. "That's all right."

The push had broken some kind of barrier between them, and from that day on, Robert and Willie were as close as any two people could be. By the time they hit sixteen they were dating, and by eighteen they were married, and by twenty they had a child. The people of Pratt City spoke about them in one breath, their names one name: RobertnWillie.

The month after Carson was born, Willie's father died, and the month after that her mother followed. Miners weren't meant to live long. Willie had friends whose fathers had died when those friends were still swimming in their mothers' bellies, but knowing this didn't lessen the hurt.

She was inconsolable those first few days. She didn't want to look at Carson, didn't want to hold him. Robert would take her up in his arms at night, kissing her never-ending tears while the baby slept. "I love you, Willie," he'd whisper, and somehow that love hurt too, made her cry even harder, because she didn't want to believe that anything good could still be in the world when her parents had left it.

Willie sang lead in the funeral procession, the weeping and wailing of all the mourners carrying sound down into the very mines themselves. She had never known sadness like that before, nor had she known the fullness of hundreds of people gathering to send her parents off. When she started the song, her voice quivered. It shook something in her.

"I shall wear a crown," Willie sang, her voice booming, bouncing from the bottom of the pit and coming back up to meet them all as they walked around the mines. Soon they passed the old potter's field where hundreds of nameless, faceless men and boys were buried, and Willie was glad that, at least, her father had died free. At least that.

"I shall wear a crown," Willie sang again, holding Carson in her arms. His mewling cry was her accompaniment, his heartbeat her metronome. As she sang, she saw the notes float out of her mouth like little butterflies, carrying some of her sadness away, and she knew, finally, that she would survive it.

Soon Pratt City started to feel like a speck of dust in Willie's eye. She couldn't be free of it. She could tell that Robert was itching to leave too. He had always been a little delicate for coal mining. At least that's what the bosses thought every time he got a mind to go ask them for a job, which was about once a year since his thirteenth birthday. Instead, he worked as a clerk in the Pratt City store.

Then, after Carson was born, the store suddenly didn't seem like enough for Robert. He could spend whole weeks complaining about it.

"There ain't no honor in it," Robert said to Willie one night. She was seated stomach to stomach with little Carson while he tried to snatch the light that was reflecting off her earrings. "There's honor in mining," Robert said.

Willie had always thought that her husband would die in the mines if ever he got a chance to go down. Her father had stopped working in the mines years and years before he died. He was twice the size of Robert, ten times as strong. Yet, still, he almost never stopped coughing, and sometimes when he coughed a string of black mucus would escape his mouth, his face would contort, and his eyes bulge out, so that it looked to Willie as though some invisible man were behind him, hands wrapped around the large trunk of his thick neck, choking him. Though she loved Robert more than she had ever thought it possible to love, when she looked at him she did not see a man who could handle hands around his neck. She never told him this.

Robert began to pace the room. The clock on the wall was five minutes behind, and the click of the second hand sounded to Willie like a man clapping off beat at a church revival. Awful, but sure.

"We should move. Go north, somewhere I can learn a new trade. Ain't nothing in Pratt City for us now that your folks are gone."

"New York," Willie said, just as soon as she had thought it. "Harlem." The word hit her like a memory. Though she had never been there, she could sense its presence in her life. A premonition. A forward memory.

"New York, huh?" Robert said with a smile. He took Carson into his arms and the boy cried out, startled, missing the light.

"You could find some kinda work. I could sing."

"You gon' sing, huh?" He dangled his finger in front of Carson's eyes, and they followed him. This way, then that. "Whatchu think about that, Sonny? Mama singing?" Robert brought the dangling finger down to Carson's soft belly and tickled. The baby screamed with laughter.

"I think he likes that idea, Mama," Robert said, laughing too.

Everyone knew someone who was headed north, and everyone knew someone who was already there. Willie and Robert knew Joe Turner back when he was just Lil Joe, Joecy's smart boy in Pratt City. Now he worked as a schoolteacher in Harlem. He took them into his place on West 134th Street.

For as long as she lived, Willie would never forget the feeling of being in Harlem for the first time. Pratt City was a mining town and everything about it was focused on what lay beneath the ground. Harlem was about the sky. The buildings were taller than any Willie had ever seen before, and there were more of them, tense, shoulder to shoulder. The first inhale of Harlem air was clean, no coal dust traveling in through the nose to hit the back of the throat, to taste. Just breathing felt exciting.

"First thing we gotta do is get me somewhere to sing, Lil Joe. I heard these ladies on the street corner, and I know I'm better than them. I just know it." They had brought in the last of their three suitcases and were finally settling into the small apartment. Joe hadn't been able to afford it on his own, and said that he was all too happy to have old friends to share it with.

Joe laughed. "You should hope you sing better than a girl on the street corner, Willie. How else you gon' make it out the street and into a building?"

Robert was holding Carson, bouncing him a little bit so that the boy wouldn't fuss. "That ain't the first thing we gotta do. First thing we gotta do is set me up with a job. I'm the man, remember?"

"Oh, you the man, all right," Willie said, winking, and Joe rolled his eyes.

"Don't y'all bring no more babies into this house, now," he said.

That night, and for many nights after, Willie and Robert and Carson all slept on the same mattress, laid out in the tiny living room on the fourth floor of the tall brick building. On the ceiling above the bed there was a large brown spot, and on that first night they lay there, Willie thought that even that spot looked beautiful.

The building that Lil Joe lived in was full of nothing but black folks, nearly all of them newly arrived from Louisiana, Mississippi, Texas. On the way in, Willie heard the distinct drawl of an Alabamian. The man had been trying to push a wide couch through a slim door. There was a similar-sounding voice on the other side of the door, giving directions: more to the left, a little to the right.

The next morning, Willie and Robert left Carson with Lil Joe so they could walk around Harlem, maybe look to see if any *For Hire* signs were up in their neighborhood. They walked around for hours, people-watching and talking, taking in everything that was different about Harlem, and everything that was the same.

Once they rounded the block past an ice cream parlor, they noticed a hiring sign on a store door, and decided to go in so that Robert could talk to someone. As they walked in, Willie tripped on the lip of the door stoop, and Robert caught her in his arms. He helped her get steady, and smiled at her once she was on her feet, kissing her cheek quickly. Once they were inside, Willie's eyes met those of the store clerk, and she felt a cold wind travel that sight line, from his eyes to hers, then all the way down to the coalpit of her stomach.

"Excuse me, sir," Robert said. "I saw the sign outside there."

"You married to a black woman?" the store clerk said, his eyes never leaving Willie's.

Robert looked at Willie.

Robert spoke softly. "I worked in a store before. Down south."

"No job here," the man said.

"I'm saying I have experience with—"

"No job here," the man repeated, more gruffly this time.

"Let's go, Robert," Willie said. She was already halfway out the door by the time the man had opened his mouth a second time.

They didn't speak for two blocks. They passed a restaurant with a sign hanging up, but Willie didn't have to look at Robert to know they would keep walking past it. Before long they were back at Lil Joe's place.

"Y'all back already?" Joe asked when they entered. Carson was asleep on the mattress, his little body curled up just so.

"Willie just wanted to check on the baby. She wanted to give you a chance to rest. Ain't that right, Willie?"

Willie could feel Joe looking at her as she answered, "Yeah, that's right."

Robert turned on his heel and was out of the door in a flash.

Willie sat down next to the baby. She watched him sleep. She wondered if she could watch him sleep all day, and so she tried. But after a while a strange and helpless panic set in, about what she didn't know. That he wasn't really breathing. That he didn't recognize his own hunger and therefore would not whine for her to feed him. That he wouldn't know her from any other woman in this new, big city. She woke him up just to hear him cry. And it was only then, when the cry set in, soft at first and then a shrieking, full-bellied sound, that she was finally able to relax.

"They thought he was white, Joe," Willie said. She could feel him watching her as she watched Carson.

Joe nodded. "I see," he said soberly, and then he walked away and let her be.

Willie waited anxiously for Robert to return. She wondered, for the first time really, if leaving Pratt City had been a mistake. She thought about Hazel, whom she hadn't yet heard from since leaving, and a wave of missing hit her, desperate and sad. She had another forward memory. This time of loneliness. She could feel it approaching, a condition she would have to learn to live with.

Robert came back to the apartment. He had been to the barber, his hair cut close. He had bought new clothes, with the last of their savings no doubt, Willie thought, and the clothes he had been wearing when he left were nowhere in sight. He sat down on the bed next to Willie, rubbed Carson's back. She looked at him. He didn't look like himself.

"You spent the money?" Willie asked. Robert wasn't meeting her eyes, and she couldn't remember the last time Robert had done that. Even on that first day she'd gone to play with him, even as she pushed him, even as he fell, Robert had always kept his eyes steadily, almost ravenously, on hers. His eyes were the first things she'd questioned about him, and the first thing she'd loved.

"I ain't gon' be my father, Willie," Robert said, his eyes still on Carson. "I ain't gon' be the kind of man who can only do one thing. I'm gonna make a life for us. I know I can do it."

He looked at her finally. He brushed her cheek with his hand, then cupped the back of her neck. "We here now, Willie," he pleaded. "Let's be here."

What "being here" meant for Willie: Every morning, she and Robert would wake up. She would get Carson ready to take downstairs to an old woman named Bess who watched all the building's babies for a small fee. Robert would shave, comb down his hair, button his shirt. Then the two of them would walk out into Harlem to look for work, Robert in his fancy clothes and Willie in her plain ones.

Being here meant they no longer walked together on the sidewalk. Robert always walked a little ahead of her, and they never touched. She never called his name anymore. Even if she was falling into the street or a man was robbing her or a car was coming at her, she knew not to call his name. She'd done it once, and Robert had turned, and everyone had stared.

At first, they both looked for jobs in Harlem. One store had even hired Robert, but after a week there was a misunderstanding when a white customer had leaned in close to Robert to ask him how he could resist taking any one of the Negro women who frequented the store for himself. And Robert came home that night crying to Willie that it could have been her the man was talking about, and so he'd quit.

The next day, they both went searching again. This time they only walked so far south before splitting off, and Willie lost Robert to the rest of Manhattan. He looked so white now, it only took a few seconds for her to lose him completely, just one white face among the many, all bustling up and down the sidewalks. After two weeks in Manhattan, Robert found a job.

It took Willie three more months to find work, but by December she was a housekeeper for the Morrises, a wealthy black family who lived on the southern edge of Harlem. The family had not yet resigned themselves to their own blackness, so they crept as close to the white folks as the city would allow. They could go no further, their skin too dark to get an apartment just one street down.

During the day, Willie took care of the Morrises' son. She fed him and bathed him and laid him down for his nap. Then she cleaned the apartment from top to bottom, making sure to wipe under the candelabra because Mrs. Morris always checked. In the early evening she would begin cooking. The Morrises had been in New York since before the Great Migration, but they ate as though the South was a place in their kitchen instead of one that was miles and miles away. Mrs. Morris usually came home first. She worked as a seamstress, and her hands were often pricked and bleeding. Once she got home, Willie would leave for her auditions.

She was too dark to sing at the Jazzing. That's what they told her the night she'd come in ready to audition. A very slender and tall man held a paper bag up to her cheek.

"Too dark," he said.

Wille shook her head. "But I can sing, see." She opened her mouth and took a deep breath, filling up the balloon of her belly, but then the man put two fingers to her, pushed the air out.

"Too dark," he repeated. "Jazzing's only for the light girls."

"I saw a man dark as midnight walk in with a trombone."

"I said girls, honey. If you were a man, maybe."

If she were Robert, Willie thought. Robert could have any job he wanted, but she knew he was too scared to try. Scared he'd be found out or scared that he didn't have enough education. The other night he'd told her that a man had asked him why he spoke "that way," and he'd become scared to talk. He would not tell her exactly what he did for a living, but he came back home to her smelling like the sea and meat, and he made more money in a month than she had ever seen in her entire life.

Robert was cautious, but she was wild. It had always been that way. The first night he had lain with her, he'd been so nervous that his penis had rested against his left leg, a log on the river of his quivering thigh.

"Your daddy's gon' kill me," he'd said. They were sixteen, their parents at a union meeting.

"I'm not thinkin' 'bout my daddy right now, Robert," she'd said, trying to stand the log. She'd put each of his fingers into her mouth one by one and had bitten the tips, watching him all the while. She'd eased him into her and moved on top of him until he was begging her: to stop, to not stop, to quicken, to slow. When he closed his eyes, she'd bidden him to open them, to look at her. She liked to be the star of the show.

It was what she wanted now too, now that she was still thinking about Robert. How she could put his skin to good use, be less cautious if she were him. If she could, she would put her voice in his body, in his skin. She would stand on the stage of the Jazzing and listen to the glowing words of the crowd rush back to her, like the memories of her singing on her parents' table often would. Boy, can she blow. You ain't never lied.

"Listen, we got a job cleaning the place at night if you want it," the slender, tall man said, rousing Willie from her thoughts before they could turn dark. "The pay's okay. Might get you somewhere a little later."

She took the job on the spot, and when she got home that night she'd told Robert that the Morrises needed her on night duty. She couldn't tell if he believed her, but he'd nodded. That night, they'd slept with Carson between them. He was starting to say a few words. The other day, when Willie had picked him up from Bess's apartment to take him up to Joe's, she'd heard her son call the old woman Mama, and a terrible, immovable lump formed in her throat as she clutched him to her body and took him up the stairs.

"The pay's okay," she said to Robert then, pulling Carson's thumb from his mouth. He started crying. He shouted at her, "No!"

"Hey now, Sonny," Robert said. "Don't speak to Mama that way." Carson put his thumb back into his mouth and stared at his father. "We don't need the money," he said. "We're doing all right, Willie. We can get our own place soon, even. You don't need to work."

"Where would we live?" Willie snapped. She hadn't meant to sound so mean. The idea was appealing to her: her own apartment, more time to spend with Carson. But she knew that she wasn't meant for that life. She knew that that life wasn't meant for them.

"There are places, Willie."

"What place? What world do you think we live in, Robert? It's a wonder you make it out these doors and out into *this* world without somebody knocking you down for sleeping with the nigg—"

"Stop!" Robert said. Willie had never heard that much force in his voice before. "Don't do that."

He rolled over to face the wall, and Willie stayed on her back, staring at the ceiling above them. The large brown spot on the ceiling was starting to look soft to her, as though the whole thing could come crashing down on them at any moment.

"I haven't changed, Willie," Robert said to the wall.

"No, but you ain't the same neither," she replied.

They didn't speak for the rest of the night. Between them, Carson began to snore, louder and louder, like a rumbling from his stomach was escaping through his nose. It sounded like the background music for the falling ceiling, and it started to terrify Willie. If the boy was still a baby, if they were still in Pratt City, she would have wakened him. Here, in Harlem, she could not move. She had to lie there, still, with the rumbling, the falling, the terror.

Cleaning the Jazzing was not too difficult. Willie would drop Carson off at Bess's before dinnertime, and then she would head over to 644 Lenox Avenue.

It was the same work that she did for the Morrises, but different too. The Jazzing audience was whites only. The performers who showed up on the stage every night were like the slender man said: tall, tan, and terrific. Meaning, as far as Willie could see, five foot five, light-skinned, and young. Willie would take out the trash, sweep, wipe the floors, and watch the men as they watched the people onstage. It was all so strange to her.

In one of the shows, an actor had pretended to be lost in an African jungle. He was wearing a grass skirt and had marks painted on his head and arms. Instead of speaking, he would grunt. Periodically, he would flex his pecs and pound his chest. He picked up one of the tall, tan, and terrific girls and draped her over his shoulder like she was a rag doll. The audience had laughed and laughed.

Once, Willie saw a show through the shield of her work that was meant to be a portrayal of the South. The three male actors, the darkest Willie had ever seen in the club, picked cotton onstage. Then one of the actors started complaining. He said that the sun was too hot, the cotton too white. He sat on the edge of the stage, lazily swinging his legs back and forth, back and forth.

The other two went forward and stood with their hands on his shoulders. They started singing a song that Willie had never heard before, one about how grateful they should all be to have such kind masters to take care of them. By the time they finished their singing, they were all standing up again, back to picking cotton.

This wasn't the South that Willie knew. It wasn't the South her parents had known either, but she could tell from the voices of the men in the audience that none of them had ever stepped foot in that South. All they wanted was to laugh and drink and whistle at the girls. It made Willie almost glad she was the one cleaning the stage instead of singing on it.

Willie had been working there for two months. She and Robert hadn't been doing very well since the night she asked him where they would live. Most nights, Robert didn't come home. When she got back from the club, just hours before sunrise, she would find Carson sleeping alone on the mattress. Joe had been picking him up from Bess's once he finished teaching and putting him to bed every night. Willie would crawl in next to Carson and wait, wide-eyed, for the sound of Robert's boots coming down the hall, the *clop clop clop* that meant she would have her husband that night. If she did hear it, if he did come, she would close her eyes quick, and the two of them would play the game of make-believe, acting like the people onstage at the club did. Robert's role was to slip in quietly beside her, and hers was to not question, to let him believe that she still believed in him, in them.

Willie went outside the club to put the trash away, and when she came back in, her boss started walking toward her. He looked annoyed, but Willie had never seen him look any other way. He'd been in the war, and he walked with a staggering limp that he liked to say prevented him from getting a more respectable job. The only thing that seemed to make him happy was stepping outside to lean against the ragged brick of the building and smoke cigarette after cigarette after cigarette.

"Someone vomited in the men's room," he said, heading out.

Willie just nodded. This happened at least once a week, and she knew the routine without having to be told. She grabbed the bucket and the mop and made her way over. She knocked on the door once, then twice. There was no answer.

"I'm coming in," she said forcefully. She had discovered weeks before that it was better to enter rooms forcefully than it was to do so timidly, since drunk men had a tendency to lose their hearing.

The man in the bathroom certainly had lost his. He was hunched over, his face in the sink, mumbling to himself.

"Oh, I'm sorry," Willie said. As she turned to leave, the man looked up, and caught her eye in the mirror.

"Willie?" he asked.

She knew his voice immediately, but she didn't turn. She didn't answer him. All she could think about was the fact that she had not recognized him.

There was a time, when they were still just sweethearts dating and at the beginning of their marriage, when Willie thought she knew Robert better than she knew herself. This was more than a matter of knowing what his favorite color was, or knowing what he wanted for dinner without him having to tell her. It was a matter of knowing the things that he could not yet let himself know. Like that he was not the kind of man who could handle invisible hands around his neck. That Carson's birth had changed him, but not for the better. It had made him deeply afraid of himself, always questioning his choices, never measuring up to a standard of his own making, a standard that was upheld in his own father's generous love, a love that had made a way for him and his mother, even when the cost had been great. That Willie could recognize these things in Robert, but be unable to recognize his hunched back, his hanging head, frightened her.

Two white men walked into the room, not noticing Willie. One wore a gray suit, and the other a blue one. Willie held her breath.

"You still in here, Rob? The girls are about to get onstage," the blue suit said.

Robert sent Willie a desperate look, and the gray suit, who hadn't yet spoken, followed his gaze to her body. He looked her up and down, a smile slowly spreading across his face.

Robert shook his head. "All right, boys. Let's go," he said. He tried to smile, but the corners of his lips tugged down almost immediately.

"Looks like Robert's already got him a girl," the gray suit said.

"She's just in here to clean up," Robert said. Willie saw that his eyes had started to plead, and it was not until then that she knew she was in trouble.

"Maybe we don't even need to go back out," the gray suit said. His shoulders relaxed, his body leaned against the wall.

The blue suit started grinning too.

Willie clutched the mop. "I should go. My boss will be looking for me," she said. She tried to change her voice as Robert had. She tried to sound like them.

The gray suit eased the mop away. "You still have cleaning to do," he said. He caressed her face. His hands started to move down her body, but before it could reach her breast she spit in his face.

"Willie, don't!"

The two suits turned to look at Robert, the gray suit wiping the spit from his face. "You know her?" the blue suit asked, but the gray suit was two steps ahead of him. Willie could see him collecting all the clues in his mind: the dusk of Robert's skin, the thick voice, the nights spent away from home. He sent Robert a withering look. "She your woman?" he asked.

Robert's eyes had started to fill up. His skin was already sallow from his being sick, and he looked like he might be sick again any minute. He nodded.

"Well, why don't you come over here and give her a kiss?" the gray suit asked. He had already unzipped his pants with his left hand. With his right hand, he stroked his penis. "Don't worry, I won't touch her," he said.

And he kept his word. Robert did all the work that night while the blue suit guarded the door. It wasn't more than a few tear-stained kisses and carefully placed hands. Before the gray suit could ask for Robert to enter her, he came, a shuddering, breathy thing. Then, immediately after, he grew bored with his game.

"Don't bother coming to work tomorrow, Rob," he said as he and the blue suit made their way out.

Willie felt a small breeze come in from the closing door. It raised the hairs on her skin. Her whole body was stiff like a piece of wood. Robert reached for her, and it took her a second to realize that she still controlled her body. He was already touching her by the time she moved away.

"I'll leave tonight," he said. He was crying again, his brown, green, gold eyes shimmering behind the wet.

He left the room before Willie could tell him he was already gone.

*

Carson was still licking his ice cream. He held it in one hand. His other hand held Willie's, and the feel of her son's skin on hers was enough to bring tears to her eyes. She wanted to keep walking. All the way to Midtown if need be. She couldn't remember the last time she'd seen her son so happy.

After that day with Robert, Joe offered to marry her, but Willie couldn't bear the thought of it. She took Carson and left in the middle of the night, found a place the next morning far enough away that she figured she wouldn't see anyone she knew anymore. But she couldn't leave Harlem, and that little corner of the great city had started to feel like it was pressing in on her. Every face was Robert's and none was his.

Carson wouldn't stop crying. It seemed like for whole weeks at a time, the boy just wouldn't stop crying. In the new apartment Willie had no Bess to leave him with, and so she left him by himself on days she went to work, making sure to shut the windows and lock the doors and hide the sharp things. At night she would find that he had put himself to sleep, the mattress soaked with his ever-present tears.

She worked odd jobs, mostly cleaning, though every once in a while she would still go out for an audition. The auditions would all end the same way. She would get onstage, feeling confident. Her mouth would open, but no sound would come from it, and soon she would be crying, and begging the person in front of her for forgiveness. One auditioner told her she had better make her way to a church if forgiveness was what she wanted.

And so she did. Willie hadn't been to church since leaving Pratt City, but now it seemed she couldn't get enough of it. Every Sunday she would drag Carson, who had just turned five years old, out with her to the Baptist church on West 128th between Lenox and Seventh. It was there she met Eli.

He was only a once-in-a-while churchgoer, but the congregation still called him Brother Eli because they thought he had a fruit of the spirit in him. Which fruit, Willie didn't know. She'd been going for about a month, sitting in the very last row with Carson on her lap even though he was too old to be a lap baby and his weight hurt her legs. Eli walked in with a bag of apples at his side. He leaned against the back door.

The preacher said, "The fire of God is fallen from Heaven, and hath burned up the sheep, and the servants, and consumed them; and I only am escaped alone to tell thee."

"Amen," Eli said.

Willie looked up at him, then returned her gaze to the preacher, who was saying, "And, behold, there came a great wind from the wilderness, and smote the four corners of the house, and it fell upon the young men, and they are dead; and I only am escaped alone to tell thee."

"Bless God," Eli said.

The bag crinkled, and Willie looked up to see Eli pulling out an apple. He winked at her as he took a bite, and she quickly snapped her head back as the preacher said, "The Lord gave, and the Lord hath taken away; blessed be the name of the Lord."

"Amen," Willie murmured. Carson started to fuss, and she bounced him on her leg a bit, but that only made him squirm more. Eli gave him an apple, and he held it in his hands, opening his mouth very wide to take just a tiny bite.

"Thank you," Willie said.

Eli tipped his head toward the door. "Take a walk with me," he whispered. She ignored him, helping Carson hold the apple so that it would not drop to the floor.

"Take a walk with me," Eli said, louder this time. An usher shushed him, and Willie worried that he would say it again, but louder, and so she got up from her seat and left with him.

Eli held Carson's hand as they walked. In Harlem, Lenox Avenue was impossible to avoid. It was where all the dirty, ugly, righteous, and beautiful things were. The Jazzing was still there, and as they passed it, Willie shuddered.

"What's wrong?" Eli asked.

"Just caught a chill is all," Willie said.

It seemed to Willie that they had walked all of Harlem. She couldn't remember the last time she'd walked so much, and she couldn't believe that they had gone so far without Carson crying. As they walked, her son kept working on his apple, and he seemed so content that Willie wanted to hug Eli for giving her that little bit of peace.

"What do you do?" Willie asked Eli once they had finally found a place to sit.

"I'm a poet," he said.

"You write anything good?" Willie asked.

Eli smiled at her and took the apple core Carson was dangling from his hands. "No, but I write a lot of bad."

Willie laughed. "What's your favorite poem?" she asked. He scooted a bit closer to her on the bench, and she felt her breath catch, something it had not done for a man since the day she first kissed Robert.

"The Bible's the best poetry there is," Eli said.

"Well, then why don't I see you in church more often? Seems like you should be studyin' the Bible."

This time Eli laughed. "A poet's got to spend more time livin' than he does studyin'," he said.

Willie found out that Eli did a lot of what he called "livin'." In the beginning she called it that too. It was a rush, being with him. He took her all around New York City to places she never would have dreamed of going before him. He wanted to eat everything, try everything. He didn't care that they didn't have any money. When she got pregnant, his adventurous spirit only seemed to grow. It was the opposite of Robert. Carson's birth had made him want to set roots, whereas Josephine's birth made Eli want to grow wings.

The baby was barely out of her stomach before Eli flew. The first time, it was for three days.

He came home to her smelling of booze. "How's my baby doin'," he said. He wiggled his fingers in front of Josephine's face, and she followed them with wide eyes.

"Where you been, Eli?" Willie said. She was trying not to sound angry, though anger was all she felt. She remembered how she had stayed quiet on the nights that Robert used to come home after being gone awhile, and she didn't intend to make the same mistake twice.

"Aw, you mad at me, Willie?" Eli asked.

Carson tugged on his pants leg. "You got any apples, Eli?" he asked. He was starting to look like Robert, and Willie couldn't stand it. She'd just cut his hair that morning, and it seemed the more hair he lost, the more Robert started to peek through. Carson had kicked and screamed and cried the whole time she cut. She'd spanked him for it, which had quieted him, but then he had given her a mean look, and she was not sure which was worse. Seemed like her son was starting to hate her as much as she was fighting not to hate him.

"Sure, I got an apple for you, Sonny," Eli said, fishing one from his pockets.

"Don't call him that," Willie hissed through her teeth, remembering again the man she was trying to forget.

Eli's face fell a little bit. He wiped at his eyes. "I'm sorry, Willie. Okay? I'm sorry."

"My name's Sonny!" Carson shouted. He bit into the apple. "I like to be Sonny!" he said, bits of juice squirting from his mouth.

Josephine started crying, and Willie grabbed her up and rocked her. "See what you done started?" she said, and Eli just kept wiping his eyes.

The kids grew older. Sometimes Willie would see Eli every day for a month. That's when the poems were flowing and the money wasn't too bad. Willie would come home from cleaning this or that house, and find scraps and stacks of papers all around the apartment. Some of the papers would have just one word on them like "Flight" or "Jazz." Others would have whole poems. Willie found one that had her name on the top, and it had made her think that perhaps Eli was there to stay.

But then he would go. The money would stop. At first, Willie took baby Josephine to work with her, but she lost two jobs that way, so she started leaving her with Carson, whom she couldn't ever seem to keep in school. They were evicted three times in six months, though by that time everyone she knew was getting evicted, living with twenty strangers in a single apartment, sharing a single bed. Each time they got evicted, she would move what little they had no more than a block down. Willie would tell the new landlord that her husband was a famous poet, knowing full well that he was neither husband nor famous. One time, when he'd come home for just a night, she had yelled at him. "You can't eat a poem, Eli," she said, and she didn't see him again for nearly three months.

Then, when Josephine was four and Carson ten, Willie joined the choir at church. She had been wanting to do it since the first day she heard them sing, but stages, even those that were altars, made her remember the Jazzing. Then she'd met Eli and stopped going to church. Then Eli would leave and she'd start going again. Finally, she went to a rehearsal, but she would stand in the back, quietly, moving her lips but letting nothing escape them.

Willie and Carson were nearing the limits of Harlem. Carson crunched on his cone and looked up at her skeptically, and she just smiled back reassuringly, but she knew, and he knew, that they would have to turn soon. When the colors started changing, they would have to turn.

But they didn't. Now there were so many white people around them that Willie started to feel scared. She took Carson's hand in hers. The days of Pratt City mixing were so far behind her, she almost felt as though she had dreamed them. Here, now, she tried to keep her body small, squaring her shoulders in, keeping her head down. She could feel Carson doing the same thing. They walked two blocks like this, past the place where the black sea of Harlem turned into the white rush of the rest of the world, and then they stopped at an intersection.

There were so many people walking around them that Willie was surprised she noticed at all, but she did.

It was Robert. He was bent down on one knee, tying the shoe of a little boy of maybe three or four. A woman was holding the little boy's hand on the other side of him. The woman had finger-curled blond hair cut short so that the longest strands just barely licked the tip of her chin. Robert stood back up. He kissed the woman, the little boy smushed between them for only a moment. Then Robert looked up and across the intersection. Willie's eyes met his.

The cars passed, and Carson tugged on the end of Willie's shirt. "We gon' cross, Mama?" he asked. "The cars are gone. We can pass," he said.

Across the street, the blond woman's lips were moving. She touched Robert's shoulder.

Willie smiled at Robert, and it wasn't until that smile that she realized she forgave him. She felt like the smile had opened a valve, like the pressure of anger and sadness and confusion and loss was shooting out of her, into the sky and away. Away.

Robert smiled back at her, but soon he turned to talk to the blond woman, and the three of them continued on in a different direction.

Carson followed Willie's gaze to where Robert had been. "Mama?" he said again.

Willie shook her head. "No, Carson. We can't go any further. I think it's time we go back."

That Sunday, the church was packed. Eli's book of poems was set to be published in the spring, and he was so happy that he had stayed put longer than Willie could remember him ever staying before. He sat in a middle pew with Josephine in his lap and Carson at his side. The pastor went up to the pulpit and said, "Church, ain't God great?"

And the church said, "Amen."

He said, "Church, ain't God great?"

And the church said, "Amen."

He said, "Church, I tell you God done brought me to the other side today. Church, I put down my cross and I ain't never gon' pick it back up."

"Glory, hallelujah," came the shout.

Willie was standing in the back of the choir holding the songbook when her hands began to tremble. She thought about H coming home every night from the mines with his pickax and his shovel. He would set them down on the porch and take his boots off before he came in because Ethe would give him an earful if he tracked coal dust into the house she kept so clean. He used to say the best part of his day was when he could put that shovel down and walk inside to see his girls waiting for him.

Willie looked into the pews. Eli was bouncing Josephine on his knees and the little girl was smiling her gummy smile. Willie's hands trembled still, and in a moment of complete quiet, she dropped the songbook down on the stage with a great thud. And everyone in the sanctuary, the congregants and pastor, Sisters Dora and Bertha and the whole choir, turned to look at her. She stepped forward, trembling still, and she sang.

Yaw

THE HARMATTAN WAS COMING IN. Yaw could see dust sweeping up from the hard clay and being carried all the way to his classroom window on the second floor of the school in Takoradi where he had been teaching for the last ten years. He wondered how bad the winds would be this year. When he was five, still living in Edweso, the winds were so strong that they snapped tree trunks. The dust was so thick that when he held out his fingers, they disappeared before him.

Yaw shuffled his papers. He had come to his classroom on the weekend before the start of the second term to think, perhaps write. He stared at the title of his book, *Let the Africans Own Africa*. He had written two hundred pages and thrown out nearly as many. Now even the title offended him. He put it away, knowing that if he didn't he would do something rash. Open his window, maybe, let the winds carry the pages away.

"What you need is a wife, Mr. Agyekum. Not that silly book."

Yaw was eating dinner at Edward Boahen's house for the sixth night that week. On Sunday, he would eat there for the seventh. Edward's wife liked to complain that she was married to two men, but Yaw complimented her cooking so often that he knew she would continue to welcome him.

"Why do I need a wife when I have you?" Yaw asked.

"Eh, careful now," Edward said, pausing his steady food-shoveling for the first time since his wife put his bowl in front of him.

Edward was the maths teacher at the same Roman Catholic school in Takoradi where Yaw taught history. The two had met at Achimota School in Accra, and Yaw cherished their friendship more than he cherished most things.

"Independence is coming," Yaw said, and Mrs. Boahen sighed one of her deep-chested sighs.

"If it's coming, let it come. I am tired of hearing you talk about it," she said. "What good is independence to you if you don't have some-one to cook your dinner!" She rushed off into the small stone house to collect more water for them, and Yaw laughed. He could picture the caption they would put under her name in the revolutionist papers: "Typical Gold Coast woman, more concerned with dinner than with freedom."

"What you should be doing is saving your money to go to England or America for more schooling. You can't lead a revolution from behind your teacher's desk," Edward said.

"I'm too old to go to America now. Too old for revolution, too. Besides, if we go to the white man for school, we will just learn the way the white man wants us to learn. We will come back and build the country the white man wants us to build. One that continues to serve them. We will never be free."

Edward shook his head. "You are too rigid, Yaw. We have to start somewhere."

"So let us start with ourselves." This was what his book was about, but he didn't say anything more, for he already knew the argument that would come from it. Both men had been born around the time the Asante were absorbed into the British Colony. Both had fathers who had fought in the various wars for freedom. They wanted the same things, but had different ideas of how to get them. The truth was, Yaw didn't think he could lead a revolution from anywhere. No one would read his book, even if he did finish it.

Mrs. Boahen came back with a large bowl of water, and the two men began to rinse their hands in it.

"Mr. Agyekum, I know a nice girl. She is still in her childbearing years so there is no need to worry—"

"I should be going," Yaw said, cutting her off. He knew it was rude.

After all, Mrs. Boahen was not wrong. It was not her place to cook for him, but he didn't feel that it was her place to lecture him either. He shook hands with Edward, and with Mrs. Boahen too, then made his way back to his own small house on the school grounds.

As he walked the mile length of the school grounds, he saw the young boys playing football. They were agile boys, in full control of their bodies. They had a boldness to their movements that Yaw had never possessed when he was their age. He stood and watched them for a moment, and soon the ball came flying toward him. He caught it, and was grateful for that small bit of athleticism.

They waved at him, and sent a new student over to fetch the ball. The boy walked up, smiling at first, but as he got closer, the smile fell from his face and a look of fear replaced it. He stood in front of Yaw, saying nothing.

"Do you want your ball?" Yaw asked, and the boy nodded quickly, staring still.

Yaw threw the ball at him, more forcefully than he meant to, and the young boy caught it and ran.

"What's wrong with his face?" Yaw heard him ask as he approached the others, but before they could answer, Yaw was already walking away.

It was Yaw's tenth year of teaching at the school. Every year was the same. The new crop of schoolboys would begin to flower the school grounds, their hair freshly cut, their school uniforms freshly pressed. They would bring with them their timetables, their books, what little money their parents or villages had been able to collect for them. They would ask each other whom they had for this or that subject, and when one said Mr. Agyekum, another would tell the story that his elder brother or cousin had heard about the history teacher.

On the first day of the second term, Yaw watched the new students amble in. They were always well-behaved children, these boys, having been handpicked for their brightness or their wealth in order to attend school, learn the white man's book. In the walkways, on the way to his classroom, they would be so boisterous that it was possible to imagine them as they must have been in their villages, wrestling and singing and dancing before they knew what a book was, before their families knew that a book was a thing a child could want—need, even. Then, once they reached the classroom, once the textbooks were placed on their small wooden desks, they would grow quiet, spellbound. They were so quiet on that first day that Yaw could hear the baby birds on his window ledge, begging to be fed.

"What does the board say?" Yaw asked. He taught Form 1 students, fourteen- and fifteen-year-olds mostly, who had already learned to read and write in English in their lower-level classes. When Yaw had first gotten the post, he had argued with the headmaster that he should be able to teach in the boys' regional tongues, but the headmaster had laughed at him. Yaw knew it was a foolish hope. There were too many languages to even try.

Yaw watched them. He could always tell which boy would raise his hand first by the way he pushed forward in his seat and moved his eyes from left to right to see if anyone else would challenge his desire to speak first. This time, a very small boy named Peter raised his hand.

"It says, 'History is Storytelling,'" Peter answered. He smiled, the pent-up excitement releasing.

"'History is Storytelling,'" Yaw repeated. He walked down the aisles between the rows of seats, making sure to look each boy in the eye. Once he finished walking and stood in the back of the room, where the boys would have to crane their necks in order to see him, he asked, "Who would like to tell the story of how I got my scar?"

The students began to squirm, their limbs growing limp and wobbly. They looked at each other, coughed, looked away.

"Don't be shy," Yaw said, smiling now, nodding encouragingly. "Peter?" he asked. The boy, who only seconds before had been so happy to speak, began to plead with his eyes. The first day with a new class was always Yaw's favorite.

"Mr. Agyekum, sah?" Peter said.

"What story have you heard? About my scar?" Yaw asked, smiling still, hoping, now, to ease some of the child's growing fear.

Peter cleared his throat and looked at the ground. "They say you were born of fire," he started. "That this is why you are so smart. Because you were lit by fire."

"Anyone else?"

Timidly, a boy named Edem raised his hand. "They say your mother was fighting evil spirits from Asamando."

Then William: "I heard your father was so sad by the Asante loss that he cursed the gods, and the gods took vengeance."

Another, named Thomas: "I heard you did it to yourself, so that you would have something to talk about on the first day of class."

All of the boys laughed, and Yaw had to stifle his own amusement. Word of his lesson had gotten around, he knew. The older boys told some of the younger ones what to expect from him.

Still he continued, making his way back to the front of the room to look at his students, the bright boys of the uncertain Gold Coast, learning the white book from a scarred man.

"Whose story is correct?" Yaw asked them. They looked around at the boys who had spoken, as though trying to establish their allegiance by holding a gaze, casting a vote by sending a glance.

Finally, once the murmuring subsided, Peter raised his hand. "Mr. Agyekum, we cannot know which story is correct." He looked at the rest of the class, slowly understanding. "We cannot know which story is correct because we were not there."

Yaw nodded. He sat in his chair at the front of the room and looked at all the young men. "This is the problem of history. We cannot know that which we were not there to see and hear and experience for ourselves. We must rely upon the words of others. Those who were there in the olden days, they told stories to the children so that the children would know, so that the children could tell stories to their children. And so on, and so on. But now we come upon the problem of conflicting stories. Kojo Nyarko says that when the warriors came to his village their coats were red, but Kwame Adu says that they were blue. Whose story do we believe, then?"

The boys were silent. They stared at him, waiting.

"We believe the one who has the power. He is the one who gets to write the story. So when you study history, you must always ask yourself, Whose story am I missing? Whose voice was suppressed so that this voice could come forth? Once you have figured that out, you must find that story too. From there, you begin to get a clearer, yet still imperfect, picture."

The room was still. The birds on the ledge were still waiting for their food to come, still crying for their mother. Yaw gave the boys some time to think about what he had said, to respond, but when no one did, he continued. "Let us open our textbooks to page—"

One of the students was coughing. Yaw looked up to see William with his hand raised. He nodded at the boy to speak.

"But, Mr. Agyekum, sah, you still have not told us the story of how you got your scar."

Yaw could feel all the boys directing their gazes toward him, but kept his head down. He resisted the urge to put his hand up to the left side of his face, feel the raised and leathery skin there with its many ripples and lines that, when he was still just a child, reminded Yaw of a map. He had wanted that map to lead him out of Edweso, and in some ways it had. His village could hardly look at him and had collected money to send him to school so he could learn, but also, Yaw suspected, so they would not have to be reminded of their shame. In other ways, the map of Yaw's scarred skin had led him nowhere. He had not married. He would not lead. Edweso had come with him.

Yaw did not touch his scar. Instead, he set his book down carefully and reminded himself to smile. He said, "I was only a baby. All I know is what I've heard."

What he'd heard: That the Crazy Woman of Edweso, the wanderer, his mother, Akua, had set the hut on fire while he, still a baby, and his sisters slept. That his father, Asamoah, the Crippled Man, had only been able to save one, the son. That Crippled Man had kept Crazy Woman from burning. That Crazy Woman and Crippled Man had been exiled to the outskirts of town. That the town had collected money to send the scarred son to school, when he was still so young he had yet to forget the taste of his mother's breast. That Crippled Man had died while the scarred son was still in school. That Crazy Woman lived on.

Yaw had not been to Edweso since the day he left for school. For many years, his mother sent letters, each written in the hand of whom-ever she'd convinced to write for her that day. The letters begged Yaw to come see her, but he never responded, and so, eventually, she stopped. When he was still in school, Yaw spent his leaves with Edward's fam-ily in Oseim. They took him in as though he were one of their own, and Yaw loved them as though he belonged to them. An unapologetic, unquestioning love like that of the stray dog that follows the man home from work every evening, happy, simply, to be allowed to walk nearby. It was in Oseim that Yaw had met the first girl he would ever be inter-ested in. In school, he had loved the Romantic poets best, and he had spent nights in Oseim copying Wordsworth and Blake onto tree leaves that he scattered around the spot near the river where she went to fetch water.

He spent a whole week doing this, knowing that the words of white Englishmen would mean nothing to her, that she could not read them. Knowing that she would have to come to him to find out what the leaves said. He would think about it every night. The girl bringing her bundle of leaves to him so that he might recite "A Dream" or "A Night Thought" to her.

Instead, she went to Edward. It was Edward who read the lines to her, and afterward, it was Edward who told her that the leaves were Yaw's doing.

"He likes you, you know," Edward said. "Maybe he will one day ask you to marry him."

But the girl shook her head, clucked her tongue in distaste. "If I marry him, my children will be ugly," she declared.

That night, lying next to Edward in his room, Yaw listened as his best friend told him that he had explained to the girl that you could not inherit a scar.

Now, nearing his fiftieth birthday, Yaw no longer knew if he believed this was true.

The semester passed. In June, Kwame Nkrumah, a political leader from Nkroful, started the Convention People's Party and Edward joined soon thereafter. "Independence is coming, my brother," he was fond of saying to Yaw on the nights when Yaw still joined him and his wife for dinner. This happened less and less. Mrs. Boahen was expecting her fifth child and the pregnancy was difficult. So difficult that the Boahens stopped entertaining. First just the other teachers and town friends that they had acquired, but then Yaw, too, noticed that even his welcome began to wear.

And so, Yaw got a house girl. He had been resistant to having other people in his house for as long as he could remember. He could cook a few dishes for himself competently enough. He could fetch his own water and wash his own clothes. He did not keep his house as neat as he had been forced to keep his room in school, but none of this bothered him. He preferred the clutter and the plain meals if it meant he would not have to have another person in his house, looking at him.

"That's ridiculous!" Edward said. "You're a teacher. People stare at you all day."

But for Yaw that was different. At the front of the classroom he was not himself. He was a performer in the tradition of village dancers and storytellers. At home, he was who he really was. Shy and lonely, angry and embarrassed. He did not want anyone to see him there.

Edward examined all of the candidates himself, and in the end Yaw ended up with Esther, an Ahanta from right there in Takoradi.

Esther was a plain girl. Maybe even ugly. Her eyes were too large for her head and her head too large for her body. On the first day of work, Yaw showed her to her room at the back of the house and told her that he spent most of his time writing. He asked her not to disturb him and then went back out to sit at his desk.

The book was getting unruly. The Gold Coast independence movement's political leaders, the Big Six, had all come back from school in America and England, and as far as Yaw could tell they were all like Edward, patient but forceful, confident that independence would indeed come. Yaw had been reading more and more about the black people of America's movement toward freedom, and he was attracted to the rage that lit each sentence of their books on fire. He wanted that from his book. An academic rage. All he could seem to muster was a long-winded whine.

"Ess-cuse me, sah."

Yaw looked up from his book. Esther was standing in front of him with the long handmade broom she had insisted on bringing with her, even though Yaw told her that his house had many brooms.

"You don't have to speak in English," Yaw said.

"Yes, sah, but my sis-tah say you ah teach-ah, so I must speak English."

She looked terrified, her shoulders hunched and her hands gripping the broom so tightly that Yaw could see the area around her knuckles begin to stretch and redden. He wished he could cover his face, put the young woman at ease.

"You understand Twi?" Yaw said in his mother tongue, and Esther nodded. "Then speak freely. We hear enough English as it is."

It was like he had opened a gate. Her body began to slip into an easy stance, and Yaw realized that it was not his scar that had terrified her, but rather the problem of language, a marker of her education, her class, compared with his. She had been terrified that for the teacher of the white book, she would have to speak the white tongue. Now, released from English, Esther smiled more brightly than Yaw had seen anyone smile in ages. He could see the large, proud gap that stood like a doorway between her two front teeth, and he found himself training his gaze through that door as though he could see all the way down into her throat, her gut, the home of her very soul.

"Sir, I have finished cleaning the bedroom. You have a lot of books in there. Did you know? Do you read all of those books? Can you read English? Sir, where do you keep the palm oil? I could not find it in the kitchen. It is a nice kitchen. What will you have for dinner? Should I go to market? What are you writing?"

Did she breathe? If she had, Yaw didn't hear it. He shuffled the pages of his book and set it aside as he thought about what to say next.

"Make whatever you want for dinner. I don't care what."

She nodded, not dissatisfied, it seemed, with the fact that he had answered only one of her questions. "I'll make goat pepper soup," she said, her eyes cast downward, moving this way and that, as though searching the floor for any thoughts she might have dropped there. "I will go to market today." She looked up at him. "Would you like to go to market with me?"

Suddenly Yaw was angry or nervous. He couldn't quite tell which, and so he chose to respond with anger. "Why should I go to market with you? Don't you work for me?" he shouted.

Her mouth closed, the portal to her soul hidden. She cocked her head to the side and stared at him as though it was just then occurring to her that he had a face, that his face had a scar. She studied it for one second more, and then smiled again. "I thought you might want a break from your writing. My sister said teachers are very serious because they do all their work in their minds and so sometimes they have to be reminded that they must use their bodies. Will you not use your body if you walk to the market?"

Now it was Yaw's turn to smile. Esther laughed, her whole wide mouth open, and suddenly Yaw had the strange urge to reach in and pull something of that happiness out for himself so that he might keep it with him always.

They went to the market. Fat women with babies at their breasts sold soup, corn, yams, meat. Men and young boys stood bartering with each other. Some sold food, others sold carvings and wooden drums. Yaw stopped by the stand of a boy who looked to be about thirteen who was using a slim knife to carve symbols into a drum. The boy's father stood careful watch beside him. Yaw recognized the man from last year's Kundum. He was one of the best drummers Yaw had ever seen, and as the man stared at his son, Yaw could see that he wanted the boy to be even better.

"You like to drum?" Esther asked.

Yaw didn't realize she had been watching him. It was so rare that he had to be concerned with other people. He hadn't been angry after all. Just nervous.

"Me? No, no. I never learned how."

She nodded. She led the freshly purchased, roped goat behind her, and at times while they walked, the animal grew obstinate, digging its hooves into the ground and nudging its head against the air, its horns reflecting light. She tugged it forcefully, and it bleated, perhaps at her, though perhaps it would have done so anyway.

Yaw realized that he should say something. He cleared his throat and looked at her, but his words stuck. She smiled at him.

"I make a very good goat pepper soup," she said.

"Is that right?"

"Yes, so good you would think your mother made it. Where is your mother?" she asked in her breathless way.

The goat stood still, screamed. Esther wrapped the rope once more around her wrist and tugged. It occurred to Yaw that he should offer to walk the goat for her, but he didn't.

"My mother lives in Edweso. I haven't seen her since the day I turned six." He paused. "She did this to me." He pointed to the scar, angled his body so that she could see it more clearly.

Esther stopped walking and so Yaw stopped too. She looked at him, and for a second he worried that she would reach out and try to touch him, but she didn't.

Instead she said, "You're very angry."

"Yes," he said. It was something he rarely admitted to himself, let alone to anyone else. The longer he looked at himself in a mirror, the longer he lived alone, the longer the country he loved stayed under colonial rule, the angrier he became. And the nebulous, mysterious object of his anger was his mother, a woman whose face he could barely remember, but a face reflected in his own scar.

"Anger doesn't suit you," Esther said. She gave the goat one more good tug, and Yaw listened to it bleat as the two of them walked ahead of him.

He was in love with her. Five years passed before he realized it, though perhaps he knew on that first day. It was summer, and the insistent fog of heat was upon them, so ever-present it felt like a low hum, a heat you could hear. Yaw didn't have to teach summer term, and so he had hours, whole days, to sit and read and write. Instead, he watched Esther clean from his spot at the desk. He pretended to be annoyed when she rolled off her list of endless questions, but since that first day, he always answered them all, each and every one. When it was not raining, he would sit outside under the shade of a big, bushy mango tree while she drew water from the well. She carried it back to the house in two buckets, and the swollen muscles of her arms would flex, and the sheen of sweat would appear on them, and when she passed him she would smile, the gap so lovely it made him want to cry.

Everything made him want to cry. He could see the differences between them as long ravines, impossible to cross. He was old; she was young. He was educated; she was not. He was scarred; she was whole. Each difference split the ravine wider and wider still. There was no way.

And so, he didn't speak. In the evenings, she would ask him what he wanted for dinner, what he was working on, whether he had heard any updates about the independence movement, whether he was still considering traveling for more education.

He said what needed to be said, nothing more.

"The *banku* is too sticky today," she said while they ate one night. In the beginning, she had insisted on taking her meals separately from him, saying that it wouldn't be proper for them to eat together, which was true enough. But the thought of her alone in her room with nowhere for all of her questions to go seemed to him to be the worse option. So now, this and every night, she ate across from him at his small wooden table.

"It's good," he said. He smiled. He wished he were a beautiful man, with skin as smooth as clay. But he was not the kind of man who could win a woman just with his presence. He would have to do something.

"No, I've made much better in the past. It's okay. You don't have to eat it if you don't like it. I'll make something else for you. Would you like soup?"

She was starting to pick up his plate, so he held it down.

"This is good," he said again, more forcefully. He wondered what he should do to win her. For the past five years she had been drawing him more and more out of himself. Asking him questions about his schooling, about Edward, about the past.

"Would you like to go to Edweso with me?" Yaw asked. "To visit my mother?" As soon as he said it, he regretted it. For years, Esther had been nudging him to go, but he either deflected or ignored her. Now, his love had made him desperate. He didn't even know if the Crazy Woman of Edweso was still alive.

Esther looked uncertain. "You want me to go?"

"In case I need someone to cook for me as I travel," he said hurriedly, trying to cover his tracks.

She considered this for a moment, and then she nodded. For the first time since he had met her, she had no further questions.

*

There were 206 kilometers between Takoradi and Edweso. Yaw knew because he could feel each kilometer as though it were a stone lodged in his throat. Two hundred and six stones collected in his mouth, so that he could not speak. Even when Esther asked him a question, like how much longer were they to travel, how would he explain her presence to the townspeople, what would he say to his mother when he saw her, the stones blocked his words from passing. Eventually, Esther too grew silent.

He remembered so little of Edweso, so he could not say if things had changed. When they reached the town, they were greeted first by a sweltering heat, the sun's rays stretched out like a cat after a nap. There were only a few people standing about the square that day, but the ones who were there stared freely, shocked at the sight either of the car or of the strangers.

"What are they looking at?" Esther whispered miserably. She was worried about herself, that people would think it improper for them to be traveling together, unmarried. She had not said this to him yet, but he could see it in the way she lowered her eyes and walked behind him.

Before long, a little boy, no older than four, holding the long train of his mother's wrapper, pointed at Yaw with his tiny index finger. "Look, Mama, his face! His face!"

The boy's father, who stood on the other side of him, snatched his hand away. "Stop that nonsense!" he said, but then he looked more closely along the line the boy's finger had drawn.

He approached Yaw and Esther where they stood, uncertain, holding one bag each. "Yaw?" he asked.

Yaw dropped his bag to the ground and walked closer to the man.

"Yes?" he said. "I'm afraid I don't remember you." He held his hand above his brows to shield his eyes from the sun, but was soon extending it again to shake the man's hand.

"They call me Kofi Poku," the man said, shaking back. "I was about ten when you left. This is my wife, Gifty, and my son Henry."

Yaw shook hands all around and then turned toward Esther. "This is my . . . This is Esther," he said. And Esther too shook hands all around.

"You must be here to see Crazy Woman," Kofi Poku said before realizing his mistake. He covered his mouth. "I'm so sorry. I mean Ma Akua."

Yaw could tell from the way his eyes searched and his mouth slowed that Kofi Poku had not had to call his mother by her name in years. Perhaps ever. As far as Yaw knew, the Crazy Woman of Edweso could have earned her title well before his birth. "Please, don't worry," Yaw said. "We are here to see my mother, yes."

Just then, Kofi Poku's wife leaned in to his ear to whisper something, and the man's eyebrows lifted, face brightening. When he spoke, it was as though the idea had been his all along.

"You and your wife must be very tired from your journey. Please, my wife and I would like you to stay with us. We will make you dinner."

Yaw started to shake his head, but Kofi Poku waved his hand, as though trying to counteract Yaw's shake with his own. "I insist. Besides, your mother keeps odd hours. It would not be good for you to go to her today. Wait until tomorrow evening. We will send someone to tell her you are coming."

How could they refuse? Yaw and Esther had planned on going straight to Akua's house to stay, but instead they walked the short mile's distance from the town square to the Poku house. When they got there, Kofi Poku's other children, three daughters and one son, were beginning dinner. One of the girls, the tallest and most slender, sat before a great big mortar. The boy held the pestle, which was nearly twice his height. He held it straight up and then would send it crashing down just as the girl's hand finished turning the *fufu* in the mortar, barely escaping the impact.

"Hello, my children," Kofi Poku called, and all of the children stopped what they were doing and stood, so that they could greet their parents, but when they saw Yaw their voices hushed and their eyes widened.

The one who looked like the youngest girl, with two puffs of hair on either side of her head, pulled on her brother's pants leg. "Crazy Woman's son," she whispered. Yet still, all could hear, and Yaw knew for certain now that his story had become legend in his hometown.

Everyone stood there, embarrassed for a minute, and then Esther with her large and muscular arms snatched the pestle from the older boy and quickly struck the *fufu* in the mortar before anyone had time to think or react. The ball of *fufu* flattened, and the *fufu* stick fell with a thud against the clay earth.

"Enough!" Esther shouted once they had all turned to stare at her. "Has this man not suffered enough that he should come home to this?" she asked.

"Please excuse my child," Mrs. Poku said, using her voice to speak instead of her husband's for the first time since they'd met her. "It's just that they have heard the stories. They will not make the mistake again." She turned, allowed her gaze to rest on each of the five children, even the toddler at her feet, and quickly, without any need for further explanation, they understood.

Kofi Poku cleared his throat, and motioned for the two of them to follow him to their seats. As they did, Yaw whispered, "Thank you," and Esther shrugged. "Let them think that I am the crazy one," Esther said.

They sat down to their meal. The kids served them, frightened but kind. Kofi Poku and his wife told them what to expect from Yaw's mother.

"She lives with only a house girl in that place your father built for her on the edge of town. She rarely goes out anymore, though sometimes you can see her outside, tending to her garden. She has a lovely garden. My wife often goes there to admire the flowers that grow there."

"Does she speak when you see her?" Yaw asked Mrs. Poku.

The woman shook her head. "No, but she has always been kind to me. She even gives me some flowers to take home. I put them in the girls' hair before we go to church, and I think it will bring them good marriages."

"Don't worry," Kofi Poku said. "I'm sure she will know you. Her heart will know you." His wife and Esther both nodded, and Yaw looked away.

It was dark in the courtyard, but the heat had not lessened, only transformed, buzzing with mosquitoes and humming with gnats.

Yaw and Esther finished their food. They said thank you. They were taken to their room, where Esther insisted on the floor while Yaw got the mattress, a tough, springy thing that fought his back. Like that, and there, they slept.

They spent the morning preparing, walking around Edweso, and eating many times. They had been told that Yaw's mother rarely slept and seemed to prefer evenings to mornings. And so they bided their time. Esther had left Takoradi only once in her life, and Yaw loved seeing the wonder in her eyes as they took in the strangeness of this new town.

Everyone thought they were married. Yaw did not correct them, and, to his delight, Esther did not correct them either, though Yaw wondered if this was more a factor of her politeness than her desire. He was too afraid to ask.

Soon, the sky began to darken and with each new shade, Yaw's stomach began to tighten. Esther kept glancing at him carefully, taking in his face as though it held instructions for how she herself should feel.

"Don't be afraid," she said.

Since they'd met five years before, Esther had been the one to encourage his homecoming. She said it had something to do with forgiveness, but Yaw wasn't certain that he believed in forgiveness. He heard the word most on the few days he went to the white man's church with Edward and Mrs. Boahen and sometimes with Esther, and so it had begun to seem to him like a word the white men brought with them when they first came to Africa. A trick their Christians had learned and spoke loudly and freely about to the people of the Gold Coast. Forgiveness, they shouted, all the while committing their wrongs. When he was younger, Yaw wondered why they did not preach that the people should avoid wrongdoing altogether. But the older he got, the better he understood. Forgiveness was an act done after the fact, a piece of the bad deed's future. And if you point the people's eye to the future, they might not see what is being done to hurt them in the present.

When it was finally evening, Kofi Poku led Yaw and Esther to Yaw's mother's house on the outskirts of town. Yaw knew it immediately from the lush things that grew in her garden. Colors that Yaw had never seen before bloomed off of long green stalks that rustled from the wind or the small creatures that moved beneath them.

"This is where I leave you," Kofi Poku said. They had not even reached the door yet. For any other family, in this and many other towns, it would have been considered rude for a townsperson to be so close to a person's house and not greet the master of the house, but Yaw could see the discomfort in the man's face, and he waved to him and thanked him again while he made his way off.

The door to the house was open, but still Yaw knocked twice, Esther standing behind him.

"Hello?" a confused voice called. A woman who looked older than Yaw, carrying a clay bowl, rounded the corner. When she saw Yaw, saw his scar, she gasped, and the bowl fell to the ground, shattering, scattering pieces of red clay from the door all the way into the garden. Tiny pieces of clay that they would never find, that would be absorbed into that earth from which they came.

The woman was shouting. "We thank God for all of his mercies! We thank him that he is alive. Our God, he does not sleep-oh!" She danced around the room. "Old Lady, God has brought you your son! Old Lady, God has brought you your son so you do not have to go to Asamando without seeing him. Old Woman, come and see!" she yelled.

Behind him, Yaw could hear Esther clapping her hands together in her own mini praise. He didn't turn, but he knew she was smiling brightly, and the warmth of that thought emboldened him to step a bit further into the room.

"Does she not hear me?" the woman mumbled to herself, turning sharply toward the bedroom.

Yaw kept moving, at first following the woman, but then continuing straight until he reached the living room. His mother sat in the corner.

"So you have returned home at last," she said, smiling.

If he had not already known that the woman in this house was his mother, he would not have known by looking at her. Yaw was fifty-five, which meant she would be seventy-six, but she seemed younger. Her eyes had the unburdened look of the young, and her smile was generous, yet wise. When she stood up her back was straight, her bones not yet hunched from the weight of each year. When she walked toward him, her limbs were fluid, not stiff, the joints never halting. And when she touched him, when she took his hands in her own, her scarred and ruined hands, when she rubbed the backs of his hands with her crooked thumbs, he felt how soft her own burns were, how very, very soft.

"The son has come home at last. The dreams, they do not fail to come true. They do not fail."

She continued to hold his hands. In the entryway, the servant woman cleared her throat. Yaw turned to find her and Esther standing there, grinning at them.

"Old Woman, we will make dinner!" the woman shouted. Yaw wondered if her voice was always this loud or if the volume was for him.

"Please, don't go to any trouble," he begged.

"Eh? The son comes home after all these years, does the mother not kill a goat?" She sucked her teeth on the way out of the door.

"And you?" Yaw asked Esther.

"Who will boil the yam while the woman kills the goat?" she asked, her voice mischievous.

Yaw watched them go, and for the first time he grew nervous. Suddenly, he felt something he had not felt in a long, long time.

"What are you doing?" he shouted, for his mother had put her hand on his scar, running her fingers along the ruined skin that he alone had touched for nearly half a century.

She continued, undeterred by the anger in his voice. She took her own burned fingers from the lost eyebrow to the raised cheek to the scarred chin. She touched all of it, and only once she had finished did Yaw begin to weep.

She pulled him down to the ground with her, pulled his head to her bosom, and began to chant, softly, "My son-o! My son! My son-o! My son!"

The two stayed like this for a long while, and after Yaw had cried more tears than he had ever cried before, after his mother had finished calling his name out into the world, he peeled himself away so that he could look at her.

"Tell me the story of how I got my scar," he said.

She sighed. "How can I tell you the story of your scar without first telling you the story of my dreams? And how do I talk about my dreams without talking about my family? Our family?"

Yaw waited. His mother got off the ground and motioned for him to do the same. She pointed to a chair on one side of the room, and she took the chair on the other. She looked at the wall behind his head.

"Before you were born, I began to have bad dreams. The dreams started out the same—a woman made of fire would visit me. In her arms, she carried her two fire children, but then the children would disappear and the woman would turn her anger toward me.

"Even before the dreams began, I was not well. My mother died at the hands of the Missionary at the school in Kumasi. Do you know it?"

Yaw shook his head. He had never heard this before, and even if he had, he would have been too young to remember it.

"The Missionary raised me. My only friend was a fetish priest. I was always a sad girl because I did not know that there was any other way to be. When I married your father, I thought I could be happy, and when I had your sisters . . ."

Here, her voice caught, but she lifted her shoulders, began again.

"When I had your sisters, I thought I was happy, but then I saw a white man burn in the square in Edweso and the dreams began. Then the war began and the dreams grew worse. Your father came back without a leg, and the dreams grew worse. I had you, and the sadness did not stop. I tried to fight sleep, but I am human and sleep is not. We were not equally matched. In my sleep one night, I set the hut on fire. They say your father could only save one, you. But that is not entirely true. He also saved me from the townspeople. For many years I wished that he had not.

"They only let me see you so that I could feed you. Then they sent you away, and would not tell me where. I have lived here in this house with Kukua since that day."

As if summoned, Kukua, the old servant, came in with wine. She served Yaw first and then his mother, but the woman refused. Kukua left as quietly as she had entered.

Yaw drank from the wine as though it were water. When the cup lay empty at his feet, he turned his attention back to his mother. She took a deep breath and began again.

"The dreams didn't stop. Not after the fire, not even to this day. I started to get to know the firewoman. Sometimes, as on the night of the fire, she would take me to the ocean in Cape Coast. Sometimes she would take me to a cocoa farm. Sometimes to Kumasi. I didn't know why. I wanted answers, so I went back to the missionary school to ask about my mother's family. The Missionary told me that he had burned all of my mother's belongings, but he lied. He had kept one thing for himself."

His mother pulled Effia's necklace from her neck then and held it out to Yaw. It glowed black in her hand. He touched it, felt the smoothness of it.

"I took the necklace to the fetish man's son so that I could make offerings to our ancestors so that they might stop punishing me. Kukua was maybe fourteen at this time. When we did the ritual, the fetish man's son stopped. He dropped the necklace very suddenly and said, 'Do you know there is evil in your lineage?' I thought he was talking about me, the things I had done, and so I nodded. But then he said, 'This thing you are carrying, it does not belong to you.' When I told him about my dreams, he said that the firewoman was an ancestor come back to visit me. He said that the black stone had belonged to her and that was why it grew hot in his hand. He said that if I listened to her, she would tell me where I came from. He said I should be glad that I was chosen."

Yaw grew angry again. Why should she be glad she was chosen if she was now a ruined woman and he a ruined man? How could she be content with this life?

His mother must have sensed his anger. Old woman that she was, she went to him and knelt before him. Yaw knew she was crying by the wetness of his feet.

She looked up at him and said, "I can't forgive myself for what I've done. I won't. But when I listened to the firewoman's stories I began to see that the fetish priest was right. There is evil in our lineage. There are people who have done wrong because they could not see the result of the wrong. They did not have these burned hands as warning."

She held her hands out to him, and he looked at them carefully. He recognized her skin in his own.

"What I know now, my son: Evil begets evil. It grows. It transmutes, so that sometimes you cannot see that the evil in the world began as the evil in your own home. I'm sorry you have suffered. I'm sorry for the way your suffering casts a shadow over your life, over the woman you have yet to marry, the children you have yet to have."

Yaw looked at her surprised, but she simply smiled. "When someone does wrong, whether it is you or me, whether it is mother or father, whether it is the Gold Coast man or the white man, it is like a fisherman casting a net into the water. He keeps only the one or two fish that he needs to feed himself and puts the rest in the water, thinking that their lives will go back to normal. No one forgets that they were once captive, even if they are now free. But still, Yaw, you have to let yourself be free."

Yaw took his mother up from the ground and into his arms while she kept chanting, "Be free, Yaw. Be free." He hugged her, surprised by how light she was.

Soon Esther and Kukua came in carrying pot after pot of food. They served Yaw and his mother well into the night. They ate until the sun came up.

Sonny

JAIL GAVE SONNY time to read. He used the hours before his mother bailed him out to thumb through *The Souls of Black Folk*. He'd read it four times already, and he still wasn't tired of it. It reaffirmed for him the purpose of his being there, on an iron bench, in an iron cell. Every time he felt the futility of his work for the NAACP, he'd finger the well-worn pages of that book, and it would strengthen his resolve.

"Ain't you tired of this?" Willie said when she stormed through the doors of the police station. She was holding her tattered coat in one hand and a broom in the other. She had been cleaning houses on the Upper East Side for as long as Sonny could remember, and she didn't trust the brooms white people kept around and so she always brought her own, carrying it from subway station to subway station to street to house. When he was a teenager, that broom used to embarrass Sonny no end, seeing his mother lug it around like it was a cross. If she held it on the days she called his name while he played with his friends on the basketball court, he would deny her like Peter.

"Carson!" she'd yell, and as he answered her with silence, he would think that he was justified in not responding, for he'd long since gone by "Sonny." He'd let her call out "Carson" a few times more before he finally said, "What?" He knew he'd pay for it when he got back home. He knew his mother would bring out her Bible and start pray-shouting over him, but he did it anyway.

Sonny took up *The Souls of Black Folk* while the officer opened the door. He nodded at the other men who'd been arrested during the march and brushed past his mother.

"How many times they gotta throw you in jail, huh?" Willie called after him, but Sonny kept walking.

It wasn't like he hadn't asked himself the same thing a hundred times or more. How many times could he pick himself up off the dirty floor of a jail cell? How many hours could he spend marching? How many bruises could he collect from the police? How many letters to the mayor, governor, president could he send? How many more days would it take to get something to change? And when it changed, would it change? Would America be any different, or would it be mostly the same?

For Sonny, the problem with America wasn't segregation but the fact that you could not, in fact, segregate. Sonny had been trying to get away from white people for as long as he could remember, but, big as this country was, there was nowhere to go. Not even Harlem, where white folks owned just about everything an eye could see or a hand could touch. What Sonny wanted was Africa. Marcus Garvey had been onto something. Liberia and Sierra Leone, those two efforts had been a good thing, in theory at least. The problem was that in practice things didn't work the way they did in theory. The practice of segregation still meant that Sonny had to see white people sitting at the front of every bus he took, that he got called "boy" by every other snot-nosed white kid in sight. The practice of segregation meant that he had to feel his separateness as inequality, and *that* was what he could not take.

"Carson, I'm talking to you!" Willie shouted. Sonny knew he was never too old for a knock on his head, and so he turned to face his mother.

"What?"

She gave him a hard look, and he gave it right back. For the first few years of his life, it had just been him and Willie. Try as hard as he might, Sonny could never conjure up a picture of his father, and he still hadn't forgiven his mother for that.

"You's a hardheaded fool," Willie said, pushing past him now. "You need to stop spendin' time in jail and start spendin' it with your kids. That's what you need to do."

She muttered the last part so that Sonny could barely hear her, but he would have known what she said even if she hadn't said it. He was mad at her because he didn't have a father, and she was mad at him because he'd become as absent as his own.

Sonny was on the housing team at the NAACP. Once a week, he and the other men and women on the team went around to all the different neighborhoods in Harlem to ask people how they were faring.

"We got so many roaches and rats, we got to keep the toothbrushes in the fridge," one mother said.

It was the last Friday of the month, and Sonny was still nursing Thursday night's headache. "Mm-hmm," he said to the woman, sweeping a hand over his brow, as though he could mop up a bit of the pain that pulsed there. While she talked, Sonny pretended to take notes in his notepad, but it was the same thing he'd heard at the last place, and the one before that. In fact, Sonny could have not gone to a single apartment and he still would have known what the tenants would say. He and Willie and his sister, Josephine, had lived in conditions like these and much worse.

He could remember with clarity a time when his mother's second husband, Eli, left and took the month's rent with him. Sonny had held baby Josephine in his arms while they all went from block to block, begging anyone who would listen to take them in. They'd ended up in an apartment that had forty people living in it, including a sick old woman who'd lost control of her bowels. Every night the woman would sit in a corner, shaking and crying and filling her shoes with her own shit. Then the rats would come to eat it.

Once, when his mother was desperate, she'd taken them to stay in one of the Manhattan apartments that she cleaned while that family was on vacation. The apartment had six bedrooms for only two people. Sonny didn't know what to do with himself with all that space. He spent the whole day in the smallest room, too scared to touch anything, knowing that his mother would have to dust off his fingerprints if he was to leave them.

"Can you help, mister?" a boy said.

Sonny dropped his notepad down and looked at him. He was small, but something about the look in his eyes told Sonny that he was older than he looked, maybe fourteen or fifteen. The boy came up to the woman and put a hand on her shoulder. He stared at Sonny longer, and so Sonny had time to study his eyes. They were the biggest eyes Sonny had ever seen on a man or a woman, with eyelashes like the long, glamorous legs of a terrifying spider.

"You can't, can you?" the boy said. He blinked twice quickly, and, watching his spider-leg lashes entangle, Sonny was suddenly filled with fear. "You can't do a single thing, can you?" the boy continued.

Sonny didn't know what to say. He just knew he had to get out of there.

The boy's voice rang in Sonny's head for the rest of that week, month, year. He'd asked to be moved off the housing team, lest he see him again.

"You can't do a single thing, can you?"

Sonny was arrested at another march. And then another. And then another. After the third arrest, when Sonny was already handcuffed, one of the police officers punched him in the face. As his eye started to swell shut, Sonny puckered his lips as if to spit, but the officer just looked him in his one good eye, shook his head, and said, "Do that and you'll die today."

His mother saw his face and started to weep. "I didn't leave Alabama for this!" she said. Sonny was supposed to go to her house for Sunday dinner, but he skipped it. He skipped work that week too.

"You can't do a single thing, can you?"

Reverend George Lee of Mississippi was fatally shot while trying to register to vote.

Rosa Jordan was shot while riding a newly desegregated bus in Montgomery, Alabama. She was pregnant.

"You can't do a single thing, can you?"

Sonny kept skipping out on work. Instead, he sat on a bench next to the man who swept the barbershops on Seventh. Sonny didn't know the man's name. He just liked to sit and talk to him. Maybe it was the fact that the man held a broom like his mother did. He could talk to him in a way he'd never been able to talk to her. "What do you do when you feel helpless?" Sonny asked.

The man took a long drag off his Newport. "This helps," he said, waving the cigarette in the air. He pulled out a small glassine bag from his pocket and placed it in Sonny's hand. "When that don't help, this do," he said.

Sonny fingered the dope for a while. He didn't speak, and soon the barber sweep took up his broom and left. Sonny sat on that bench for nearly an hour, just running that small bag from finger to finger, thinking about it. He thought about it as he walked the ten blocks home. He thought about it as he fried an egg for dinner. If nothing he did changed anything, then maybe he was the one who would have to make a change. By midafternoon the next day, Sonny had stopped thinking about it.

He called up the NAACP and quit his job before flushing the bag down the toilet.

"What are you gonna do for money?" Josephine asked Sonny. He couldn't keep his apartment now that he didn't have an income, so he was staying at his mother's house until he could figure things out.

Willie stood over the sink, washing dishes and humming her gospel tunes. She hummed loudest when she wanted to appear as though she wasn't listening in.

"I'll figure something out. I always do, don't I?" His voice was a dare, and Josephine didn't accept, leaning back into her seat and becoming, suddenly, silent. His mother hummed a little louder and started to dry the dishes in her hands.

"Let me help you with that, Mama," Sonny said, hopping up.

Immediately, she started in on him so that he knew that she had been listening. "Lucille came by here yesterday asking for you," Willie said. Sonny grunted. "Seem like maybe you should give the girl a call."

"She know how to find me when she want to."

"What about Angela or Rhonda? They know how to find you too? Seem like they only know how to get to my house on days you *ain't* here."

Sonny grunted again. "You don't got to give 'em nothing, Mama," he said.

His mother snorted. She stopped humming and started singing instead. Sonny knew he had to get out of the apartment, and fast. If his women were after him and his mama was singing gospel, he had better find himself a place to be.

He went to see his friend Mohammed about a job. "You should join the Nation of Islam, man," Mohammed said. "Forget the NAACP. They ain't doing shit."

Sonny accepted a glass of water from Mohammed's eldest daughter. He shrugged at his friend. They'd had this conversation before. Sonny couldn't join the Nation of Islam as long as his mother was a devout Christian woman. He would never hear the end of it. Besides, his days of sitting in the back of his mother's church had not left him immune to ideas about the wrath of God. It was not the kind of thing you wanted to attract. "Islam ain't getting shit done neither," he said.

His friend Mohammed used to be named Johnny. They'd met shooting hoops in courts all around Harlem when they were boys, and they'd kept up their friendship, even as their basketball days ended and their midsections grew.

When they'd met, Sonny had still gone by "Carson," but on the court he liked the quickness, the ease of "Sonny," and so he'd adopted that name as his own. His mother hated it. He knew it was because his father used to call him that, but Sonny didn't know a thing about his father and there was no sentimental pull to the name for him other than the sound of the other kids saying "Yeah, Son! Yeah, Sonny!" when he sunk one.

"It's dry out there, Sonny," Mohammed said.

"You gotta know somethin'. Anything, man."

"How much school you had?" Mohammed asked.

"Couple years," Sonny said. In truth, he couldn't remember finishing one year in any one place, so much had he skipped school, moved around, gotten kicked out. One year, out of sheer desperation, his mother had tried to get him into one of the fancy white schools in Manhattan. She'd marched into the office wearing glasses and carrying her best pen. While Sonny looked at the pristine building, clean and shiny, with smartly dressed white children entering and exiting as calmly as can be, he'd thought about his own schools, the ones in Harlem that had the ceiling falling in and smelled of some unnameable funk, and he was surprised that both things could even be called "schools." Sonny could remember how the white school officials had asked his mother if she wanted some coffee. They'd told her that it just wasn't possible for him to go there. It just wasn't possible. Sonny could remember Willie squeezing his hand with one of hers as they walked back to Harlem, wiping away tears with the other. To comfort her, Sonny said he didn't mind his schools because he never went, and Willie said the fact that he never went was what was wrong with them.

"That ain't enough for the one thing I heard about," Mohammed said.

"I gotta work, Mohammed. I got to."

Mohammed nodded slowly, thinking, and the next week he gave Sonny the number of a man who had left the Nation and now owned a bar. Two weeks later Sonny was taking drink orders at Jazzmine, the new jazz club in East Harlem.

Sonny moved his things out of his mother's house the night he found out he got the job. He didn't tell her where he was working because he already knew she didn't approve of jazz or any other kind of secular music. She sang for the church, used her voice for Christ, and that was it. Sonny had asked her once if she had ever wanted to be famous like Billie Holiday, singing so sweet that even white people had to pay attention, but his mother just looked away and told him to be careful of "that kind of life."

Jazzmine was too new to attract the big-time clients and players. Most days, the club was half-empty, and the workers, many of whom were musicians themselves, hoping to be seen by the kind of people who could make their careers, quit before the club was even six months old. It wasn't long before Sonny became head bartender.

"Gimme a whiskey," a muffled voice called to Sonny one night. He could tell it was a woman's voice, but he couldn't see her face. She was sitting all the way down at the end of the bar, and her head was in her hands.

"Can't serve ya if I can't see ya," he said, and slowly she lifted her head. "Why don't you come on down here and get your drink?"

He had never seen a woman move that slowly. It was like she had to wade through deep and mucky waters to get to him. She couldn't have been more than nineteen years old, but she moved like a world-weary old woman, like sudden movements would break her bones. And when she plopped herself down on the stool in front of him, she still seemed in no hurry.

"Long day?" Sonny asked.

She smiled. "Ain't all days long?"

Sonny got her the drink, and she sipped it just as slowly as she had done everything else.

"My name's Sonny," he said.

She slipped him another smile, and her eyes grew amused. "Amani Zulema."

Sonny chuckled. "What kind of name is that?" he asked.

"Mine." She stood up, and with the same slow stroll took her drink across the bar and up onto the stage.

The band that had been playing seemed to bow before her. Without Amani needing to say anything at all, the pianist stood up to give her the stool and the others cleared the stage.

She set her drink on top of the piano and started running her hands along the keys. Here, on the piano, was the same lack of urgency that Sonny had noticed before, just fingers lazily ambling along.

It was when she started singing that the room grew really quiet. She was a small woman, but her voice was so deep, it made her look much larger. There was a gravelly quality to the sound too, like she had been gargling with pebbles to prepare herself. She swayed while she sang. First one way, then a cock of the head before moving the other way. When she started to scat, the small crowd grunted and moaned and even shouted "Amen!" once or twice. A few people came in off the street and stood in the doorway, just trying to catch sight of her.

She ended in a hum, a sound that seemed to come from the fullest part of her gut, where some said the soul lived. It reminded Sonny of his childhood, of the first day his mother sang out in church. He was young, and Josephine was just a baby bopping on Eli's knee. His mother had dropped her songbook on the ground and the whole congregation had been startled by the noise, looking up at her. Sonny felt his heart catch in his throat. He remembered that he had been embarrassed for her. Back then, he was always angry at or embarrassed by her. But then she had started to sing. "I shall wear a crown," she sang. I shall wear a crown.

It was the most beautiful thing Sonny had ever heard, and he loved his mother then, like he had never loved her before. The congregation said, "Sing, Willie" and "Amen" and "Bless God," and it seemed to Sonny then that his mother didn't have to wait for Heaven for her reward. He could see it; she was already wearing her crown.

Amani finished her humming and smiled at the crowd as they started to roar with clapping and praise. She picked her drink up from the top of the piano and drank it all the way down. She walked back toward Sonny and set the empty glass in front of him. She didn't say another word as she made her way out.

Sonny was staying in some projects on the East Side with some folks he kind of knew. Against his better judgment, he had given his mother his address, and he knew she had given it to Lucille when the woman showed up holding his daughter.

"Sonny!" she shouted. She was standing on the sidewalk outside the apartment building. There could have been upwards of a hundred Sonnys in Harlem. He didn't want to admit that this one was him.

"Carson Clifton, I know you up there."

There was no back door to the apartment, and it would only be a matter of time before Lucille figured out a way up.

Sonny leaned the top half of his body out of his third-floor window.

"Whatchu want, Luce?" he asked. He hadn't seen his daughter in nearly a year. The child was big, too big to be cocked against her tiny mother's hip, but Lucille had always had strength enough to spare.

"Come let us up!" she hollered back, and he sighed one of what Josephine called his "old lady sighs" before going down to get them.

Lucille wasn't in the room but ten seconds before Sonny regretted letting her in.

"We need money, Sonny."

"I know my mama been payin' you."

"What I'm supposed to feed this child? Air? Air can't grow a child."

"I ain't got nothin' for you, Lucille."

"You got this apartment. Angela told me you gave her somethin' just last month."

Sonny shook his head. The lies these women told each other and themselves. "I ain't seen Angela in longer than I seen you."

Lucille harrumphed. "What kind of father are you!"

Sonny was angry now. He hadn't wanted any children, but somehow he had ended up with three. The first was Angela's girl, the second Rhonda's, and the third was Lucille's girl, who had come out a little slow. His mother gave them all some money each month even though he had told her to stop and told each of his women to stop asking her. They didn't listen.

When Angela had given birth to their daughter, Etta, Sonny was only fifteen years old. Angela was only fourteen. They'd said they were gonna get married and do things the right way, but when Angela's parents found out she was pregnant and that the baby was Sonny's, they'd sent her down to Alabama to stay with her family there until the baby was born, and then they wouldn't let him see either girl when Angela came back up.

Sonny really had wanted to do right by Angela, by his daughter, but he was young and unemployed, and he figured Angela's parents were probably right when they said he was basically good for nothing. It nearly broke his heart the day Angela married a young pastor who worked the revival circuits down south. The pastor would leave Angela in Harlem for months at a time, and Sonny thought if he could have her, he would never leave her.

But then he'd look at himself in the mirror sometimes, and he'd see features he didn't recognize from his mother's face. His nose wasn't hers. Nor were his ears. He used to ask his mother about these features when he was young. He used to ask her where his nose, his ears, his lighter skin came from. He used to ask her about his father, and all she would say was that he didn't have a father. He didn't have a father, but he had turned out all right. "Right?" he would tease the man in the mirror. "Right?"

"She ain't even a baby no more, Lucille. Look at her."

The girl was hobbling around the apartment on her little sea legs. Lucille shot Sonny a killing look, snatched the child up, and left.

"And don't go calling my mama for money now neither!" he shouted after her. He could hear her stomping all the way down the stairs and out into the street.

Two days later, Sonny was back at Jazzmine. He had asked the other folks who worked there when Amani would be back, but none of them knew.

"She go where the wind blow," Blind Louis said, wiping down the bar. Sonny must have sighed a little, because soon Louis said, "I know that sound."

"What sound?"

"You don't want none, Sonny."

"Why not?" Sonny asked. What could an old blind man possibly know about wanting a woman just from the sight of her?

"Ain't just about the way a woman look, you gotta think about what's in 'em too," Louis answered, reading his mind. "Ain't nothin' in that woman worth wanting."

Sonny didn't listen. It took three more months for him to see Amani again. By that time he'd gone looking for her, dropping in at club after club, waiting to see some slow stroll make its way up to the stage.

When he found her, she was sitting at a table in the back of the club, sleeping. He had to get close to know this, so close he could hear the inhale and exhale of her breath as she snored. He looked around the room, but Amani was in a dark corner of the bar, and no one seemed to be looking for her. He pushed her arm. Nothing. He pushed her arm again, harder this time. Still nothing. On the third push, she rolled her head to one side so slowly, it was like a boulder moving. She blinked a couple of times, a slow, deliberate movement that brought her heavy lids and thick eyelashes together.

When she looked at him finally, Sonny could see why she might need to blink. Her eyes were bloodshot, the pupils dilated. She blinked twice more, this time quickly, and watching her, it suddenly occurred to Sonny that he hadn't considered what he would do once he'd found her.

"You singing tonight?" he asked meekly.

"Do it look like I'm singing?"

Sonny didn't answer. Amani started to stretch her neck and shoulders. She shook her whole body out. "What do you want, man?" she asked, seeing him again. "What do you want?"

"You," Sonny admitted. He had wanted her since the day he saw her sing. It wasn't her slow gait or the fact that her voice had reminded him of his favorite memory of his mother. It was that he had felt something in himself open up when she started singing that night, and he wanted to capture just a little bit more of that feeling, keep it for himself.

She shook her head at him and smiled a little. "Well, come on."

They went out into the street. Sonny's stepfather, Eli, liked to walk, and when he was around he used to take Sonny and Willie and Josephine all around town. Maybe that was how his mother had grown to like walking too, Sonny thought. He still remembered the day that she had walked with him all the way down into the white part of the city. He'd thought they would keep on going forever and ever, but she had stopped suddenly, and Sonny found himself disappointed, though he hadn't been able to figure out why.

With Amani, Sonny passed by places he knew from his days on the housing team, jazz joints for the down-and-out, cheap food stands, barbershops, all with junkies on the street holding hats outstretched in their hands.

"You ain't told me 'bout your name yet," Sonny said as they stepped over a man lying in the middle of the street.

"Whatchu want to know?"

"You Muslim?"

Amani laughed at him a little. "Naw, I ain't Muslim." Sonny waited for her to speak. He had already said enough. He didn't want to keep pressing her, showing her his desire, his weaknesses. He waited for her to speak. "*Amani* means 'harmony' in Swahili. When I started singing, I felt like I needed a new name. My mama named me Mary, and ain't nobody gonna hit it big with a name like Mary. And I ain't into all that Nation of Islam and Back to Africa business, but I saw Amani and I felt like it was mine. So I took it."

"You ain't into the 'Back to Africa business,' but you using an African name?" Sonny had put his politics behind him but could feel them creeping up. Amani was nearly half his age. The America she was born into was different from the one he had been born into. He resisted the urge to wag his finger at her.

"We can't go back, can we?" She stopped walking and touched his arm. She looked more serious than she had all night, like she was only just considering that he was a real person and not someone she had dreamed up when he found her asleep. "We can't go back to something we ain't never been to in the first place. It ain't ours anymore. This is." She swept her hand in front of her, as though she were trying to catch all of Harlem in it, all of New York, all of America.

They finally got to a housing project way out in West Harlem. The building wasn't locked, and when they entered the hallway, the first thing Sonny noticed was the row of dope fiends lining the walls. They looked like dummies, or like the corpse Sonny had seen when he walked into a funeral home to find the mortician manipulating a body, hooking the elbow up, turning the face left, bending the body at its back.

No one was manipulating these bodies in the hallway—no one that Sonny could see—but he knew immediately that it was a dope house, and suddenly what he hadn't wanted to know about Amani's slow, sleepy movements, her dilated pupils, became all too apparent. He grew nervous, but swallowed it down, because it was important to him that Amani not see that the longer he was with her, the more he began to feel that he had no control over himself.

They entered a room. A man cradling his own body curled up against the wall on a dirty mattress. Two women were tapping their arms, readying themselves for the needle a second man was holding. They didn't even look up as Sonny and Amani entered.

Everywhere he looked, Sonny saw jazz instruments. Two horns, a bass, a sax. Amani set her things down and sat next to one of the girls, who finally looked up, nodded at them. Amani turned to Sonny, who was still hanging back, his hand still grazing the doorknob.

She didn't say anything. The man passed the needle to the first girl. That girl passed the needle to the second. The second passed the needle to Amani, but she was still looking at Sonny. She was still silent.

Sonny watched her plunge the needle into her arm, watched her eyes roll back. When she looked at him again, she didn't have to speak for him to hear her say, "This is me. You still want it?"

*

"Carson! Carson, I know you in there!"

He could hear the voice, but at the same time, he couldn't hear it. He was living in his own head, and he could not tell where that ended and where the world began, and he didn't want to answer the voice until he was sure he knew which side of things it was coming from.

"Carson!"

He sat quietly, or at least what he thought was quietly. He was sweating, his chest heaving up and down, up and down. He would need to go score soon to keep himself from dying.

When the voice outside the door started praying, Sonny knew it was his mother. She had done it a few times before, when he was still mostly sober, when dope was still mostly fun and he felt like he had some control over it.

"Lord, release my son from this torment. Father God, I know he done gone down to Hell to take a look, but please send him back."

Sonny might have found it soothing if he weren't feeling so sick.

He heaved, nothing at first, but soon he was vomiting in the corner of the room.

His mother's voice grew louder. "Lord, I know you can deliver him from what ails him. Bless him and keep him."

Deliverance was exactly what Sonny wanted. He was a forty-five-year-old dope fiend, and he was tired but he was also sick, and the sickness of trying to come off the dope outweighed his exhaustion with staying on it every single time.

His mother was whispering now, or maybe Sonny's ears were no longer working. Soon he couldn't hear anything at all. Before long, somebody would be home. One of the other fiends he lived with would come in and maybe they would have scored something, but probably they wouldn't have and Sonny would have to begin the ritual of trying to score himself. Instead, he began it now.

He pushed himself up off the ground and put his ear against the door to make certain his mother had gone. Once he knew, he went out to greet Harlem.

Harlem and heroin. Heroin and Harlem. Sonny could no longer think of one without thinking of the other. They sounded alike. Both were going to kill him. The junkies and the jazz had gone together, fed each other, and now every time Sonny heard a horn, he wanted a hit.

Sonny walked down 116th Street. He could almost always score on 116th Street, and he had trained himself to spot junkies and dealers as quickly as possible, letting his eyes scan the folks walking by until they landed on the people who had what he needed. It was a consequence of living inside his own head. It made him aware of others who were doing the same thing.

When Sonny came across the first junkie, he asked if she was holding, and the woman shook her head. When he came across the second one, he asked if he would let him carry, and the man shook his head too, but pointed him along to a guy who was dealing.

Sonny's mother didn't give him money anymore. Angela sometimes did if her Bible-slinging husband had made some extra cash on the revival circuit. Sonny gave the dealer every last dollar he had, and it bought him so little. It bought him next to nothing.

He wanted to shoot it before going back just in case Amani was there. She would take him for the next to nothing he had. Sonny went into the bathroom of a diner and shot up, and instantly he could feel the sickness moving away from him. By the time he made it back home, he felt almost well. Almost, which meant that he would have to score again soon to get a little closer, and again to get a little closer, and again, and again.

Amani sat in front of a mirror, braiding her hair. "Where you been?" she asked.

Sonny didn't answer. He wiped his nose with the back of his hand and started rummaging around the fridge for food. They lived in the Johnson Houses on 112th and Lexington, and their door was never locked. Junkies came and went, from one apartment to the next. Someone was passed out on the floor in front of the table.

"Your mama was here," Amani said.

Sonny found a piece of bread and ate around the mold. He looked at Amani as she finished her hair and stood up to look at herself. She was getting thick around the middle.

"She say she want you to come home for Sunday dinner."

"Where you going?" he asked Amani. He didn't like it when she got dressed up. She had promised him a long time ago that she would never give up her body for dope, and, in the beginning, Sonny hadn't believed she would be able to keep her promise. A dope fiend's word didn't count for much. Sometimes, for assurance, he would follow her as she walked around Harlem on those nights when she did her hair up, put makeup on her face. Every time he did, it ended the same sad way: Amani begging a club owner to let her sing again, just once more. They almost never did. One time, the dingiest joint in all of Harlem had said yes, and Sonny had stood in the back as Amani got up onstage to blank stares and silence. Nobody remembered what she used to be. All they could see was what she was now.

"You should go see your mama, Sonny. We could use some money."

"Aw, c'mon, Amani. You know she ain't gon' give me nothing."

"She might. If you cleaned yourself up. You could use a shower and a shave. She might give you something."

Sonny went up to Amani. He stood behind her and wrapped his arms around her belly, felt the firmness of its weight. "Why don't *you* give me something, baby?" he whispered into her ear.

She started to wriggle, but he held firm and she softened, leaned into him. Sonny had never loved her, not really. But he had always wanted her. It took him a while to learn the difference between those two things.

"I just did my hair, Sonny," she said, but she was already offering him her neck, bending it to the left so that he could run his tongue along the right side. "Sing me a li'l something, Amani," he said, reaching for her breast. She hummed at his touch, but didn't sing.

Sonny let his hand wander down from her breast, down to meet the tufts of hair that awaited him. Then she started. *"I loves you, Porgy. Don't let him take me. Don't let him handle me and drive me mad."* She sang so softly it was almost a whisper. Almost. By the time his fingers found her wet, she was back at the chorus. When she left that night to go out to the jazz clubs, they wouldn't let her sing, but Sonny always did.

"I'll go see my mama," he promised when she left the front door swinging.

Sonny kept a glassine bag of dope in his shoe. It was a reassurance. He walked the many blocks between his house and his mother's house with his big toe clenched around the bag as though it were a small fist. He'd clench it, then release it. Clench it, then release it.

As Sonny passed the projects that filled the distance between his apartment and Willie's, he tried to remember the last time he'd really spoken to his mother. It was 1964, during the riots, and she had asked him to meet her in front of her church so that she could lend him some money. "I don't want to see you dead or worse," she'd said, passing Sonny what little change hadn't made it into the offering plate. As he took the money, Sonny had wondered, What could be worse than dead? But all around him, the evidence was clear. Only weeks before, the NYPD had shot down a fifteen-year-old black boy, a student, for next to nothing. The shooting had started the riots, pitting young black men and some black women against the police force. The news made it sound like the fault lay with the blacks of Harlem. The violent, the crazy, the monstrous black people who had the gall to demand that their children not be gunned down in the streets. Sonny clutched his mother's money tight as he walked back that day, hoping he wouldn't run into any white people looking to prove a point, because he knew in his body, even if he hadn't yet put it together in his mind, that in America the worst thing you could be was a black man. Worse than dead, you were a dead man walking.

Josephine answered the door. She cradled her baby girl in one arm and her son held her other hand. "You get lost or somethin'?" she asked, shooting him a dirty look.

"Behave," his mother hissed from behind her, but Sonny was glad to see his sister treating him the same way she always had.

"You hungry?" Willie asked. She took the baby from Josephine and started walking toward the kitchen.

"I'ma use the bathroom first," Sonny said, already making his way over. He closed the door and sat on the commode, pulling the bag from his shoe. He hadn't been there a minute, but he was already nervous. He needed something to tide him over.

When he came back out, his mother had already fixed him a plate. His mother and sister watched him while he ate.

"Why you ain't eating?" he asked them.

"Because you 'bout an hour and a half late!" Josephine said through gritted teeth.

Willie put an arm on Josephine's shoulder, then pulled a little money out from inside her bra. "Josey, why don't you run go get these kids something?" she said.

The look Josephine sent Willie hurt Sonny more than anything she had said to him yet. It was a look that asked if Willie would be safe left alone with him, and the uncertain nod Willie gave back just about broke Sonny's heart.

Josephine collected her children and left. Sonny had never seen the baby before, though his mother had come to tell him about the birth. The toddler Sonny had seen once, when he passed Josephine on a quiet street one day. He'd kept his head down and pretended not to see them.

"Thanks for the food, Mama," Sonny said. He was almost finished with his food, and he was starting to feel a little sick from eating so fast. She nodded and heaped another helping onto his plate.

"How long it been since you ate something proper?" she asked.

Sonny shrugged and his mother continued to watch him. He was uncomfortable again; the small hit he took was wearing off too quickly, and he wanted to excuse himself to go do more, but too many trips to the bathroom would only make her suspicious.

"Your father was a white man," Willie said calmly. Sonny nearly choked on the chicken bone he had been working over. "You used to ask me about him, long time ago, and I ain't never told you nothing, so I'm tellin' you now."

She got up to pour a glass from the pitcher of tea she kept by the sink. She drank the whole glass of tea while Sonny watched her back. When she finished that glass, she poured herself another and took it back to the table.

"He didn't start out white," she said. "He was black when I met him, more yellow than black, really. But still, he was colored."

Sonny coughed. He started fingering the chicken bone. "Why you ain't told me before?" he asked. He could feel himself getting angry, but he held it back. He had come here for money, and he couldn't fight with her now. Not now.

"I thought about tellin' you. I did. You saw him once. Day we walked all the way to West 109th Street, you remember that? Your daddy was standing across the street with his white woman and his white baby, and I thought maybe I should tell Carson who that man is, but then I figured it'd be better just to let him go. So I let him go, and we went back to Harlem."

Sonny snapped the chicken bone in half. "Mama, you shoulda stopped him. You shoulda told me, and you shoulda stopped him. I don't know why you always lettin' people walk all over you. My father, Eli, the goddam church. You ain't never fought for nothin'. Not nothin'. Not a day in your life."

His mother reached across the table, put her hand on his shoulder, and squeezed hard until he had to look her in the eyes. "That ain't true, Carson. I fought for you."

He returned his eyes to the two pieces of chicken bone on his plate. He toed the bag in his shoe.

"You think you done somethin' cuz you used to march? I marched. I marched with your father and with my li'l baby all the way up from Alabama. All the way to Harlem. My son was gon' see a better world than what I saw, what my parents saw. I was gon' be a famous singer. Robert wasn't gon' have to work in a mine for some white man. That was a march too, Carson."

Sonny started looking toward the bathroom. He wanted to excuse himself and finish up the bag in his shoe. He knew it would probably be the last he could afford for a long, long while.

Willie cleared his plate and refilled her tea. He could see her standing at the sink, drinking in long, deep breaths, her chest and back rising and falling as she tried to collect herself. She came back and sat down right in front of him, looking at him all the while.

"You was always so angry. Even as a child, you was angry. I used to see you lookin' at me like you was like to kill me, and I didn't know why. Took me a long time to figure out that you was born to a man who could choose his life, but you wouldn't never be able to choose yours, and it seemed like you was born knowing that."

She took a sip of her drink and stared off into space. "White men get a choice. They get to choose they job, choose they house. They get to make black babies, then disappear into thin air, like they wasn't never there to begin with, like these black women they slept with or raped done laid on top of themselves and got pregnant. White men get to choose for black men too. Used to sell 'em; now they just send 'em to prison like they did my daddy, so that they can't be with they kids. Just about breaks my heart to see you, my son, my daddy's grandson, over here with these babies walking up and down Harlem who barely even know your name, let alone your face. Alls I can think is this ain't the way it's s'posed to be. There are things you ain't learned from me, things you picked up from your father even though you ain't know him, things he picked up from white men. It makes me sad to see my son a junkie after all the marchin' I done, but makes me sadder to see you thinkin' you can leave like your daddy did. You keep doin' what you doin' and the white man don't got to do it no more. He ain't got to sell you or put you in a coal mine to own you. He'll own you just as is, and he'll say you the one who did it. He'll say it's your fault."

Josephine came back in with the kids. They had ice cream smeared on their shirts and contented little smiles on their faces. Josephine didn't wait to hear more. She just took the kids straight into the bedroom to lay them down to sleep.

Willie pulled a wad of cash out from between her breasts and slapped it on the table in front of him. "This what you came for?" she asked.

Sonny could see tears forming in her eyes. He kept toeing the glassine bag, his fingers itching to get at the money.

"Take it and go if you want to," Willie said. "Go if you want to."

What Sonny wanted was to scream, to take the money, take what was left in the bag in his shoe and find somewhere to go shoot up until he could no longer remember the things his mother had told him. That was what he wanted to do. But he didn't do that. Instead, he stayed.

Marjorie

"ESS-CUSE ME, SISTAH. I take you see Castle. Cape Coast Castle. Five cedis. You come from America? I take you see slave ship. Juss five cedis."

The boy was probably around ten years old, only a few years younger than Marjorie herself was. He had been following her since she and her grandmother's housekeeper got off the tro-tro. The locals did this, waiting for tourists to disembark so that they could con them into paying for things Ghanaians knew were free. Marjorie tried to ignore him, but she was hot and tired, still feeling the sweat of the other people who had been pressed against her back and chest and sides on the nearly eight-hour tro-tro ride from Accra.

"I take you see Cape Coast Castle, sis. Juss five cedis," he repeated. He wore no shirt, and she could feel the heat radiating off of his skin, coming toward her. After all the traveling, she couldn't stand another strange body so near hers, and so she soon found herself shouting in Twi, "I'm from Ghana, stupid. Can't you see?"

The boy didn't stop his English. "But you come from America?"

Angry, she kept walking. Her backpack straps were heavy against her shoulders, and she knew they would leave marks.

Marjorie was in Ghana visiting her grandmother, as she did every summer. Some time ago, the woman had moved to Cape Coast to be near the water. In Edweso, where she had lived before, everyone called her Crazy Woman, but in Cape Coast they knew her only as Old Lady. So old, they said, she could recite the entire history of Ghana from memory alone.

"Is that my child coming to me?" the woman asked. She was leaning on a cane made of curved wood, and her back mimicked that curve, rounding down so that the woman looked like she was in constant supplication. *"Akwaaba. Akwaaba. Akwaaba,"* she said.

"My Old Lady. I've missed you," Marjorie said. She hugged her grandmother too forcefully and the woman yelped.

"Eh, have you come to break me?"

"Sorry, sorry."

Old Lady called her house boy to take Marjorie's bag, and slowly, gingerly, Marjorie pulled the straps from her aching shoulders.

Her grandmother saw her wince and asked, *"Are you hurt?"*

"It's nothing."

The response was a reflex. Whenever her father or grandmother asked her about pain, Marjorie would say she had never known it. As a young child, someone had told her that the scars her father wore on his face and her grandmother on her hands and feet were born of great pain. And because Marjorie had no scars that resembled those, she could never bring herself to complain of pain. Once, when she was just a little girl, she had watched a ringworm on her knee grow and grow and grow. She'd hidden it from her parents for nearly two weeks, until the worm overtook the curve where thigh met calf, making it difficult for her to bend. When she'd finally shown her parents, her mother had vomited, and her father had snatched her in his arms and rushed her to the emergency room. The orderly who came to call them back had been startled, not by the worm, but by her father's scar. She'd asked if he was the one who needed help.

Looking at her grandmother's hands now, it was almost impossible to distinguish scarred from wrinkled skin. The whole landscape of the woman's body had transformed into a ruin; the young woman had been toppled, leaving this.

They took a cab back to Old Lady's house. Marjorie's grandmother lived in a big, open bungalow on the beach, like the kind the few white people who lived in town had. When Marjorie was in third grade, her father and mother had left Alabama and returned to Ghana in order to help Old Lady build it. They stayed for many months, leaving Marjorie in the care of a friend of theirs. When summer came and Marjorie was finally able to go visit them, she fell in love with the beautiful house with no doors. It was five times the size of her family's tiny apartment in Huntsville, and its front yard was the beach, not a sad slab of dying grass like the yard she had always known. She spent that whole summer wondering how her parents could leave a place like this.

"Have you been good, my own child?" Old Lady asked, handing Marjorie some of the chocolate she kept in the kitchen. Marjorie had a sweet tooth reserved for chocolate. Her mother often joked that Marjorie must have been birthed from a cocoa nut, split open and wide.

Marjorie nodded, accepting the treat. "Are we going to the water today?" she asked, her mouth full, the chocolate melting.

"Speak Twi," her grandmother answered sharply, knocking Marjorie on the back of her head.

"Sorry," Marjorie mumbled. At home in Huntsville, her parents spoke to her in Twi and she answered them in English. They had done this since the day Marjorie had brought a note home from her kindergarten teacher. The note read:

Marjorie does not volunteer to answer questions. She rarely speaks. Does she know English? If she doesn't, you should consider English as a Second Language classes. Or perhaps Marjorie would benefit from special care? We have great Special Ed classes here.

Her parents were livid. Her father read the note aloud four times, shouting, "What does this foolish woman know?" after each repetition, but from then on they had quizzed Marjorie on her English every night. When she tried to answer their questions in Twi, they would say, "Speak English," until now it was the first language that popped into her head. She had to remind herself that her grandmother required the opposite.

"Yes, we will go to the water now. Put away your things."

Going to the beach with Old Lady was one of Marjorie's favorite things in the world to do. Her grandmother was not like other grandmothers. At night, Old Lady spoke in her sleep. Sometimes she fought; sometimes she paced the room. Marjorie had heard the stories about the burns her grandmother carried on her hands and feet, about the one on her father's face. She knew why the Edweso people had called her Crazy Woman, but to her, her grandmother had never been crazy. Old Lady dreamed dreams and saw visions.

They walked to the beach. Old Lady moved so slowly, it was like she wasn't moving at all. Neither of them wore shoes, and when they got to the edge of the sand, they waited for the water to come up and lick the spaces between their toes, clean the sand that was hidden there. Marjorie watched as her grandmother closed her eyes, and she waited patiently for the old woman to speak. It was what they had come for, what they always came for.

"Are you wearing the stone?" her grandmother asked.

Instinctively, Marjorie raised her hand to the necklace. Her father had given it to her only a year before, saying that she was finally old enough to care for it. It had belonged to Old Lady and to Abena before her, and to James, and Quey, and Effia the Beauty before that. It had begun with Maame, the woman who had set a great fire. Her father had told her that the necklace was a part of their family history and she was to never take it off, never give it away. Now it reflected the ocean water before them, gold waves shimmering in the black stone.

"Yes, Old Lady," she said.

Her grandmother took her hand and once more they fell silent. "You are in this water," she finally said.

Marjorie nodded her head soberly. The day she was born, thirteen years ago, all the way across the Atlantic, her parents had mailed her umbilical cord to Old Lady so that the woman could put it into the ocean. It was Old Lady's only request, that if her son and daughter-in-law, both old themselves by the time they decided to get married and move to America, ever had a child they would send something of that child back to Ghana.

"Our family began here, in Cape Coast," Old Lady said. She pointed to the Cape Coast Castle. "In my dreams I kept seeing this castle, but I did not know why. One day, I came to these waters and I could feel the spirits of our ancestors calling to me. Some were free, and they spoke to me from the sand, but some others were trapped deep, deep, deep in the water so that I had to wade out to hear their voices. I waded out so far, the water almost took me down to meet those spirits that were trapped so deep in the sea that they would never be free. When they were living they had not known where they came from, and so dead, they did not know how to get to dry land. I put you in here so that if your spirit ever wandered, you would know where home was."

Marjorie nodded as her grandmother took her hand and walked her farther and farther out into the water. It was their summer ritual, her grandmother reminding her how to come home.

Marjorie returned to Alabama three shades darker and five pounds heavier. Her period had come while she was with her grandmother, and the old woman had clapped her hands and sang songs to celebrate Marjorie's womanhood. She didn't want to leave Cape Coast, but school was starting and her parents wouldn't let her stay any longer.

She was entering high school, and while she had always hated Alabama, the newer, bigger school had instantly reminded her of why. Her family lived on the southeast side of Huntsville. They were the only black family on the block, the only black people for miles and miles and miles. At her new high school, there were more black children than Marjorie was used to seeing in Alabama, but it took only a few conversations with them for Marjorie to realize that they were not the same kind of black that she was. That indeed she was the wrong kind.

"Why you talk like that?" Tisha, the leader of the pack, had asked her the first day of high school when she joined them for lunch.

"Like what?" Marjorie asked, and Tisha had repeated it, her accent turning almost British in order to capture her impression of Marjorie. *"Like what?"*

The next day Marjorie sat by herself, reading *Lord of the Flies* for English class. She held the book in one hand and a fork in the other.

She was so engrossed in the book that she didn't realize that the chicken she had pierced with her fork hadn't made it into her mouth until she tasted air. She finally looked up to see Tisha and the other black girls staring at her.

"Why you reading that book?" Tisha asked.

Marjorie stammered. "I—I have to read it for class."

"*I have to read it for class,*" Tisha mimicked. "You sound like a white girl. White girl. White girl. White girl."

They kept chanting, and it was all Marjorie could do to keep from crying. In Ghana, whenever a white person appeared, there was always a child there to point him out. A small group of children, dark and shiny in the equatorial sun, would extend their little fingers toward the person whose skin was different from theirs and shout, *"Obroni! Obroni!"* They would giggle, delighted by the difference. When Marjorie had first seen children do this, she'd watched as the white man whose skin color had been told to him grew shocked, offended. "Why do they keep saying that!" he'd asked the friend who was showing him around.

Marjorie's father pulled her aside that night and asked her if she knew the answer to the white man's question, and she had shrugged. Her father had told her that the word had come to mean something entirely different from what it used to mean. That the young of Ghana, itself an infant country, had been born to a place emptied of its colonizers. Because they didn't see white men every day the way people of his mother's generation and older had, the word could take on new meaning for them. They lived in a Ghana where they were the majority, where theirs was the only skin color for miles around. To them, to call someone *"obroni"* was an innocent act, an interpretation of race as skin color.

Now, keeping her head down and fighting back tears as Tisha and her friends called her "white girl," Marjorie was made aware, yet again, that here "white" could be the way a person talked; "black," the music a person listened to. In Ghana you could only be what you were, what your skin announced to the world.

"Don't mind them," Marjorie's mother, Esther, said that night as she stroked Marjorie's hair. "Don't mind them, my smart girl. My beautiful girl."

The next day Marjorie ate lunch in the English teachers' lounge. Her teacher, Mrs. Pinkston, was a fat, walnut-skinned woman with a laugh that sounded like the slow build of an approaching train. She carried a large pink handbag that she would pull books out of unendingly, like a magician's hat. In her head Marjorie called the books rabbits. "What do they know?" Mrs. Pinkston said, passing Marjorie a cookie. "They don't know a thing."

Mrs. Pinkston was Marjorie's favorite teacher, one of two black teachers in a school that served almost two thousand students. She was the only person Marjorie knew who had a copy of her father's book, *The Ruin of a Nation Begins in the Homes of Its People.* The book was her father's lifework. He was sixty-three when he finished it, approaching seventy when he and her mother finally had her. He'd taken the title from an old Asante proverb and used it to discuss slavery and colonialism. Marjorie, who had read every book on her family's bookshelves, had once spent an entire afternoon trying to read her father's book. She'd only made it to page two. When she told her father this, he'd said that it was something she wouldn't understand until she was much older. He said that people need time in order to be able to see things clearly.

"What do you think about the book?" Mrs. Pinkston said, pointing to the copy of *Lord of the Flies* that dangled from Marjorie's hands.

"I like it," Marjorie said.

"But do you love it? Do you feel it inside you?"

Marjorie shook her head. She didn't know what it meant to feel a book inside of her, but she didn't want to tell her English teacher that, lest it disappoint her.

Mrs. Pinkston laughed her moving-train laugh, leaving Marjorie to her reading.

And so Marjorie spent three years this way, searching for books that she loved, that she could feel inside of her. By senior year, she had read almost everything on the south wall of the school's library, at least a thousand books, and she was working her way through the north wall.

"That's a good one."

She had just brought down *Middlemarch* from the shelf and was taking in the smell of the book when the boy spoke to her.

"You like Eliot?" Marjorie asked. She had seen him around recently, but she couldn't quite remember where. With blond hair and blue eyes, he looked like a little boy she'd seen in a Cheerios commercial once, now grown up.

He put his index finger to his lips. "Don't tell anyone," he said, and she smiled despite herself.

"My name's Marjorie."

"Graham."

They shook hands and Graham told her about *Pigeon Feathers,* the book he was reading. He told her that his family had just moved there from Germany, that his father was in the military, that his mother had died long ago. Marjorie must have spoken too, but she couldn't remember what she had said, only that she had smiled so much her cheeks ached. Before they knew it, the bell rang and lunch hour was over and they went on to their next class.

From then on, they saw each other every day. They read together in the library while everyone else ate lunch. They sat only inches apart at a big, long table that could have seated thirty or more, the many empty seats giving them no excuse to explain their proximity. They stopped talking as much as they had that first day. Reading together was enough. Sometimes Graham would leave a note with his own writing for Marjorie to find. They were mostly little poems or fragmented stories. She was too shy to show him the things that she had written. At night, when she went home, she would wait for her parents to go to bed before turning on her lamp to read Graham's notes in the soft light.

"Daddy, when did you know you liked Mama?" she asked at breakfast the next day. Her father had suffered from a heart attack two years before and now ate a bowl of oatmeal every day. He was so old that Marjorie's teachers always assumed he was her grandfather.

He wiped his lips with his napkin and cleared his throat. "Who told you I like your mother?" he asked. Marjorie rolled her eyes as her father started to laugh. "Did your mother tell you that? Eh, Abronoma, you are too young to like anyone. Concentrate on your studies."

He was out the door, headed to teach his history course at the community college, before Marjorie could protest. She had always hated it when her father called her Dove. It was her special name, the nickname born with her because of her Asante name, but it had always made Marjorie feel small somehow, young and fragile. She was not small. She was not young, either. She was old, so old her breasts had grown to the size of her mother's, so large she sometimes had to carry them in her hands when walking naked through her bedroom to keep them from slapping against her chest.

"Who do you like?" Marjorie's mother asked, coming into the room with fresh laundry in her hands. Though her parents had lived in America for nearly fifteen years, Esther still would not use a washing machine. She washed all the family's undergarments by hand in the kitchen sink.

"No one," Marjorie said.

"Has someone come to ask you to prom?" Esther asked, grinning widely. Marjorie sighed. Five years ago she had watched a 20/20 special on proms across America with her mother, and her mother had been delighted by it. She said that she had never seen anything like the girls in their long dresses and the boys in their suits. The thought that her daughter could be one of those special girls was a hope that flickered like light in Esther's eye, just as it stung like dust in Marjorie's. Marjorie was one of thirty black people at her school. None of them had been asked to prom the year before.

"No, Mama, God!"

"I am not God, and I have never been," her mother said, pulling a lacy black bra from the depths of the sink water. "If a boy likes you, you have to make it known that you like him too. Otherwise, he will never do anything. I lived in your father's house for many, many years before he asked me to marry him. I was a foolish girl, hoping he would see that I wanted the same thing he did, without ever making it known.

Were it not for Old Lady's intervention, who knows if he would have ever done anything. That woman has strong powers of will."

That night, Marjorie tucked Graham's poem under her pillow, hoping she had inherited her grandmother's willpower, that the words he'd written would float up into her ear as she slept, blossom into a dream.

Mrs. Pinkston was putting on a black cultural event for the school, and she asked Marjorie if she would read a poem. The event, called The Waters We Wade In, was unlike anything the school had ever done before, and it was to take place at the beginning of May, well after Black History Month had passed.

"All you have to do is tell your story," Mrs. Pinkston said. "Talk about what being African American means to you."

"But I'm not African American," Marjorie said.

Though she couldn't exactly read the look on Mrs. Pinkston's face, Marjorie knew instantly that she had said the wrong thing. She wanted to explain it to Mrs. Pinkston, but she didn't know how. She wanted to tell Mrs. Pinkston that at home, they had a different word for African Americans. *Akata.* That *akata* people were different from Ghanaians, too long gone from the mother continent to continue calling it the mother continent. She wanted to tell Mrs. Pinkston that she could feel herself being pulled away too, almost *akata,* too long gone from Ghana to be Ghanaian. But the look on Mrs. Pinkston's face stopped her from explaining herself at all.

"Listen, Marjorie, I'm going to tell you something that maybe nobody's told you yet. Here, in this country, it doesn't matter where you came from first to the white people running things. You're here now, and here black is black is black." She got up from her seat and poured them each a cup of coffee. Marjorie didn't really even like coffee. It was too bitter; the taste clung to the back of her throat, like it couldn't decide whether it wanted to enter her body or be breathed out of her mouth. Mrs. Pinkston drank the coffee, but Marjorie just looked at hers. Briefly, for only a second, she thought she could see her face reflected in it.

That night Marjorie went to see a movie with Graham. When he came to pick her up, she asked him if he would park his car one street over. She wasn't ready to tell her parents yet.

"Good idea," Graham said, and Marjorie wondered if his father knew where he was.

When the movie ended, Graham drove her into a clearing in the woods. It was one of those places that other kids supposedly went to make out, but Marjorie had been through it a couple of times, and it was always empty.

It was empty this night. Graham had a bottle of whiskey in his backseat, and though she detested the taste of alcohol, Marjorie sipped from it slowly. While she drank, Graham pulled out a cigarette. After he lit it, he kept playing with the lighter, making the fire appear, then disappear again.

"Would you stop that, please?" Marjorie asked once he started waving the lighter around.

"What?" Graham asked.

"The lighter. Would you put it away, please?"

Graham gave her a strange look, but he didn't say anything, and so she didn't have to explain. Ever since she had heard the story of how her father and grandmother got their scars, she had been terrified of fire. When she was just a little girl, the firewoman of her grandmother's dreams had haunted Marjorie's own waking hours. She had only heard about her from her grandmother's stories on those days when they walked to the water so that her grandmother could tell her what she knew of their ancestors, and yet Marjorie thought she could see the firewoman in the blue and orange glow of the stove, in hot coals, in lighters. She feared that the nightmares would come for her too, that she too would be chosen by the ancestors to hear their family's stories, but the nightmares never came, and so, with time, her fear of fire had waned. But every so often she could still feel her heart catch when she saw fire, as though the firewoman's shadow still lurked.

"What'd you think of the movie?" Graham asked, putting the lighter away.

Marjorie shrugged. It was the only response she could manage because she hadn't been thinking at all about the movie. Instead, she'd thought about the location of Graham's hands in relationship to the popcorn or the armrest they shared. She'd thought about his laugh when he'd found something funny, about whether or not the tilt of his head toward the left, toward her, was an invitation for her to tilt her own head toward him or to rest it on his shoulders. In the weeks they had spent getting to know each other, Marjorie had become more and more enamored with the blue of his eyes. She wrote poems about them. The blue like ocean water, like clear sky, like sapphire—she couldn't capture it. At the movies, she had thought about how the only real friends she had were characters in novels, not real at all. And then Graham had appeared and swallowed up a bit of her loneliness with his blue whale eyes. The next day she wouldn't for the life of her be able to remember what the movie was called.

"Yeah, I felt the same way," Graham said. He took a long drag from the whiskey bottle.

Marjorie wondered if she was in love. How could she know? How did anyone know? In middle school she had been into Victorian literature, the sweeping romance of it. Every character in those books was hopelessly in love. All the men were wooing, all the women being wooed. It was easier to see what love looked like then, the embarrassingly grand, unabashed emotion of it. Now, did it look like sitting in a Camry, sipping whiskey?

"You still haven't let me read any of your writing," Graham said. He stifled a burp, passing the bottle back to Marjorie.

"I have to write a poem for Mrs. Pinkston's assembly next month. Maybe you can read that one."

"That's a few weeks after prom, right?"

Her mouth went dry at the mention of the dance. She waited for him to say more, but he didn't, and so she just nodded.

"I'd love to read it. I mean, if you want me to." The bottle was back in his hands, and though it was dark, Marjorie could make out the deeply wrinkled lines of his knuckles, turning red from clutching.

· · ·

That week the Bradford pear trees started to bloom. At school everyone said they smelled like semen, like sex, like a woman's vagina. Marjorie hated the smell of them, a reflection of her virginity, her inability to liken the smell to anything other than rotting fish. Every year, by summer, she would grow accustomed to the smell, and by the time the blossoms fell, the smell would be nothing more than a distant memory. But then spring would come and the smell would resurface, loudly announcing itself.

Marjorie was working on her poem for The Waters We Wade In when her father got a call from Ghana. Old Lady was frail. Her caretaker couldn't tell if the dreams were the same or different. Old Lady didn't leave the bed as often as she used to—she, the woman who had once been afraid of sleep.

Marjorie wanted her family to go to Ghana immediately. She stopped writing the poem, snatched the phone away from her confused father—an act that on another day would have earned her a knock on the head—and demanded that the caretaker put Old Lady on the phone, even if it meant waking her.

"Are you sick?" she asked her grandmother.

"Sick? I will soon be dancing with you by the water this summer. How can I be sick?"

"You won't die?"

"What have I told you about death?" Old Lady said sharply into the phone, her voice sounding stronger than it had at the beginning of their conversation. Marjorie tugged at the cord. Old Lady said that only bodies died. Spirits wandered. They found Asamando, or they didn't. They stayed with their descendants to guide them through life, to comfort them, sometimes to scare them into waking from their fog of unloving, unliving.

Marjorie reached for the stone at her neck. Her ancestor's gift. "Promise me you won't leave until I can see you again," Marjorie said. Behind her, Yaw placed a hand on her shoulder.

"I promise I will never leave you," Old Lady said.

Marjorie handed the phone back to her father, who gave her a strange look. She went back to her room. On her desk, the piece of paper that was supposed to hold a poem simply said, "Water. Water. Water. Water."

Marjorie and Graham went on another date, this time to the U.S. Space & Rocket Center. Graham had never been before, but Marjorie and her parents went once a year. Her mother liked to look at all the pictures of astronauts that lined the halls and her father loved to walk through the museum, examining every rocket as though he were trying to learn how to build one himself. In some ways, Marjorie thought, her parents had already traveled through space, landing in a country as foreign to them as the moon.

Graham didn't heed the *Do Not Touch* signs. He left ghostly finger-prints on fiberglass cases, prints that disappeared almost as soon as he left them.

"America wouldn't have a space program if it weren't for the Germans," Graham said.

"Do you miss Germany?" Marjorie asked. Graham hardly ever talked about the place where he had done most of his growing up. He didn't wear the country on his sleeve the same way she wore Ghana on hers.

"Sometimes, but military brats get used to moving around." He shrugged and pressed his fingers against a case that held a space suit. Marjorie pictured his hand pushing through the glass, lifting his body into the case, fitting him into the suit, then losing gravity until his body started to float up, up.

"Marjorie?"

"What?"

"I said, would you ever move back to Ghana?"

She thought for a moment, of her grandmother and the sea, the Castle. She thought of the frantic commotion of cars and bodies on the streets of Cape Coast, the wide-hipped women selling fish out of large silver bowls, and the young girls whose breasts had not yet come in walking down the road's median, pressing their faces into the windows of the taxis, saying "Ice water," and "Please, I beg."

"I don't think so."

Graham nodded and started to move forward, on to the next case. Marjorie took his hand just as he was lifting it to press it against the fiberglass. She stopped him, and said, "I mostly just feel like I don't belong there. As soon as I step off the airplane, people can tell that I'm like them but different too. They can smell it on me."

"Smell what?"

Marjorie looked up, trying to capture the right word. "Loneliness, maybe. Or aloneness. The way I don't fit here or there. My grandmother's the only person who really sees me."

She looked down. Her hand was shaking, so she let go of Graham's, but he took it back. And when she looked up again, he was leaning down, pressing his lips to hers.

For weeks, Marjorie waited for word about her grandmother. Her parents had hired a new caretaker to watch her every day, which only seemed to infuriate her. She was getting worse. Marjorie didn't know how she knew, but she knew.

At school, Marjorie was quiet. She didn't raise her hand in any of her classes, and two of her teachers stopped her to ask if everything was all right. She brushed them off. Instead of eating lunch in the English lounge or reading in the library, she sat in the cafeteria, at the corner of a long rectangular table, daring anyone who passed by to do their worst. Instead, Graham came over and sat across from her.

"You okay?" he asked. "I haven't really seen you since . . ."

His voice trailed off, but Marjorie wanted him to say it. Since we kissed. Since we kissed. That day, Graham was wearing the school's colors—an obnoxious orange, calmed, only slightly, by a soothing gray.

"I'm fine," she said.

"You worried about your poem?" he asked.

Her poem was a collection of fonts on a piece of paper, an experiment in box lettering, cursive, all caps. "No, I'm not worried about that."

Graham nodded carefully, and held her gaze. She had come to the cafeteria because she wanted to be alone while surrounded by people. It was a feeling she sometimes liked, like stepping off the plane in Accra and being met by a sea of faces that looked like her own. For those first few minutes, she would capture that anonymity, but then the moment would drop. Someone would approach her, ask her if he could carry her bag, if he could drive her somewhere, if she would feed his baby.

While she stared back at Graham, a brunette girl Marjorie recognized from the hallways approached them. "Graham?" she asked. "I don't normally see you here at lunch. I would remember seeing you."

Graham nodded, but didn't say anything. The girl had yet to notice Marjorie, but Graham's lack of attention pulled her glance away from him, toward the person who had won it.

She looked at Marjorie for only a second, but it was long enough for Marjorie to notice the wrinkle of disgust that had begun to form on her face. "Graham," she whispered, as though lowering her voice would keep Marjorie from hearing. "You shouldn't sit here."

"What?"

"You shouldn't sit here. People will start to think . . ." Again, a quick glance. "Well, you know."

"No, I don't know."

"Just come sit with us," she said. At this point, she was scanning the room, her body language turning anxious.

"I'm fine where I am."

"Go," Marjorie said, and Graham turned toward her. It was as if he had forgotten whom he had been arguing for in the first place. As if he'd been fighting simply for the seat, and not the girl who sat across from it. "Go, it's fine."

And once she had said it, she stopped breathing. She wanted him to say no, to fight harder, longer, to take her hand across the table and run his reddened thumbs between her fingers.

But he didn't. He got up, looking almost relieved. By the time Marjorie noticed the brunette girl slipping her hand into his to pull him along, they were already halfway across the room. She had thought Graham was like her, a reader, a loner, but watching him walk away with the girl, she knew he was different. She saw how easy it was for him to slip in unnoticed, as though he had always belonged there.

*

Prom was themed The Great Gatsby. In the decorating days that preceded it, the school's floors were littered with sparkles and glitter. The night of prom, Marjorie was sandwiched between her parents on their couch, watching a movie on the television. She could hear her parents whispering about her when she got up to make popcorn.

"Something's not right," Yaw said. He had never been good at whispering. At regular volume his voice was a boom from the belly, deep and loud.

"She's just a teenager. Teenagers are like this," Esther said. Marjorie had heard the other LPNs at the nursing home where Esther worked talk like this, as if teenagers were wild beasts in a dangerous jungle. Best to leave them alone.

When she came back, Marjorie tried to look brighter, but she couldn't tell if she was succeeding.

The phone rang, and she rushed to pick it up. She had asked her grandmother to call her once a month as an assurance, even though she knew it was cumbersome for the old woman to have to do so. But, when she answered the phone, she was greeted by Graham's voice.

"Marjorie?" he asked. She was breathing into the phone, but she had yet to speak. What was there to say? "I wish I could take you. It's just that . . ."

His voice trailed off, but it didn't matter. She'd heard it before. He was going to go with the brunette. He had wanted to take Marjorie, but his father didn't think it would be proper. The school didn't think it was appropriate. As a last defense, Marjorie had heard him tell the principal that she was "not like other black girls." And, somehow, that had been worse. She had already given him up.

"Can I still hear your poem?" he asked.

"I'm reading it next week. Everyone will hear it."

"You know what I mean."

In the living room, her father had started snoring. It was the way he always watched movies. She pictured him leaning down onto her mother's shoulders, the woman's arms wrapped around him. Maybe her mother was sleeping too, her own head leaning toward Yaw's, her long box braids a curtain, hiding their faces. Theirs was a comfortable love. A love that didn't require fighting or hiding. When Marjorie had asked her father again when he had known he liked Esther, he said he had always known. He said it was born in him, that he breathed it in with the first breeze of Edweso, that it moved in him like the harmattan. There was nothing like love for Marjorie in Alabama.

"I have to go," she said to Graham on the phone. "My parents need me." She clicked the phone onto its receiver and went back into the living room. Her mother was awake, staring ahead at the television, though she wasn't watching it.

"Who was that, my own?" she asked.

"No one," Marjorie said.

The auditorium sat two thousand. From backstage, Marjorie could hear the other students filing in, the insistent chatter of their boredom. She was pacing the room, too scared to look out past the curtain. Beside her, Tisha and her friends were practicing a dance to music that played faintly from the boom box.

"You ready?" Mrs. Pinkston asked, startling Marjorie.

Her hands were already shaking, and she was surprised she didn't drop the poem she was holding.

"No," she said.

"Yes, you are," Mrs. Pinkston said. "Don't worry. You'll be great." She kept moving, off to check on all the other performers.

When the program started, Marjorie's stomach began to hurt. She had never spoken in front of so many people before, and she was ready to attribute the pain to that, but then it settled more deeply. A wave of nausea accompanied it, but soon both passed.

This feeling came from time to time. Her grandmother called it a premonition, the body registering something that the world had yet to acknowledge. Marjorie sometimes felt it before receiving a bad test score. Once, she got it before a car accident. Another time, she got it only moments before she realized she had lost a ring her father had given her. He argued that these things would have happened whether she had felt the feeling or not, and perhaps that was true. All Marjorie knew was that the feeling told her to brace herself.

And so, bracing herself, she stepped onto the stage once Mrs. Pinkston introduced her. She knew the lights would be bright, but she had not factored in their heat, like a million brilliant suns shining down on her. She began to sweat, passed a palm across her forehead.

She set her paper down on the podium. She had practiced a million times, under her breath in class, in front of the mirror in her bathroom, in the car while her parents drove.

The sound of silence, cut by the occasional cough or shuffling of feet, taunted Marjorie. She leaned into the mic. She cleared her throat, and then she read:

> Split the Castle open,
> find me, find you.
> We, two, felt sand,
> wind, air.
> One felt whip. Whipped,
> once shipped.
>
> We, two, black.
> Me, you.
> One grew from
> cocoa's soil, birthed from nut,
> skin uncut, still bleeding.
> We, two, wade.
> The waters seem different
> but are same.
> Our same. Sister skin.
> Who knew? Not me. Not you.

She looked up. A door had creaked open, letting more light in. There was enough light for her to see her father standing in the doorframe, but not enough for her to see the tears running down his face.

. . .

The only promise Old Lady, Akua, the Crazy Woman of Edweso, broke was the last one she made. She died in the middle of a sleep she used to fear. She wanted to be buried on a mountain overlooking the sea. Marjorie took the rest of the school year off, her grades so good it didn't make much of a difference.

She walked with her mother behind the men who were tasked with carrying her grandmother's body up. Her father had insisted on carrying too, though he was so old, his presence was more of a burden than a help. When they got to the grave site, the people began weeping. Everyone had been crying for days and days on end, but Marjorie had yet to.

The men began digging out the red clay. Two mounds stood on either side of the big rectangular hole, growing deeper. A woodworker had crafted Old Lady's coffin in a wood the same color as the ground, and when the coffin was lowered, no one could tell where it ended and the earth began. They began to return the clay to the hole. They packed it in tight, patting it with the back of the shovel once they had finished. The sound echoed off of the mountain, into the valley.

Once they put a marker on the grave, Marjorie realized that she had forgotten to drop in her poem, built from the dream stories Old Lady used to tell when she walked Marjorie to the water. She knew her grandmother would have loved to hear it. She pulled the poem from her pocket, and her trembling hands made the words wave even though there was little wind.

Marjorie threw herself onto the funeral mound, crying finally, *"Me Mam-yee, me Maame. Me Mam-yee, me Maame."*

Her mother came to lift her up off the ground. Later, Esther told her that it looked like she was going to fly off the cliff, down the mountain, and into the sea.

Marcus

MARCUS DIDN'T CARE FOR WATER. He was in college the first time he saw the ocean up close, and it had made his stomach turn, all that space, that endless blue, reaching out farther than an eye could hold. It terrified him. He hadn't told his friends he didn't know how to swim, and his roommate, a redhead from Maine, was already seven feet under the surface of the Atlantic before Marcus even stepped his toes in.

There was something about the smell of the ocean that nauseated him. That wet salt stink clung to his nose and made him feel as though he were already drowning. He could feel it thick in his throat, like brine, clinging to that place where his uvula hung so that he couldn't breathe right.

When he was young, his father told him that black people didn't like water because they were brought over on slave ships. What did a black man want to swim for? The ocean floor was already littered with black men.

Marcus always nodded patiently when his father said things like this. Sonny was forever talking about slavery, the prison labor complex, the System, segregation, the Man. His father had a deep-seated hatred of white people. A hatred like a bag filled with stones, one stone for every year racial injustice continued to be the norm in America. He still carried the bag.

Marcus would never forget his father's early teachings, the alternative history lessons that got Marcus interested in studying America more closely in the first place. The two had shared a mattress in Ma Willie's cramped apartment. In the evenings, lying on the mattress with springs like knives, Sonny would tell Marcus about how America used to lock up black men off the sidewalks for labor or how redlining kept banks from investing in black neighborhoods, preventing mortgages or business loans. So was it a wonder that prisons were still full of them? Was it a wonder that the ghetto was the ghetto? There were things Sonny used to talk about that Marcus never saw in his history books, but that later, when he got to college, he learned to be true. He learned that his father's mind was a brilliant mind, but it was trapped underneath something.

In the mornings, Marcus used to watch Sonny get up, shave, and leave for the methadone clinic in East Harlem. It was easier to follow the movements of his father than it was to watch a clock. At six thirty he got up and had a glass of orange juice. By six forty-five he was shaving, and by seven he was out the door. He would get his methadone and then he would head over to work as a custodian at the hospital. He was the smartest man Marcus knew, but he never could get completely out from under the dope he used to use.

When he was seven, Marcus once asked Ma Willie what would happen if some part of Sonny's schedule was to change. What would happen if he didn't get the methadone. His grandmother just shrugged. It wasn't until Marcus was much older that he started to understand just how important his father's routine was. His entire life seemed to hang in this balance.

Now Marcus was near the water again. A new grad school mate had invited him to a pool party to celebrate the new millennium, and Marcus had, hesitantly, accepted. A pool in California was safer than the Atlantic, sure. He could lounge on the chair and pretend he was just there for the sun. He could make jokes about how he needed a tan.

Someone yelled, "Cannonball!" sending a cold, wet splash onto Marcus's legs. He wiped it off, grimacing, after Diante handed him a towel.

"Shit, Marcus, how long we gon' stay out here, man? It's hot as hell. This some Africa heat right here."

Diante was always complaining. He was an artist whom Marcus met at a house party in East Palo Alto, and even though Diante had grown up in Atlanta, something about him reminded Marcus of home. They'd been like brothers ever since.

"We ain't been here but ten minutes, D. Chill," Marcus said, but he was starting to feel restless too.

"Naw, nigga. I ain't about to burn up in this damn heat. Let me catch you later." He got up and shot a small wave to the people in the pool.

Diante was always asking to go to school events with Marcus and then leaving almost as soon as they arrived. He was looking for a girl he'd met at an art museum once. He couldn't remember her name, but he told Marcus that he could tell she was a schoolgirl, just from the way she talked. Marcus didn't feel the need to remind him that there were about a million universities in the area. Who could say the girl would end up at one of his parties?

Marcus was getting his Ph.D. in sociology at Stanford. It was something he would never have been able to imagine doing back when he was splitting a mattress with his father, and yet, there he was. Sonny had been so proud when he told him he'd been accepted to Stanford that he cried. It was the only time Marcus had ever seen him do it.

Marcus left the party soon after Diante, making up some excuse about work. He walked the six miles home, and when he got there he was sweating through his shirt. He got into the blue-tiled shower and let the water beat over his head, never lifting his face up toward it, still scared of drowning.

"Your mama says hi," Sonny said.

It was their weekly phone call. Marcus made it every Sunday afternoon, when he knew his aunt Josephine and all the cousins would be in Ma Willie's house cooking and eating after church. He called because he missed Harlem, he missed Sunday dinners, he missed Ma Willie singing gospel at the top of her voice, as if Jesus would be there in ten minutes if she would only just summon him to come fix a plate.

"Don't lie," Marcus said. The last time he'd seen Amani was his high school graduation. His mother had dressed up in some outfit Ma Willie had given her, no doubt. It was a long-sleeved dress, but when she lifted her arm to wave at him while he crossed the stage to get his diploma, Marcus was almost certain he could see the tracks.

"Humph" was all Sonny replied.

"Y'all doing good over there?" Marcus asked. "The kids an' 'em all okay?"

"Yeah, we good. We good."

They breathed into the phone for a bit. Neither wanting to speak, but neither wanting to hang up the phone, either.

"You still straight?" Marcus asked. He didn't ask often, but he asked.

"Yeah, I'm good. Don't you worry 'bout me. Keep yo head in dem books. Don't be thinkin' 'bout me."

Marcus nodded. It took him a while to realize that his father wouldn't be able to hear that, and so he said, "Okay," and they finally hung up the phone.

Afterward, Diante came by to get him. He was dragging Marcus to a museum in San Francisco, the same one where Diante had met the girl.

"I don't know why you sweating this girl, D," Marcus said. He didn't really enjoy art museums. He never knew what to make of the pieces that he saw. He would listen to Diante talk about lines and color and shading. He would nod, but really, it all meant nothing to him.

"If you saw her, you'd understand," Diante said. They were walking around the museum, and neither of them was really taking in any of the art.

"I understand she must look good."

"Yeah, she look good, but it ain't even about that, man."

Marcus had already heard it before. Diante had met the woman at the Kara Walker exhibit. The two of them had paced the floor-to-ceiling black paper silhouettes four times before their shoulders brushed on the fifth pass. They'd talked about one piece in particular for nearly an hour, never remembering to get each other's name.

"I'm telling you, Marcus. You gon' be at the wedding soon. Alls I gotta do is find her."

Marcus snorted. How many times had Diante pointed out "his wife" at a party only to date her for a week?

He left Diante to himself and wandered the museum alone. More than the art, he liked the museum's architecture. The intricate stairways and white walls that held works of vibrant colors. He liked the walking and the thinking that the atmosphere allowed him to do.

He had been to a museum once on a class field trip back in elementary school. They'd taken the bus, then walked the remaining blocks on the buddy system, each child holding the next child's hand. Marcus could remember feeling awed by the rest of Manhattan, the part that wasn't his, the business suits and feathered hair. In the museum, the ticket taker had smiled at them from way up in the glass booth. Marcus had been craning his neck in order to see her, and she'd rewarded his efforts with a little wave.

Once they'd gone inside, their teacher, Mrs. MacDonald, had led them through room after room, exhibit after exhibit. Marcus was at the end of the line, and LaTavia, the girl whose hand he held, had dropped his in order to sneeze, and so Marcus had taken the opportunity to tie his shoe. When he lifted his head again, his class had moved on. Thinking back, he should have been able to find them quickly, a line of little black ducklings in the big white museum, but there were so many people, and all so tall, that he couldn't see his way around them, and he quickly grew too frightened to move.

He was standing there, paralyzed and quietly crying, when an elderly white couple found him.

"Look, Howard," the woman said. Marcus could still remember the color of the woman's dress, a deep bleeding red that only served to scare him even more. "Poor thing's probably lost or something." She studied him carefully, said, "He's a cute one, isn't he?"

The man, Howard, was carrying a slender cane, and he tapped at Marcus's foot with it. "You lost, boy?" Marcus didn't speak. "I said, you lost?"

The cane kept hitting at his foot, and for a second Marcus had felt as though at any moment the man would lift the cane all the way up toward the ceiling and send it crashing over his head. He couldn't guess why he felt that way, but it had scared him so badly, he could start to feel a wet stream traveling down his pant legs. He'd screamed and ran from one white-walled room to another to another, until a security guard had chased him down, called the teacher over the intercom, and sent the whole class back out into the street, back onto the bus, back home to Harlem.

Diante found him after a while. "She ain't here," he said. Marcus rolled his eyes. What did he expect? The two of them left the museum.

A month passed, and it was time again for Marcus to return to his research. He had been avoiding it because it wasn't going well.

Originally, he'd wanted to focus his work on the convict leasing system that had stolen years off of his great-grandpa H's life, but the deeper into the research he got, the bigger the project got. How could he talk about Great-Grandpa H's story without also talking about his grandma Willie and the millions of other black people who had migrated north, fleeing Jim Crow? And if he mentioned the Great Migration, he'd have to talk about the cities that took that flock in. He'd have to talk about Harlem. And how could he talk about Harlem without mentioning his father's heroin addiction—the stints in prison, the criminal record? And if he was going to talk about heroin in Harlem in the '60s, wouldn't he also have to talk about crack everywhere in the '80s? And if he wrote about crack, he'd inevitably be writing, too, about the "war on drugs." And if he started talking about the war on drugs, he'd be talking about how nearly half of the black men he grew up with were on their way either into or out of what had become the harshest prison system in the world. And if he talked about why friends from his hood were doing five-year bids for possession of marijuana when nearly all the white people he'd gone to college with smoked it openly every day, he'd get so angry that he'd slam the research book on the table of the beautiful but deadly silent Lane Reading Room of Green Library of Stanford University. And if he slammed the book down, then everyone in the room would stare and all they would see would be his skin and his anger, and they'd think they knew something about him, and it would be the same something that had justified putting his great-grandpa H in prison, only it would be different too, less obvious than it once was.

When Marcus started to think this way, he couldn't get himself to open even one book.

He couldn't remember exactly when the need for studying and knowing his family more intimately had struck him. Maybe it was during one of those Sunday dinners at Ma Willie's house, when his grandmother had asked that they all hold hands and pray. He would be shoved between two of his cousins or his father and Aunt Josephine, and Ma Willie would begin one of her prayers with a song.

His grandmother's voice was one of the wonders of the world. It was enough to stir in him all of the hope and love and faith that he would ever possess, all coming together to make his heart pulse and his palms sweat. He'd have to let go of someone's hand in order to wipe his own hands, his tears.

In that room, with his family, he would sometimes imagine a different room, a fuller family. He would imagine so hard that at times he thought he could see them. Sometimes in a hut in Africa, a patriarch holding a machete; sometimes outside in a forest of palm trees, a crowd watching a young woman carrying a bucket on her head; sometimes in a cramped apartment with too many kids, or a small, failing farm, around a burning tree or in a classroom. He would see these things while his grandmother prayed and sang, prayed and sang, and he would want so badly for all the people he made up in his head to be there in that room, with him.

He'd told his grandmother this after one of the Sunday dinners, and she'd told him that maybe he had the gift of visions. But Marcus never could make himself believe in the god of Ma Willie, and so he'd gone about looking for family and searching for answers in a more tangible way, through his research and his writing.

Now Marcus jotted down a few notes and headed out to meet Diante. His friend's mission to find the mysterious woman from the museum had ended, but his taste for parties and outings had not.

They ended up in San Francisco that night. A lesbian couple Diante knew had opened up their house into a gallery night/Afro-Caribbean dance party. When they walked in, they were greeted by the tinny sound of large steel drums. Men with brightly colored kente cloths wrapped around their waists held drum mallets with round pink tips. A woman stood at the end of this row of men, wailing out a song.

Marcus pushed farther in. The art on the walls frightened him a little, though he would never admit it to Diante if, or more likely when, his friend asked his opinion. The piece Diante had contributed was of a woman with horns strung around a baobab tree. Marcus didn't understand it at all, but he stood under it for a short while, his head tilted to the left, nodding slightly whenever someone appeared next to him.

Soon the person next to him was Diante. His friend poked him in the shoulder repeatedly, all the jabs in quick succession, so that he had finished before Marcus could tell him to stop.

"What, nigga?" Marcus said, turning to look at him.

It was like Diante didn't even realize someone else was there. His body was angled away, and he suddenly turned it back toward Marcus.

"She's here."

"Who?"

"The fuck you mean, who? The girl, man. She's here."

Marcus turned his gaze toward where Diante was pointing. There were two women standing side by side. The first was tall and skinny, light-skinned like Marcus himself was, but with dreadlocks that drifted down past her ass. She was playing with her locs, twirling them around her finger or taking the whole lot of them and piling them onto the very top of her head.

The woman next to her was the one who caught Marcus's eye. She was dark—blue-black, they would have called her on playgrounds in Harlem—and she was thick with sturdy, large breasts and a wild Afro that made her look as though at some point very recently she had been kissed by lightning.

"C'mon, man," Diante said, already walking toward the women. Marcus walked a little bit behind him. He could see Diante trying to play it cool. The calculated slouch, the careful lean. When they got to the women, Marcus waited to see which one was *the* one.

"You!" the woman with the dreadlocks said, slapping Diante's shoulder.

"I thought I recognized you, but I couldn't remember where I woulda known you from," Diante said. Marcus rolled his eyes.

"We met at the museum, a couple of months ago," the woman said, smiling.

"Right, right, of course," Diante said. He was on his best behavior now, standing straight and smiling. "I'm Diante, and this is my friend Marcus."

The woman flattened her skirt and picked up another loc, started to twirl it around her finger. Preening, it seemed. The woman next to her hadn't said a word yet, and her eyes were mostly trained on the ground, as though if she didn't look at them, she could pretend they weren't there.

"I'm Ki," the dreadlocked woman said. "And this is my friend. Marjorie."

At the mention of her name, Marjorie lifted her head, the curtain of wild hair parting to reveal a lovely face and a beautiful necklace.

"Nice to meet you, Marjorie," Marcus said, extending his hand.

*

When Marcus was just a little boy, his mother, Amani, had taken him for the day. Stolen him, really, for Ma Willie and Sonny and the rest of the family had no idea that Amani, who had asked just to say hi, would lure him away from the apartment with the promise of an ice cream cone.

His mother couldn't afford the cone. Marcus could remember her walking with him from one parlor to another shop to another and another in the hope that the prices would be better at a place just a little bit farther down. Once they reached Sonny's old neighborhood, Marcus knew two things with certainty: first, that he was somewhere he was not supposed to be, and second, that there would be no ice cream.

His mother had dragged him up and down 116th Street, showing him off to her dope fiend friends, the broke jazz crew.

"Dis your baby?" one fat, toothless woman said, squatting so that Marcus was looking straight down the barrel of her empty mouth.

"Yep, dis Marcus."

The woman touched him, then waddled on. Amani kept navigating him through a part of Harlem that he knew only through stories, through the salvation prayers the church congregants put up each Sunday. The sun got lower and lower in the sky. Amani started crying, and yelling at him to walk faster though he was going as fast as his little legs could carry him. It was nearly dusk before Ma Willie and Sonny found him. His father had snatched his hand and tugged him away so fast, he thought his arm would escape its socket. And he'd watched as his grandmother struck Amani hard across the face, saying loud enough for anyone to hear, "Touch this child again and see what happens."

Marcus thought about that day often. He was still amazed by it. Not by the fear he'd felt throughout the day, when the woman who was no more than a stranger to him had dragged him farther and farther from home, but by the fullness of love and protection he'd felt later, when his family had finally found him. Not the being lost, but the being found. It was the same feeling he got whenever he saw Marjorie. Like she had, somehow, found him.

Months had passed, and Diante and Ki's relationship fizzled, leaving only Marcus and Marjorie's friendship as evidence of its ever having been. Diante teased Marcus about Marjorie constantly, saying, "When you gon' tell that girl you into her?" But Marcus couldn't explain to Diante that it wasn't about that, because he didn't really understand himself what it *was* about.

"So this is the Asante Region," Marjorie said, pointing to a map of Ghana on her wall. "This is technically where my family's from, but my grandmother moved down to the Central Region, right here, to be closer to the beach."

"I hate the beach," Marcus said.

At first Marjorie smiled at him, like she was going to start laughing, but then she stopped, and her eyes turned serious. "Are you scared of it?" she asked. She let her finger drift slowly from the edge of the map down to the wall. She rested her hand against the black stone necklace she wore every day.

"Yeah, I guess I am," Marcus said. He had never told anyone before.

"My grandmother said she could hear the people who were stuck on the ocean floor talking to her. Our ancestors. She was kind of crazy."

"That don't sound crazy to me. Shit, everybody in my grandma's church caught a spirit at one point or another. Just because somebody sees or hears or feels something other folks can't, doesn't mean they're crazy. My grandma used to say, 'A blind man don't call us crazy for seeing.'"

Now Marjorie gave him a real smile. "You want to know what I'm scared of?" she asked, and he nodded. He had learned not to be surprised by how forthcoming she was. How she never gave in to small talk, just dove right into deep waters. "Fire," she said.

He had heard the story of her father's scar in the first week of meeting Marjorie. Her answer didn't surprise him.

"My grandmother used to say we were born of a great fire. I wish I knew what she meant by that."

"You ever get back to Ghana?"

"Oh, I've been busy with grad school and teaching and all of that." She paused and looked into the air, counting. "I haven't been back since my grandmother died, actually," she said softly. "She gave me this. A family heirloom, I guess." Marjorie pointed to the necklace.

Marcus nodded. So that was why Marjorie never took it off.

It was getting late, and Marcus had work to do, but he couldn't move from this particular spot in Marjorie's living room. There was a large bay window that let in so much light that his shoulder felt brushed with warmth. He wanted to stay for as long as he could.

"She would have hated to know that it's been so long. Almost fourteen years. When my parents were alive, they used to try to make me go, but it was too painful, losing her. And then I lost my parents, and I guess I just didn't see the point anymore. My Twi's so rusty, I don't know if I could even get around anyway."

She forced a laugh, but looked away as soon as it escaped her lips. She hid her face from him for what seemed like a long stretch of time.

The sun finally reached a place where the window couldn't catch its light. Marcus could feel the heat lifting off of his shoulder, and he wanted it back.

Marcus spent the rest of the school year avoiding his research. He couldn't see the point anymore. He had gotten a grant that would take him to Birmingham so that he could see what was left of Pratt City. He went with Marjorie, and all they'd been able to find was a blind, and probably crazy, old man who claimed he knew Marcus's great-grandpa H when he was just a boy.

"You could do your research on Pratt City," Marjorie had suggested when they left the man's house. "Seems like an interesting town."

When the old man had heard Marjorie's voice, he said he wanted to feel her. That this was how he got to know a person. Marcus had watched, amazed and somewhat embarrassed, as she let the man run his hands along her arms and, finally, her face, like he was reading her. It was her patience that had amazed him. In the short time that he'd known her, he could already tell that she had enough patience to take her through almost any storm. Marcus sometimes studied with her in the library, and he would watch out of the corners of his eyes as she devoured book after book after book. Her work was in African and African American literature, and when Marcus asked her why she chose those subjects, she said that those were the books that she could feel inside of her. When the old man touched her, she had looked at him so patiently, as though while he read her skin, she was also reading him.

"That's not the point," he said.

"What is the point, Marcus?"

She stopped walking. For all they knew, they were standing on top of what used to be a coal mine, a grave for all the black convicts who had been conscripted to work there. It was one thing to research something, another thing entirely to have lived it. To have felt it. How could he explain to Marjorie that what he wanted to capture with his project was the feeling of time, of having been a part of something that stretched so far back, was so impossibly large, that it was easy to forget that she, and he, and everyone else, existed in it—not apart from it, but inside of it.

How could he explain to Marjorie that he wasn't supposed to be here? Alive. Free. That the fact that he had been born, that he wasn't in a jail cell somewhere, was not by dint of his pulling himself up by the bootstraps, not by hard work or belief in the American Dream, but by mere chance. He had only heard tell of his great-grandpa H from Ma Willie, but those stories were enough to make him weep and to fill him with pride. Two-Shovel H they had called him. But what had they called his father or his father before him? What of the mothers? They had been products of their time, and walking in Birmingham now, Marcus was an accumulation of these times. That was the point.

Instead of saying any of this, he said, "You know why I'm scared of the ocean?"

She shook her head.

"It's not just because I'm scared of drowning. Though I guess I am. It's because of all that space. It's because everywhere I look, I see blue, and I have no idea where it begins. When I'm out there, I stay as close as I can to the sand, because at least then I know where it ends."

She didn't speak for a while, just continued walking a little bit ahead of him. Maybe she was thinking about fire, the thing she had told him she most feared. Marcus had never seen so much as a picture of her father, but he imagined that he had been a fearsome man with a scar covering one whole side of his face. He imagined that Marjorie feared fire for the same reasons he feared water.

She stopped beneath a broken lamppost that flickered an eerie light on and off and on and off. "I bet you would like the beach in Cape Coast," she said. "It's beautiful there. Not like anything you would see in America."

Marcus laughed. "I don't think anyone in my family's ever left the country. I wouldn't know what to do on a plane ride that long."

"You mostly just sleep," she said.

He couldn't wait to get out of Birmingham. Pratt City was long gone, and he wasn't going to find what he was looking for in the ruins of that place. He didn't know if he would ever find it.

"All right," he said. "Let's go."

Marcus

*

"Ess-cuse me, sah! You want go see slave castle? I take you see Cape Coast Castle. Ten cedis, sah. Juss ten cedis. I take you see nice castle."

Marjorie was rushing him through the tro-tro stop, hurrying them toward a cab that would take them to their beach resort. Days before, they had been in Edweso, paying respects to her father's birthplace. Only hours before, they'd been in Takoradi, doing the same for her mother's.

Everything was brilliant here, even the ground. Everywhere they went, Marcus would notice sparkling red dust. It coated his body by the end of every night. Now there would be sand to join it.

"Don't mind them," Marjorie said, moving Marcus past the group of young boys and girls who were trying to draw him toward them to buy this or that, take him here or there.

He stopped Marjorie. "You ever seen it? The Castle?"

They were in the middle of a busy street, and cars were blaring their horns, though it could have been at anyone—the many thin girls with buckets on their heads, the boys selling newspapers, the whole, entire country with skin like his, hustling about, making driving near impossible. Still, they found a way to pass.

Marjorie clutched at her backpack straps, pulled them away from her body. "No, actually. I've never been. That's what the black tourists do when they come here." He lifted an eyebrow at her. "You know what I mean," she said.

"Well, I'm black. And I'm a tourist."

Marjorie sighed and checked her watch, though they had nowhere they needed to go. They had come for the beach, and they had all week to see it. "Okay, fine. I'll take you."

They took a cab to their resort to set down their things. From the balcony, Marcus caught his first real glimpse of the beach. It seemed to stretch for miles and miles. Sunlight bounced off of the sand, making it shimmer. Sand like diamonds in the once gold coast.

There was almost no one milling around the Castle that day, save for a few women who were gathered around a very old tree, eating nuts and plaiting each other's hair. They looked at Marcus and Marjorie as the two of them walked up, but they didn't move. Marcus started to wonder if he was really seeing them in the flesh. If ever there was a place to believe was haunted, this was it. From the outside, the Castle was a glowing white. Powder white, like the entire thing had been scrubbed down to gleaming, cleansed of any stains. Marcus wondered who made it shine like that, and why. When they entered, things started to look dingier. The dirty skeleton of a long-past shame that held the place together began to show itself in blackening concrete, rusty-hinged doors. Soon a man so skinny and tall he looked like he was made from stretched rubber bands greeted them and the four others who had signed up for the tour.

He said something to Marjorie in Fante, and she spoke back in the halting, apologetic Twi she had been speaking all week.

As they walked toward the long row of cannons that looked out at the sea, Marcus stopped her. "What did he say?" he whispered.

"He knew my grandmother. He wished me *akwaaba*."

It was one of the few words Marcus had learned in his time here. "Welcome." Marjorie's family, strangers on the street, even the man who had checked them in at the airport, had been saying it to her their entire stay. They had been saying it to him too.

"This is where the church was," the rubber band man said, pointing. "It stands directly above the dungeons. You could walk around this upper level, go into that church, and never know what was going on underneath. In fact, many of the British soldiers married local women, and their children, along with other local children, would go to school right here in this upper level. Other children would be sent to England for school and they would come back to form an elite class."

Next to him, Marjorie shifted her weight, and Marcus tried not to look at her. It was the way most people lived their lives, on upper levels, not stopping to peer underneath.

And soon they were headed down. Down into the belly of this large, beached beast. Here, there was grime that could not be washed away. Green and gray and black and brown and dark, so dark. There were no windows. There was no air.

"This is one of the female dungeons," the guide said finally, leading them into a room that still smelled, faintly. "They kept as many as two hundred and fifty women here for about three months at a time. From here they would lead them out this door." He walked further.

The group left the dungeon and moved together toward the door. It was a wooden door painted black. Above it, there was a sign that read *Door of No Return.*

"This door leads out to the beach, where ships waited to take them away."

Them. Them. Always them. No one called them by name. No one in the group spoke. They all stood still, waiting. For what, Marcus didn't know. Suddenly, he felt sick to his stomach. He wanted to be somewhere else, anywhere else.

He didn't think. He just started to push at the door. He could hear the guide asking him to stop, yelling at Marjorie in Fante. He could hear Marjorie too. He could feel her arm on his hand, then he could feel his hand push through, then, finally, there was light.

Marcus started running onto the beach. Outside, there were hundreds of fishermen tending their bright turquoise nets. There were long handcrafted rowboats as far as the eye could see. Each boat had a flag of no nationality, of every nationality. There was a purple polka-dotted one beside a British one, a blood-orange one beside a French one, a Ghanaian one next to an American one.

Marcus ran until he found two men with dark, gleaming, shoe-polish skin who were building a dazzling fire with flames that licked out and up, crawling toward the water. They were cooking fish on the fire, and when they saw him, they stopped, stared.

He could hear her feet behind him before he could see her. The sound of feet hitting sand, a light, muffled sound. She stopped many paces away from him, and when she spoke, her voice was a distant thing carried by sea-salted wind.

"What's wrong?" Marjorie shouted. And he just kept staring out into the water. It went every direction that his eye could see. It splashed up toward his feet, threatening to put out the fire.

"Come here," he said, finally turning to look at her. She glanced at the fire, and it was only then he remembered her fear. "Come," he said again. "Come see." She stepped a little bit closer, but stopped again when the fire roared into the sky.

"It's okay," he said, and he believed it. He held out his hand. "It's okay."

She walked to where he stood, where the fire met the water. He took her hand and they both looked out into the abyss of it. The fear that Marcus had felt inside the Castle was still there, but he knew it was like the fire, a wild thing that could still be controlled, contained.

Then Marjorie released his hand. He watched her run, headlong, into the crashing waves of the water, watched her dip under until he lost her and all he could do was wait for her to resurface. When she did, she looked at him, her arms moving circles around her, and though she didn't speak, he knew what she was saying. It was his turn to come to her.

He closed his eyes and walked in until the water met his calves, and then he held his breath, started to run. Run underwater. Soon, waves crashed over his head and all around him. Water moved into his nose and stung his eyes. When he finally lifted his head up from the sea to cough, then breathe, he looked out at all the water before him, at the vast expanse of time and space. He could hear Marjorie laughing, and soon, he laughed too. When he finally reached her, she was moving just enough to keep her head above water. The black stone necklace rested just below her collarbone and Marcus watched the glints of gold come off it, shining in the sun.

"Here," Marjorie said. "Have it." She lifted the stone from her neck, and placed it around Marcus's. "Welcome home."

He felt the stone hit his chest, hard and hot, before finding its way up to the surface again. He touched it, surprised by its weight.

Marjorie splashed him suddenly, laughing loudly before swimming away, toward the shore.

Acknowledgments

I am incredibly grateful to Stanford University's Chappell-Lougee Fellowship, the Merage Foundation for the American Dream Fellowship, the University of Iowa's Dean's Graduate Research Fellowship, and the Whited Fellowship for supporting this work over the last seven years.

Many, many thanks to my agent, Eric Simonoff, for being so sure and so wise, a fierce advocate for this novel. I am also grateful for the rest of the wonderful team at WME, especially Raffaella De Angelis, Annemarie Blumenhagen, and Cathryn Summerhayes for so brilliantly representing me to the rest of the world.

Enormous thanks to my editor, Jordan Pavlin, for her encouragement and graceful editing, her steadfast belief in this novel, and for taking such great care. Thanks also to everyone at Knopf for their boundless enthusiasm. Another thanks goes to Mary Mount and everyone at Viking UK.

For the bedrock of friendship: Tina Kim, Allison Dill, Raina Sun, Becca Richardson, Bethany Woolman, Tabatha Robinson, and Faradia Pierre.

Thank you to Christina Ho, first reader and beloved friend, for seeing this novel in every messy iteration and for assuring me, at each turn, that it was worth pushing forward.

It was such a privilege to spend two years at the Iowa Writers' Workshop. Thank you Deb West, Jan Zenisek, and Connie Brothers.

Thanks also to my classmates there, especially to the ones who gave advice, encouragement, and a home-cooked meal, sometimes all in the same night: Nana Nkweti, Clare Jones, Alexia Arthurs, Jorge Guerra, Naomi Jackson, Stephen Narain, Carmen Machado, Olivia Dunn, Liz Weiss, and Aamina Ahmad.

I have had the extraordinary good fortune of having teachers who made me feel, even when I was just a child, that my dream of becoming a writer was not only possible, but a foregone conclusion. I cannot say thank you enough for that early support, but I will continue to try. In Alabama: Amy Langford and Janice Vaughn. At Stanford: Josh Tyree, Molly Antopol, Donna Hunter, Elizabeth Tallent, and Peggy Phelan. At Iowa: Julie Orringer, Ayana Mathis, Wells Tower, Marilynne Robinson, Daniel Orozco, and Sam Chang. I must say another thank-you to Sam Chang for believing in this book from the very first word, for making sure I had everything I needed in order to work, and for that phone call in 2012.

Thank you to Hannah Nelson-Teutsch, Jon Amar, Patrice Nelson, and, in loving memory, Clifford Teutsch for their support and warm welcome.

I owe so much to my parents, Kwaku and Sophia Gyasi, who, like so many immigrants, are the very definition of hard work and sacrifice. Thank you for cutting a path so that it might be easier for us to walk. Thank you to my brothers, Kofi and Kwabena, for walking with me.

Another special thank-you to my father and Kofi for fielding countless research questions. In addition to their helpful answers and suggestions, some of the books and articles I consulted were: *The Door of No Return* by William St. Clair, *Mission from Cape Coast Castle to Ashantee* by Thomas Edward Bowdich, *The Fante and the Transatlantic Slave Trade* by Rebecca Shumway, *The Human Tradition in the Black Atlantic, 1500–2000* edited by Beatriz G. Mamigonian and Karen Racine, *A Handbook on Asante Culture* by Osei Kwadwo, *Spirituality, Gender, and Power in Asante History* by Emmanuel Akyeampong and Pashington Obeng, *Black Prisoners and Their World, Alabama 1865–1900* by Mary Ellen Curtin, "From Alabama's Past, Capitalism Teamed with Racism to Create Cruel Partnership" by Douglas A. Blackmon, *Twice the Work of Free Labor: The Political Economy of Convict Labor in the New South* by Alex Lichtenstein, "Two Industrial Towns: Pratt City and Thomas" from the Birmingham Historical Society, *Yaa Asantewaa and the Asante-British War of 1900–1* by A. Adu Boahen, and *Smack: Heroin and the American City* by Eric C. Schneider.

Finally, most urgently, thank you to Matthew Nelson-Teutsch, best reader and dearest heart, who brought to each reading of this novel all of the generosity, intelligence, goodness, and love that he brings to my days. We, this novel and I, are better for it.

Yaa Gyasi was born in Ghana and raised in Huntsville, Alabama. She holds a BA in English from Stanford University and an MFA from the Iowa Writers' Workshop, where she received a Dean's Graduate Research Fellowship. She lives in Berkeley, California.

A NOTE ON THE TYPE

This book was set in Scala, a typeface designed by the Dutch designer Martin Majoor (b. 1960) in 1988 and released by the FontFont foundry in 1990. While designed as a fully modern family of fonts containing both a serif and a sans serif alphabet, Scala retains many refinements normally associated with traditional fonts.

Composed by North Market Street Graphics,
Lancaster, Pennsylvania

Printed and bound by Berryville Graphics,
Berryville, Virginia

Designed by Soonyoung Kwon